AS GOOD AS IT GETS?

Fiona was born in a youth hostel in Yorkshire. She started working on teen magazine *Jackie* at age 17, then went on to join *Just Seventeen* and *More!* where she invented the infamous 'Position of the Fortnight'. Fiona now lives in Scotland with her husband Jimmy, their three children and a wayward rescue collie cross called Jack.

For more info, visit www.fionagibson.com. You can follow Fiona on Twitter @fionagibson.

By the same author:

Mum On The Run
The Great Escape
Pedigree Mum
Take Mum Out
How the In-Laws Wrecked Christmas: a short story

AVON

AVON

A division of HarperCollins*Publishers*
1 London Bridge Street,
London SE1 9GF

www.harpercollins.co.uk

A Paperback Original 2015

3

First published in Great Britain by
HarperCollins*Publishers* 2015

A catalogue record for this book is
available from the British Library

ISBN-13: 978-1-84756-366-8

Set in Sabon LT Std by Palimpsest Book Production Ltd,
Falkirk, Stirlingshire

Printed and bound in Great Britain by CPI Group (UK) Ltd, Croydon CR0 4YY

Acknowledgements

Enormous thanks to super-agent Caroline Sheldon, and to my fabulous new editor, Helen Huthwaite at Avon. Here's to lots more books and carrot cake! For 15 years I've had the good fortune to belong to a brilliant writing group. Tania, Vicki, Amanda, Pauline, Hilary and Sam – dreaming up plotlines wouldn't be half as much fun without you. My Facebook friends also help me enormously – I love your banter and jokes. Special thanks to Rachel Millward, who alerted me to the fact that spliff/ weed (or whatever the young 'uns call it these days) is sometimes known as 'cheese' – it's in the book, Rachel! And a big hello and hug to lovely Kim Lock who won a little competition I ran. See, I did remember!

I turned 50 as I finished writing this book. Thank you to my lovely friends who travelled so far (Belgium! The Netherlands! *Australia*!) for a week of japes and gin, and who make me feel lucky every day. Jen, Kath, Lode, Susan and her boyfriend Jack D, Wendy R, Wendy V,

Marie, Ben, Iain, Chris, Elisabet, Gayle, Esther, Ellie, Lesley, Jackie, Keith, Sumishta, Seori, the inimitable Curries, Cragga C, Andy, Mickey and Jennifer – you made it the best birthday of my life. And you're the Mary Berry of Lanarkshire, Elaine Hughes.

My mum moved into a care home this year; I don't know what I'd have done without my dog walks and chats with Adele, Tania and Carolann. Finally, thank you to Jimmy, Sam, Dexter and Erin, for being all-round brilliant. Love you so much.

facebook.com/pages/Fiona-Gibson
twitter@FionaGibson
fionagibsonauthor.blogspot.co.uk

For Jane Parbury with love

February 14, 1997

Dear Fraser,

Happy Valentine's Day! Sorry this is late. You see, a few of the girls at work got flowers today and that made me think of you.

It also made me wonder why your phone number's unavailable. Perhaps it's broken? And maybe you've injured your hand and haven't been able to write? If so, I sympathise. I know you don't handle pain well. I'm still smirking at the memory of you being agonisingly constipated after wolfing that massive bag of toffees on the train to Amsterdam.

Surely, though, phone issues aside, you could have got in touch somehow? You know – just to tell me you're okay and haven't died (maybe you ARE dead? But then, wouldn't someone have tracked me down and let me know?). In fact I don't really think of any of that. You know what I do think?

That you're scared, Fraser. You're a terrified boy who – despite all your promises – has decided to run away.

BLOODY COWARD!!!

Honestly, I didn't expect this from you. 'It'll be fine,' you told me, that day when we drove down to Brighton. 'It'll be amazing. I'm so happy. Please don't worry about a thing.' Do you remember saying all that? The ensuing silence suggests you were lying through your very nice, very posh teeth.

So I've made a decision. I've stopped hoping you'll get back in touch at some distant point and throw me a crumb of support. I'm not scrabbling around like a fat pigeon, waiting for your scraps. You were right – our baby and I will be just fine. We don't need you.

Goodbye, Fraser.

Charlotte

PS Actually, I wish I could be a pigeon for just long enough to shit on your head.

*

February 19, 1997

Dear Charlotte,

I hope this finds you well. My name is Arlene Johnson and I am Fraser's mother. After receiving your charming letter he wishes to have no further contact with you. I trust you will find both the enclosed cheque and small gift useful, and sincerely hope that there will be no further correspondence between yourself and my son. Please remember that he is only 19 years old and has a promising future ahead of him.

Yours,

Arlene

Enclosed:
1 cheque for £10,000
1 packet Chirpy Nut and Seed Mix For Wild Birds

*

February 23, 1997

Dear Arlene,

That was kind of you, trying to pay me off. Thanks, too, for reminding me of Fraser's age. I am aware of how old he is. I'm only 21 myself and some might say I have a promising future too. The last time I saw him, we drove down to Brighton in the middle of the night and sat on the seafront watching the sun coming up. He seemed very happy about the baby. We both were. It might not have been planned but we decided we could make it work and that we wanted to be together.

Obviously, he's had a change of heart. I'd be grateful if you could ask him to contact me. I know he's a very capable boy and I'm sure he could manage to write a letter himself instead of getting his mummy to do it for him.

Charlotte

Enclosed: 1 torn-up cheque. Perhaps you could use it as confetti, when Fraser marries a more suitable (preferably un-pregnant) girl?

*

February 28, 1997

Letter returned to sender. No further correspondence.

Chapter One

Present Day

'Hey, beautiful!' the blond boy yells, nudging his friend. They watch, admiring, as the shopping crowds mill around us. There are more glances as we walk: some fleeting, others more direct. All this attention isn't for me; Christ no, that hasn't happened since Madonna vogued in a gold conical bra. Even then, it pretty much amounted to a bloke up some scaffolding yelling, 'Your arse looks like two footballs!' I'd adored my stretch jeans until that sole cruel comment killed the love affair stone dead. Not that I'm the kind of woman to take any notice of construction workers' remarks. I mean, I've only festered over it for *twenty-three years . . .*

Anyway, of course it's not me who's causing virtually every young male in this over-heated shopping mall to perform a quick double-take. I am thirty-eight years old with wavy, muddy brown hair that's supposed to be shoulder-length but has outgrown its style, yet isn't properly long – it's just long-ish. That's what my hair is: *ish*. I am also laden with copious bulging bags, like a yak. Judging by the odd glimpse in mirrored surfaces, I note that I have acquired a deathly pallor beneath the mall's unforgiving lights. I also have what the magazines term 'a shiny breakthrough' on my nose and cheeks.

The cruel lighting, of course, is not detracting from my daughter Rosie's beauty. Leggy and slender, with a cascade of chestnut hair which actually *gleams*, like polished wood, she's marching several paces ahead, lest someone might assume we're together. Faster and faster she goes, on the verge of breaking into a trot, while I scuttle behind, tasked with carrying the shopping. Incredibly, Rosie doesn't seem to notice the glances she's attracting from all these good-looking young males. Perhaps, when you're so often admired, you simply become immune to it.

I stop, dumping the bags on the floor and checking my hands for lacerations while she courses ahead. 'Rosie!' I call after her. 'Rosie – wait!' While there are no open wounds, I have acquired a callus on my left palm from lugging Will's birthday presents through the mall. Sure, I could have bought them online, but when we stumbled upon a closing down sale earlier, I couldn't resist grabbing a quality turntable, headphones and speakers (yes, I am transporting speakers – i.e., virtually *furniture*) at bargain prices.

At first, I comforted myself with the thought that my husband will enjoy unearthing his vinyl collection from the loft, and be able to re-live those heady, music-filled evenings of his youth. Now, though, I'm concerned that Will, who's been without gainful employment for six months, might view my purchases as 'something to fill your copious spare time'-type gifts – i.e., faintly patronising, and not something I'd have thought of buying when he was busy being a senior person with an environmental charity. It's his birthday tomorrow; he'll be forty-one. I have already stashed away a blue cashmere sweater and the delicious figgy fragrance he likes. Maybe that was enough. I don't want him to think I'm festooning him with presents because I feel sorry for him . . . oh, *God*. Things were so much simpler when he went off to work every day, either by Tube to his Hammersmith office or off in his car to some marshy bit of London, with his waders and big waxy jacket stashed in the boot. He doesn't even have his own car anymore. He sold it, saying, 'I don't need it, do I? So what's the point of keeping it?'

'Better for the environment anyway,' our son Ollie added, in an attempt to cheer him up.

Through the shopping crowds I glimpse Rosie in her baggy red top and skinny black jeans which make her legs even longer than they really are. They are limbs of a foal, or a sleek gazelle. She canters past Gap and Fat Face with her hair billowing behind her before performing a swift left turn into Forever 21.

Please, no – *not* Forever 21. The shop is vast, almost a city in itself, with its own transport system (about fifty escalators) and populated by millions of hot-cheeked teenagers snatching at skirts in sizes that didn't even exist (six! *four!!*) when I was that age. Size ten was considered tiny then. I'm what's commonly termed a 'curvy' fourteen: neatish waist nestling between ample hips and sizeable boobs, which aren't quite the blessing one might imagine. In the wrong kind of outfit, they make me look as if I have one of those huge German sausages – a *kochwurst*, I believe they're called – stuffed up my top. Or a bolster, like you find on posh hotel beds. Those weird cylindrical pillows you never know what to do with and end up throwing on the floor. Chest-wise, I have to be careful with necklines so as to avoid a stern matronly look. Yes, a big rack can be sexy in the right context. Too often, though, it gives off an 'I am unfazed by bedpans' sort of vibe.

I peer through the enormous glass frontage of Forever 21. It's packed in there, virtually a scrum, as if these highly-charged girls are terrified that the supply of sequinned T-shirts and iridescent leggings is about to run dry. I can imagine the pained looks I'd attract if I dared to hobble in with my sacks of stereophonic equipment, never mind tried to enter the changing rooms and try anything on. They'd probably call security and wrestle me out of the building.

I hover at the doors with my bags clustered around my feet, like someone who has unexpectedly become homeless. I'll *never* find Rosie in there. She might as well have gone to China. Another woman, presumably a mother, loiters nearby, pursing her lips and stabbing irritably at her phone. There's also a scattering of boys and men, all waiting, presumably wondering what the heck their girlfriends and daughters have been doing in there for eighteen hours.

After what I regard as an acceptable browsing period, I call Rosie's mobile. No answer. I actually don't know why she has a phone – or at least, why I pay the contract for it. It's supposed to enable us to stay in contact. When she was younger, she'd constantly call and message me while she was out. These days, she texts me about once a month. They usually say 'ok' or 'yeah', although she does still put a kiss, for which I'm grateful.

A woman strolls by with a little girl who looks about seven years old. 'Shall we go for ice cream, darling?' the woman asks.

'Yeah,' the girl enthuses. 'Can we go to that place where they sprinkle Smarties on?'

'Of course,' the woman replies, causing a wave of nostalgia to crash over me. How excited she is, out shopping with her mum, like Rosie used to be with me. I'd only suggested coming here so we could spend some mum-and-daughter time together, because I know she prefers shopping malls with their weird, artificial atmosphere and piped music to actual streets with proper weather and pigeons and sky. But I'd imagined that we'd at least stroll around together, and stop off for hot chocolate and cake.

My phone rings, and I snatch it from my jeans pocket. 'Mum, where *are* you?'

'Outside Forever 21,' I reply.

'Come in!' she commands.

'It's okay thanks, darling. I'll wait here.' *I would rather spear my own eye than enter the Emporium of Cropped Tops.*

'Mum, please—'

'I need at least a week's warning to go in,' I explain. 'I have to rev myself up for it and get special breathing equipment. I'm sure the atmosphere's thinner up at the top, the fifth floor or whatever it is, where the underwear is—'

'Mum, something's *happened*!'

'What? Are you okay?' I grab at my bags, realising it'll be quite a feat to carry them all while clutching my phone.

'Yeah, I'm fine,' Rosie says.

'Where are you exactly? What's happened?'

'You'll never believe this, Mum. I've been scouted!' What pops into my mind is the actual Scouts, which

Rosie chose over Guides because they did all the fun stuff like camping and cooking on fires. She was a tomboyish, outdoorsy kid who shunned pink. She never used to gallop ahead, or spend an entire morning choosing a nail polish. 'What d'you mean, scouted? Are you *sure* you're okay?'

'Yeah, just hurry up. There's someone here from a model agency and they want to do pictures . . .'

Ah, that kind of scouted. *Nice try,* I decide, finishing the call. So a random stranger's trying to sweet-talk my daughter with that old 'could be a model' line? I can imagine how *that* goes. All she has to do is come along to his 'studio', which happens to be a dingy flat with filthy net curtains above a fried chicken shop . . .

The security man eyes me in the manner of a suspicious immigration officer as I barge my way into the store. I stride up the escalators, barely noticing the weight of my carrier bags now.

I arrive, panting, at the summit of Forever 21 and scan the floor for a man with paedo glasses, smiling too much and telling Rosie she has a *great future ahead of her*. I'm fine – well, sort of – when boys of her own age look at her. Of course they do: she's a lovely girl. I'm aware that teenagers are supposed to find each other attractive and, while there's been nothing serious yet, she's never short of attention from boys. I'm okay with that – truly. Honestly. Well, mostly . . . What I'm *not* fine about is the idea of some fifty-year-old perv with nicotine fingers and winking gold jewellery thinking he can take advantage of my daughter . . .

No sign of her anywhere. My hair seems to crackle as I push it out of my face, probably due to the static electricity generated by millions of nylon knickers and bras.

'Mum! Hey, Mum, over here!'

I turn and spot Rosie, who's waving excitedly. Beside her stands a tall, slim and elegant woman – late-forties perhaps – in a cream linen jacket and faded skinny jeans, her ash-blonde hair scooped up artfully into a tousled bun. Not quite the chicken-shop perv I had in mind, but we'll see . . .

'Hi.' I stride over and look expectantly at the stranger.

'Hi,' she says, fixing on a wide smile, 'I'm Laurie and I work for a model agency called Face . . .'

'I'm Charlotte.' I dump the bags at my feet and shake her hand.

'I hope you don't mind,' she goes on, 'but I spotted your daughter a few minutes ago. We've been chatting.' She casts Rosie a fond glance, in the manner of a glamorous aunt, before turning back to me. 'I really think she has the potential to be a model.'

'Really?' I wipe a slick of sweat from my upper lip. 'Well, you see, she's still at school . . .'

'Yes, she told me. That's fine, lots of our girls are. I love her look, the stunning blue eyes and dark hair . . . it's very dramatic.' She turns back to Rosie. 'You have *fantastic* bone structure, sweetheart. I can't believe you've never been scouted before . . .'

'I'm not really sure,' I say firmly. 'We'd need to think it over.'

'Oh, of course,' Laurie says, addressing Rosie again: 'How tall are you, darling?'

Rosie frowns. 'Er, what would you say, Mum? About five-foot-eight?'

'Yes, around that,' I reply, noticing Laurie looking her up and down. This is more unsettling than the admiring looks she was attracting in the mall. She is sizing up my precious firstborn as a commodity, a *thing*, tilting her head this way and that, as if my daughter were a bookshelf and she's trying to imagine if she'd fit in that corner behind the sofa.

'I'd say more like five-nine,' she observes, 'at the very least. And you said you're sixteen, Rosie?'

'Only just,' I cut in.

'Mum,' Rosie splutters, 'I'm seventeen in August. That's next month!' She cuts me from her vision. 'I'm actually *nearly seventeen*.'

'I still think it's a bit young,' I remark. 'And anyway, she has a lot on at school over the next few months—'

Rosie emits a dry laugh. 'Yeah, like the summer holidays. *That's* what I'm doing over the next few months. I've nothing planned at all. We're not even going away, are we, Mum?'

'We might,' I say defensively.

'Well, this is exactly the age we like them to start,' Laurie cuts in, delving into her tan leather bag for a business card which she presses into my palm. 'Some join us even younger, but of course they're always chaperoned on castings and jobs . . . Okay if I take a quick picture, Rosie?'

'Er, sure,' she replies with a shy smile. Don't ask me, then. I'm only her mother.

I squint at the card as Laurie takes the shot with her phone. She seems genuine; it says *Laurie Piper, Head Booker, Face Models*, not *Creepy Weirdo Who Prowls Around Shops Where Teenagers Go*. The agency is in Long Acre in Covent Garden, not some godforsaken suburb I've barely heard of. In fact, with her cool grey eyes and pronounced cheekbones, Laurie has the air of an ex-model herself. 'That's beautiful,' she enthuses, studying the image on her phone. 'Such a fresh, pretty face.'

'Thank you,' Rosie says, blushing. Oddly enough, whenever I tell my daughter how lovely she is, she fixes me with a rather beleaguered, *you're-only-saying-that* sort of look.

'So,' Laurie goes on, 'perhaps you'd both like to think it over? Give me a call and pop into the agency sometime for a chat. You can meet the team and we'll explain how everything works . . .'

'Okay,' Rosie says brightly.

'I'm *really* not sure,' I tell Laurie, irritated now that she doesn't seem to have listened to a word I've said. 'Next year's really important for Rosie. She needs good grades in her A-levels because she's hoping to do a veterinary degree . . .'

'Huh?' Laurie says distractedly.

'Rosie wants to be a vet,' I explain.

'Mum, it's *fine*!' Rosie throws me a pleading look.

'Don't worry about that,' Laurie says. 'We can always work around school . . .' What the hell does that mean? '. . . And we nurture our girls. We're like a surrogate family really . . .'

She doesn't need a surrogate family!

'Anyway,' Laurie adds, turning back to my daughter as if I've conveniently melted into the shiny white floor, 'lovely to meet you. Do think it over, won't you?'

Rosie grins. 'I definitely will.'

'Bye then.' We watch her striding towards the escalator.

'God, Mum,' Rosie breathes. 'I can't believe you did that.'

'Did what?'

'Went on about me wanting to be a vet!'

I frown, prickling with hurt. 'I didn't *go on*. I just mentioned it. You've been saying for years that that's what you want to do. She can't just expect you to drop all your plans—'

'She doesn't. Weren't you listening? She said they *work around* school.' She lets out an exasperated gasp as we step onto the escalator. 'I can't understand why you're not happy for me.'

Oh, for crying out loud. 'I am. Of course I am. You're lovely and you'd make an amazing model. But I just think, I don't know . . .' I scrabble for the right words. 'I didn't think it'd be your kind of thing.'

She blinks at me. 'Why not?' How can I put this – that I can't imagine my bright, sparky daughter fitting into a vacuous, appearance-obsessed world? Maybe that's unfair, and the truth is that I just don't *want* her to do it, because it's scary and unknown and, actually, I'd prefer things to stay the way they are. 'You think I want to be huddled over my books all my life,' Rosie mutters.

'No, I'm not saying that. But you've got loads going on, love. I don't see how modelling will fit into all of that.'

We fall into silence as we leave the shop. I glance at Rosie, feeling guilty for dampening her excitement. 'I just think it'd be fun,' she murmurs finally.

'I'm sure it would be,' I say.

She musters a small smile. 'Sorry for being snappy.'

'It's okay. And I don't want to be a killjoy, you know. It's just, I didn't realise agency people worked that way . . .'

'You mean scouting girls?'

'Yes.'

'Well, Kate Moss was scouted,' she says, taking a couple of carrier bags from me without even being asked. 'That's how they find new models.'

'What, by prowling around shops?'

She laughs. 'Laurie wasn't *prowling,* Mum. You're so suspicious! She was really nice.'

'Yes, she did seem nice, but, you know . . . we'll have to see.' As we make our way out of the mall, I try to figure out how to put her off modelling without spoiling what was clearly a thrilling encounter for her. The truth is, what's so lovely about Rosie is that there's so much more to her than the way she looks. She excels at school, even in the subjects she struggles with, because she works hard. Yes, she can be rather spiky at times, but isn't that part of being a sixteen-year-old girl?

As we drive home, I try to imagine her dad's reaction to today's encounter. Will's handsome, strong-jawed face shimmers into my mind, and it's not awash with delight. He's very protective, and I know he regards the fashion industry as a load of fluff and nonsense. Rosie's too smart for all that, he'll decide. He was pretty taken aback when she started to fill the bathroom with a baffling array of skincare and hair products. 'She's just a normal teenage girl,' I explained.

Plus, while he may have been persuadable at one time, Will has become rather grumpy of late. I can guess why; he is stressed about our precarious finances. Until January, he was employed by Greenspace Heritage, a charity which protects wildlife and its habitats within the M25. Unfortunately, the new Director's views were at odds with Will's. While my husband felt it was all about encouraging the public to enjoy London's hidden wildernesses – i.e., to get messy and have fun – the boss believed they should focus on negotiating corporate deals to bring in huge injections of cash. And so Will was 'let go' from the job he'd loved, and which had consumed him for the past decade.

'Something'll come up,' he keeps saying, which is having the opposite effect of reassuring me. I've become conscious of treading carefully around him – of picking my moment before asking anything even faintly controversial. For instance, while I know he's applying for jobs, are any interviews likely to happen in the near future – i.e., *at some point this year*? I can't help worrying that his redundancy pay-off must have all but run out by now. 'There's enough in the joint account isn't there?' he asked tersely, last time I raised it. Yes, there was, just about – thanks to my full-time job. However, we both know I don't earn enough to keep the four of us long-term.

In fact, occasionally I wonder if it's *not* Will's redundancy, but something far scarier that's driving us apart: that, quite simply, he's stopped fancying me. I caught him glancing at me the other night as I undressed for bed, and he didn't look as if he were about to explode with desire. By the time I'd pulled off my bra – a sturdy black number capable of hoisting two porpoises to safety from an oil-slicked sea – he was already feigning sleep.

I lay awake for ages, studying the back of his head. *Do we still love each other?* I wondered, not for the first time. *Or are we only together for the kids, or because we're too old or scared to break up and start all over again?* It's not that I expect full-on passion all the time, not when we've been married for thirteen years. But, more and more often these days, I find myself wondering, is this as good as it gets?

I glance at Rosie as we make our slow journey home through the outer reaches of East London. 'You do remember it's Dad's birthday tomorrow?' I prompt her.

'God, yes.' She pulls a horrified face.

'You haven't bought him anything?'

'Sorry, Mum. I was going to today, but after we'd met Laurie it went right out of my mind . . .' *First whiff of modelling stardom and she forgets her dad's birthday. Not good.*

'Could you make him a card, at least?'

'Yeah, of course,' she replies, pausing before adding, 'D'you think they'll take me on?'

So she really wants to do this. 'Let's see what happens. Maybe it's best not to get too excited about it.'

'Why not?' she exclaims. 'It *is* exciting, Mum! Why are you being so negative?'

'I'm not, Rosie. We just need to think about what it might mean for you. And of course,' I add, trying to sound as if it's no big deal at all, 'we'll have to talk it over with Dad.'

Chapter Two

We arrive home to find Ollie, who's eleven, poring over his laptop at the kitchen table. 'This is so cool, Mum,' he announces without shifting his gaze from the screen.

'Lovely. Anyway, *hello,* hon. Had a good afternoon?'

'You didn't even look!' I glance over his shoulder – he's studying a rather professional-looking microscope, with numerous levers and knobs – then stash the bags containing Will's presents out of sight in the cupboard under the stairs.

Ollie shares his dad's passion for science and nature – triggered, I suspect, by the sweetly entitled 'field trips' Will used to take the kids on, from which they'd return all excited and mud-splattered and present me with larvae and bugs. Sometimes he'd take them off camping for a couple of days. While Ollie still ventures out with him occasionally, Rosie hasn't pulled on her waders for several years now. Maybe, I reflect, Will feels redundant in more ways than one.

I wave at him through the kitchen window. He grins from our back garden – his arms are laden with bits of shrub – and motions that he won't be a minute. 'I'd love this for my birthday,' Ollie muses, still peering at the screen.

'We'll see, love. But it's not until December and Dad's is tomorrow, okay? So it's *slightly* more urgent. Hope you've remembered.'

'Oh! Yeah, yeah,' he says blithely as Will strides in, dispenses a quick kiss on my cheek and says, 'I'll just get cleaned up. Did you have a good time at the shops?' Without waiting for an answer he bounds upstairs.

Rosie, who'd wandered off to see her rabbit, emerges from the utility room with him snuggled in her arms. Sixteen she may be, and the proud owner of a Babyliss hot brush, yet she still adores her pet. Guinness is getting on a bit now, and Rosie insisted we took him to the vet (I suspect she wanted an excuse to nosy about at the surgery) for a bunny MOT. Being unable to find anything wrong with him, the vet suggested that perhaps he shouldn't spend all his time outdoors, for which he charged a £45 consultation fee. And so Guinness now 'divides his time' between a luxury hutch and adjoining run in the garden, and a large hay-filled box in our utility room.

'Where's Dad?' Rosie asks, stroking back Guinness's ears.

'Having a shower,' I reply. 'He's been gardening all day.'

'Can't wait to tell him!' Her eyes are shining, her cheeks flushed with excitement.

'Tell him what?' Ollie mutters, zooming in for a closer look at the microscope.

'I was scouted today.'

'What?' Ollie turns to face her. 'By a model agency, you mean?' Christ, even he is familiar with the term.

'Yeah,' Rosie says with a grin.

'Like, they reckon you could be on the cover of magazines and stuff?'

'Yes, Ollie.'

'*You*, with your funny little sticky-up nose?' He jumps up from his seat and mimics a supermodel strut across the kitchen. With a gasp of irritation, and with Guinness still clutched to her chest, Rosie stomps up to her room.

'What's up with her?' Ollie asks.

'Oh, she's just excited and thinks you're not taking it seriously.'

He pushes back choppy dark hair from his grey-blue eyes. 'But Rosie's not interested in modelling. It's a crap job, Mum. They're a load of bitchy anorexics—'

'You can't say that,' I retort, still amazed that he has any awareness of the business at all. 'You don't know anything about it. Neither do I . . .'

'Who's a bitchy anorexic?' Will strolls into the kitchen, all fresh and smelling delicious from his shower.

'No one,' I say quickly.

'Dad, look at this,' Ollie pipes up, beckoning him over to the laptop. Will peers at the microscope.

'Yeah, that looks great. That's pretty serious kit.'

'. . . It's got incident *and* transmitted illumination,' Ollie explains, 'and look how powerful that eyepiece is . . .'

I watch them, flipping from one image to the next, whilst attempting to communicate silently to Ollie that he mustn't blurt out anything about Rosie being scouted today. *That modelling thing*, I urge him, *please do not speak of it until I can be sure that Dad's in the right sort of mood.* In fact, I'm pretty certain he'll view modelling as completely wrong and ridiculous for his beloved Rosie. Whenever I explain to anyone that Will isn't her biological dad – she was eighteen months old when we met – I quickly point out that he is her dad in every other possible way. He's been a brilliant father to her.

Some women go for charm or money or incredible prowess in bed. I realised I'd fallen madly in love with Will Bristow when he appeared at my flat with the wooden toy garage he'd built for Rosie, complete with an actual working lift, for her collection of toy cars.

'I know she's not old enough for it really,' he said apologetically, 'but I had some wood kicking about and got a bit carried away . . .' Sure, my heart had already been flipped by his wide, bright smile, his deep blue eyes and lean, delicious body. But it was that *lift*, that you wound up and down with a tiny handle, which made me realise that this kind, rather shy man, who cared about plants and the dwindling red squirrel population, could quite possibly be the love of my life.

Will glances up from the laptop. 'What were you saying about bitchy anorexics?'

'Oh, nothing, hon. We'll talk about it later.' I throw Ollie a *don't-say-anything* look, then delve into a carrier bag and thrust him a present – the mini silver Maglite torch he's been after.

'Aw, great! Thanks, Mum!'

I smile, watching him admire its powerful beam. He is less enthusiastic about his other gift, and merely flings it over a chair. 'Ollie,' I prompt him, 'could you *admire* your new sweatshirt, please? It's for school. You said you needed one and I actually went into Hollister for that, because Maria said they do the nicest ones for boys and you complained that the last ones were thin and cheap-looking.' I blink at him, awaiting gratitude. 'I could have just gone to BHS,' I add.

'Uh-huh,' he mutters.

'D'you realise it's completely dark in Hollister?' I continue. 'It's like venturing down towards the earth's core. They should issue miners' helmets with lamps on for us ordinary people who don't have special night vision . . .'

Ollie smirks. 'It's *meant* to be dark, Mum.'

'Yes, I realise that. If I'd bought your torch before I went in, then I wouldn't have been stumbling about, treading on people's feet. Also, I can't believe the looks policy they have in there. I mean, all the staff look like models . . .' Damn, the M-word pops out before I can stop it.

Ollie turns to Will. 'Guess what, Dad . . .'

Please, do not speak of it . . .

'What?' Will asks.

'Rosie's gonna be a model!'

Oh, bloody hell . . .

Will frowns at me. 'Huh? What's going on?'

I grab his hand and smile broadly. 'Nothing, darling. Nothing's going on. Well, not much. Come and show me what you've been doing in the garden and I'll tell you all about it.'

It worries me, as we step out into the warm July afternoon, this occasional tendency I have of addressing Will as if he were about eight years old. It started after his redundancy, and I'm only trying to be supportive and kind. However, I fear it can come out sounding as if I might try to check his hair for a nit infestation, or arrange his pizza toppings to make a face.

Will seems more relaxed as we sit side by side on our worn wooden bench in the late afternoon sunshine. We bought this place – a redbrick terrace in dire need of an upgrade – when Ollie was a toddler, figuring that two children with limitless energy really needed a lawn to run about on. What we'd failed to realise was that if you own a garden, you actually have to *garden* it. But we'd had our hands full with the children and our jobs, and the previous owners' immaculate borders soon ran amok, much to the consternation of Gerald and Tricia next door.

'It's fine,' I'd say, whenever one of them peered over the fence and asked what our 'plans' for it were. 'You don't want precious plants with kids running about. We far prefer it like this.' I talked as if it were an actual lifestyle choice, and not sheer neglect, that had made our garden that way. It grew even more jungly – with Tricia making the occasional barbed comment that we might 'get someone in to, you know, *give you a hand*' – until Will found himself with acres of time to tackle it. And when he's not gardening, he's out on his bike, foraging for wild food in the leafy pockets of East London; we've had elderflower, sorrel and armfuls of watercress. He's turned into quite the hunter-gatherer, and it suits him. He looks like the kind of man who, should you find yourself trapped on a mountain in a freak storm, would be capable of knocking up a sturdy shelter from a couple of sticks and a bread wrapper and cook a hearty meal out of some lichen.

'So,' Will says now, shielding his eyes from the sun, 'what's this about modelling?'

'Oh, a woman from an agency spotted Rosie in Forever 21 and said she has potential. It's not a big deal . . .'

'Forever 21?' Such places don't feature on Will's radar.

'Clothes shop the size of Belgium. I wouldn't recommend going in without a ration pack and some kind of paper trail to help you find your way back out . . .'

'Well,' he says, 'I hope you told her where to get off.'

I look at him, momentarily lost for words. 'Of course I didn't. D'you honestly think I'd speak to anyone like that?'

Will shrugs. 'What did you tell her then?'

'I didn't tell her *anything*. It's not as if she was offering Rosie an actual job or a contract or however they do it. I mean, she wasn't about to drag her off by her hair and throw her onto a catwalk . . .' He flares his nostrils, a relatively new habit of his. 'Anyway,' I add, 'I said we'd think it over.'

'What is there to think about?' Will asks. 'You know what the modelling world's like . . .'

'No, I don't,' I say firmly, 'and neither do you.'

He turns to me, eyes guarded. 'Well, I can imagine. Half a tomato a day, hoovering up a ton of coke—'

'What?' I splutter. 'That's a bit of a leap, isn't it?'

'I don't think so. And what about photographers preying on young girls?'

Deep breath. Keep calm. Focus on the blue haze of cornflowers. 'Well, yes, I s'pose that does happen occasionally . . .'

'And you'd be okay with that, would you?'

'Of course I wouldn't. God. What a thing to say, Will!' I glare at him, knowing he's only acting this way because he's concerned, and wants the best for Rosie. However, he wasn't snippy like this when he had barely a moment to himself, often working evenings and weekends if Greenspace required it. And, whilst I'm hugely impressed that he's learnt how to make food shoot up from the earth, I also worry that he's become a little . . . *anchorless*. 'Face is a proper agency,' I add huffily. 'The woman gave me her card.'

'Oh, her card! She couldn't have faked that then.'

'You're suggesting she prints up bogus cards to lure girls to her office?'

Will shrugs again. 'Maybe.'

I clamp my back teeth together and fix my gaze on

our unlovely shed which is huddled, slowly sagging and rotting, at the bottom of the garden. 'Look,' I say carefully, 'this obviously means a lot to Rosie. You should have seen her – she was thrilled to bits. I'm not madly keen on the idea either, but I think it's only fair to let her visit the agency so we can find out what it's all about.' Will slides his gaze towards me. 'It's just a *chat*,' I add. 'I know you're being protective, but surely you realise I'd never say yes if I thought she was going to be exploited in any way . . .'

Will digs a trainer toe into the gravel path. 'Sorry. You're right. I'm just being a jerk.'

I link my arm through his. His arms are lightly tanned, his skin warm to the touch. 'No, you're not. You're her dad and you love her and just want to keep her safe.'

He musters a smile. 'Wonder what Mum'll have to say?'

'God, yes, I hadn't thought of that.' Gloria, my mother-in-law, was a beauty queen in the 70s and she's coming round later for dinner. I can't decide whether her input will be helpful; she's never seemed especially keen to discuss her glamorous past. But maybe, as it concerns Rosie, she'll be happy to offer advice.

Then it hits me: my friend Liza's daughter, Scarlett, appeared in a couple of catalogues before going to university. Liza will have a more up-to-date view of modelling than Gloria does and, more importantly, she's brilliant company and gets along with everyone. I call her to invite her to dinner and, thankfully, she sounds delighted to come. Diluting the mother-in-law effect, I think it's called.

Chapter Three

Gloria's golden hair – it's actually *gold*, rather than merely blonde – is set in stiff waves, as if piped on top of her head. She has a neat, narrow nose and large, carefully made-up pale blue eyes, involving several toning shades of iridescent shadow. The overall effect is of refined beauty, although, if small children were around, you'd be worried that they might cut themselves on her cheekbones. 'Hello, Gloria,' I say, kissing her powdered cheek. 'You look lovely.'

'You too,' she says briskly. 'That's a very pretty dress.' Reed thin and wearing a peach blouse and immaculate navy blue trouser suit, she eyes my pistachio Ghost dress. I still love it, despite it being of a similar vintage to Guinness, who's reappeared, still being cradled by Rosie as she greets her grandma. I reassure myself that a girl who still adores her bunny is unlikely to have her head turned by a load of coke-hoovering fashion types.

I also note that Will appears to have acquired a new jumper at some point during his trip to collect Gloria, which is odd. Even stranger, it's *identical* to the one I bought for his birthday.

'Present from Mum,' he says, giving me a wink. 'She wanted to make sure it fitted.'

'Doesn't it suit him?' she observes.

'Er, yes, it really does,' I reply, trying to keep down a smirk. 'You have lovely taste, Gloria.'

She smiles and eagerly snatches the glass of wine he offers her. 'Now you mustn't keep topping me up, Will.' *Enthusiastic sip.* 'I'm not supposed to be drinking, you know. My nutritionist . . .' *Massive gulp.* 'Mmm, it does smell good in here . . .'

'All Will's work,' I explain. 'He's doing roast chicken and all these clever things with vegetables. Me and Rosie have been out shopping . . .'

'. . . Spending your money, Will?' she titters, a comment so clearly ill-chosen it causes sweat to spring from my armpits. 'Oh, I know you work hard, Charlotte,' she adds, 'at that . . . *place*.' You'd think, by the accompanying curl of her lip, that she means a sauna or lapdancing club. In fact it's a crisp factory in Essex. A posh crisp factory, I might add, offering fancy varieties such as crushed pink peppercorn and the alarming-sounding lobster bisque. It's all very upmarket. In fact we don't even call them crisps but *hand-cooked potato chips*. But they're still basically fried potatoes, and my job is to market them. I am a flogger of fat-drenched Maris Pipers coming in at around 1025 calories per family pack, and Gloria, whose diet appears to consist mainly of Chilean sauvignon and the occasional olive, cannot bring herself to speak of it.

'So how *is* the job-hunting going, Will?' she asks, turning to her son.

'Really well, thanks,' Will replies, peering through the oven's glass door.

'Any interviews yet?'

I see his jaw tighten as he straightens up. Now I realise why he invited Gloria over this evening instead of tomorrow. While he's always been happy to take care of her – especially since his father died four years ago – he couldn't face being grilled about his future career plans on his actual birthday. 'I'm sure something'll come up soon,' he replies firmly as Ollie and I set the kitchen table and Rosie returns Guinness to the utility room.

'Have you thought about the police force?' Gloria asks, glugging more wine.

Will grimaces. 'It's not *quite* my area of expertise, Mum.'

'I know that,' she concedes, 'but they have excellent training and pension schemes . . .'

'Isn't Dad a bit old to be a cop?' Ollie asks.

'Thanks, Ollie,' Will chuckles, giving me a look.

'Well, I'm sure they do a mature entry scheme,' she goes on, clearly an expert in such matters. 'Or what about the prison service?'

'Dad can't work in a prison!' Rosie exclaims with a loud guffaw.

Gloria frowns. 'Why not?'

'Because . . .' Rosie smirks. 'I just . . . can't imagine it.'

'Working with a load of murderers,' Ollie adds, eyes widening. 'That'd be interesting, wouldn't it, Dad?'

'Fascinating,' Will agrees, turning his attention to a saucepan of gravy on the hob.

'But what if he was attacked?' Rosie asks. 'Can you imagine Dad managing to fight someone off?' Both she and Ollie peal with laughter.

'Well, er, I'd imagine that's not necessary,' Gloria says curtly.

'He'd be scared witless,' Ollie adds.

'Thanks, everyone,' Will cuts in, pushing back his dark hair with an oven-gloved hand. 'I do appreciate all your career advice but don't worry, I actually have everything under control . . .' Really? I'd love to believe it's true. He brightens as Liza arrives, greeting us with a bottle of wine and hugs all round – even Gloria, as if she's an old friend – and having the miraculous effect of instantly lightening the atmosphere. Fair and pretty with a slim, boyish body, Liza looks a decade younger than her fifty-two years. She never bothers with make-up beyond a lick of mascara. Her lilac embroidered top and skinny jeans were probably thrown on, but she looks radiant and lovely. Liza calls herself a 'slasher'; i.e., Spanish-teacher-slash-yoga-instructor-slash-wholefood-store-employee. Her life is full and varied and she seems to thrive on it. I start to relax as we catch up on each other's news; unlike Gloria, Liza knows to avoid quizzing Will directly about his job hunt.

'So, how are you, Rosie?' she asks as Will and I bring a myriad of dishes to the table.

Rosie grins, taking the seat next to her. 'I got scouted today. A woman from an agency thought I could be a model.'

'Wow!' Liza looks impressed. 'Are you going to do it?'

'Yeah, of course,' she exclaims.

'Well, um, we still need to talk about that,' I say quickly.

'I was the same,' Liza remarks, smiling her thanks as Will fills her wine glass. 'Freaked out when Scarlett first mentioned it. Remember she entered that competition without telling me? And then only went and *won*?'

I laugh. 'But you knew she could look after herself . . .'

'. . . And so can Rosie.' She turns to my daughter. 'You'll be *fine*, honey. You'll be an amazing model . . .'

'It's not a fait accompli, Liza,' Will remarks.

'Oh, Dad.' Rosie rolls her eyes. 'You did some modelling, didn't you, Grandma? Weren't you in pageants or something when you were young?'

Gloria purses her lips. 'That's the American term. We called them beauty contests and yes, I did take part in a few . . .'

'You're beautiful, Gloria,' Liza says truthfully. 'I can imagine you all glammed up.'

'Wasn't it fun?' Rosie asks. Gloria pauses to tip the rest of her wine down her throat, seemingly without making any swallowing motion at all.

'No,' she says finally, 'it certainly wasn't.'

We all stare at her. 'Why not?' Ollie asks.

'Was it horribly pressurised?' Will enquires gently. 'I can imagine it was a very competitive world.'

She emits a little cough, as if preparing to make an important announcement. 'No, it wasn't that. I was very successful actually. I was Miss Foil Wrap in 1972 . . .' To avoid an attack of the giggles, I focus hard on the deliciousness of Will's glazed carrots.

'What's foil wrap?' Ollie wants to know.

'You know, *foil*,' I explain, 'like you wrap a chicken in.'

Confused, Ollie peers at her. 'Why did they have a "Miss Foil Wrap"?'

'I was a brand ambassador,' Gloria says grandly. 'For the sashing ceremony I wore a dress entirely made of foil.'

'Wow,' Rosie breathes. 'Bet that was amazing.'

'Very futuristic,' Will says with a grin, but Gloria's face has clouded. Maybe she thinks he's taking the piss. She has that effect: of making those around her feel intensely uncomfortable, without actually doing very much. I note that, while the rest of us have been tucking into Will's delicious roast dinner, she has consumed a sliver of chicken roughly the size of a fingernail clipping.

'Actually,' she says, 'it wasn't. An unfortunate incident happened, but I don't want to talk about it in front of the children.' Now, of course, we're all agog.

'We're not children,' Rosie points out gently. 'I'm sixteen, Grandma. I'm not shockable, honest . . .'

Gloria shakes her head and pushes away her plate.

'Did the foil rip?' Ollie asks. 'Did everyone see your—'

'*Ollie,*' I say sharply, although I'm as keen as he is to hear the story. 'Just leave it, love. I don't think Grandma wants to—'

'I mean,' he goes on, mouth crammed with roast potato, 'foil's just thin aluminium. We did the properties of metals at school. I s'pose it's good for a dress, though, 'cause it doesn't rust . . .'

Will clears his throat. 'I think we can move on from the foil now, Ollie.'

'No,' Gloria says tersely, 'it's quite all right. I *will* tell you what happened, but only because I hope it'll serve as a warning to Rosie.'

A rapt silence descends, interrupted only by the rustle of Guinness shuffling about in his box. 'Grandma . . .?' Rosie prompts her.

Gloria twiddles her empty glass. 'I was *accosted*.'

'You mean during a contest?' I gasp, wishing now that we'd never brought this up.

'No, at a photo call,' Gloria explains. 'All the local papers were there. *Everyone*. It was a major event. All the reporters wanted to talk to me. And there was a nasty little man from the *Sorrington Bugle* . . .'

I glance at Will in alarm. Poor Gloria. She's clearly

harboured an unspeakable secret all these years. Maybe that's what's caused her to develop a rather critical edge.

'Mum,' Will says, 'you needn't talk about it. We don't want to stir up horrible memories for you.'

She peers down at her lap. 'It's okay. If Rosie's even considering modelling, then I think she should know about this . . .'

'What did the man do?' Ollie asks eagerly, tilting his head.

'He . . . poked me.'

Oh, Christ. Does that mean what I think it means? Now I'm slugging *my* wine, Gloria-style.

'Where?' Rosie asks, aghast.

'In the car park in front of everybody.'

'With his *Sorrington Bugle*?' Ollie blurts out, crumpling with laughter.

'Ollie!' I bark at him. 'It's not funny, you know, being poked—'

'I mean where in the *body*, Grandma,' Rosie explains as I top up the adults' glasses with wine, except for Will's, as he's driving his mother home to East Finchley later. I catch him eyeing the wine bottle greedily.

'In the bottom, darling,' Gloria replies, mouthing the word *bottom* in the way that people say *tumour*.

'Were you still wearing the aluminium dress?' Ollie asks.

'Yes, that's right—'

'Did he make a hole in it with his finger?'

'Ollie, that's *enough*, thank you,' Will says firmly. 'I think we've heard all we need to about the dress.'

'So, um . . . is that why you gave up, Grandma?' Rosie asks, clearly having difficulty keeping a straight face.

'Well, no,' Gloria replies. 'I became a Mum. Will was

my priority and of course, my figure was never the same after that . . .'

Will catches my eye. *Sorry,* he mouths, making me smile.

'So now you know what can happen in the modelling world,' Gloria adds. 'It's not safe, Rosie. There are people out there who'll want to take advantage of a beautiful young girl like you.'

Rosie turns to me with a stricken face.

'Of course, Gloria,' Liza starts, 'no one should think it's acceptable to behave in that way . . .'

'I agree,' Will cuts in, 'so, obviously, Rosie shouldn't get involved.'

'What?' she gasps. 'You mean we can't even go to the agency?'

'Well,' he starts, 'I don't think it's—'

'Dad, that's not fair! *Please!*'

He frowns, catching my eye in a silent plea for me to back him up.

'Horrible little man,' Gloria mutters. 'I always remember he wore a banana yellow tie—'

'I can't believe this,' Rosie cries. 'No one cares what I think. You're all discussing this as if it was nothing to do with me at all!'

'Rosie,' I say quickly, 'we'll talk about this later, okay?'

'Dad's saying no,' she wails, 'because of something that happened, like, fifty years ago!'

'Forty-three actually,' Gloria murmurs, placing her cutlery neatly on her plate.

Rosie doesn't appear to have heard her. 'For God's sake, Dad. Things are different now . . .'

'Yeah,' Ollie cuts in. '*Everyone* was a perv in the seventies. It was on the news, they've got this thing called Operation Yew Tree where they're rounding them all up—'

'Good God,' Will mutters as we clear the table together and he sets down the chocolate cake he made earlier. While it's normally one of my favourite things, right now I'm not sure I can stomach a crumb. What on earth made me think it would be helpful to chat to Gloria about modelling?

'This looks amazing,' Liza enthuses, darting me a quick look. I glance at Rosie, whose eyes are brimming with tears.

'Mum,' she mutters, glaring at Will's cake as if he'd scraped it up off the pavement, 'tell Dad how nice Laurie was.'

I look at both of them, trapped in the middle as I so often seem to be these days. They adore each other, but recently, during their frequent spats, I've noticed Will stepping carefully around Rosie as if she were made of the finest porcelain. And I've begun to suspect that there's something else she wants to add, but doesn't quite dare: *You're not my real dad so you can't tell me what to do.*

'The seventies were well weird,' Ollie continues cheerfully. 'Everyone wore massive flares and there was this programme on telly with these little pink creatures on another planet. We saw it at the TV museum. They didn't even speak . . .'

'*The Clangers*,' I mutter.

'All paedos,' Ollie observes.

'*The Clangers* weren't paedos,' I retort. 'They were innocent little knitted mice . . .'

Liza turns to Gloria. 'Er, I don't mean to belittle your experience, and I'm sure it was traumatic . . .' Gloria nods. '. . . But my daughter Scarlett did some modelling too, before she went to Bristol. She had a fantastic time and saved all her earnings and she's paying her own way through university. It's meant she hasn't had to take out a loan.'

Rosie's eyes widen. 'Wasn't she in some catalogues?'

Liza nods. 'Yes. Boden, mostly—'

'Boden?' I repeat. 'I didn't know that.' Liza has always played down Scarlett's foray into modelling. It had been over very quickly, as far as I could gather; now I suspect she just didn't want to seem boastful.

Liza nods proudly. 'She still does the occasional job, but only in holiday time and it doesn't get in the way of her studies at all.' She smiles at Gloria. 'She's studying English and Philosophy . . .'

'I'm not saying it's *all* bad,' Gloria says reluctantly.

'And the beauty of it is,' Liza continues, 'all her friends have bar jobs or are waitressing, and Scarlett hasn't had to do any of that.'

A hush fills our over-heated kitchen. 'I could pay my own way through vet school,' Rosie remarks.

'Well,' I say carefully, 'it sounds like Scarlett's had a really good experience.'

Liza nods. 'Yes, she has. D'you want to see some of her pictures?' She laughs. 'Sorry, I'm such an embarrassing mum. She'd hate me for this . . .'

'Go on,' I urge her, 'I'd love to see.' She fetches her phone from her bag and we all cluster round it. The pictures are from a Boden shoot; sunny and smiley with Scarlett's corn-coloured hair blowing across her freckled face.

'She looks amazing,' Rosie exclaims.

'Well, I think so,' Liza says with a grin.

She scrolls through pictures of Scarlett scampering through the dunes and balancing, with arms outstretched, on a fallen-down tree. 'Aren't they great?' I enthuse, shooting a quick look at Will.

He nods, seeing as I do that Scarlett is wearing the least provocative items of clothing known to womankind: a polo neck sweater. Jolly spotty wellies. A duffel coat, for goodness' sake. Could anything be more wholesome? 'So it's really been okay?' Will asks her. 'I mean, nothing awful's happened?'

'Of course not,' Liza replies. 'If it had, I'd have put a stop to it. Anyway, it's not as if she was a timid thirteen-year-old. She was eighteen when she started . . .'

'Rosie's only sixteen,' I remind her.

'Yes, Mum,' Rosie groans, 'and in Viking times I'd have at least seven children by now.'

'God forbid,' Will splutters, and even Gloria emits a wry chuckle.

I catch her eye as she prods at her cake with a fork. 'Look, I do understand what you're saying, Gloria, about the foil dress poking. And I know you're only concerned. But from what Liza's said about Scarlett's experience . . . well, maybe we shouldn't just dismiss it.'

Liza nods. 'It really improved her confidence and she met some lovely people. Honestly, it's been an amazing opportunity for her . . .'

I smile and turn to Will. 'I think the final decision should actually rest with Rosie . . . don't you, darling?'

'Dad, *please*,' Rosie blurts out. 'I can look after myself. I'm not an idiot . . .'

He frowns at me. 'But I thought we said—'

'We didn't say anything,' I cut in, 'because we haven't actually found out what it might entail. How about I call the agency on Monday? We can at least all go in for a chat.'

'You mean all of us,' Rosie asks, aghast, 'like a family outing?'

I nod firmly. 'Absolutely. Well, Ollie could go to a friend's . . .'

Will stares. 'You mean *me*? You're saying I've got to come too?'

'Yes. You obviously have concerns so I think it's important that you're there, don't you?'

'Er, I don't think . . .'

'You're coming, Will,' I say, surprising myself with my bossiness.

He gives me a look as if he's about to protest, then busies himself by fetching more wine from the fridge.

'*Why*, Mum?' Rosie cries. 'This'll be so embarrassing!'

'Because we're your family and we love you,' I say brightly, giving Liza a wink across the table as I refill her glass.

Chapter Four

I am woken at 7.27 next morning by the whine of a lawnmower. Must be Tricia next door, making a point about how grass should be immaculately shorn, and that her neighbours – especially us, the Bristows at number 27 – are letting the area down. Ours is more your abundant, bursting-with-blooms kind of garden, and all the more beautiful for it.

By late May, as everything started to grow like crazy, Tricia blinked at our explosion of flowers and remarked, 'Startling colour combo, in my opinion! But each to their own . . .' Damn cheek. In fact, I far prefer Will's approach. Tricia and Gerald's petunias and marigolds have been planted at regular intervals (10 cm), and their lawn – a perfect rectangle with edges neatly clipped – looks like an IKEA rug.

I slip out of bed, peer through the window and see that it's not Tricia who's toiling away out there, but Will. Immediately, it's apparent that this isn't just ordinary grass cutting. It's *sulky*-mowing, undertaken to make a point. On and on he goes, striding back and forth without pausing to pick up stones or admire his blooms, as he usually does. Our ancient petrol mower drones away like a vexed insect.

It doesn't seem a terribly *birthdayish* thing to do. Maybe he's miffed because I didn't hear him get up, and have therefore failed to festoon him with gifts and birthday kisses. Unlikely, though. Will isn't the kind of man who expects – or even enjoys – a fuss being made. It's more probable that he's making a point about something. Yes, that's it: the energetic mowing is probably due to being railroaded yesterday into agreeing to visit the model agency. Or maybe it's *not* that. Perhaps he's reached the tipping point of his gardening, foraging, cake-baking life, and this is his final attack on our little plot before he starts a new job. Maybe he *has* a new job, and is planning to surprise me. How ironic that would be, after his mother going on about the prison service and police force last night.

I pull on my dressing gown and venture out onto the landing. 'Rosie?' I call through her closed bedroom door.

Silence.

'Ro, are you awake?' I push it open, momentarily calmed by a lingering scent. Although strewn with knickers and tights and Kit Kat wrappers, her room at least smells good, unlike the rest of the house. With its hint of vanilla candles and jasmine body spray, it has a sweet, heady atmosphere all of its own.

She emits a low moan from her bed. 'What time is it?'

'It's Dad's birthday, *that's* what time it is. Did you manage to get anything together?'

'Ohhhh . . . I forgot.'

'Didn't you make him a card?'

Her sleepy face emerges from the duvet. 'No, sorry. Haven't you got something in reserve?'

I hear Will coming in from the garden and pottering about downstairs. 'What d'you mean, in reserve?'

'Like, in your gift drawer or something?' Ah, the magic, bottomless gift drawer: a treasure trove of stale lavender hand lotions and long-forgotten boxes of Milk Tray, no doubt fuzzed with white bloom.

'No, Rosie, I don't.'

'But you always have something . . .'

'Well, yes, there's that brown satin nightie Auntie Sally gave me last Christmas but I'm not sure Dad'll go for that.' Sally is Will's younger sister, and adored by their mother, despite deigning to visit roughly three times a year; she only lives in the Cotswolds, for goodness' sake. 'Anyway, he won't expect a present. Just a card'll do fine . . .'

'Could you sneak out and buy one for me?' She picks a fleck of sleep from her left eye.

'No,' I retort. 'Why should it be my job? Come on – you need to do *something*.' She closes her eyes again as if exhausted by our brief exchange. Sometimes I'm driven to distraction by the inertness of teenagers. As a child, Rosie would be up with the lark, poking at my face as I lay in bed, demanding to finger paint or lash a pile of sticks together with rope to make a raft, which she would then proceed to 'sail' across our garden. These days, if it weren't for school, she would spend her days cocooned in duvet, jabbing at her phone or flipping idly through a book.

I turn to leave, stepping over a scattering of nail polishes and battered old shoes, and enter Ollie's room, which smells of stale bedding and socks. It's crammed with the artefacts he's collected over the years (prime exhibits include a preserved crocodile head, donated by Liza when she'd been to the Natural History Museum in New York, and an abandoned wasps' nest we found in the attic). 'Wake up, Ollie,' I command, looming over him. 'It's Dad's birthday.'

'Oh, er, yeah . . .'

'You need to draw him a card. Quick! Come on, get up. Where are your pens?'

'*Mum.*' Ollie sits up slowly. 'He doesn't care about stuff like that.'

Actually, this year, I think he will. He needs to know we love him, that he still has a role here beyond chief gardener and cook, and that today of all days is about him. Of course, I don't tell Ollie that. 'I just think he'll appreciate it if you make an effort, love.'

'But I'm no good at drawing.' His hair is jutting up at all angles and there's a pillow crease on his cheek.

'You are, but it doesn't matter. Just find some card and write happy birthday in wiggly type.'

He snorts. 'That's not very original.'

'Well, I'll leave you to think of something better. I'm off for a shower.'

I sluice myself quickly and, when I emerge, I spot two bras drying on the radiator. Rosie's is a wisp of duck-egg blue Top Shop lace. Mine is the sturdy black contraption for hoisting porpoises. Maybe I should start jogging, like Tricia does – run off some of those Archie's Hand-Cooked Potato Chips I keep ramming into my face. Maybe then Will would be more inclined to ravage me on a Sunday morning instead of attacking the lawn.

With this thought in mind, I shun my usual weekend attire of old jeans and a T-shirt and wriggle into my favourite dress: black with spriggy red flowers, figure-hugging but stretchy and therefore pretty forgiving. Rather than creating the singular *kochwurst*-boob, it cleverly creates just enough cleavage without triggering bilious looks from the kids. Effortlessly foxy is the look I'm aiming for, not desperate middle-aged woman who hasn't had sex for fourteen weeks. Then – although I only wear make-up for work these days – I apply a quick slick of BB cream, some mascara and a dab of sheer, berry-coloured lipstick.

'Shall I run out and buy him a box of After Eights?' Ollie asks, ambling into my bedroom.

'Um, no.'

'Why not?'

'He hates them.'

Ollie frowns. 'Celebrations then?'

'No, darling, he'd rather have *nothing* than a box of panic-bought chocolates from Londis—'

'Why?' He looks baffled.

I consider how to explain this. 'It's not really about the *thing*, Ollie. It's about the planning and thought that's gone into it – the effort.'

'It'd be quite an effort to go out to the shop,' he reasons, 'when really, I'd rather stay here.'

'Oh, come on, Ollie. You know what I mean. Presents do matter, you know.'

He exhales through his nostrils. 'What did Dad get *you* last birthday?'

'Er . . .' I clear my throat. 'We decided not to do presents last year. We had the house repointed instead.' And now I'm recalling Tricia, at first admiring the handiwork and then, when I let slip that the lovingly applied mortar was my actual *present*, chuckling, 'Oh, poor you!

Well, you're being very stoical about it, I have to say. Gerald bought me a day of treatments at Henley Grange. But I suppose your place did need urgent attention . . .'

'You know how it is,' I replied brightly. 'Priorities and all that. No point in having lovely smooth pores if your house falls down.'

Having instructed Ollie to create an artistic masterpiece, I find Will in the kitchen and give him a hug. 'Happy birthday, darling.'

'Thanks.'

'Everything okay?' I ask, stepping away.

'Sure.' He's still retaining a trace of the grumpiness he'd displayed while mowing, and I sense my patience fraying. Birthdays didn't used to involve frenetic mowing at dawn. In fact, practical tasks of any nature would be banned for the day. There'd be cheap champagne at breakfast, plus smoked salmon, scrambled eggs and lots and lots of kisses. Sex, too, once the kids had been dispatched to school. We'd had a tradition of always taking the day off on our birthdays.

'Feel okay about turning forty-one?' I ask brightly.

''Course I do,' Will says, adding, 'you look lovely today.'

'Thanks. So do you.' It's true; his light tan brings out the azure of his eyes, and his strong, lean legs and taut stomach and bottom all add up to a physique a man of thirty would envy.

He smiles wryly. 'Reckon gardening leave suits me, then?'

'Yes,' I say, 'I really do.' And, tempting though it is to ask, 'Any news, though? About interviews, I mean?', I force myself not to, because at forty-one he is surely capable of sorting out his own life. Anyway, I reflect, calling the kids downstairs and gathering everyone together in the living room, perhaps I was wrong about the angry-mowing. Maybe he was just feeling *energetic*.

He seems genuinely delighted with the kids' hastily-drawn cards and my pile of presents. 'This is too much,' he exclaims, examining the turntable and speakers which I hauled around that godforsaken mall. 'Thank you, darling.' He examines the fragrance and soft blue sweater. 'But . . . isn't this the one Mum gave me?'

'I bought you an identical one,' I say, laughing. 'Gloria and I obviously have the same taste.'

He grins and kisses the top of my head. 'Bloody hell. That's worrying.'

Ollie and Rosie edge away at the sight of us expressing affection, as if the next step may be some enthusiastic snogging (unlikely). 'Look, Mum,' Rosie remarks, poised at the front window, 'people are moving in over the road.' I join her to watch several powerful-looking men unloading furniture from a removal van. There's a woman, too – skinny and bird-like in tight black jeans and a faded denim jacket, with a torrent of wavy auburn hair cascading down her back. A tall, rangy teenage boy appears to be watching the proceedings with interest, without offering to help.

Actually, I decide, this family looks interesting. Our corner of East London has a villagey feel; well-scrubbed women march around in Breton tops and boot-cut jeans, ferrying photogenic children to and from numerous activities. Some local mums fill their entire lives with bake sales and ensuring our little community runs precisely as it should. While I'm happy here, occasionally I find our neighbourhood a little *too* well behaved. The one time I took Ollie to a music workshop as a toddler, I was politely asked by a statuesque blonde to 'please remove that beaker he's holding – we don't want other children seeing it'. It was only Ribena, not Scotch.

Now the woman and removal men are all standing around and chatting in the bright sunshine. 'Shall we go out and say hi?' I suggest.

'No,' Will exclaims, followed by a derisive laugh. 'God, Charlotte.'

'Why not?'

'Mum, no!' Rosie cries. 'You can't just march over there. You don't know them.'

'I wouldn't *march*. I'd just walk normally . . .'

'What would you say?' she demands.

I smirk. 'How about, "Hello"? I find that's usually a good way to start things off.' Outside, the woman tosses back her head and laughs long and hard at something one of the men has said.

'Mum's so nosy,' Ollie sniggers to his dad.

'Yeah, she's turned into a curtain-twitcher,' Will agrees, which prickles me; we're *all* standing here, peering out, after all.

'Well,' I announce, 'I'm going out to welcome them. C'mon, Will, let's be neighbourly.'

'You can't!' Rosie cries. But I'm already making for the door, with Rosie shouting, 'Dad, stop her!' and actually *grabbing* at my arm, as if I were naked and about to ruin her young life.

Chapter Five

The woman and boy are chatting companionably at their front door. As we approach, I realise her trousers aren't in fact jeans, but black leather. How very racy.

'This is a bit embarrassing,' Will mutters.

'No it's not. It's just a nice thing to do,' I whisper back, rearranging my face into a wide smile. 'Hello,' I say brightly. 'We live across the road. Just thought we'd come over and say hi.'

'Oh, hi,' the woman says, seeming genuinely pleased. 'Lovely to meet you.'

'I'm Charlotte and this is my husband Will . . .'

'I'm Sabrina,' the woman says, 'and my husband . . .' She turns to the open front door and yells: 'Tommy? Come outside! Our new neighbours are here . . .'

A tall, broad-chested man in a faded black Rolling Stones T-shirt and jeans a tad on the tight side emerges and greets us warmly. While Sabrina is tiny and astonishingly pretty – early forties at a guess – Tommy is a hulking bear of a man, perhaps heading for fifty, with clippered greying hair and a bone-crushing handshake.

'Great to meet you both. Lovely area this is.' He has the kind of deep, gravelly voice that's perfect for relating dirty jokes.

'It really is,' I agree, glancing at the boy who's now perched on the low front wall, lighting a roll-up. 'That's our son Zach,' Sabrina adds with an eye roll. 'Helping enormously as you can tell.'

We all laugh, and I can't help being transfixed by the way he's puffing nonchalantly in full view of his parents. He can't be much older than Rosie. Will would have a heart attack if he ever saw her with a ciggie in her mouth. 'D'you have to smoke that out here?' Tommy growls, which Zach chooses to ignore.

'Er, are you going to be starting at Harrington High, Zach?' I ask him.

He shakes his head. 'Nah.'

'Oh, are you going to St Jude's?'

Another head shake, causing his mop of black hair to flop into his dark, guarded eyes. 'I'm not at school.'

'He left last year,' Sabrina explains. 'Wants to pursue music . . .'

'Are you going to music college?' I ask, sensing Will shooting me a sharp look.

'He's doing his own thing,' his mother explains with a resigned smile.

'Meaning sod all, basically,' Tommy chortles. 'He's studying at the college of fuck-all, then possibly graduating to the university of sitting-on-his-arse. Bloody exhausting, isn't it, Zach?'

We laugh again, and Zach gazes at us as if we're a collection of random strangers waiting for a bus. 'Well,' Will says, growing impatient now, 'if there's anything you need . . .'

'Great, thanks,' Sabrina says warmly.

'There *is* something,' Tommy adds. 'Don't suppose you know if there are any good cycling trails around here? Trail biking, I mean.'

I pause for Will to answer this time, thinking that perhaps he might like to contribute, seeing as he's the one who zooms around parks and marshlands on his foraging expeditions. But he just stands there, mute, as if Tommy had enquired about some obscure local facility – an accordion supplier, perhaps, or a breeder of guinea pigs. 'Er, you cycle a lot, don't you?' I prompt Will, widening my eyes.

'Um, yeah, just round and about really,' he says vaguely. Oh, for Christ's sake. I know he's eager to get away, but he doesn't have to be so uncommunicative. It's like having another teenager in tow.

'Would you say the marshes are the best place?' I suggest.

'Yeah.' Will nods. 'Depends what you're looking for really . . .'

'Well, I guess we'd better let you get on.' I smile brightly, realising I'm trying to compensate for Will's standoffishness, and feel decidedly out of sorts as we troop back to our house.

'Did you have to do that?' Will hisses as we cross the road.

'Do what?'

'Interrogate the boy . . .'

I gawp at him as we reach our house. 'I didn't interrogate him. I just asked a few questions. At least I was interested. It's better than being rude, like you were, pretending you couldn't quite remember what a bicycle is . . .'

Will emits a gasp of irritation.

'Charlotte! Just a minute . . .' I turn to see Sabrina, her ravishing hair shining like copper as she hurries towards us. 'Sorry,' she adds, 'I should've said. We're having a few friends around for a barbecue next Saturday. A sort of christen-the-house thing. It'd be great if you and your family could come . . . we'd love to meet you all properly.'

Clearly, *she* wasn't appalled by me 'interrogating' her son. 'That's kind of you,' I reply. 'We'd love to, wouldn't we, Will?'

'Uh . . . yeah,' he says, in an overly bright voice, unable to disguise the fact that he'd rather clean our tiling grout than fraternise with the new neighbours.

*

Will's mood has lifted by the time we're all installed in our favourite local Malaysian restaurant for his birthday dinner (well, it's everyone's favourite apart from Ollie's – he nagged to go to the Harvester and is beyond thrilled that Rosie's best friend Nina started working there recently). 'You should have heard Mum, grilling the poor boy,' Will chuckles.

'I only asked a few polite questions,' I correct him, not minding a bit of light ribbing as long as we have a fun evening out.

Will laughs, tucking into fiery prawns. 'You didn't *ask* questions. You fired them at him like a machine gun. He was virtually ducking for cover.' He shields his head with his hands and grins at Ollie. 'She wanted to know all about his future career plans, what he intends to do with the rest of his life . . .'

Rosie sniggers. 'Yeah. You were out there for ages, Mum. And they were obviously dead busy . . .'

'. . . And the boy—' Will starts.

'Zach,' I cut in. 'His name's Zach.'

'. . . he was smoking in front of his parents,' Will goes on, 'and it wasn't just a roll-up either.'

'Wasn't it?' I ask.

'What was it then?' Ollie demands, eyes wide.

'D'you mean it was pot?' I blurt out, at which Rosie snorts with laughter.

'Pot? Who calls it *pot*?'

Everyone is sniggering now as the waiter clears our table. 'Mum does, obviously,' Will says with a grin. 'She thinks it's still 1972.'

'I wasn't even *born* in 1972, Will. And what am I meant to call it?'

'Pot!' Ollie mimics me. 'Look, we're having a groovy night out! Would anyone like some *pot*?'

The waiter glances back and smirks.

'Hash, then?' I suggest with a shrug. 'Ganja? Whacky baccy? *Assassin of youth*?'

Ollie and Rosie convulse with laughter. 'Where d'you hear that?' she exclaims.

'In a film,' I reply, in mock indignation, to which Ollie enquires – of course, I should have sensed the question hurtling towards me, like the thundering rock in *Raiders of the Lost Ark* – 'Have *you* ever smoked pot, Mum?'

I sip my wine while formulating an appropriate response. Outright lying doesn't feel right – but then, do my children need a full inventory of every misdemeanour from my distant past? Anyway, as far as they're concerned I was never a young person. I was born a middle-aged woman forever stuffing sweaty pants into the washing machine and moaning about the loo being left unflushed.

'I, uh . . . had a nibble of a space cake once,' I say, hoping that'll satisfy them.

'What's a space cake?' Ollie asks eagerly.

'It's a little bun with, er, stuff baked into it.'

'Like *pot*?' Rosie giggles.

'That's right,' I say in a small, regretful voice. 'I thought it was an ordinary cake actually.'

'Like from Starbucks?' Will smirks.

'Yes. A sort of . . . *herbal muffin*.'

'No, you didn't,' Ollie teases. 'You knew it was drugs, Mum. You wanted that cake, I can tell . . .'

'She only had a little nibble,' Will adds, his mouth twitching with mirth.

'Where did you have it?' Rosie asks. 'At a party?'

I pour myself a glass of sparkling water to prove how *pure* I am now, and not the type to consume suspect bakery goods of any description. 'Yes,' I reply simply, 'it was at a party.' In fact it was Fraser, Rosie's real father, who I'd sampled space cakes with – in Amsterdam, unsurprisingly, on our Inter-railing trip. It had become 'our' trip by chance. I'd planned to travel with Angie, a school friend, and when she'd contracted glandular fever I'd decided to go on my own. En route to Paris I'd met Fraser, whose refined features and floppy fair hair suggested a privileged upbringing involving rugby and cricket and an expensive education. Certainly, he had enough cash in the seemingly bottomless pockets of his khaki shorts to spend four months drifting around Europe, stopping off to see various wealthy friends, whereas I'd only been able to scrape together enough for three weeks. From then on we'd travelled together, and by the time we rolled up at an Amsterdam hostel, we were in love.

'What was it like?' Ollie wants to know, making my

heart jolt. *Oh my God, it was heaven. Lying in Vondelpark with him kissing crumbs from my lips, and not knowing if it was the druggy cake making my head swirl, or the beautiful blond boy who looked like one of those carved marble angels you see in cathedrals . . .*

'Mum?' Ollie prompts me.

'Er, yes?' I nearly knock over my glass of water.

'What did it taste of?'

I take a fortifying glug of wine. 'It was horrible,' I fib. 'The most disgusting thing I ever ate. It made me very, very sick, and if either of you are ever offered anything like that, just say no.'

Rosie grins. 'They actually call it weed these days, Mum. Weed or spliff or cheese.'

'Cheese?' I repeat, feeling decrepit. 'Are you sure?'

'Yeah, you hear people saying they're gonna score some cheese . . .'

I splutter involuntarily. 'Who are these people?'

She shrugs. 'Just *people*.'

'Are you sure that's what they mean, though?' I ask.

'They could just be going to buy a Camembert,' Will offers, sending the kids into hysterics again.

I smile and squeeze his hand under the table. If only it could always be like this, with Will being funny and sweet, like he used to be, before redundancy and angry-mowing and refusing to talk to me about anything important. Yet the fact that our marriage is hardly sparkly these days isn't *all* his fault; it's mine too. Occasionally, when Liza mentions a date she's been on, I can't help sensing a twinge of envy. Life can feel terribly grown up sometimes, when I come home to a barely communicative husband, then get on with the business of shovelling Guinness's droppings out of his hutch (Rosie refuses to involve herself in his toileting. What kind of vet will she make, if she can't bring herself to deal with a few innocuous pebble-like poos?).

Sometimes, I tell myself, this is just how adult life is, and I should stop mourning the loss of spontaneity and passion and accept how things are. The way Will flinches when I touch him in bed, as if jabbed with a red hot toasting fork with a smouldering marshmallow on the end . . . at our age it's just normal, isn't it? Everyone looks back at their younger selves occasionally, and feels all dreamy and wistful. Then they give themselves a mental slap and get on with hoiking a mass of gunky hair out of the shower drain and book in the car for its MOT.

'Good birthday, sweetheart?' I ask, my hand still wrapped around his.

Will smiles warmly. 'Lovely, thanks.'

'So, am I forgiven interrogating our new neighbours?'

'Guess so.' He squeezes my hand back.

'What did you think of Sabrina? Isn't she beautiful?'

'Hmm, s'pose so,' he says with a shrug.

'Come on,' I tease him. 'What about that stunning red hair? And her body! So slim and fit-looking. D'you think she's a dancer?'

Will looks genuinely baffled. 'I've no idea. Why d'you say that?'

'Oh, I don't know – she has that lean, sinewy vibe about her, a bit like Liza . . .' I pause. 'Maybe she's something to do with the music business? Or a make-up artist?'

Rosie chuckles. 'Why d'you do this, Mum?'

'Do what?'

'Take such a massive interest in other people's lives.'

'I don't,' I retort. 'I'm just interested. So, are we all going to their party next Saturday?'

'Oh, I'm not sure,' Will says with a shrug. 'We won't know anyone, will we?'

'But we could *get* to know them,' I point out.

'Will there be anyone my age?' Ollie wants to know.

'I've no idea,' I say briskly, 'but anyway, *I'm* looking forward to it, and I'd appreciate it if you could all be positive because I'd really like us to all go as a family.' I cough and sip my wine. In fact, I'm not that desperate myself. I'm out of practice when it comes to strangers' parties; what to wear, what to say, how to *be* . . . I can't recall the last time Will and I went to a social event where we didn't know practically everyone. In fact, the last party I went to was my work Christmas do – seven months ago. The factory guys tore into the cheap fizz, and Frank, a strapping six-footer with a deep Spanish accent, remarked, 'You're very attractive, Charlotte . . . *for your age*.'

'I s'pose,' Will says, draining his glass, 'it'd be pretty rude of us not to go.'

'I might be busy,' Rosie announces, perusing the dessert menu.

'Actually,' I say firmly, 'you won't be, hon. It's only one night and it's not too much to ask.'

Sniggering again, Ollie leans towards Rosie and Will. 'You know why Mum really wants to go? She thinks they might have *herbal buns*.'

Chapter Six

My mother-in-law calls at 8.07 on Wednesday morning, perfectly timed to coincide with the kids grabbing breakfast and my frenzied hunt for Ollie's elusive trainers. 'Hello, Gloria, how are you?' I say, indicating to Will who's calling. *I'm-not-here*, he mouths, accompanied by vigorous hand waving as if trying to actually rub himself out.

'Is Will there?' No pleasantries; no, how lovely it was to see us all on Saturday. Perhaps she's still feeling prickly about us rekindling the memory of the *Sorrington Bugle* sleazebag.

'Is everything okay?' I ask. 'Has something happened?'

'Yes, I've found the perfect job for him. Can you put him on?'

I stare at Will.

No! Will mouths. *I'll call her later* . . . 'He's, erm, out on his bike at the moment, I'm afraid.'

'At this time?'

'Yes, he likes to get out early if he's . . . foraging. That way he gets the best stuff.'

'Really? Does it *run out*, then, like at a jumble sale?'

She emits a dry, humourless laugh. 'Well, never mind that. There's a job here in the paper and it sounds ideal for Will . . .'

'Thanks, Gloria, but I really think he's fine, you know? I don't want to keep bombarding him with suggestions . . .'

'. . . They offer full training and excellent prospects,' she witters on, as if I hadn't spoken. 'I was worried when I saw him on Saturday. He seemed a little . . . *flat*.'

'No, he's fine, really – he's great. So, um, what kind of job is it, just out of interest?'

'Traffic warden. Sounds like there's a shortage and, let's face it, they're always needed—'

'Gloria,' I cut in, catching Will's eye, 'I'm not sure he'd want to be a traffic warden.'

Will splutters his coffee.

'Is that him, is he back?'

'No, no, that's Ollie,' I say quickly, wondering at which point she'll tire of being his personal career advisor: when he *does* find paid work, presumably. Another reason for him to ramp up the job hunt . . .

'I think he should at least consider it,' Gloria says, sounding put out.

'I'm sure he will,' I say, having difficulty maintaining a serious voice with Will miming throat-cutting motions across the kitchen. 'Sorry, Gloria, but I really need to get off to work . . .' I finish the call and kiss Ollie goodbye as he rushes off to meet his friend Saul, then head upstairs to find Rosie. Normally, she doesn't need any chivvying to get ready for school. 'Hon,' I say, finding her hunched over her laptop on her bed. 'You should be gone by now. It's really late . . .'

'Yeah-in-a-minute,' she murmurs, eyes fixed on the screen. I can sense her mentally shooing me away.

'What are you looking at? Is it a homework thing?'

'No, it's a fashion site . . .'

'At twenty past eight? Come *on*, Rosie—'

'I need to study this stuff,' she mutters.

'You mean you're studying fashion? Is this for art or something?'

Ignoring me, she leans closer to the laptop. I peer over her shoulder. Models with haunted eyes and matted, dirty-looking hair are wearing baggy beige shifts in a setting which looks, to my untrained, un-fashiony eye, like a derelict psychiatric hospital. There are rusting iron beds, a sinister-looking trolley and, lurking in a corner, a concerned-looking man with Clark Kent spectacles and a clipboard. I glance at Rosie's open notepad, in which she has written: *Key trends. Unstructured nudes in pale plaster hues . . .*

'What's an unstructured nude?' I ask.

'Um, I don't really know,' she admits.

'It sounds a bit worrying,' I add with a smile.

Rosie sniffs and writes: *Washed-out colour palette.* 'Wow,' I mutter. 'The fashion industry must be populated by geniuses if this is what we've got to look forward to. Looks more like *One Flew Over the Cuckoo's Nest* . . .'

'Huh?' She turns to me.

'Classic film with Jack Nicholson set in a psychiatric hospital. Brilliant, but not really known for the outfits. I mean, it's not *Breakfast at Tiffany's* . . .' I break off, realising I've lost her. 'Why are you looking at this stuff anyway?'

'For the thing after school.'

Ah, the agency meeting. 'You don't have to swot, you know. They're not going to quiz you about hem lengths and trouser shapes . . .'

She pushes away a frond of dark hair that's escaped from her sensible ponytail. While Rosie enjoys rummaging through the rails in Top Shop, she's never been remotely interested in cutting-edge trends. She errs towards the casual: jeans, baggy sweaters and pretty embellished tops. 'Look,' she says, sighing, 'I'll feel better if I'm prepared, okay? You're always telling me that.'

'Yes, for an English or history exam. This is different . . .' I glance at her dressing table, on which she appears to have tipped out every item of make-up she owns. Not that there's much; she only tends to wear it for a night out. 'Remember they want you to look natural,' I add.

'Yes, Mum, I *know*. Why are you and Dad coming anyway? I mean, I'm not going to get lost, you know. And it's not a family outing. It's not like we're going to Madame Tussaud's . . .'

'We're coming, Rosie, and that's that. No need to be so snappy.'

With another dramatic sigh she shuts her laptop. 'Sorry. I'm just a bit nervous, Mum . . .'

'Hey,' I say, pulling her in for a hug, 'it'll be fine. And it's no big deal, is it? It's just—'

'A chat,' she chips in, mustering a big, brave smile, before grabbing her jacket and scampering off.

Back downstairs, I give Will a hasty kiss goodbye as I, too, should have set off by now. As I step out into the bright sunshine, I thank my lucky stars – not for the first time – that I have a job to go to.

I enjoy my drive to work, despite the strange whiff in my car – fermenting apple cores, laced with stale biscuits – which I think is a hangover from when the kids were little, and couldn't cope with a ten-minute journey without a huge array of snacks, and which never seems to fade, no matter how vigorously I go at it with the hoover. In fact, driving is *blissful* compared to dealing with Gloria's well-meaning natterings, and ogling 'pale plaster' tabards, which reminds me that our kitchen desperately needs a lick of paint. We went for bare plaster walls, seduced by pictures in a magazine where it seemed to evoke a sort of faded beauty, like a Toast catalogue. In fact, it just looks like we couldn't be bothered to finish the room. We can't afford decorators, and I'm holding off suggesting that Will does it, in case it further delays his return to the world of paid employment.

As I'm heading out of London, and away from the worst of the traffic, I soon make up for lost time, and by the time I pull into the car park at Archie's, I'm all soothed. I have a quick chat with Freya and Jen, who run the visitors' centre and shop, then trot upstairs to the light, airy office. Our website implies that our potato chips are hand crafted in our home kitchen, deep in the Essex countryside. It *is* the country, just about; i.e., we're not quite on the Tube, and are surrounded by flat, scrubby fields, and the building I work in is a converted village school with a small, tidy garden in front. But this isn't where our crisps are actually made. That happens in an ugly gunmetal-grey manufacturing plant, concealed by a dense row of conifers. It's why we don't offer factory tours. The public would come expecting to see a kindly granny carving Maris Pipers, and discover a terrifying slicing machine and several enormous vats of bubbling oil manned by twenty-odd employees.

I pull off my jacket, and consider texting Rosie to ask if she's feeling okay about the model agency meeting – as she clearly isn't – then decide against it. She'll be at school, and anyway, the more I try to reassure her that it'll be okay, the more terrified she'll be. That's a thing I've noticed about teenagers: how very *opposite* they are. If you want to put them off buying some terrible shoes, all you have to do is go on about how gorgeous they are.

I click on my computer and check my inbox. There's a 'missive' – as my boss calls his perky team emails – from Rupert, AKA King of Crisps.

Wednesday, July 9

From: rupert@archies-chips.co.uk
To: all teamsters
Subject: Just a few odds & sods!

Hi folks,

How's tricks, my lovelies? Just a line to say thanks for all being so awesome! We've had a crazy time and you've all been incredible. No distribution probs lately, and we're all set to take the world by storm, or at least the highlight of our crisp calendar – The Festival of Savoury Snacks!

Just a tiny thing. With a few new peeps having joined the team, can I just – sorry to be a pain here – mention a few words we don't use here at Archie Towers?

I should point out that there aren't actually any towers. It's just one of those cuddly things that Rupert likes to say.

You know how pernickety I am! he goes on, sprinkling exclamation marks around as liberally as his favoured hand-harvested sea salt. *Just give me a punch next time you see me, haha. Anyway, here goes:*

- *Instead of staff we say* ***team*** *(singular =* ***teamster****)*
- *Not company but* ***family*** *(i.e. you're now welcomed into the bosom of the Archie family!)*
- *Not fry but* ***cook*** *(yes, I realise that's technically what we do here, but we all know the connotations of the word 'fry' – i.e., greasy, artery-clogging and frankly pretty horrid. Which isn't our bag here at Archie's, right?)*
- *Not meeting but* ***gathering***
- *Not supplier but* ***friend*** *(i.e., our potatoes come from our friend Mickey Hunter's farm in Kent)*

Okie-doke?
Love,
Rupe xxx

'Sounds like someone's said "fry" again,' I tell Dee, who's arrived pink-cheeked, having cycled from her village a couple of miles away.

'Oh, Christ,' she sniggers, removing her jacket and helmet and dropping a contraband snack (raspberry Pop Tart) into the toaster. Dee and I look after events, PR and social media together. I'm also in charge of updating our touchy-feely website. Rupert insists on lots of photos of 'teamsters' doing fun stuff together, to convey the message that we're a happy gang, forever larking about, and never have to do anything as mundane as sit at a desk or attend a meeting. I've had to stage garden parties and bike rides to show what a jolly time we all have. However, despite the tweeness and Rupert's relentless enthusiasm for making everything 'fun', I do enjoy working here, especially since – and I feel awful even admitting this – Will's been at home. It's my escape, of sorts. Is it okay to want to run away from your own husband? I don't mean in a packing-my-bags, forever sort of way. But I'm aware that I cherish my time away from the house.

'I still don't get the family thing,' remarks Dee, who's fairly new here, as she makes coffee.

'I thought it was weird at first,' I reply, scrolling through the rest of my mail, 'and I did try to point out to Rupert that we're not really a family, in that we're not a biologically related unit who all go on holiday together . . .'

She laughs. 'How did he take that?'

'He said that to him, we *are* family.'

'Scary,' Dee says, handing me a mug of coffee and proceeding to make the first of a barrage of phone calls with remarkable efficiency. At twenty-four, she is probably the most grown-up person I know. She buys scented oil burners from John Lewis and pounces on White Company bed linen at sale time. She knows what an Oxford pillowcase is, for goodness' sake. She explained it to me. At her age, I was already a mother, so I probably *looked* like a bona fide adult as I pushed Rosie on the swings in the park – but our tiny flat whiffed of wet laundry and potties and stress.

'Look what Mike bought yesterday,' Dee enthuses, during a break in calls, beckoning me over to look at her phone. She has photographed a chrome standard lamp with a hot orange shade – that's how proud of it she is.

'It's lovely,' I say.

'Isn't it? And we're choosing rugs on Saturday . . .' She has just moved into a tiny, impossibly cute cottage with her handsome builder boyfriend who sent possibly the world's biggest bouquet of red roses to our office on her birthday.

'So how is it?' I ask. 'Living together, I mean?'

'Oh, it's great. I love it that we're together more, you know? And it didn't make sense to keep two places going.'

'No, I understand that . . .' I glance at Dee. Her hair is pale blonde, straightened and shiny as glass, and her elfin features are defined with a flick of liquid liner and a touch of lip gloss. She seems so young for cosy, rug-choosing domesticity.

'So, um . . . what d'you and Mike do in the evenings?' I ask.

She shrugs. 'Well, we do dinner – okay, *I* do dinner – and then we watch a box set.'

'But you do go out sometimes?' I realise I probably seem overly fascinated by her lifestyle: the habits and behaviour of a young person. It's just . . . she seems so *content*. Why can't I be like that, all excited by John Lewis home fragrances?

'Occasionally,' Dee replies, 'but to be honest, we'd rather get the house finished than waste our money in pubs and restaurants.'

Hmm. Perhaps it's because my freedom was curtailed so abruptly – by having a baby at twenty-two – that I can't help feeling youth is something to be cherished and clung on to for dear life.

'Anyway,' Dee says, 'isn't it Rosie's big day today? With the model agency, I mean?'

'Yes, we're due there at four.' The sound of tuneless

whistling announces Rupert's arrival as he bounds upstairs to our office.

'What's this about modelling?' He beams at us – his 'girls', which in my case is stretching things a bit – and rakes back a mop of curly dark hair.

'Rosie was scouted on Saturday,' I explain. 'We were out shopping and a woman from an agency came up to us. She seems keen to take Rosie on.'

He feigns a crestfallen face. 'Only Rosie? What about you? I'd have thought they'd have snapped you up!'

'Don't think so, Rupert,' I reply, laughing, 'unless they have a special division for people to model stair lifts, or those easy-care slacks you get in the Sunday supplements.'

'Oh, come on,' he blusters, grinning fondly and perching on the edge of my desk. In his faded checked shirt and scruffy jumbo cords, he's actually impossible to dislike. Not bad looking either, although not my type; mid-forties, glinting grey eyes and long, skinny legs, which lend him an endearing foal-like quality. Archie's is his baby. Realising his own name – Rupert Plunkett-Knowles – was perhaps a little too fancy for something as earthy as crisps (even *posh* crisps), he named the company after his beloved Golden Retriever.

I start to update Rupert on our plans for the snacks festival in Bournemouth, which Dee and I are pulling together. Competitions, goodie bags and live cookery demonstrations: Rupert greets our every suggestion with his customary enthusiasm. 'Sounds excellent!' he booms as we wrap things up. 'Anyway, I know you're heading off early today so I'll let you get on . . . sounds like an *amazing* opportunity for Rosie.'

'Yes, I suppose it is.' He strides to the window and peers

out, as if surveying his kingdom. Rupert and his wife Marcelle have four daughters with flowing blonde manes, like thoroughbred ponies; I have no idea how they manage to hold everything together. 'Rupert,' I say hesitantly, 'what would you do if one of your girls wanted to be a model?'

He turns and shrugs. 'I'm fine about whatever they want to do, as long as it makes them happy. How d'you feel about it?'

I consider this. 'You know, I think it's actually okay. It could be a good experience for her, doing the shoots, maybe a bit of travel . . .'

'You don't sound completely convinced,' Dee remarks.

'Well, no. Of course there's the worry about the pressure to be super-skinny – having a thigh gap and all that . . . I mean, what's that all about?'

'Horrible,' Dee agrees with a shudder.

I sip my coffee. 'I don't think it's an especially healthy thing – the whole business, I mean – and she's not madly confident. She pretends she is, but it's just an act, really. And she still seems so young—'

'But if it doesn't work out,' Rupert cuts in, 'she can just stop, can't she?'

I nod, hoping it's that simple. Giving me a reassuring pat on the arm, he snatches his trilling mobile from his pocket and lollops back downstairs. Dee and I spend the rest of the day finalising plans for the festival and, despite my doubts, I'm starting to feel pretty excited for Rosie as I head downstairs and through the shop, where baskets of new crisp varieties have been set out for testing. Always a dangerous time for me, this, and my favourite work skirt is already feeling a little pinchy on the waist. 'Go on, try these,' Freya urges me from behind the counter.

'What are they?' I ask, hand hovering as I try to resist the urge to snatch one.

'Mature Cheddar and vintage ale.'

'Hmm. Doesn't seem quite right, eating beer.' I pop one into my mouth; scrumptious, I decide, heading out to my car, although if truth be known you can't beat good old salt and vinegar. My phone rings as I start the ignition. 'Where are you?' Will barks.

'Just setting off. Don't worry, there's plenty of time—'

'It's just, you need to have a word with Rosie *right now*.'

'What's wrong?'

Will sighs. 'She came home from school and hid in her room for ages and next thing she's bloody plastered in make-up . . .'

'Oh God, she really doesn't need—'

'And when I mentioned it,' he interrupts, 'I mean, I only said, "You're wearing quite a lot of make-up, Ro", she started crying and now her eyes are all red and puffy and she said she can't possibly go. Can you please have a word with your daughter?'

Ah, *my* daughter now. Technically accurate, but he never says that. 'She's just sensitive,' I start, 'and pretty nervous, I think. I'll have a word when I get home.'

'You need to,' he declares. 'I can't handle this, Charlotte. I don't know what to say to her.'

And he thinks I do? 'All right,' I mutter as Frank from the factory saunters past, slugging a can of Coke. 'Listen,' I add, 'I can't do anything sitting here, can I? Try to calm her down and, whatever you do, don't criticise her. In fact don't comment on her appearance at all.'

'What should I say then?'

'Nothing. Just talk about . . . *nothing*. The weather or something.'

'Oh, that'll help. That'll sound really natural. As you know, Rosie and I often have long discussions about cold fronts and cloud formations . . .'

For crying out loud. 'Don't say anything then,' I snap, watching Frank stop and light up an extremely un-Archie's cigarette. A moment later, Dee comes out too and he offers her one from his packet. The sight of them chatting and laughing in the sunshine makes me feel extremely old and tired.

'Okay then,' Will says. 'I won't say another word to her. I'll be *mute*.'

'Sounds like a good plan,' I growl, pulling out of the car park and hoping my husband's mood has improved by the time I get home. After all, we're going on a *family outing*.

*

'How is she now?' I ask Will, tossing my jacket over a kitchen chair.

He shrugs. 'I did what you said. I haven't attempted further communications.' Why is he speaking like this, as if English isn't his mother tongue?

'I'll talk to her.' I brush past him and march up to her room. She's had permission to leave school early today; Ollie will head over to his friend Saul's after school. 'Rosie, are you okay?' I call through her bedroom door.

'Yup.' She sounds deflated.

'It's just, we're supposed to be at the agency at four. Are you getting ready?'

Silence.

'Rosie, d'you think we could possibly have a conversation that's not through a two-inch-thick door?'

There's a shuffling noise, then the door opens slowly. Will was right: inexpertly applied foundation cakes her lovely face. She's applied smudgy black eyeliner and a ton of red lipstick. Her cheeks bear swirls of violent pink blusher, like scorch marks, and her eyes are bloodshot from crying. 'Oh, darling.' I bite my lip. 'You look a bit upset.'

'I *am* upset,' she snivels. 'You know what Dad said? "What've you done to your face?" How d'you think *that* made me feel?'

Um, he had a point. 'What he meant was—' I start.

'He's always criticising me,' she exclaims, which is patently untrue, 'and on a day like this which is *so* important to me. Look at the state of me, Mum!' As if Will had strapped her to a stool in the middle of Debenhams and proceeded to pile on the slap like an over-zealous Benefit counter girl.

'Dad just wants what's best for you,' I say firmly. 'But if it's going to be a huge drama then maybe we should cancel this meeting . . .'

'No!' she wails. 'I don't want that, Mum. Please.'

At a long-ago yoga class, I remember Liza telling us all about breathing through your bellybutton. It sounded bizarre, but she said it was calming and now I wish I'd learnt how to do it. 'Okay,' I say slowly, 'if we're going, then please take off your make-up and let's get ready.'

Rosie sighs and wipes her eyes on the sleeve of her top. Miraculously, she does tissue off most of her make-up and, after much splashing of cold water, her eyes lose some of their pinkness. 'Hey,' Will says as we meet in the kitchen, 'that's better, love. You look great.' He does too, having swapped his usual gardening attire for a smart chambray shirt and dark jeans, accessorised with an expression of grim stoicism. He just cares, I remind myself, kissing him on the cheek.

'What was that for?' He smiles.

'Nothing. I just love you, that's all.' I wait for him to add, *I love you too.*

'Well, we'd better be going,' is all he says.

Chapter Seven

It's not Laurie who greets us at Face Models but a bored-looking girl with a blunt dark fringe and a gleaming pink nose stud, like a pomegranate seed, on reception. In fact, when I say greet, that's not quite what she does. She continues to stare at her laptop for a few moments before deigning to acknowledge our arrival. 'We're here to see Laurie,' I say, sensing nervousness radiating from my daughter's every pore as she hovers at my side.

The girl glances up. 'She just popped out. Have a seat . . .' She indicates the sole chair in the small reception area, brightening suddenly as she registers Will's presence. 'God, am I glad to see *you*. Weren't you meant to come this morning? The whole place is going mental!'

'Sorry?' Will looks baffled.

'Wifi's down. I've been onto your people five times now. Complete nightmare—'

'Er, I'm not here to fix your Wifi,' Will explains. 'I'm just, er . . .'

'He's with us,' I cut in, realising at once that it's wrong of me to speak for him. The girl twitches her nose, in precisely the way Guinness does, and Laurie rushes in clutching a carton of coffee.

'Oh, hi – Rosie! Sorry, darling. Sorry, sorry . . .' She gives her a fleeting hug, which seems to turn Rosie rigid with alarm, whilst holding her carton aloft. 'You look great. Wow – you've *all* come. Dad too. Quite the family outing!' We all laugh awkwardly and follow her into a bright open-plan office buzzing with trilling phones. 'Bit manic today,' Laurie adds, quickly naming the half dozen young people who are all seated around a large oval table strewn with paperwork, coffee cartons and phones. 'Sasha, Milly, Greg, Claudia, Ryan, Jojo . . .' I nod, trying to take it all in, but none of the names are lodging in my head. 'They're the bookers,' Laurie adds. 'Well, Claudia's the boss. But we all pitch in here, we're like *family* . . .' Hmm, just like Archie's. There's the odd half-hearted smile, hastily dispensed in between intense phone conversations and the odd outburst of shouting.

'Marla's had a meltdown at the Burberry shoot,' wails a young man (Ryan? Or Greg?) with a shock of sandy hair and a brow piercing. 'For fuck's sake. That girl needs to get a grip.' Unperturbed by his outburst, a gaggle of incredibly tall, angular girls are gossiping and sipping from water bottles in a far corner. Of course, Rosie's tall too – but she's my *daughter*, I'm used to her lofty height, and barely register it. I mean, I don't go around feeling all gnome-like at home. But among all these towering strangers I seem to have become a sort of sub-species.

The three of us wait uncertainly as Laurie falls into an unintelligible exchange about rates and options with one of the girls at the table. I'd hardly expected to waltz in here and blend right in. But I hadn't expected to feel quite so . . . *alien*. I wish I'd made an effort, like Will has, and changed out of my work clothes. My cream shirt and black needlecord skirt looked fine this morning. Now, though, I'm conscious of a distinct 'I spent the morning in a crisp factory in Essex' air about myself. I also wish I'd cleaned my teeth when I got home. What if I smell of cheddar and vintage ale?

'Sorry about that,' Laurie says, beckoning us into a smaller, glass-walled office furnished with an acid-yellow coffee table and two squashy, pale grey sofas. 'It's less shouty in here,' she adds. We arrange ourselves on the sofas. On the white walls are several framed magazine covers and adverts, the most prominent featuring a not entirely unpleasant-looking young man wearing nothing but a pair of snugly fitting white Armani briefs. 'So, Rosie,' Laurie says, 'did you bring some photos?'

'Yes,' Rosie says, sounding a little breathless. She delves into her battered suede bag and pulls out a small plastic wallet of snapshots. 'Sorry, they're not very good,' she murmurs.

'These are fine,' Laurie says, flicking through them quickly: Rosie on holiday in Brittany last summer, when we could still afford holidays, and sitting cross-legged on a rug in our overgrown garden, pre its Will-instigated make-over. In the background are Ollie's old, sun-faded plastic tractor and a wash stand draped with knickers and bras. It looks a little tawdry. 'You have a lovely face,' Laurie muses, 'but would you mind taking your make-up off please?'

'Oh.' Rosie throws me a startled glance. 'I already did.'

Laurie smiles kindly. 'It's just, I need the team to see the real you, darling, and you still have quite a lot of eye make-up on. Come on, I'll show you to the bathroom. There's cleanser and wipes in there. And don't worry, girls do this all the time. You tell them natural and they come in absolutely *caked*.' We all laugh stiffly as Rosie and Laurie head for the loos.

'When are Chanel going to confirm if they want Courtney?' yells someone in the main office. I glance at Will and squeeze his hand.

'Hey,' he says with a wry smile.

'This is a bit weird, isn't it?'

He nods, then indicates pants-man on the wall. 'Maybe I should give it a go?'

I chuckle. 'I'm sure they'd snap you up.'

'Seriously, d'you think this place is okay? I mean, is it a proper, bona fide company?'

'Yes, don't worry – I've checked.' In fact, Rosie isn't the only one who's been conducting a little research about the modelling business. I've learnt from late-night Googling sessions that Face is a highly-respected establishment, and not one of those rogue agencies where they'll say, 'Of course you can be a model at four-foot-eleven, height doesn't matter at all' – then politely ask for £950 to 'cover costs' and ping you back out, cackling at your gullibility, with no more hope of becoming a model than being asked to take over the helm of the BBC. I've also discovered that Face represents many 'top girls', and that a gap between the front teeth is very 'now', along with fierce eyebrows and cheekbones like knives. It's all very mysterious – the idea that certain types of facial features fall in and out of fashion, like clothes – and, although I'm reluctant to admit it, it's quite fascinating in a perverse sort of way. I've found myself reading about famous models and their 'industry' (a word I'd formerly associated with car manufacturing plants, belching fumes), and tried to figure out how Rosie might fit into all of that, and how it might affect our family.

Admittedly, I'm nervous. Everything feels a little precarious as it is.

'Look,' I whisper. 'D'you think she's a new girl too?'

We both watch as a tall, teenage girl with a froth of blonde curls wanders into the main office with her mum (not *both* parents, I note). 'Yeah, poor thing looks terrified,' Will notes. 'You have to ask yourself if it's good for girls of that age to be judged on their looks. I mean, they're self-conscious enough as it is. Then they're thrown into this world where they're going to be scrutinised every single day . . .'

I bite my lip. 'I know, but we're here now, aren't we? And remember, the whole thing's completely in our control. If we don't feel it's right for Rosie . . .'

'I guess you're right,' he says as a pixie-haired Asian woman flicks through the snapshots the girl has brought with her. There's a brief chat, inaudible to us in our little glass cube, and the woman pulls a *sorry, not quite right for us* sort of face. The girl tries to look brave but seems visibly deflated as she turns to leave, like some of the air has been let out of her. Even her curls seem to have lost their bounce.

'Rosie's been ages,' I murmur.

'I know. D'you think she's having another meltdown?'

'God, I hope not . . .' I glance through the window where a bunch of the staff have gathered on the pavement. They are all puffing urgently on their cigarettes, as if told that they have precisely ten seconds to finish them.

'Here we are!' Laurie trills, striding towards us with Rosie at her side. My daughter, face as shiny as a polished apple, smiles meekly. 'I'm just going to introduce her to the team,' she adds. 'Are you okay waiting here, Mum and Dad?'

I feel myself ageing rapidly. 'Er, yes, of course.'

We wait as Rosie is whisked around the table, then Laurie beckons us to join them. I am aware of the staff taking more interest in us now: Will in his smartest jeans – would these agency people describe them as Dad-jeans, I wonder? – and me in my provincial officey outfit, with my muddy brown hair lacking any specific shape or style.

'The way things work,' Laurie explains, 'is that we'll handle Rosie's bookings and manage her career. Clients pay us, the agency, and we deduct fifteen per cent commission and then the money is paid into Rosie's account.'

Her directness slightly floors me. 'Does this mean you want to take her on?'

'Yes, but let's see how it goes. Sometimes a girl takes off right away, and she's doing all the shows and amazing editorial, covers and fashion and fabulous campaigns – and other times . . .' Laurie falters. 'Nothing. You simply never can tell.' She turns to Rosie. 'First of all, we'll need to get some decent test shots done. That way, you'll build up your book – that's a portfolio of your pictures, showing different looks – and we can start sending you on go-sees and castings . . .'

'Great,' Rosie says, clearly delighted.

'You do remember she's still at school?' I point out.

'Yep, don't worry – it'll be holidays and out-of-school-hours only. You'll find all the info you need in this pack –' she hands me a thick white folder with Face's logo in elegant type on the front – 'and there's lots of advice in there too. So, is there anything else you'd like to ask?'

I glance at Will, urging him to speak. 'Erm, I'm sure there will be,' he replies, 'when we've read through all the info.'

Laurie smiles warmly. 'Call me anytime. I've attached

a card with the pack and my mobile's on there. I know it's worrying for parents but I can assure you, she'll be in excellent hands with us.'

'I'm sure she will be,' I say, deciding I *do* like her – she seems to have a knack of putting Rosie at her ease – and anyway, how can I possibly deny my daughter this chance? This is a top agency; there won't be any creepy *Sorrington Bugle* types lurking about here. In fact, I'm starting to feel more comfortable with the whole thing. It's only a spot of part-time modelling, like Liza's daughter Scarlett does, frolicking about in a Boden duffel coat. It's hardly Agent Provocateur.

'You're absolutely stunning, darling,' Laurie adds, giving Rosie another unexpected hug, 'and I have an instinct where our girls are concerned . . .' She laughs, checking herself. 'I shouldn't say this because there are no guarantees, but I have a *very* good feeling about you.'

'Me too,' pipes up the sandy-haired man from the table. 'She's a stunning girl. And isn't she the absolute *image* of her dad?'

Chapter Eight

Rosie is so thrilled about being signed up by Face that the comment seems to bounce right off her. But it sticks with me – as I'm sure it does with Will – following us home and niggling away in my head like a small, persistent worm.

Of course, Rosie knows Will isn't her biological father, and I've never made any secret of that. 'Your birth daddy,' I explained when she was little, 'is someone I met when I was travelling around Europe, and it just didn't work out with us.' She'd ask where he was now, and I'd say – truthfully – that I didn't know. That was enough back then. She'd accept it and get on with playing with her cars and garage. Then, by the time she was eight or nine, the questions became trickier:

Did you love my birth daddy?

We were both so young, darling.

I know, but were you IN LOVE?

(Gigantic swallow.) Yes, I suppose we were at the time. We weren't together for very long, though, so I didn't know him like I know Daddy.

Did you love him as much as you love Daddy?

It was just different . . .

How different?

Well, Daddy and me . . . we're a family and it's a deep, real love.

The sort that lasts for ever and ever?

Yes. (Said with certainty then. These days, I'm not sure I'd be able to answer with such rock-solid confidence.) So I dealt with her questions as best I could – although at times it felt like being pelted with tennis balls. And, although I try to reassure myself that I've always been honest and open, I've never told her about Fraser's sudden disappearing act, or his mother's subsequent letter with the bird seed and cheque. It would sound far too hurtful and rejecting. Anyway, luckily, Rosie has seemed pretty satisfied with my explanations so far. Although she knows Fraser's name, she has made no attempt to track him down, as far as I am aware. In fact, just a year or so ago, when the subject came up – she asked if I thought he might live in London – she quickly added, 'He's not a big deal to me, you know, Mum. *Dad's* my dad. He always will be. I don't care about genes and stuff like that.'

Plus, while we use the phrase 'birth daddy', it's misleading as Fraser was presumably 200 miles away in Manchester, in his fancy turreted house, when Rosie was born (my own parents were with me, holding my hand and being completely fantastic). But what else to call him? 'Biological' brings to mind warfare – or washing powder – and 'real dad' wouldn't be right either. Will is Rosie's real father, in every way that matters.

And what a dad he is, throwing together an impromptu feast when we arrive home to celebrate Rosie's success at the agency, despite not really approving of modelling at all. We invite Liza, plus Nina, who's been Rosie's best friend since their first day at school, and Ollie appears with his friends Saul and Danny. 'When d'you think they'll call me?' Rosie asks when we're all tucking into marinated lamb around our garden table.

'Soon, I bet,' Nina says, her light brown hair shining in the evening sun. 'It's going to be amazing, Ro. Oh my God. Your whole life's going to change! You'll get loads of free clothes and meet famous people. You'll be invited to film premieres and parties . . .'

'Just wait and see what happens,' Liza says, placing a hand over Rosie's. 'Try not to stress about it, love.'

'I won't,' she asserts. 'I'm not stressed at all. It's just . . .' She bursts out laughing. 'I'm just so excited!' I look at my daughter, and can almost see the joy radiating from her. It's like the old Rosie – or rather, the *younger* Rosie – who'd whoop with delight when we arrived at the beach, and pelt to the sea, still in a T-shirt and shorts, desperate to plunge in. She didn't march ahead in shopping malls. She held my hand whenever we were out, and we'd spend hours at the kitchen table together, making pictures with glitter and glue.

Isn't she the absolute image of her dad? the agency man had remarked. Well, yes – both she and Will have striking blue eyes and generous, expressive mouths. But of course, any similarities are coincidental.

In fact, she *really* looks like Fraser. I pretend she doesn't – that she's far more like me – but occasionally she'll look a certain way, and it's him, the boy I fell for on a train to Paris. We'd caught each other's eye as a bunch of rowdy Scousers had burst into a rendition of 'Bohemian Rhapsody' at the other end of the carriage. 'Don't know about you,' Fraser murmured, leaning across the aisle towards me, 'but I can't stand Queen. I actually can't listen to them. They make me feel ill.'

'Me too,' I'd replied, and we'd quickly agreed that this song in particular had a fervently sick-making effect. It had bonded us, stifling laughter as the boys filled the carriage with raucous singing; by the time they reached the Beelzebub part, we were in hysterics. From that day on, we were inseparable. Although I'd had a few boyfriends before, I'd never been properly in love. And here I was, not Inter-railing alone after all but hopping around Europe with a beautiful blond boy with posh vowels and perfect teeth.

After our travels I'd wait at Euston for him to step off the Manchester train. My life revolved around our weekends together. I try not to think about it but occasionally, especially when Will seems to be inhabiting his own, private universe and stomps about with his hoe, I can't help it. Why did Fraser just leave us like that? It seemed completely un-him. He'd always phoned every day – until he stopped phoning – and would always bring a small present for me: a necklace, a battered paperback we'd talked about, or a CD to boost my meagre collection.

'Maybe you didn't really know him,' Mum said gently, meaning well but causing me to fly on the defensive. Of course I had! I'd known him for a whole eight months. Okay, put like that it didn't seem long, but to me it had felt as if my life had been divided into two parts – before and after Fraser. I'd never met anyone I felt so *right* with, from the very start. Trouble was, the 'after' part soon lurched from our lovely weekends together, to being without him with no explanation at all.

It's getting closer, too – the moment when Rosie will

announce that she wants to track him down. It's as inevitable as her falling in love, and leaving home and having her heart broken for the first time, and it's terrifying.

'Let me help with those,' Liza says, breaking off from her conversation with Will as I gather up the plates.

'No, it's fine, honestly. It's lovely out here in the sunshine. Just relax and enjoy it.'

In the kitchen, I set about loading the dishwasher, trying not to fixate on what we'll do if Fraser turns out to be un-track-downable, or dead – or if we *do* find him, and he's a whopping disappointment to Rosie. Or, perhaps worse, he turns out to be completely fantastic and she adores him instantly, and thereafter regards Will as a substandard fake dad. There's always the option of ignoring the whole issue, and hoping it'll miraculously go away – like when my last car started making strange grinding noises. I pretended it wasn't happening, gamely driving around until the grinding turned into an almighty racket of things crunching and snapping and that was it, the big end – whatever that was – had 'gone'. *If only you'd dealt with it sooner,* the garage mechanic told me, *you'd have avoided a disaster like this.*

Of course, I reflect, Fraser Johnson probably has a family of his own now and might refuse to see Rosie at all. How would *that* feel, to be rejected by the person who half-made her? There are so many possible outcomes, all of which make me feel a little bit sick. Through the window, I watch Will and Liza laughing at the garden table and mentally tell myself off for imagining problems when, as yet, there aren't any. 'We'll deal with it if – and when – it happens,' has been Will's rather brave, reassuring line on the whole Fraser issue.

Just like he's dealing with this, the prospect of Rosie launching into a world we know nothing about, which seems to involve lots of shrieking at the agency, and girls photographed with filthy hair. Really, I should just give myself a damn good shake and be grateful for what I have.

Chapter Nine

With the festival rattling towards us, work is frantic for the rest of the week. In fact, I'm grateful to have too much to do as it's allowed me precious little time to fret over the agency man's comment about Fraser. Thankfully, neither Rosie nor Will has mentioned it, and at home, things seem fairly harmonious. Although I suspect Rosie is on tenter-hooks, waiting for a call from the agency, she is putting on a good show of pretending not to care. By the time Saturday rolls around, I'm relieved that we're all going out, to our new neighbours' party, with the addition of Ollie's friend Saul who's been hanging out with us for the day.

'Why are you wearing *that*?' Ollie asks as I trot down-stairs, ready to go.

'You mean a dress?' I look down at it. It's a simple pale blue shift, and is – I thought, until a moment ago – quite flattering.

'Yeah. We're only going to the neighbours' . . .'

'Yes, our neighbours' *party*. I just thought I'd make an effort, Ollie. It's customary, you know – to try and look nice when you're socialising.'

Will comes over and kisses me on the cheek. 'You look lovely. That colour really suits you.'

'Thanks, darling.' I smile, sensing my cheeks flushing; compliments are so rare these days, I've almost forgotten what to do with them.

'How long are we staying?' Ollie wants to know.

I grin. 'We'll leave at precisely 12.07 a.m.'

'What?' he barks. 'What are we gonna do for all that time?'

'Bring Scrabble,' Will mutters with a smirk.

I snigger, grateful that at least *he's* not moaning, and that Rosie is ready to go – fresh-faced and casual in soft, old jeans and a pretty embroidered top. 'Only kidding,' I tell Ollie. 'We won't be too late, okay? Come on, let's try to be pleasant and sociable and meet some new people, like normal families do.'

Sabrina greets us at the door in a leopard print dress which clings to her taut, skinny body, her auburn hair blow-dried big and bouncy, like Cindy Crawford's in her 90s heyday. 'I'm so glad you've come,' she gushes, beckoning us into the cluttered kitchen.

'Hope it's okay that Ollie's brought a friend,' I say.

''Course it is! The more the merrier.' A jumble of fairy lights is strewn over shelves and packing cases, and an oak dining table is cluttered with wine and beer bottles, vases of flowers and Welcome to Your New Home cards. 'Excuse the state of the place,' Sabrina adds with a husky laugh. 'I know it seems mad, having a party so soon after moving in but I couldn't wait. Tommy's always saying how impatient I am, like a little kid.'

'Well, I'm glad you did,' I say truthfully. 'There aren't enough parties around here.'

'Yeah, it was all her idea, the raving loony,' Tommy

remarks fondly, greeting me with a kiss on the cheek and hastily introducing us to the guests in the kitchen: a cluster of middle-aged men in regulation T-shirts (mostly black) and jeans (faded and a little tight). There's the odd greying man-ponytail and a smattering of studded leather belts. While I'm not usually one to check out men's footwear, there's something about an embellished cowboy boot that draws the eye down.

The women are all lightly tanned, like Sabrina, with bare legs, polished cleavages and big, brightened smiles. Feeling somewhat lacking in high-octane glamour, I give small thanks that I chose to wear a dress tonight. 'Here you go, guys,' Tommy says, handing the kids a Coke each. 'Come out into the garden and meet Zach and his merry band of men. They might look a bit scary but don't worry – they don't bite.' Obediently, they follow him through to the back of the house, which I can see leads onto a long, narrow, unloved garden filled with billowing smoke from a barbecue.

'So what d'you do, Charlotte?' Sabrina asks, handing me a glass of wine.

'I work in marketing for a crisp company – Archie's . . .'

'Ooh, the posh crisps?'

'They are pretty posh,' I agree with a smile.

'I love them,' she enthuses, 'especially the new kind with sage. My God, they're so good! I always buy those 'cause I know Tommy won't touch them.' She rolls her eyes affectionately. 'He's more your Chilli Heatwave Doritos kind of man. Common as muck.'

We both laugh, and my stomach rumbles, activated by the barbecue smells wafting in through the open back door. 'So how about you, Sabrina?' I ask, noticing with relief that Will has fallen into conversation with a jovial-looking bald man who's swigging a beer by the fridge. At least Will is unlikely to be grilled about his job prospects here.

'I run my own company,' she explains. 'Wedding dresses – Crystal Brides, it's called. I specialise in sparkle.' She chuckles and waves a tanned hand, which is heavily bedecked with ornate silver rings. 'I *love* a bit of glitz.'

'D'you make the dresses yourself?' I ask.

'No, no, I have girls who do that. I just design them . . .' She breaks off as one of the ponytailed men hands us each a glass of champagne, despite the fact that we have wine too. I glance at Will again, conscious that I'm checking on him to make sure he's okay. Of course he is. We might not socialise much these days, and I know he felt dragged along tonight – but he's a grown man who can handle himself at parties. I don't need to worry about him being 'left out'.

Sabrina and I drift out to the back garden. 'Don't look at it too closely,' she says. 'Place is a bloody state.'

'Well,' I remark, 'you've only been here a week.'

'Oh, we'll never get around to doing anything with it. We don't even have a watering can.' She grins and indicates the pale green shed at the bottom of the garden. 'See that, though? It's already been christened.' She laughs loudly as I try to figure out whether she means what I think she means.

'Really?' I ask. 'You mean you've . . .' – I drop my voice – '*done it* in there?'

'Yeah! What a laugh that was.' I smile, conscious of a hollow feeling in my gut. 'You know what it's like with teenagers in the house,' she goes on. 'Impossible to get any privacy . . .' Although I want to know more, I'm also a little startled by her honesty. She's right, though:

on the rare occasions that Will and I manage to get it together, we proceed with extreme caution, as if over-hearing the merest creak of a bed would traumatise the kids. And when I say *rare*, I mean precisely that. The reason I remember the precise date of our last 'session' (which implies enthusiastic, thrashing-around sort of sex; in fact mice do it more noisily than we do) is because it occurred at precisely 7.15 a.m. on Mother's Day. Afterwards, Will jokingly said it was my present. The time before that was Christmas Eve; in the periphery of my vision was a heap of wrapped presents, plus the holly garland we'd never got around to nailing on the door. It's not that I keep a detailed account of our activities. Just that we only seem to get around to doing it on significant dates.

'Got to grab your chance when you can,' Sabrina adds with a wink.

'Wasn't it a bit *splintery* though?' I ask, picturing our own, equally unlovely shed.

'Yeah,' she laughs, lighting a cigarette, 'but we like that. A bit of danger, you know. An element of risk.'

I turn this over in my mind. Whenever people talk about risky sex, I imagine they mean doing it where there's the possibility of being discovered – in the car, for instance, or up an alley or something. I've never considered it might involve a Black and Decker work-bench. I have a fortifying gulp of champagne.

'It was his idea,' she adds, indicating Tommy, who's grappling at something charred and black with enormous barbecue tongs. 'You know what men are like. *Insatiable . . .*'

'Oh yes,' I say, wondering whether Will and I could possibly cram ourselves into our much smaller shed, alongside the mower, the strimmer and God knows what else is in there. A load of spiders, probably. I never go in. Perhaps I should, to assess its potential as a love den . . . .

We install ourselves with a group of women who are all chatting on embroidered cushions on the overgrown lawn. There are quick introductions, and a woman called Abs – fittingly, she has the sinewy body of a fitness instructor – says, 'D'you like live music, Charlotte?'

'I do,' I say truthfully, 'but I haven't seen any for ages.'

'You should come and see Zach's band,' Sabrina adds, 'next time they have a gig.'

'That'd be great,' trying to sound enthusiastic. 'What kind of stuff do they play?'

'Indie rock, I suppose you'd call it.' She beams proudly at her son, who's now deep in conversation with Rosie, while the other teenage boys are kindly letting Ollie and Saul hang out with them. My glass is topped up by a passing bearded man in a leather jacket who joins us on the cushions.

At the risk of sounding like a Miss World contestant, I realise I'm enjoying meeting new people. Will and I don't do this enough, I reflect. We don't do anything enough: have sex, go to gigs or parties . . . *and we're going to start doing all of those things loads more*, I decide, realising the wine and champagne have whooshed to my head as I haven't eaten anything yet. I can't grumble that we're in some kind of marital rut when I'm hardly making an effort to haul us out of it. Everyone I meet seems to have full, exciting lives: Abs, it turns out, isn't a fitness instructor but Sabrina's business partner in Crystal Brides. I meet a hat designer, a gallery owner and someone who caters for band tours. The atmosphere is lively and fun, and the music becomes gradually louder as the evening wears on.

'Me and Tommy run a management company,' explains Brian-with-the-beard. 'We used to work for one of the majors but decided to go it alone.' I'm ridiculously pleased that I've managed to deduce that he means band management, and major record label. He indicates the teenagers who have now gathered on a stripy rug on the lawn, where Zach is inexpertly strumming an acoustic guitar. 'See that crew over there? Lots of potential . . . Christ, what *is* Tommy doing with that food?'

We all turn to watch as he squirts lighter fuel over blackening sausages on the barbecue. 'What are you doing that for?' Sabrina shouts, leaping up and rounding on her husband like a ferocious bird.

Tommy frowns. 'They weren't cooking fast enough. They're burning outside but the middles are raw . . .'

'That's because it's not hot enough yet, idiot! You say *I'm* impatient?' She snatches a cooked sausage with her bare hands, stuffs it into a roll and bites into it. 'Tastes like petrol, you bloody nutter. God, Tommy, we've got forty-odd people here and they're all pissed and need something to eat. What're you gonna do now?'

He shrugs and sips from a can of lager. 'We'll have to get them something else.'

'Like what?' Sabrina snorts. 'There's nothing in the house. Just some dried spaghetti and a packet of Club biscuits. What d'you plan to do with that, Barbecue Man?'

She strides back to rejoin us on the cushions. 'Damn fool. He can't cook, he's *never* done a barbie before, but of course Mr-bloody-Masterchef had to buy a top-of-the-range barbecue and then fuck it up.' Brian and I try, unsuccessfully, not to laugh.

'Is everything ruined?' Will asks, appearing at Tommy's side.

'Er, yeah, mate. It just squirted out of the can really fast.' Now the teenagers have gathered round, clearly enjoying the spectacle as Sabrina delivers another barrage of abuse.

'Could Dad help?' Rosie murmurs.

I turn to Will with a hopeful smile. 'Do we have anything we could bring over?'

'Um . . . maybe. I could see what we could do . . .'

Sabrina smiles squiffily. 'No, it'd be far too much trouble.'

'It's no trouble at all,' he says. 'But, um, I don't want to get in the way of your plans . . .'

'What plans?' Sabrina cackles. 'We don't have any, apart from Tommy planning to poison us all.'

Will's face breaks into a grin – a proper, relieved-to-be-useful grin – as he turns towards the house, summoning Ollie and Saul to join him. 'C'mon, boys, give me a hand and we'll see what we can rustle up.'

Sabrina and Abs watch them leave. 'What a man,' Abs breathes. 'So he's your new neighbour, Sabs?'

Just as I'm just processing this – that the friends are called *Sabs and Abs* – Sabrina tosses her flame-coloured hair and giggles, 'Mmm, and isn't he hot? Wonder if Charlotte loans him out?'

Chapter Ten

Will, Ollie and Saul return laden with enough delicious offerings for everyone. There are lamb and chicken kebabs with a minty marinade, a huge bowl of spicy slaw and an impressive array of salads. Guests gather around the barbecue, entranced by the mouth-watering aromas (or perhaps my *hot* husband). 'Christ,' Tommy marvels, slapping Will on the back, 'this is a bit better than a jumbo packet of Iceland sausages.'

It's truly impressive, and I watch from the sidelines as everyone fusses around Will and hands him drinks. I know I've tended to focus on his rather prickly, defensive side these past few months. In contrast, everyone here seems to appreciate what a brilliant all-round human being he is. Of course, they're not hovering around him, tentatively asking how the job search is going. They haven't over-ridden his decision that Rosie shouldn't have gone to the model agency. Without intending to, I seem to have been stressing him out lately – cranking up his grumpiness – whereas everyone here is just raving about his spectacular cooking. I feel proud, actually. Proud that my husband has saved the day and appears to be mingling happily.

Music pounds from the kitchen, guests start dancing on the lawn and I find myself installed, a little fuzzy myself, next to Sabrina on a rickety wrought iron bench. 'So how long have you two been together?' she asks.

'Fifteen years,' I reply, to which she darts a quick glance at Rosie, who's laughing at something Zach has said. 'Will isn't Rosie's real dad,' I add.

'Oh, right! I just assumed—'

'I mean, I hate that term. Of course he is. But she was a toddler when I met him.'

Sabrina smiles. 'She looks like Will, though . . .'

'Yes, I know. Everyone says that.'

She pauses. 'So, er . . . d'you have any contact with—'

'Her real father?' I shake my head. 'No, not since before she was born.'

'Really? God!'

We break off to thank Will for platefuls of barbecued deliciousness, and wait until he's resumed his position as head chef before continuing. 'I met him when we were Inter-railing,' I add, 'and he's never even seen her.'

'Bastard,' Sabrina splutters.

I shrug. 'You know, I don't really feel like that. Not anymore. He obviously couldn't cope with the idea of being a dad. At least, he put on a great show *pretending* he could, but then . . .' I nibble a chicken skewer before adding, in a brisker tone, 'He just disappeared when I was pregnant. There was a terse letter from his mother, warning me off, then nothing.' *And of course, I haven't thought about him at all . . .*

Sabrina frowns, processing this. 'But that's outrageous, Charlotte. What an absolute dick . . .'

'I know, and of course, I did try to get in touch. I tried calling his parents' place, where he lived, but they'd changed the number and any letters were sent back to me. Anyway, my parents stepped in, and were fantastic – and then I met Will and it's all worked out.' I beam brightly to show how precisely fantastic everything is.

'You mean he's never even contributed?' Sabrina checks herself. 'Sorry, Charlotte, that's so nosy of me. Tell me to shut the hell up . . .'

I smile, enjoying her lack of restraint. She is fun and refreshingly honest, and I think – I *hope* – we'll be friends. 'It's fine, honestly. There was a cheque from his mum, but . . .' I tail off as a bunch of men burst out through the back door, hooting with laughter and carrying a life-sized blow-up doll. She is a vision in marshmallow-pink plastic with a mass of bouncy red hair, rather lethal-looking pointy breasts and a circular, red-lipped mouth. 'Who invited her?' I exclaim, laughing.

Sabrina cackles. 'Oh, that's Chloe. Friend of Tommy's gave her to him for Christmas.' I catch Will's startled expression and laugh even harder. 'Classy, huh?' she adds. 'She always makes an appearance at parties.'

Ollie and Saul appear at my side. 'What's that?' Saul asks, eyes agog.

'It's, er, a sort of doll.'

'A *doll*?' He guffaws and nudges Ollie.

I glance at Sabrina, who's in hysterics now, with her blow-dry mussed up and her lipstick worn off, bar the pencilled outline. 'It's Tommy's,' I explain as Chloe is paraded past us, as if about to be given her birthday bumps. Even Will is creasing up with laughter now.

'But what's it *for*?' Ollie wants to know.

'It's, er, a sort of pretend girlfriend,' Sabrina replies, trying to keep a straight face.

Saul looks incredulous. 'What does he do with her?'

She smirks and takes a big swig of wine.

'What's she for, Mum?' Ollie demands.

'Er, they probably sit and watch TV together,' I explain, noticing Saul nudging Ollie, then the two of them dissolving in laughter – my cue, I think, to whisk the kids off home. It's gone eleven; amazingly, none of the neighbours have complained about the thumping music.

'We're heading back,' I tell Will, finding him chatting away to Tommy, 'but you stay as long as you like.'

'Hey,' Tommy chuckles, 'you've got a late pass, mate,' which isn't what I meant at all, but never mind. At least he's enjoying himself, which sparks a tiny flicker of optimism that he'll soon put his special foraging gloves into retirement and rejoin the human race. A job, and colleagues, and the odd rowdy night out – that's what he needs, urgently. Then we'll start to have fun again, like in the old days. This party has proved that Will can shake off his grumpiness and be charming and lovely, like he used to be.

Wrapping a matey arm around Will's shoulders, Tommy hands him a beer. Will grins, clearly enjoying being made so welcome and having his barbecuing skills praised to the hilt. And my heart does a little skip, forcing the trials of late into the background: my lovely, *hot* Will, whom women joke about 'borrowing'. Does it matter that we haven't done it since Mother's Day? It's normal, I think. All couples' sex lives fall into a pattern eventually, and ours now seems to happen quarterly, like a VAT return.

Even so, as I hug Sabrina goodbye I make a supreme effort not to even *glance* at her shed.

*

Tired and yawning, the boys shuffle straight off to Ollie's room, leaving Rosie and me in the kitchen. How lovely, I think: some mum – daughter time. Who cares that it's almost midnight? No school or work tomorrow. 'You seemed to be getting on well with Zach,' I say lightly, clicking on the kettle for tea.

'Yeah, he's all right.' She perches on the edge of the worktop, swinging her almost endless, denim-clad legs. Her feet are bare and pretty, her nails painted duck-egg blue. 'We were just talking,' she adds.

'I wasn't suggesting anything else, love.'

Her face softens. 'He's nice. Interesting. We had a laugh.'

I try to arrange my features into a casual expression. What I'd love to do now is ask her about boys, and if there's anyone around whom she likes at the moment. But it doesn't feel right to quiz her. I'd always imagined we'd have one of those lovely, discuss-anything mother/daughter relationships – boys, sex, the whole caboodle – but it hasn't quite happened that way. Whenever I've tried, tentatively, to touch upon sensitive matters, she's shuffled uncomfortably as if I'm a PSE teacher about to thrust a wad of embarrassing leaflets at her. It's so hard to know how to be with her these days. I know she doesn't want me checking her homework, or running her a bath, or doing any of those motherly things I used to do for her – yet she's not quite grown-up either. She seems incapable of fixing herself breakfast without leaving a scattering of Frosties in her wake, and I've found her prodding nervously at the washing machine buttons as if the appliance might blow up in her face.

She jumps down from the worktop. 'Think I'll get some sleep, Mum.'

'What about your tea? Want to take it up with you?' I fish out the teabag and add a generous slosh of milk, plus two sugars, just the way she likes it.

'Thanks, Mum, but I'm pretty tired.' She allows me to hug her, then pulls back and meets my gaze. 'That was a bit weird for me, you know,' she murmurs.

'What, the party? I thought you were enjoying it . . .'

'No, that thing the man said at the agency.' I frown at her, genuinely uncomprehending for a moment. 'About me being the image of Dad,' she adds.

'Oh.' My heart drops like a stone.

She picks at a fingernail. 'I've thought about it all week. I can't *stop* thinking about it.'

I blink at her, shimmeringly sober now despite all the wine and champagne I've knocked back tonight. At least Will's not here. That's a relief. 'I'm sure it was a bit weird for you,' I manage. 'But, you know . . . you *do* look like him. Like Dad, I mean. Like Will.'

The pause is filled by faint music drifting across from Tommy and Sabrina's house. 'So am I like my real dad too?' she asks.

'Er, yes, I suppose you are. But to be honest, it's so long since I've seen him, I can't really picture—'

'You can't picture his *face*?' She looks aghast.

'Well, yes, of course I can but, you know – it's kind of . . . blurry.'

'Blurry?' she repeats. 'That's nice, Mum.'

Well, yes, being sent a packet of bird seed and a sod-

off-don't-bother-us-again cheque was nice too. 'I'm just trying to be honest,' I say gently.

She wrinkles her nose. 'You mean you can hardly remember him at all?'

'No, of course I can.' I can sense my cheeks sizzling, and my heart seems to be rattling away at twice its normal speed. In fact, his face *has* faded in my mind, like an old tea towel where the pattern's nearly gone. Yet the *essence* of Fraser – his huge, bright smile, his raucous, head-turning laugh, the way he made me feel as we giggled our way around Europe – is indelibly imprinted on my mind.

'D'you have any photos of him?' Now Rosie, who professed to be so tired, is showing no sign of heading up to bed.

'No, sorry, I don't.'

'Why not?'

'They must've all got lost,' I mutter, at which she utters a little *pfff* of disdain and trots up to her room.

And of course, I know my response wasn't in any way adequate. What I should do now is follow her up and coax her to talk, and find out what she wants to do next – track him down somehow? And arrange to meet him? I would, if Will and I felt closer at this moment in time. But we need to handle this together, and right now, together is the *last* thing I feel.

Crushingly tired now, I pad lightly upstairs. I've made up a bed on Ollie's bedroom floor for Saul; the light is off and it looks as if they've crashed out already. While Rosie's is still on, I can sense *do-not-disturb* vibes seeping out beneath her closed bedroom door. So I go to bed and try to calm myself by thinking about positive things: the people I've met tonight, and the way Will saved the day with his minted lamb and glamorous salads. *You're lucky,* I remind myself, *and we'll handle the Fraser thing carefully, when the time's right. There's absolutely nothing to worry about.*

It's gone 2 a.m. when Will slips into bed beside me. His beery breath is oddly alluring, reminding me as it does of our earlier days when we went out nearly every night and woke up entangled in each other's arms, a time before he even owned a strimmer.

'Enjoy the rest of the party?' I murmur.

'Yeah. Sorry, didn't mean to wake you.'

'It's okay, I haven't managed to drop off yet.'

I want to tell him about Rosie, and the whole blurted-out thing about Fraser, but now's not the time, not in the middle of the night when he's fuzzy with booze. Instead, I snuggle closer, spooning around his naked body. I'm ridiculously pleased when he takes my hand and wraps my arm around him. It's a gesture which I interpret to mean he wouldn't be completely appalled if I were to become a little, uh . . . amorous. I mean, he's not giving the impression that he'd throw me off and scream for the police. So I edge my hand downwards.

Will flinches, as if an electric current has shot out of my fingers. Perhaps I'm being too tentative, and just tickling him. Better be firmer – not too languorous, either, as I can tell by his deep, steady breathing that he's moments away from sleep. My foot brushes his, and I detect a fine knit: M&S lambswool blend, at a guess. He's forgotten to take his socks off. That's good, I decide. It means he's pretty pissed, which might make him less worried about anyone hearing, or any of the other possible reasons he'll only do it with me four times a year.

Yep, socks I can handle. Christ, I'd do it with him

wearing a fake fur tiger outfit if that's what it took. I mean, I'm not *fussy*—

'Hahaha!' Laughter rings out from Ollie's room. 'That inflatable doll, that was *so* funny . . .'

Ah, it would appear that my darling son and his friend are not slumbering after all. 'Yeah,' Saul agrees. 'What did your mum say again?'

'That it was for watching telly with.'

'HAHAAAA!' They both hoot with mirth while Will grunts into his pillow and politely removes my hand from his nether regions. Well, that's that then. It'll probably be Halloween before the next opportunity comes up. Perhaps I could wear Dracula fangs and a cape.

I tune in as the boys resume their chat. 'Think she really believes that?' Saul asks.

'Yeah, I reckon. She's a bit . . . y'know . . .'

A bit *what*? Prudish? A buttoned-up old hag? I try, fruitlessly, to steady my breathing in order to bring on the blissful release of sleep.

'You know what those dolls are really for,' Saul adds sagely.

'Yeah,' Ollie sniggers, 'for men to have sex with 'cause they can't get a real woman.' They both peal with laughter until Rosie thumps her bedroom wall to shut them up.

All is silent again. Then my son's voice booms out, loudly and clearly through the wall: 'You'd think my mum'd know that at her age. God, she's naive.'

Chapter Eleven

Will's hangover hovers over the house like a damp, rather rank-smelling flannel. 'Feel like my liver's about to give up,' he moans, flipping through the Sunday papers at the kitchen table.

'Oh, come on,' I say briskly. 'It was only a few beers.'

'That's easy for you to say.'

I consider this. 'It is, actually. I mean, I had tons to drink too. More than normal, anyway, and I feel fine—'

'Well,' he says wearily, 'I *don't,* so please stop rubbing it in how amazingly full of joie de vivre you are.'

Whoo, touchy-pants this morning. 'Maybe you're just out of practice,' I suggest. 'We should go out more often, Will. It was really fun last night. We don't even have to take the kids. Rosie's old enough to look after Ollie—'

'You'd pay me, though?' she asks, only partly joking as she strolls into the kitchen, flings open a cupboard and groans in disappointment. 'Why's there *never* anything to eat?'

I laugh. 'What are you talking about? The house is stuffed with food. There are tons of crisps—'

'*Crisps!*' she repeats witheringly. 'It's always crisps. Crisps, crisps, crisps . . .'

'. . . and the freezer's so full,' Will cuts in, 'I could hardly squeeze a little packet of lovage into it—'

She frowns at him. 'What's lovage?'

'A herb,' he replies flatly.

'You mean a weed?' She is teasing him now, and, miraculously, he raises a small smile.

'Technically, yes, but I think you'll find it's delicious.'

'Why can't we eat normal food?' she asks him, then turns to me. 'And why wouldn't you pay me for doing a responsible job?'

I blink at her. 'Sorry?'

'I mean looking after Ollie so you and Dad could start going out again, and doing stuff and having a nice time together . . .' I glance at Will. Has Rosie detected the malaise between us, or am I just being paranoid? I have to say, he doesn't look thrilled at the idea of regular date nights with me.

'Look, Rosie,' I say carefully, 'we've talked about this before – how Dad and I don't really believe in paying you and Ollie for doing jobs, because before we know it you'll be demanding 50p for washing a teaspoon or passing us the remote control—'

'Nina gets paid,' she insists. 'She's paid for everything she does.'

I meant the teaspoon/remote control thing as a joke, but it's fallen flat. 'I doubt that, but anyway, you've told me she doesn't get an allowance and that's why she's waitressing at weekends. And we *do* give you money, and part of the deal is that you're generally helpful around the house.'

With a despairing shake of her head, Rosie opens

the fridge, extracts a bottle of chocolate milk and takes a generous swig. While I'm not a fan of bottle-slurping – I mean, we have glasses, and even neon-coloured straws if desired – I decide to let it go this time. I need to get out of here, away from Will, who is coughing feebly into a tissue now, and behaving as if death is imminent, and Rosie, who's mumbling that there's nothing she fancies to eat in the fridge either. Thank goodness Ollie and Saul have already been whisked off to the West End by Maria, Saul's ever-obliging mum.

'It's a gorgeous day,' I announce, grabbing my laptop from on top of the fridge. 'I'm going to sit in the garden.' I head out, closing the back door behind me, in the hope that that'll deter Rosie and Will from following me, and install myself at our old, sun-bleached wooden table.

I glance at our house as my laptop whirrs into life. For God's sake – a few weak beers and Will's acting as if he's an urgent candidate for a liver transplant. And complaining that I'm exhibiting too much joie de vivre! Well, sorry if I'm not *ill* enough for him. Maybe he'd have been happier to see me spewing into the toilet. Sex thing aside, I'm starting to realise that Will behaves as if he isn't especially fond of me anymore. I mean, he seems to find me irritating on a pretty regular basis. We don't treat each other like lovers, or partners, or anything really – we're just *there*. When I suggested not giving each other birthday presents last year, I hadn't actually meant it. I suppose, pathetically, I'd been testing him to see how he'd react. The correct response would have been, 'The thing is, darling, I've bought you something already' – i.e., beautiful, fragile, utterly impractical lingerie – 'and we're going to dinner tonight.' So I was a little taken aback when I came home from work to find two workmen on ladders, slapping mortar onto the front of our house.

Oh, stuff Will and his hangover. I may stay out here for a very, very long time. I might not even come in tonight, but make myself a cosy little den in the shed to sleep in. If Sabrina and Tommy can manage to do it in theirs, without impaling themselves on a rake, then surely it'd be possible to make the space in ours to create a little nest.

I squint at my laptop. The bright sunshine is making it impossible to read so I carry it down to the bottom of the garden and plonk myself on a paving slab in the shade of the shed. Inhaling a lungful of warm air, I type two words into Google:

Fraser Johnson.

There. I've actually done it. Admittedly, it's not the first time. On several occasions over the years, I've done precisely this, and gawped at the figure – something like 9,230,000 results. Then, fearing that my laptop would start shrieking, 'GOOGLING EX ALERT! GOOGLING EX!' I've shut it down in a sweat.

Not this time, though. Rosie's questions about Fraser from last night are still ringing shrilly in my ears. Obviously, he's on her mind. I need to start trying to track him down and at least find out if he's alive.

Still prickling from Will's ill humour, I start scrolling through the results. I find Fraser Johnsons who are bakers, artists, investment bankers and undertakers. They are located in St Ives and Aberdeen and, seemingly, every place in between. There's a Fraser Johnson making craft beers in Cumbria. Hmm. Bet he'd be able to handle a few drinks without spending the whole of the next day whimpering about his traumatised liver.

I glance towards the rabbit run. Guinness is peering at me through the wire meshing. My skin prickles with unease, but I refuse to be freaked out by a staring bunny. I turn back to the screen, eyes lighting upon a Fraser Johnson who's a plasterer in Lewisham: ideal for sorting out our frankly atrocious kitchen walls.

Perhaps I should feel guilty, mentally setting myself up with all of these strangers, imaging myself being festooned with fine ales and beautiful paintings and even having the perfect coffin selected and set aside. But these are only random men. I don't for one second imagine that any of them is the Fraser I loved, and with whom I assumed – idiotically – I'd be raising a child. It's such a common name, that's the problem. I could spend all day poring over thousands of Frasers and be none the wiser as to where he is, or what he's doing now. He might not even be living in Britain. His family were loaded, and despite his ramshackle appearance on our trip, he was all set to be taken on by some investment company, via a friend of his dad's. With his breezy confidence and seemingly no worries about how things might turn out, there was a sense even then that he was heading for a glittering future. Meanwhile, I was part-way through a marketing course with a grotty flat, a cranky flatmate and a couple of part-time waitressing jobs.

I do a Google Images search. I know, this is really pushing things. It reveals a baffling array of males varying from a young, grinning boy in a Chelsea football strip to a formal portrait of an elderly man sitting behind a polished desk.

'Working on a Sunday?'

I flinch and look up. It's Tricia, looming over the fence, her no-nonsense straw-coloured hair held back from her pink-cheeked face by means of a striped towelling headband.

'Yep, just a few things to tie up,' I reply, sensing my own cheeks glowing hot.

'Looks like you're burning!' she observes cheerfully. 'You should wear block, Charlotte. There's nothing more ageing than the sun.'

I smile tightly, trying to transmit the message: *thank you for the beauty tip. Now, if you don't mind, I'm hard at work on a crucial report* . . . Her curranty eyes are fixed upon my screen. Although she can't possibly see anything from where she's standing, I quickly shut down the page. A burst of high-pitched yapping – for no reason that I can fathom – announces Nipper's arrival in her garden. Nipper is a tiny, beige-coloured hound of no discernible breed – he looks like a purse with teeth. *Where did they get him?* Liza whispered recently. *Accessorize?*

'Meant to ask,' Tricia goes on, now scooping up Nipper into her arms, 'were you disturbed by that awful racket last night?'

I frown. 'Um . . . I don't think so?'

She presses her lips together. 'That party, I mean, over the road. Awful music blaring half the night. I was on the verge of calling the police . . .'

'Oh, Tommy and Sabrina's party. We were there, actually—'

'You know them?' she exclaims.

'Not really. We'd only met them once before.' I force a big, bright smile. 'They're really nice people.'

'Oh. Well, I hope it's not going to be a regular thing.'

'I wouldn't imagine so, no . . .' I shut down my laptop and stand up, making it clear that our neighbourly exchange is over.

'Charlotte?' Will has appeared at our back door, clutching the phone.

''Scuse me, Tricia, looks like I'm being summoned.' I stride towards him.

'It's Mum,' he hisses, thrusting the phone at me.

I frown. 'She wants to talk to *me*?'

'Yeah,' he adds in a ridiculous stage whisper, 'she wants to know what's happening with this modelling thing.'

I blink at him and take the phone. 'Hi, Gloria, how are you?'

'Fine, just wondered if you'd thought over what I'd said?'

'Er, what specifically?' I ask, wandering into the kitchen to observe a scattering of bread crusts and juice sloppages on the table, presumably left by Rosie, to mark where she's been.

'About being extremely careful,' Gloria says, 'when dealing with photographers. I'm very concerned, Charlotte. It's not a world I think Rosie is especially suited to.'

Of course, she couldn't have discussed this with Will, not with him still in recovery from last night – at two o'clock in the bloody afternoon. It irks me, too, this implication that I am perfectly happy to propel my daughter into a world of pervs and predators just to get her picture on the cover of a magazine. But I know Gloria takes a dim view of my parenting abilities. She 'cried for three days', she once let slip, on learning that her darling son had fallen in love with a hapless single mother when she'd always thought he'd end up with Emily Forrest who, while I was up to my elbows laundering bibs, was studying the oboe at the Royal College of Music.

'Please don't worry, Gloria,' I say firmly. 'It's all in hand and we'll be keeping a close eye on things. In fact, she's doing her first test shoot tomorrow after school. The agency are keen for her to get some proper professional shots to build up her portfolio . . .'

'It's called a *book*, Mum,' Rosie corrects me, lurking in the hallway.

'She will be chaperoned, though?' Gloria wants to know. 'Because if you don't have time, with your *job* and everything, I can always take—'

'No, no, I'm leaving work early so I can go with her,' I say, at which Rosie's face falls.

'Mum,' she hisses, 'there's no need . . .'

'*Yes there is*,' I mouth at her, adding, 'It's fine, Gloria. I know you're concerned, but honestly, there's nothing to worry about at all.'

Chapter Twelve

Rosie is perched on a high chrome stool in a brightly-lit alcove, having her make-up applied by a girl called Boo. Despite it being rather stuffy in the photographer's studio, Boo has topped off her black linen shift dress with a sort of Peruvian hat with hanging-down ear flaps in hairy brown wool. She must be boiling in that, I muse, then realise how silly I'm being for worrying about a young girl's sweaty scalp. This is *fashion*, I remind myself. Comfort doesn't come into it. Bet the photographer – an unshaven, rather irritated-looking man called Parker – like the posh pens – doesn't nurture such thoughts. And nor will his stocky, ginger-cropped assistant, who's been introduced to me merely as 'my assistant'. Perhaps Parker doesn't feel he's important enough to warrant a name.

'So it's your first shoot, Rosie?' Boo says pleasantly, while I leaf through the copy of *Vogue* that was lying on the low table in the studio. I have myself installed in the furthest corner of the room, on a rather grimy tan leather sofa, so as to be as unobtrusive as possible.

'Yes,' Rosie replies. 'I don't really know what to expect . . .'

'Oh, you'll be fine. Parker's great. You're so lucky to be working with him.'

'Yes, I know, Laurie said he's amazing . . .' Already, after just a few brief phone chats with her booker, Rosie has adopted a slight model-agency inflection. Am*aaaa*zing . . .

'You mean Laurie at Face?' Boo asks.

'Yeah, she scouted me—'

'Oh-my-God, you're so lucky! D'you *realise* how lucky you are?'

Rosie chuckles. 'Um, guess so.'

'She's the best!' Boo shrieks. 'She, like, owns the industry!' As they fall into companionable chatter, I can't help feeling impressed at how relaxed Rosie seems in this unfamiliar environment. The hairdryer is switched on and, feeling pretty redundant, I continue flicking through the magazine.

'Looks like we've got Cassandra for Friday's shoot,' Parker tells his assistant. Models, I've realised, rarely have surnames.

'She's a great girl, amazing attitude,' the assistant remarks approvingly. Also: they are not women but *girls*.

'She's got that androgynous sexy insouciance thing going on,' Parker drawls, opening a small fridge and extracting beers for the assistant and himself. I sip my tap water from a glass with a brownish lipstick smear on it, realising that I'll never understand this world, not when I look at a picture of a swimsuit – a 'simple one-piece' at that – and wonder what kind of maniac would pay £795 for it. I mean the cossie (and I do know that no one in such circles says *cossie*) is plain black with a thin white belt and a tiny gold buckle. For that kind of money, I'd expect a flashing fairylight neckline and a sticky-out skirt bit, with martinis perched upon it.

Having expertly appraised the fashion pages, I check my watch. Rosie has been having her hair and make-up done for three quarters of an hour. I stifle a yawn. Of course, I didn't expect anyone to talk to me, or for Parker to be eager to know about the inner workings of a premium crisp company in Essex. In fact, Rosie's right, in that I probably shouldn't have come at all. Parker's studio is on the top floor of an old, weather-beaten warehouse near Old Street; she would have been capable of finding it by herself. 'You do realise there'll be nothing for you to do,' she pointed out on the Tube journey here. I joked that there might be a box of jigsaws and colouring-in books.

When she emerges from the alcove, it's all I can do not to gasp. She is *breathtakingly* lovely: made up, certainly, but so skilfully you can barely detect Boo's handiwork at all. My daughter has been sort of smoothed over, her eyes and lips subtly enhanced and her cheekbones defined with expert brushwork. She is wearing the dark skinny jeans she arrived in, but has swapped her checked shirt for a simple white vest.

'Lovely!' Parker says approvingly. 'You look beautiful, darling. Now, all I need you to do is stand in front of the background so we can test the lights. And don't worry, there's no need to pose as such. Just be yourself. It's all about a nice, relaxed feel . . .'

I stare from the sofa, transfixed. I know Rosie would prefer me not to watch, and that I should still be forensically examining *Vogue*, but I can't help myself. The background is a roll of pale grey paper, and Rosie looks a little unsure as she stands in front of it. 'Just relax your face and part your lips a little,' Parker says encouragingly. 'That's it. That's gorgeous.'

She fixes her gaze on the lens and, as Parker starts to shoot, something incredible happens. She is no longer my daughter, still partial to snacking on cookies and milk on the sofa with Guinness plonked on her lap. She's not the schoolgirl with her hair in a scrunchie who comes home and tips out the contents of her battered old schoolbag – dog-eared jotters, Milky Bar wrappers, a brush so matted with hair it could be classed as a rodent – on the kitchen table. Right here, in Parker's sun-filled studio, she is wearing the most casual clothes imaginable, and her hair has merely been lightly mussed up. Yet something magical is happening. Her beauty is shining out of her.

My eyes fill up. Even Will would be moved if he could see our lovely girl now.

'These are amazing,' Parker says, continuing to shoot. Am*aaaa*zing . . .

Watching her, I can hardly believe I am fifty per cent responsible for her genes. People are wrong when they assume mothers envy their daughters' beauty. How could I? I feel proud, actually. In front of the camera, she is other-worldly, like a beautiful cat.

'Is this really your first shoot?' Parker asks, pausing to flick through the images on his camera.

'Yes,' Rosie says meekly.

'You're a natural. You really are.'

'I'm a bit nervous,' she admits, with an apologetic grin.

'Don't worry, darling. These are looking great, your agency's going to love them . . .' He resumes shooting as, somewhere at the far end of the studio, a mobile rings. 'Get that, Fletch?' Parker says distractedly. So that's the assistant's name. Is no one in fashion called Linda or John? There's a mumbled conversation, and Fletch holds out the phone.

'It's Joely.'

'Tell her I'm shooting,' Parker says without looking round.

'She says it's urgent.'

He grimaces, grabs the phone and mutters, 'Sorry, Rosie, won't be a sec. It's my sister. Always some bloody drama . . .'

He marches off with his phone. Rosie twists her fingers together and looks around, obviously wondering what to do with herself. I jump up from the sofa and stroll towards her, not to get involved or anything; just to reassure her that she's doing really well. Her eyes widen with alarm as I approach, as if I am about to dab at her face with a spat-on tissue. 'Mum!' she hisses. 'What are you *doing*?'

'Nothing, I just—'

'Go and sit down,' she commands, 'or go for a walk or something. Have a look around—'

I frown at her. 'There's nothing around here to look at.'

'There must be *something*.'

'Um, I don't really fancy just wandering the streets, love . . .'

She lets out an exasperated gasp, then switches on a big, beaming smile as her new best friend Boo appears with her little pot of powder and brush and proceeds to sweep it over Rosie's face.

'Yeah, yeah, nightmare,' Parker is saying, phone still clamped to his ear, as I slink back to the sofa. 'You should call Face – they're always taking on new girls. Got one here now. She's great. A real find . . .' He's pacing around, rubbing at his bristly chin and glancing at Rosie. 'Well, yeah . . . in fact her mum's here now. Yep. First shoot. You know how they are . . .'

I glare at him. 'They' are just being parents, actually. 'They' want to make sure no one says, *And could you just whip your clothes off for this one, darling?* 'Er, not bad,' he adds, assuming an indecipherable expression. He drops his voice to a murmur. 'She's all right. She's . . . you know. Just a mum.'

What does that mean? I'm wearing newish jeans and a floral printed top from White Stuff that's a particular favourite, in that it minimises things in the boob region. After feeling so provincial-officey at the agency, I thought it best to opt for a casual mum look today. Parker glances in my direction and pulls a fake smile. I shift uncomfortably, aware that, for some reason, I am being assessed. Why on earth are they talking about me? Today, I am just a chaperone.

'I s'pose I could ask her,' Parker says, now staring blatantly at me. 'Better clear it with Face, though.' He finishes the call and holds out his phone. Fletch scampers to take it from him.

'Er, Mum?' Parker says.

Mum? I'm not his mother. He is *easily* as old as I am. 'Yes?' I say politely.

'Bit of an emergency here. My sister's a fashion journalist, writes for that new free mag, the scrappy-looking thing – what's it called again?'

'*Front*,' Fletch obliges.

Parker chuckles. 'Yeah, *Front*. It's all fashion and beauty, isn't it? So what's that about?'

Fletch shrugs. 'Front row? Y'know, like at the shows . . .'

‘Oh, *right*,’ Parker says, turning back to me. ‘Ever seen it?’

I nod. ‘Just strewn about on the Tube . . .’

‘Yeah, well, they’re doing a thing about the new London girls and their mums, how they feel about it, that kinda thing—’

‘The new London girls?’ I repeat.

‘Yeah, the new faces. *You* know. Models. The ones coming up. They want to know how their mums feel about, er . . .’ He shrugs. ‘Dunno really. My sister doesn’t half waffle on. But they’re doing a mums and daughters shoot in a studio across town and one of the models has had a strop with her mum and stormed out . . .’ He raises a hopeful smile. ‘So you’ll do it, yeah?’

I glance at Rosie, whose face has sort of *crumpled*. ‘You mean . . . I’d be photographed with Rosie?’

‘That’s right,’ he says, as if it’s no big deal at all.

‘And . . . we’d both appear in the magazine?’

‘Yeah.’

‘I’m not sure, I mean—’

‘Oh, c’mon, Mum,’ he cajoles me. ‘No one’ll see it. It’s just a crappy little magazine full of, well, I dunno really, never read it myself . . .’ Rosie stares, looking mildly stunned, as Parker rattles through the procedure: ‘I’ll do the pictures here. They’re cool with that. There’s no time to get the two of you over to the other shoot anyway . . .’ As if travel arrangements are foremost on my list of concerns. ‘It’ll be good for you, Rosie,’ he adds. ‘Get you some attention as one of the new, young crop.’ Hmm. Does he have to make her sound like a carrot?

‘So . . . what d’you think, Rosie?’ I ask her.

She looks appalled. ‘Yeah, great,’ she croaks.

Parker grins and nods to Fletch. ‘Call her agency, check

it out with them, then ring my sister back and tell her I'll do the shots here. She can speak to Rosie and Mum' – can he *please* stop referring to me as universal mum? – 'in about an hour's time.' He nods to no one in particular and marches off. Before I can talk it over properly with Rosie – to find out if this is really okay, or if she feels bullied into it – I am whisked off to the make-up alcove where Boo swaps her breezy demeanour for one of grim determination.

'Hop on the stool,' she commands, surveying my reflection in the mirror. Her face tenses, locked for a moment in extreme concentration, as if she has been challenged to transform a grotty 70s pebble-dashed bungalow into a structure of architectural splendour befitting an episode of *Grand Designs*. And now comes a torrent of products, kicking off with a shimmery cream, 'to brighten your ashen tones', Boo says charmingly, alerting me to an aspect of my appearance I'd never thought to worry about before. No less than *four* foundations are blended on a palette, bringing to mind those men mixing up mortar when they were repointing our house. The resulting shade – which looks too dark, in my inexpert opinion – is daubed on thickly with a brush. Still, at least a roller wasn't required. Powder follows – enough to create a small dust storm – then Boo moves on to my eyes. 'We want a *smoky* eye,' she chirps, proceeding to layer on many shades of brown shadow and, alarmingly, black. She finishes by painting my lips with a colossal amount of goo.

'Now for your hair,' she mutters, tugging off her woolly hat and dumping it on the make-up table. This is serious work; it's making her sweat. 'What d'you do with it normally?' she asks.

'Just wash it really,' I reply.

She peers at me with ill-disguised horror. 'You don't blow dry or style it, to give it a bit of body?'

I feel as if I have been ushered into the wrong job interview – one for which I am entirely unsuited. I'd feel no more out of my depth than if she were to suddenly ask, 'So how *would* you go about diagnosing an enlarged spleen?'

'I'm usually in a rush in the mornings,' I explain. 'Anyway, it dries in the car on my way to work.'

Boo looks quite nauseous at this, as if I have explained that I don't in fact bother with cleaning myself at all. 'You don't use any products?'

'Well, shampoo, obviously, and Rosie and I like that Body Shop banana conditioner—'

'Well, we'll need to do *something*,' she huffs, unearthing a collection of hair appliances and brushes from her bag. I am squooshed with a water spray, then blow dried and tonged – I thought tongs had died out at around the same time as fax machines – until my face is framed by a mane of billowing curls. 'What d'you think?' Boo asks, plonking a hand on her hip.

What do I *think*? I look like Brian May out of Queen, in lipstick. 'It's quite, er, eighties,' I say, my fixed smile implying that this is a positive thing.

'Yeah, you needed a bit more oomph,' Boo says blithely, producing an industrial-sized can of hairspray, like a golden fire extinguisher, and liberally squirting it all over my head. 'All done,' she announces.

I blink through the haze of spray and step out to greet my public. Rosie stares, seemingly incapable of speech. Parker and Fletch have rearranged the lights, and dragged a stylish clear Perspex chair in front of the grey background (because clearly, I am too decrepit to stand). 'Oh, good job!' Parker enthuses, as if I'm a re-sprayed car. 'She looks *all right*!'

My daughter is still gawping at me as if she's never seen me before. The shoot begins, and whereas it was all about 'a nice relaxed feel' with Rosie, it now appears to be all about many props: a navy blue curtain is hung behind us, a table is dragged into shot for me to lean on 'casually', and a lamp is plonked on it, which I'm hoping will obscure my face (but no – Parker adjusts its position to ensure that I and my massive man-perm are clearly in view).

Every so often he stops to change lenses. I do hope there's a youth-making one to make everything fuzzy, as if shot through twenty-denier tights, or a colander. Parker has asked Rosie to stand behind me with her hand resting on my shoulder. I can sense her mortification seeping down from her fingers, through my top and into my skin. Boo keeps scampering over and brushing on more powder, as if my face is dissolving into a puddle of oil. 'Bit of a shine issue,' she says, frowning. 'D'you always break out like this?'

'It's just quite hot in here,' I point out, although Rosie's face has remained perfectly matte: perhaps I have developed the sebaceous glands of a thirteen-year-old. Or maybe it's a menopausal hot flush? On a positive note, at least Parker is taking literally hundreds of pictures so, hopefully, *one* of them will be okay.

Shoot over, I am dispatched back to the sofa while Rosie is interviewed by Parker's sister on the phone. Rather than sitting beside me, she has chosen to pace back and forth across the vast studio floor: *Yeah, it's great . . . just happened when I was out shopping, yeah . . . with friends.*

Er, with *me,* actually, while I lugged that wretched

stereophonic equipment around Forever 21 – in which Will has shown no interest after the initial opening, apart from to stack it all carefully in our bedroom. An invisible 'unwanted gift' label has hovered over it ever since.

. . . *Feel so lucky,* Rosie goes on. *Yeah, well, I s'pose my ambition is to work with all the top designers . . .*

What about being a vet? I want to shriek. What about your *A-levels*?

She finishes her interview and hands the phone to me. 'Hi, Rosie's mum,' comes Joely's bright voice. 'So, er, what's your name again? Sorry, I didn't quite catch—'

'Charlotte,' I reply. 'Charlotte Bristow.'

'Great, yeah – so can I ask a few questions?' She fires them at me, and I mean *really* fires them, in the way that Will accused me of doing, when I gently quizzed Zach about his educational prospects. Yes, I find myself babbling, I'm delighted about Rosie being scouted. No, we'd never considered it before, and no, there aren't any other models in the family – then I remember. Gloria. 'Well, her grandma was Miss Foil Wrap in the seventies,' I add, hoping this'll satisfy her enough to finish this thing as swiftly as possible.

'Wow, did that lead to an amazing career?' Joely asks.

'Um . . . not exactly.'

'Oh dear . . . so what happened?'

The pause hangs in the air. Rosie is perched on a window sill with her legs dangling down, and Boo is packing up her products into a small wheeled suitcase. 'Er . . . there was a sort of thing – a *groping* thing – with a photographer. And then she got pregnant—'

'A photographer got her pregnant?' Joely gasps. 'Gosh, it's a wonder you're so relaxed about Rosie modelling at all. You must be a really cool mum!'

'No, I mean she got pregnant by her husband,' I explain limply.

'Oh. So, um . . . I'll finish with a few questions about your beauty routine, okay?'

Not this again.

'Favourite product?' Joely prompts me.

'I don't really have one,' I reply, aware of Rosie yawning and fiddling with her phone.

'Well, I need to put something,' Joely says, sounding impatient now, 'because all the other mums in my feature have told me theirs. That's the thing, you see – I want to know the beauty advice you've passed on to your daughter. That's the whole crux of the thing.'

'I don't think she needs my beauty advice,' I say, trying to keep my tone light.

Joely sighs. 'Just tell me some of the products you use, then.'

My mind is a blank. I try to picture our bathroom shelf, but all I can see is the London Dungeons mug crammed with far more toothbrushes than there are members of my family, their bristles all spayed as if gnawed by dogs. 'Elvive shampoo?' I say.

'I mean *aspirational* brands,' Joely says hotly.

Shit. My gaze falls to the copy of *Vogue*, which is lying open on the table. There's a full-page advert for some kind of serum containing real gold particles. It's packaged in a tiny, multi-faceted glass bottle with a cylindrical golden lid. It looks more like a precious object to be displayed on a shelf than something you'd put on your face. 'Erm, Belle Visage Beauty Elixir,' I blurt out, causing Rosie's head to whip round in my direction.

'Wow,' Joely says. 'You have expensive tastes, Mum!' Today, clearly, I have ceased to have an actual name.

'Um, well, you know how it is. When you find the right product . . .'

'God, yeah. I'd love to try it but it's way beyond my budget, unfortunately. So . . . what d'you like about the Elixir specifically?'

Hell, this is the part where I'm supposed to rave about its inter-molecular-cellular-plumping effects or whatever these miracle serums are meant to do. 'It smells nice,' I reply.

'Really?' She laughs. 'Well, good for you. I love hearing about mums treating themselves instead of letting themselves go. I mean, I'm not a mother, so it's all a mystery to me really, but how come so many women stop even wearing *mascara* when they have kids?'

'Er, they're just busy, I guess . . .'

'But how long does it take to apply it? Twenty seconds tops?'

I really don't know. I have never timed it and anyway, I can't even start to explain that it's *not* time – anyone can spare twenty seconds, after all – but priorities, and that the last thing you're thinking about when children are clamouring, demanding breakfast, is your eyelashes. 'I think it's more a case of forgetting,' I explain.

'Well, *I'd* never forget, and I bet you don't either. I admire you for spending all that money and putting yourself first . . .' This, I can see, is going to sound fantastic in a national magazine: a thinly veiled criticism of women who temporarily lose themselves in the fug of early motherhood. For the whole of Rosie's first year, my legs were shrouded in hair and I forgot that moisturiser even existed.

I touch my cheek as Joely witters on. It feels eerily waxy with its many layers of product, and I'm overcome by an urge to scrub my face. 'I don't want it to sound as if I'm obsessed with expensive skincare,' I say firmly.

'Oh, come on,' she retorts, 'we all know it's important to look good. Like it or not, everyone's judged by their appearance.' A chilling thought hits me: maybe she's right, maybe I need to make more of an effort and then perhaps Will wouldn't politely remove my hand from his nethers and Rosie wouldn't canter about ten metres ahead when we were out shopping together . . . 'Anyway,' Joely concludes, 'thanks so much for your time. I hope you'll like the feature when it comes out.'

'I'm sure I will,' I say, relieved to finish the call and say our goodbyes and leave the studio.

Rosie stares at me as we step outside the building. 'Are you really going home like that?'

'Of course I am. What else am I supposed to do?'

'Er . . . find somewhere to wash it off?'

'Where exactly? There's nowhere around here.' We march past a beleaguered fountain constructed from stained concrete blocks. Its surrounding pond, no bigger than a child's paddling pool, is littered with crisp packets and drinks cans. 'Perhaps I could have a quick dip in there,' I suggest, facetiously.

Rosie sighs. 'You could have taken it all off in the studio. Boo had cleansers and wipes, or you could have gone to the loo . . .'

I touch my hair, which feels as if it's sitting on my head like a giant meringue. 'I thought she might be offended,' I explain, 'as if I couldn't wait to get it off.'

'God, Mum. You look really weird! And what was that thing you were saying about the elixir stuff? What where you on about?'

'She just wanted my beauty tips,' I reply with a smirk.

Chapter Thirteen

Two days later, by which point my hair has just about returned to its normal texture, Liza comes round to hear all about it. Sabrina drops by too, returning the stack of dishes that Will used to transport his barbecue offerings, and now the three of us are working our way through a chilled bottle of sauvignon in the warmth of the early evening sun.

'So are you married, Liza?' Sabrina asks with her customary directness.

'Single since pretty much forever,' Liza replies. 'My daughter's twenty and at Bristol uni. Her dad and I split up about ten years ago but it was pretty amicable. We'd just kind of . . .' She shrugs. 'Run out of steam, I guess.'

Sabrina nods. Her white broderie anglaise dress enhances her tan; she looks astonishingly pretty. 'Well, you tend to know when there's no going back, don't you?'

'Yep, it's that point where you're just . . . *existing* together,' Liza says.

'Like housemates,' Sabrina agrees. 'Not like you and Will, Charlotte. You've got a real catch there. Bet he was all over you when you came from that shoot.' I have already filled them in on Boo's enthusiasm for 'a smoky eye', as if I had just the one, rather than a matching pair.

'Can't wait to see the pictures,' Liza adds.

I grin. 'Actually, I have one on my phone. I forced Rosie to take it when we got home.'

'Show us!' Sabrina commands, extracting a packet of cigarettes from her bag and lighting one up. I grab my phone and bring up the picture.

'Oh my God, you look . . .' Liza peals with laughter.

'. . . Amazing,' Sabrina exclaims as they peer at the screen.

'No, I don't. I look like a transvestite.'

'Are you crazy?' Sabrina shrieks. 'You look fabulous. Your hair, your make-up—'

'But they're not *my* hair and make-up,' I cut in, topping up everyone's glasses. 'Rosie said I looked weird and she was right. The make-up artist looked like she needed a stiff drink by the time she'd finished. I'm hoping they crop me out of the picture so it's just Rosie on her own.'

'You're crazy,' Sabrina chuckles. 'What did Will say?'

I smirk. 'He said, "Bloody hell", then carried on wiping his mushrooms.'

'You *are* joking . . .'

'Well,' I start, 'some of them are pretty grubby and you never know what might've peed on them . . .'

'I'm not talking about mushrooms,' she asserts. 'I mean *you*. Wasn't he overwhelmed?'

'Er, not that I noticed,' I reply.

She shakes her head in bewilderment.

'He was probably in shock,' Liza suggests. 'I mean, you're so natural, usually. He just likes you the way you are.'

We fall silent for a moment as I consider this, and try

to dredge up some evidence that, secretly, Will is still desperately in love with me. 'Actually,' I mutter, 'when you said about just existing together, Liza . . . well, that's us.'

She frowns. 'It's not really that bad, is it? I know it's frustrating, the whole job situation and Will being here all the time—'

'We are though,' I interrupt. 'We're like *housemates*. The only difference is, we sleep in the same bed.' I blink and swallow hard, glimpsing Rosie through the window, pottering about with Nina in the kitchen.

Sabrina clears her throat. 'Will's lovely, though.'

I nod, feeling slightly irritated. That's not the point; I'm not denying his attractiveness, or his talents with the barbecue tongs. 'Yes, he is,' I reply, 'but sometimes I worry that we're just not that lovely together anymore.'

She gives me a sympathetic look. 'Everyone goes through little spells like that.'

I smile wryly. 'Ours isn't so little, Sabrina.'

'You need to spice things up then,' she offers. 'What about a date night? Sometimes you have to set it up – get it in the diary. Me and Tommy go on dates all the time. And make things different at home. In bed, I mean. If Will didn't go for the full-on glamour from your shoot, how about trying something else?'

I frown, uncomprehending. 'Like what?'

'Like . . . *you* know. Role play or something. Introduce an element of surprise.'

I glance at Liza who's suppressing a laugh. 'Sorry, Sabrina. I hate to sound negative, and I know plenty of people are into the saucy nurse outfit and all that, but I don't think it'd exactly *surprise* Will . . .'

'But surely—'

'He'd have a heart attack,' I cut in, 'or give himself a

hernia from laughing. He'd be bound to burst something. Anyway, I don't really have the body for a sexy nurse outfit.' I jab at my ample chest. 'I'm more your stern matron.'

Sabrina lights another cigarette. 'That might do it for him. A matronly thing, I mean . . .'

'No, that would *hospitalise* him and anyway, I'm not sure about dressing up as someone else just to get him interested, you know?' I sip my wine.

'Maybe *he* could dress up then?'

'But what as?'

Sabrina shakes her ahead, as if I really am a lost cause. 'I don't know. Whatever your thing is . . .'

'The trouble is,' I explain, 'I don't think I have one. A *thing*, I mean. I might have had once, but I can't for the life of me remember what it was—'

'Come on, what about policemen?'

Liza and I laugh some more. 'Don't get started on uniforms,' I say, trying to compose myself. 'His mother's convinced he should be a prison officer or a traffic warden . . .'

'A traffic warden could be pretty sexy,' Liza teases. 'He could book you for parking in a restricted area.'

We all hoot with laughter. 'You could offer a personal favour to avoid getting a ticket,' Sabrina suggests.

Will appears at the back door, and we try to rearrange our expressions into some semblance of normality as he makes his way towards us with another bottle of wine.

'Thanks, darling,' I say. 'Why don't you have a drink with us?' I can hardly look at him now without imagining him marching along the street, pausing to check each parked car.

'No, I'll leave you to it,' he says, giving me a curious look. 'It's pretty late anyway.'

Sabrina watches him fondly as he heads back to the house. 'Oh, he's such a love,' she exclaims, and I wonder if she really has him down for some kind of superman, the George Clooney of London E11, or if she's just trying to make me feel warmer towards him. Thankfully, the conversation moves away from my love life and into the altogether more sparkling realm of Sabrina's wedding dress designs. We chatter away until it's dark and, when they've left, I feel oddly disorientated.

Sure, it's partly due to the wine I've guzzled. But, despite having had a lovely time, I'm also thinking: nurses, policemen, traffic wardens? Is this what it's come to, really – that I should pretend to be someone else in order to seem sexy and interesting to Will?

I loiter at the open back door, breathing in the warm evening air. A small movement gives me a start. Guinness is still in his run. I doubt very much if he'd expire if left out here, but what if he did? How bad would I feel then? I lift him up and carry him inside. It feels so comforting, cradling a warm, fluffy animal, that instead of putting him straight to bed, I sit at the kitchen table, holding him in my arms.

It's eleven-thirty and the whole house is silent. I can feel Guinness's tiny beating heart. Perhaps I'm more pissed than I realised, what with planning to have only *one* glass (maybe two) with Liza, then the three of us accidentally tippling nearly three bottles. But I actually feel quite . . . *loved.* Yes, I tell myself: Guinness loves me in his own pure, small mammal-ish way.

Christ – what am I *doing*? I snap back to reality and stare down at our pet. Of course he doesn't love me. I'm just the person who happened to notice he was still out there at night time. I mean, as rabbits go, he's cute enough – but he's basically just sitting here on my lap, twitching. And not only that. He has also, I discover as I stand up, pooped on my denim skirt. The pellets bounce on our green speckled lino before rolling under the table. I place him in his utility room bed, then, without attending to the poos, stride back outside and plonk myself on our back step.

I can't go to bed yet. There's no way I could sleep. My mind is whirring over the fact that I've become one of those 'pet people': the kind of dotty middle-aged woman who sits with a small, fluffy animal on her lap in restaurants and posts little morsels into its mouth. I'll be the kind of person who might be faintly amusing to observe from a distance, but you wouldn't want to be stuck at the same table as her.

I'm starved of *human* love, that's what it is. That's why I was Googling Fraser – not just because Rosie had asked about him. No one searches for exes if they're completely happy with their lot. It's a symptom of, of . . . well, of *something*, anyway. I gnaw at a fingernail, wishing I'd asked Sabrina to leave me a ciggie, despite the fact that I haven't had so much as a puff since 1996. Getting up from the step, I make my way to our garden table, planning to gather up the glasses to avoid Tricia beaking over the fence tomorrow and muttering to Gerald about what a bunch of lushes we are, not only boozing – on a week night – but smoking too. Sabrina's fag ends are stubbed out in a plastic plant pot.

However, instead of clearing the table, I pick up an unfinished glass of wine. It smells nasty, sour and slightly pee-like, but I still have a sip, whilst staring at our shed.

Could Will and I possibly do it in there? Maybe Sabrina just meant that I should be more proactive, and shake things up a little in the sex department. Well, that's probably true. 'Night-night,' we say, like a couple of octogenarians, before turning off our bedside lamps and assuming our positions so far apart, a caravan could trundle between us. So maybe I *should* take matters into my own hands. I mean, I do fancy Will, even after all these years; I probably still would if he was fat and bald and had turned into a farting snorer – but none of that has even happened to him. He is just an older, slightly more ruggedly handsome – and more muscular, due to all the gardening and cycling – version of his younger self.

What does Fraser look like now?

The sudden thought makes me feel quite dizzy. I try to push it out of my brain, annoyed for even letting it in. He's definitely sneaking back into my consciousness more often these days – the posh git with his upper-class accent and public-school hair. I inhale deeply, have another slug of spiteful plonk and focus instead on our shed.

It's a particularly unlovely one, it has to be said. It hasn't been painted since we moved here and is rotting at the bottom, its timbers slowly crumbling into the ground. Its sole small, square window is cracked from when Ollie and Saul were attempting to play rounders (SMASH! 'We didn't *do* anything!'). Could it really be a haven of raunch, a secret den of saucy goings-on?

Perhaps it could. Knocking back the rest of the tepid wine, I place the glass on the garden table. Then I push open the creaky wooden door – we've never had a key for it – and sneak in.

There's a light but I daren't switch it on. Our bedroom overlooks the garden, and there's a small chance that Will might happen to glance out, spot the glow from the bare bulb and assume an intruder was about to make off with his big yellow tub of hormone rooting powder. It's sitting on the shelf, illuminated in a shaft of streetlight that's struggling through the grubby window, and sounds like pretty exciting stuff. Rude, actually: *hormonal rootings*. What's happening to me? One minute I'm virtually planning a romantic minibreak with a rabbit. Then I'm sensing a stirring in my loins while glimpsing some kind of stimulating powder for plants. Perhaps I need some kind of therapy.

So what else is in here? I need a torch in order to make full inventory of all the other goodies. After all, it's Will's private lair: God knows what he gets up to in here. I sneak back to the house, enjoying myself now – feeling reckless and naughty and less the tragic middle-aged-bunny-fancier – and find Ollie's new torch under a heap of detritus on the worktop. I click it on in the kitchen. Yep, it works.

Back in the shed, I continue my explorations. There are stacks of plastic plant pots, oil cans and a polythene bag of rather sinister-sounding Blood Fish & Bone Fertiliser. Hmmm. Don't fancy *that* near my private parts. There's not much space in here either. Clearing out some of the bulkier stuff – lawnmower, Ollie's wrecked old bike and a cluster of rusty old rakes and hoes – would attract suspicion from my beloved, and make the whole enterprise less spontaneous than I'd like.

Cans of creosote and Nitromors Stripper, lined up neatly on the top shelf, are illuminated by the torch as I step on something soft and bouncy. They're Will's waders, from when he was gainfully, *happily* employed, and used to slosh about in the marshes, checking the nesting habitats of Canada Geese. I pick one up and sniff it. It's reassuringly rubbery, like the erasers we had at school.

A smile plays on my lips. Could waders be sexy? They're not my thing: as I confessed to Sabrina, I don't actually have one. But maybe Will would go for it, or at the very least find it amusing, and applaud my efforts? I could surprise him, summoning him out from the house via a call to his mobile and let him find me in here, naked – apart from the big rubber boots. Even if he thought I'd lost my mind, it'd be a laugh, wouldn't it? We should have more laughs, I decide. *That* would stop me thinking about Fraser-bloody-Johnson. The two of us could just about squeeze in here, and there's a bench – a bit splintery, granted, but I could pad it with cushions smuggled out of the house. Excited now, and fuelled by cheap Chilean booze, I place Ollie's torch on the shelf in order to free up both hands.

I tug off my blue canvas shoes, hitch up my skirt and pull on the waders. They're far too big for me. They don't even look funny, let alone sexy. So what next? I find Ollie's pair, worn on his field trips with Will, squished under the bench. They look more my size so, just out of curiosity, I pull them on. They're tight – *too* tight. Ollie must have worn them when he was about seven or eight. I stare down at my legs, beginning to think that waders possibly aren't quite right for a passionate encounter. Maybe some marriage counselling sessions would be more beneficial?

I start to try and pull them off. They seem to be stuck, as if some kind of vacuum has formed around my feet.

I pull and pull, finally wrestling one off and taking a minute to catch my breath before attacking the other. It's even harder to shift. Christ, I'm going to have to creep back into the house like this, in my T-shirt and skirt and one wader. Looking around the shed, I spot the big yellow tub and twist off its lid. Powder is what I need, of the hormone rooting variety if necessary.

Just before my fateful Inter-railing trip, my friend Angie and I had gone to a fetish club in Soho. While she'd dared to wear a red rubber crop top and a hip-hugging mini, I'd gone in a normal black dress from Miss Selfridge and loitered about by the bar, sipping my beer and feeling intimidated until it became apparent that these shiny, rubbery people were in fact extremely friendly. In the loo, a girl had explained that sprinkling talc into rubber garments made them easy to slip on and off.

It's a nugget of information I'd completely forgotten, until now. Reaching for the yellow pot, I twist off its lid and sprinkle a little into the boot. I'm trying to banish the unsettling thought that the hormone powder might cause my leg hair to sprout profusely and make Will think I'm having some kind of middle-aged testosterone surge. One normal leg, and the other, the thickly-haired limb of a mammoth – that would take some explaining. But needs must. I give the boot a sharp tug, and it *flies* off, sending me staggering backwards into the bench which slams against the flimsy wooden wall, juddering the entire shed as something very hard and heavy crashes down on top of me.

'Owww!' I scream, clamping both hands to my head. I crouch down in the dark – the torch must have rolled off the shelf, and switched off – feeling dizzy and sick.

Concussed, probably. 'My fucking head,' I bleat, gingerly patting my scalp.

There's a wet patch. I am bleeding. I remain still, staring at my hands until my eyes become accustomed to the gloom. Now I can make out dark, sticky smears on my fingers. What if I need stitches? Never mind Will – what would Ollie and Rosie think if their mother had to be carted off to hospital and sewn up? Parents are meant to set a good example. We're not supposed to get piddled on wine and injure ourselves in sheds. I'm a terrible mother and, if Will takes the kids away from me, it'll be my own fault.

I need to survey the damage properly. I pat about on the floor, trying to find Ollie's torch, and discover instead a big tin of something sticky, emitting a pungent smell. So that's what happened. The tin fell down on my head and its lid pinged off, and now creosote is pooling around my bare feet.

'Gerald!'

Shit, that's Tricia from next door, sounding horribly close.

'Gerald, come out here *right now*.'

'Tricia, it's nothing, I told you . . .'

I can hear her stomping about in her garden, muttering to herself, something about intruders and police. A horrible image forms in my mind – of Will, standing calmly with his arms around a bleak-faced Rosie and Ollie as he explains, 'I'm sorry, but Mum has some . . . *issues* right now . . .'

'Gerald?' Tricia yells, seemingly inches from our shed. 'I told you I heard something out here. For God's sake, hurry up and *help* me.'

Chapter Fourteen

Oh, Christ. Gerald. Brigadier General of the Neighbourhood Watch who spearheaded a campaign to chalk a circle around every dog poo deposit in our neighbourhood and write, WHO DID THIS? beside each one ('Scooby Doo!' Ollie scrawled beside a particularly extravagant pile). Anyway, Gerald is not to be messed with.

A slice of bright white light beams from their open back door. 'No, I *don't* know where your grey cardigan is,' Tricia snaps. 'Just put on your dressing gown and hurry up.'

My heart is thumping as I remain, motionless, crouched in the shed. I'm paddling in creosote, I realise, in my thin cotton socks. My shoes are covered in the stuff too. 'Just a fox,' Gerald mutters, his voice growing nearer. 'What's all the fuss?'

'A fox that screamed in a woman's voice?' she retorts.

'Well, they do, actually. They cry, you know that, and it can sound just like a human. Now will you just forget this and come up to bed?'

'A fox that swore?' she exclaims. 'A fox that screamed, *My fucking head*?' There follows some mumbled discussion. '. . . the Bristows' garden,' Tricia goes on. 'If he actually tried to tame it, there wouldn't be all that undergrowth for people to hide in . . .'

Undergrowth? Damn cheek. They are herbaceous borders, bursting with hollyhocks and all the other flowers I don't know the names of but make a point of admiring, to show Will that I appreciate his efforts. 'What kind of people?' Gerald retorts.

'I don't know. Drug addicts. Burglars. You don't seem remotely concerned . . .'

Another pause, then Gerald mutters, 'You said it was a woman, though?'

'Yes. At least, I think so. God, I don't know. Could've been someone in pain. A woman, a child – anyone. Maybe someone being attacked . . .'

'Right, well, we'd better have a look around . . .' Obviously, Gerald in his stripy pyjamas and tartan slippers would terrify the wits out of any lurking crack addict. There's more ill-humoured murmuring, then, having apparently satisfied themselves that no one is likely to crash through the fence and attack them, our neighbours make their way back indoors.

Shivering now, I tug down my skirt, then peer out of the shed towards Tricia and Gerald's house. Their kitchen light goes out. I step out, shutting the shed door and darting across our garden before quietly letting myself into our house.

In the hallway I peel off my ruined socks and stuff them deep into the kitchen bin. Then I hoist up one foot at a time and give it a good scrub at the sink with the dishwasher sponge, taking care to bin it when I'm done, to avoid poisoning anyone. I might be a little tipsy, and a complete fool for even considering waders as erotic attire, but at least I'm being methodical and taking care to cover my tracks – literally, as our kitchen floor needs a thorough wipe to erase my creosotey footprints. Thank God my family is asleep.

In the sanctuary of the bathroom I inspect my head. An impressive quantity of blood has seeped from the cut, which I dab at ineffectually with a dampened cotton wool pad. As it's stinging quite badly, I daub on what we used to call 'magic cream', because the last thing I need is a septic scalp. Then, still feeling a little nauseous, I tread lightly to our darkened bedroom.

Mercifully, Will doesn't seem to register me undressing or climbing into bed beside him. It's not unusual, me coming up to bed later, although I've long suspected that synchronising our bedtimes might benefit our marriage. Now, though, I'm ridiculously grateful for being able to lie down in the dark without any attention whatsoever being bestowed upon me. I close my eyes, wondering when the wound will stop smarting.

Will's hand edges over, making me flinch. 'You okay?'

'Yes, I'm fine.' *Apart from being shat on by a rabbit and attacked by a two-litre can of creosote, I'm absolutely tickety-boo.*

'What time is it?' he murmurs.

'Oh, I don't know. Late. After midnight. Night, darling.' Please, please go back to sleep . . .

A beat's silence. I think he's dropped back off, so I'm safe for now. Skin repairs itself more quickly at night, so I've heard, so by morning the hole in my head will be all healed again. At least, that's what I'd like to believe. The negative side of my brain is telling me it'll continue to bleed all night and I'll wake up with the pillowcase stuck to my scalp. It might even have to be surgically removed. I turn away from Will and pray for sleep to come.

A hand slides over my back. Then he spoons around me, and if *that's* not enough, he starts kissing the back of my neck. This is highly irregular, him cuddling in like this – and on a normal night I'd be delighted and all over him in a nanosecond. But tonight isn't a normal night. It's one of humiliation and pain.

'Hey,' he whispers.

'I'm a bit tired,' I whisper back, gritting my teeth as his hand edges round and round . . . what's going on here? All that sex talk in the garden with Liza and Sabrina . . . did some of it drift in to the house, like pollen? Or did he hear me saying we're like housemates, and vowed to put things right? Oh-my-God, now the hand is *doing* things which, again, I'd find thrilling under normal circumstances but now cannot entertain at all.

This is so weird. The last couple of times, I've been the one to instigate things. I've tried to gently ask if there's any reason why we hardly ever do it these days, and he's just brushed me off, saying it's 'just life', whatever that means. But now, it's as if another man, who looks very like Will, has broken in and snuck into our bed. Or maybe he's been taken over by an amorous alien. I wriggle uncomfortably and let out a little murmur, which I hope he'll interpret as 'I am *completely* exhausted' rather than, 'Let's do it.'

'Charlotte?' he whispers.

'Mmmrr,' I mumble unintelligibly.

'Look . . . I'm sorry.'

''S'okay.' I have no idea what he's sorry for but I don't want to hear it now. I want to sleep for six hours and wake up with a mended head.

The hand comes to rest on the soft curve of my stomach. 'Just wanted to say . . .' I realise I'm holding my breath. '. . . you've been really good about the job thing.'

''S'all right,' I whisper.

'I, um . . . I know it hasn't been easy lately . . .' Why has he decided to talk about this now, when I've tried so many times during normal daylight hours and he's never been anything other than brusque or defensive?

'I don't mind at all,' I say firmly. 'It's good, you being here, er . . . doing stuff.'

'You really think so?'

'Mmm.' He kisses the back of my neck so tenderly, I almost want to cry. *Now please go straight to sleep like you do virtually every other night* . . . But he doesn't. He keeps kissing me, and I know I'm being a bit offish, lying here rigid and not responding in any way. So I turn and plant a speedy kiss on his cheek.

He pulls away and frowns. 'Can you smell something?'

'Er, I don't think so . . .'

'Well, I can.' He sniffs loudly. 'It's sort of . . . *medicinal*. It's coming from your hair. Have you been using a new product or something?'

'No,' I say defensively.

'You must have. It's a medicated smell. D'you have dandruff?'

'I've never had dandruff in my life!' I protest.

'Well, it smells a bit like it. Or is it that tea tree stuff? D'you have nits?'

'No!'

'Let me have a look . . .' He clicks on his bedside light and starts raking through my hair.

'I don't have nits, Will! Get off—'

'Hold still. I'm just checking . . .'

'Ow!' I yelp.

He shrinks back. 'What's wrong? What have I done?'

'It's just . . . would you leave my hair alone please? It's a bit . . . sore.'

'You have sore *hair*?' He squints at the top of my head. 'My God, there's a cut here. It looks pretty bad. What on earth happened?'

'I banged it,' I mutter, feeling like a silly child.

Gently, protectively, Will eases a strand of hair away from my face. 'How did you do that?'

'I, er, fell.' Shivering, I bunch the duvet around my shoulders as Will continues to examine the wound.

'You've put something on it.'

'Yeah, Sudocrem.'

He sighs. 'It looks pretty deep. Why didn't you tell me?'

'I . . .' I clear my throat. 'I felt a bit stupid . . .'

'Oh, darling.' He puts his arms around me and pulls me close. It's so rare for him to do this, my eyes well up with tears. 'You idiot,' he murmurs. 'Bit pissed, were you?'

'A bit,' I agree.

'On a Wednesday night,' he chastises me gently. 'In the garden, too. What would Tricia and Gerald say?'

'Er, hopefully they didn't see,' I say with a feeble laugh.

Will's face turns serious. 'Did you fall outside?'

'No, I, er, bumped my head when I was coming in.'

'What, on the door or something?'

'Yes, I think so.'

He shakes his head. 'Did you trip?'

'Uh-huh.' As he's feeding me the lines, it doesn't count as lying.

'Maybe we should put a dressing on it,' he suggests.

'It'll be *fine*,' I say firmly. 'Better let the air get to it.'

He gives me another concerned look, then switches off the lamp. I expect him to turn away and say goodnight, but instead, he takes me in his arms and holds me close. And it's just what I need, after my shed trauma: being held as I drift off to sleep. 'I love you, Charlotte,' he whispers.

'I love you too, darling.'

'I love you, you drunk, crazy woman, and I know I don't tell you that enough.' I turn and kiss him again, thinking: this is lovely. This is a million times better than cuddling a rabbit. Will does care, after all, and he's being all affectionate and sweet because I am injured.

Maybe, I reflect, I should arrange to be whacked on the head by a tin of creosote more often.

Chapter Fifteen

There is no further questioning from Will regarding my wound over breakfast, and Rosie and Ollie are too concerned with the grave injustices inflicted upon their own lives to even notice it. Besides, I have carefully combed my hair over the crusty bit, like a balding man.

'My agency haven't phoned yet,' Rosie announces, with a dramatic sigh, like a seasoned model whose career is experiencing a temporary downturn.

'You've got an agent,' Ollie muses. 'I'd love that. I'd love to be able to say, "Speak to my *agent.*"'

Rosie wrinkles her nose at him. 'I'm sure they will,' I say, absent-mindedly, wondering if my husband will detect that anything untoward happened in the shed last night. Half past six, I was up this morning, to creep out and mop up the spilt creosote, plus the dark, sticky footprints leading to our back door. I even wiped the grass where I'd trampled on it, concealing the gunky rags under black bags in the wheelie bin. I'd felt like someone covering up their tracks after committing a violent crime.

'Mum?' Rosie's voice interrupts my thoughts. 'I said I thought I'd have some go-sees to go on by now.'

'D'you *go on* go-sees then?' Ollie teases. 'D'you *go-see* people?'

She frowns. 'That's why they're called go-sees, Ollie. But no, I *don't* go on them 'cause no one wants to see me.'

'We want to see you,' he says with a grin. 'We like you, Ro, even if the model agency doesn't—'

'Oh, shut up,' she snaps.

'Rosie, there's no need to be so grumpy or take it out on Ollie . . .' I tail off as he examines the sweatshirt I bought him from deepest, darkest Hollister.

'I can't wear this for school, Mum,' he announces.

I stare at it. 'Why not?'

''Cause it's dark blue, not black.'

'Oh, Christ. Is it?'

'Yeah! It's obvious. Are you colour blind or something?'

'No, I'm not, Ollie. I told you, it was completely dark in there, like a cave. Next time I'm going to Primark . . .'

'Not Primark,' he groans, catching his father's eye. Throughout all this, Will has been standing and smirking and drinking his coffee.

'Can't you take it back?' Will suggests.

'No, I can't,' I reply. 'If he'd said at the time, if he'd actually *looked* at it properly, then I might have had the receipt—' I tail off and grab my jacket and bag. 'Anyway, I'd better get off to work.'

'Head feeling better?' Will asks, somewhat belatedly, as I kiss him goodbye.

'Yes, much better, thanks.' I hug Rosie and Ollie – who don't even enquire as to what might be wrong with me – and leave.

In contrast, everyone at work not only spots the scab immediately, my comb-over having dislodged somewhat, but lavishes me with concern. Rupert even suggests that I shouldn't have come in at all. 'Head injuries can be serious,' he says gravely, towering over me in the shop. He peers at my wound like a sympathetic GP. 'Are you sure you were okay to drive?'

'I'm fine,' I say firmly, flattered by the attention.

'It's just . . .' He smiles and his eyes glint playfully. 'Um . . . maybe you should be at home . . . *resting*.'

I laugh, baffled by his concern. 'I'm okay, honestly. I just bumped it on the door. It's my age, I think. My spatial awareness isn't what it was.'

'It's not just that,' Dee says, as she and Rupert follow me upstairs to the office. 'We were just thinking, with this being such a *special* day . . .' I frown, not getting it at all.

'That's right,' Rupert adds, parking his bum on my desk, 'and I have to say, despite it all, you still look radiant . . .'

'I very much doubt that,' I reply.

'You do, truthfully.' He grins at Dee. 'Think it's that cream she uses? That stuff with the real gold particles in?'

'Yeah, probably,' chuckles Dee.

I blink at them in bewilderment. 'What are you talking about?'

'Oh, don't be bashful,' Rupert cuts in. 'We all have our little beauty secrets. Me – I use a nasal hair trimmer. Marcelle bought it for me last Christmas . . . charming, eh? Nice to see romance isn't dead!' As he barks with laughter it starts to dawn on me: the only time real gold particle cream – *serum*, actually – has entered my consciousness was at Rosie's shoot. That ad in *Vogue*, which I'd happened to glance at while being interviewed on the phone . . . Oh, Christ. 'Is it out?' I gasp.

'Sure is,' Dee says with a grin, waving a copy of *Front* magazine from her desk.

'Oh God, let me see.' I lurch over as she flicks it open to the significant page. Rosie looks lovely, and incredibly relaxed, considering this was her first shoot. I, on the other hand, am perched awkwardly on the Perspex chair as if fearful that someone might march over and snap, 'Please don't sit on that.' But worse than that – because the photo is *fine* really, despite my man make-up and guitar-player-out-of-Queen hair – is the headline.

In huge type, across two whole pages, it reads:

We're the High-Maintenance Mums Behind
Fashion's New Faces!

'Oh my God,' I croak.

'We're obviously paying you too much,' Rupert sniggers.

I glare at the page. 'But that's not what she said when she did the interview. No one mentioned anything about high-maintenance mums. I've been totally misrepresented!' It's true: I buy a supermarket moisturiser that's actually a bum cream for babies and haven't had my eyebrows shaped by anything other than my own unsteady hand and some rusting tweezers since about 2005. I've *never* had a massage, unless you count Will grudgingly rubbing my shoulders for about three seconds, before enquiring, 'Is that enough?' Guinness is more pampered than I am. At least he has his nails clipped at the vet's. My head has started to sting again with the stress of it all.

As Rupert and Dee's laughter subsides I sit down with the magazine at my desk.

Charlotte Bristow, 42, looks amazing for her age . . .

That's because I'm thirty-bloody-eight. I don't remember my age even being mentioned. With Rosie and I being last-minute participants, Joely probably forgot to ask.

. . . *Fabulous bone structure and a dewy complexion,* it goes on. *And her beauty secret? She swears by super-luxe Belle Visage Beauty Elixir containing real gold micro-particles. At £750 for 50ml, it's the most expensive serum on the market today* . . .

My wound throbs even harder as I stare at the figure. *£750.* I have owned cars that cost less than that. 'This is rubbish,' I mutter. 'I use the cheapest stuff imaginable. My shampoo's 99p—'

'No wonder,' Dee teases, 'when you spend that much on your face.'

Still grinning, Rupert peers over my shoulder. 'They're saying Rosie's fifteen . . .'

'Yes, they've got her age wrong too.'

'You're saying they made it *all* up then?'

My cheeks flush. 'Well, er, I did say I use that serum, but only because I didn't want to seem like a cheapskate . . .'

He smiles. 'Well, you certainly don't. Anyway, listen – I've got just the thing to take your mind off it.'

'Yes?' I say eagerly, closing the magazine.

'Website really needs an update. Would you mind?'

'Of course not,' I reply with genuine relief. Anything to stop me fretting about that headline.

'Great. With the festival coming up, it really needs to

look tip-top. Could you cobble together a shoot today? Something lovely and sunny with everyone having a jolly time?'

I nod. 'D'you have anything in mind?'

'Erm . . .' He rakes a hand through his unruly dark hair. 'I'll leave that to you and your creative genius. Just pull together something fun, okay?'

'Yes, no problem—'

He bounds for the door, pausing to add, 'Oh, and I meant to say, that magazine thing . . .' He beams a fond, big brotherly sort of smile. 'You do scrub up very well, Charlotte Bristow.'

'For my age,' I call after him as he clatters downstairs.

'For *any* age,' he shouts back.

Chapter Sixteen

I'm feeling better already about *Front* magazine. When I sneaked another look, I learnt that the other mothers were partial to algae body wraps and enzyme facials. So perhaps I'm small fry, in model-mum circles, where self-maintenance is concerned.

Turning my attention to work, I decide to stage a staff picnic – the sky is perfectly cloudless, it's an ideal day for it – to photograph for our website. I gather up hampers, blankets and assorted paraphernalia from the shop, then drive to the nearest supermarket and amass enormous quantities of sandwiches and cakes. Finally, I stop off at a gift shop for plastic windmills and Tibetan prayer flags to pin up about the place.

Back at work, in the spud store – the cool, dark shed where cuddly Farmer Mickey's Maris Pipers are kept – I find the enormous bundle of bunting which I used for a shoot last summer (each time the word 'shoot' forms in my mind, I imagine Parker, a *proper* photographer, snorting with derisive laughter). Although it's a bit dusty, the bunting looks fine once I've pinned it up between trees in the garden in front of the visitors' centre and shop.

In fact, with the sun beating down onto my colourful scene, it's actually very pleasing. You might even believe we were in the depths of the real countryside, rather than barely beyond the East London sprawl. Even last night's sorry episode with the waders and hormone rooting powder is fading from my consciousness as I put the finishing touches to the picnic scene. I'm further distracted when it comes to persuading 'teamsters' to take part in the shoot, whilst laughing off yet more comments about my outing as a high-maintenance mother (which everyone appears to have examined forensically, despite Parker insisting that 'no one will see it').

'What d'you want us to do?' Frank asks grumpily, rubbing his hands on the front of his factory apron and blinking in the sunshine as if he's just emerged from hibernation.

'Could you just arrange yourselves around the picnic?' I say, adding, 'And, er, would you mind taking your overalls off please, folks?'

The teamsters obligingly pull off their uniforms and sling them out of shot. Then Frank pulls out a packet of Silk Cut and lights one up, so then I have to politely ask him to dispose of that too, because no one smokes at an Archie's picnic. I realise, of course, that he's winding me up, being the naughty Spanish factory lad whom I suspect his female colleagues all secretly fancy. While he doesn't quite cut it on the jolly teamster front, I know Rupert values him for being a grafter.

'Dee, come and join the picnic,' I say as she emerges from the shop, looking lovely with her blonde hair artfully pinned up, and not just *for her age*. I notice, too, that

Frank's demeanour changes as she arranges herself on a corner of the brightly-striped blanket. 'Could you sit a bit nearer to Frank, Dee?' I ask as I start to take pictures. 'We're meant to be a family, remember? You look a bit lost, sitting there all by yourself.'

She laughs awkwardly. 'Bit closer,' I murmur, realising she's flushed bright pink, and wishing now that I'd asked Sandra to sit next to him instead, because obviously, Dee is hugely uncomfortable. Maybe she's worried about how Mike will react if he sees her on our website, cosying up to a handsome colleague. I keep snapping away, aiming to get the job done as quickly as possible, and deciding that I could appear on our site naked, draped over *all* the factory guys, and Will probably wouldn't bat an eyelid.

Shoot over, I spend the next couple of hours in the office writing the accompanying blurb, then hit upon the idea of calling Will for ideas for picnic recipes. 'Hi?' he says curtly.

'Erm, are you busy right now? It's just, I'm writing a thing about picnics for the website and I'm a bit stuck for ideas.'

'Right, er . . .'

'Sorry, are you in the middle of something?'

He clears his throat. 'No, no – it's fine, it's just, Sabrina popped by . . .'

'Oh, what does she want?' I didn't mean that the way it probably sounded. Just that it seems odd, her dropping in when I'm not there. But then, why shouldn't she? Will spends far too much time alone.

'We're just having coffee,' he says.

'Right. Great! That's . . . really good. Well, er, I was going to ask if you could help me with some recipes but I'm sure I'll think of something.'

'No, it's fine – I'll call you back, okay?' he says in an over-bright voice.

'Yeah, sure, no hurry.' Feeling a tad put out, and wondering if Sabrina's wearing that pretty white broderie anglaise dress again, or perhaps her foxy leather trousers, I finish the call and start to edit my photos. I take care to choose the ones where Dee looks least uneasy – although she's hardly a picture of relaxed, picnicky joy in any of them. Still, the site now looks pleasingly summery. I write some blurb about how we're always larking about in the garden, and add a few competitions; all I need now are some recipes. Still no call back from Will, so I start searching online.

I find Stilton tarts and falafels with a spicy Moroccan dip, plus a bevy of interesting salads, which I tweak slightly so as not to copy them directly. I even dash off a few wonky coloured pencil drawings (my 'charming illustrations' as Rupert rather generously calls them) and scan them in. There. All done. It's now two hours since I called Will and he's obviously had far too many other pressing matters on his hands to find the time to phone me back.

Anyway, I tell myself as I drive home, I don't need him to tell me how to make a bloody falafel.

*

In contrast, Sabrina is obviously *thrilled* by Will's culinary expertise, as I discover when I find her still installed in our kitchen, swooning over his finds from his latest foraging trip. 'Giant puffballs,' she marvels.

'Thanks,' I say with a grin, 'although this is meant to be a minimiser bra.'

She laughs huskily, looking especially radiant in a pale pink strappy top – it's more of a hankie, really – and old, faded jeans which hug her tiny bottom. 'I mean these mushrooms. Aren't they amazing? Would you believe you can find them in London?'

'I had no idea,' I reply.

'He's going to sauté them in breadcrumbs as a starter,' she enthuses in the manner of a cookery show presenter.

'Sounds lovely. Very impressive.' I drop my bag at my feet and tell myself there's no reason to feel miffed by this cosy domestic scene, because they're talking about *fungi*, for God's sake. While Sabrina carefully wipes one with a piece of kitchen roll, Will ambles over and plants a kiss on my cheek.

'Good day?' he asks.

'Yeah, busy,' I say breezily as Sabrina places the clean mushroom on a large white plate and gazes at it reverentially.

She sighs loudly. 'I wish *my* husband took an interest in food. There's nothing sexier than a man who knows what he's doing in the kitchen. Tommy can barely manage to rip open a bag of oven chips.'

I laugh politely, reminding myself that of course this is innocent, because for one thing the kids are here. Rosie wanders in from watching TV in the living room and flops down onto a kitchen chair. 'Hi, love,' I say, kissing the top of her head. 'Did you see the magazine?'

She nods. 'Yeah. They got my age wrong. They said I was fifteen.'

'Yes, mine too, but they added three years on for me . . .'

'I saw that too,' Sabrina chuckles. 'I'd never have had you down as a high-maintenance mum, Charlotte! But you both looked gorgeous . . .'

'They did,' Will says absent-mindedly, sautéing now and turning to add, 'You will stay for dinner, Sabrina?' I glance at him, taken aback by his sudden invitation. It's unlike him to be so spontaneous. But then, don't I often wish he'd be more sociable and loosen up a little?

'If you're sure,' she replies. 'That's very kind of you.'

'What about Tommy and Zach?' I ask. 'Would you like to ask them over too?'

'Oh, Tommy's away for a few days and Zach prefers to fend for himself . . .' She turns to Rosie. 'He asked me to mention that he'll pick you up after dinner, is that okay?'

'Yeah,' she says, blushing.

I study her face. 'Does this mean you're hanging out together?'

'Er, kind of,' she mumbles as Ollie ambles in for dinner and gives me a fleeting hug.

'That's nice,' I chirp, wondering how Will feels about this. We have seen the boy smoking *pot,* after all, but then, maybe it's par for the course for a seventeen-year-old boy? I glance at Will, who looks a little taken aback himself by the Zach announcement.

'What are these, Dad?' Ollie asks, peering at the plate.

'Mushrooms,' Will replies.

'They look like they've got skin disease,' Rosie remarks.

'No they don't,' Sabrina retorts. 'They're amazing. They're nothing like the anaemic little mushrooms you get in cartons from the shops—'

'The kind we like,' Ollie quips, stuffing one into his mouth anyway, if only to please his dad.

The main event is baked salmon, and it's so delicious – perfectly baked in foil with chilli and dill – that I've already forgiven Will for not phoning me back at work.

I *must* stop being so sensitive. As for feeling iffy about Sabrina spending all afternoon installed in our kitchen – well, that was just a flash of juvenile ridiculousness on my part.

'So are you and Zach planning to hang out here?' I ask Rosie lightly, spearing a French bean.

'Erm, no, we're going to the cinema.' Right on cue, our doorbell rings. Dinner barely touched, she throws down her cutlery and leaps up to answer it. 'Let's just go,' she says quickly, her face clouding as I hurry through to the hall.

'Hi, Zach, how are you?' I ask.

'Good, thanks.' Taller than Rosie, he's all gangly handsomeness with burnt toffee-coloured eyes and a mop of dark hair which he's constantly flicking out of his face. She throws me a *don't-you-dare-interrogate-him* look.

'What film are you going to see?' I ask pleasantly.

'We'll just see what's on,' Zach says with a shrug.

'But shouldn't you check first? You could book tickets online—'

'Mum,' Rosie cuts in, eyes wide, 'we do know how to go to the cinema.'

'Okay, okay . . .' I laugh and step away. 'So, um, are you going to finish your dinner first?'

She pulls a horrified face. 'We've got to go *now*.'

'Oh! Right. So, er, what time will you be back?'

'It's only seven,' Sabrina chuckles, appearing at my side. 'They'll be fine. Don't worry. Not planning to kidnap her, are you, Zach?'

'Nah,' he chuckles with a wry grin.

That's not the point, I reflect as they leave; of course it's fine for Rosie to date boys. It's just . . . Sabrina's spent all afternoon with Will, and now Rosie and Zach appear to be 'going out', if that's not too decrepit a phrase . . . it's starting to feel a bit much.

'Isn't it sweet,' Sabrina says, back in our kitchen, 'how well those two get on?'

I nod, trying to hide my disappointment that Rosie hadn't even mentioned tonight's date. But then, she has also appeared in a national magazine and barely uttered two sentences about it.

*

She's in a chattier mood when she returns, unscathed, just after ten. 'Well, that was awkward,' she announces, squeezing in between Will and me on the sofa.

'What was?' I ask. 'Didn't you have a good time?'

'Yeah, we did – the movie was a bit crap, some action thing Zach wanted to see . . .' She turns to me. 'I mean you making such a fuss about us going out.'

'I didn't make a fuss,' I protest. 'All I said was—'

'Zach couldn't believe it,' she adds with a smirk, 'how protective you are.'

'All I did was suggest you booked tickets. I hardly chaperoned you, Rosie.'

'. . . And you know what's funny? You're all worried about me going out to the cinema, but Dad's happy to collect mushrooms that could make our whole family die!' She peals with derisive laughter.

'Of course you can go to the cinema,' I mutter, my head wound beginning to sting again. It seems to have become a barometer of my moods.

'Hey, Mum.' She touches my arm. 'It's okay, you know. Zach's just a friend.'

'Yeah, fine,' I say sulkily, deciding she's right: I probably *do* worry too much. So she's made a new friend, and it looks as if Will has too – which is good for him, of course. I'd far rather see him being friendly and chatty and asking neighbours over for dinner spontaneously than furiously mowing our lawn.

But I'm still not completely delighted about walking in to find Sabrina fawning over his puffballs.

Chapter Seventeen

It drops next day. The bombshell, I mean, just as I'm about to set off for the Festival of Savoury Snacks.

There's just Rosie and me in the kitchen, and I'm grinning like an idiot at my phone. Dee and Rupert have gone down early to Bournemouth to set up our stand at the exhibition centre, and Dee's sent me a photo of the two of them posing proudly beside the world's biggest crisp. It'll take pride of place on our stand *and* gain a mention in the Guinness Book of Records, if anyone still cares about such a thing (Rosie was obsessed with it as a little girl; that's what our rabbit is named after, and not 'the alcoholic beverage', as Tricia put it, assuming a not-entirely-approving face).

'Rupert told us he was going to make the crisp,' I witter away, even though I suspect Rosie's not really listening, 'but he can't have fried it, at least not in one piece. You'd never find a potato big enough.' I study it again. 'I think he must've baked it. So really, it's more of a giant Pringle . . .'

Rosie mutters something whilst delving into the schoolbag at her feet.

'Yes, I think it's definitely baked,' I add.

'Mum,' she snaps, straightening up, 'could you stop going on about the crisp? It's not that interesting, okay?'

'Oh, I just thought . . .' Stung by her sharpness, I tail off and place my phone on the table. A few years ago, she'd have been thrilled by such an outstanding example of potato engineering. I'd probably have let her take a day off school so she could see it for real.

'I wasn't talking about crisps, Mum,' she adds coldly.

'Well, I couldn't hear you, Rosie, because you were actually speaking into your bag, and your voice must've been absorbed by the sweaty old T-shirt and gym shorts you've been carting about for weeks . . .' I head into the utility room and start unloading the washing machine, just to put some distance between us. I'd never imagined that the teenage stage would be quite like this. Sure, I had an idea that it was tricky, and that no one would want to come to the zoo with me anymore, or draw funny felt-tipped faces on boiled eggs – but this grumpy, sullen thing, and the see-saw moods? I'd assumed that was a cliché – a lazy sitcom view of teenhood. But now I see it's just the way things are.

Back in the kitchen, I dump the laundry basket on the worktop. 'So what *were* you talking about?' I ask, in as pleasant a voice as I can muster.

'I said, I want to meet my real dad.'

My heart seems to crash against my ribs. I lick my dry lips and grip the rim of the basket. 'Really? Are you sure?'

She juts out her chin and nods.

'Well, um . . . okay . . .' Thank God Ollie's getting ready for school upstairs and Will's in the garden as usual, digging up spuds. 'I, er, thought you'd want to at some point,' I add, trying to read her expression. For some reason, it's defiant.

'Yeah. Well, I do.' We look at each other awkwardly. In fact, it *is* okay – ish. Of course she should meet him, if that's what she wants. She is entitled to, and I have never planned to stand in her way. However, I am also aware that it's not as simple as Rosie meeting Fraser for a coffee, and her coming back and saying, 'That was nice, I liked him.' And then getting on with the rest of her life.

No, I'm fully aware that it'll be . . . *monumental.*

'So how will we get in touch with him?' she asks, her tone still frosty, as if it's my fault he has never once tried to find us, or sent her a note or a card. I can sort of understand that a nineteen-year-old boy might have a sudden panic attack over the thought of caring for a tiny, nappy-wearing thing that spits milk and screams in the night. I'd had to accept that he'd taken fright and run away, and that we were better off without him than if he'd stayed around, being useless. Yet I've never been able to understand, as the years have passed, why Fraser has never been curious enough to want to enquire about his child, let alone get to know her. He was a smart young man. Even after I'd got married, he could have found some way to track us down.

'I'll think about it when I'm away, okay?' I say carefully, as Ollie appears with his schoolbag slung low on his back. 'Remember I'm staying over at Grandma and Grandpa's tonight.'

'Think about what?' he asks.

'Nothing, hon. Just find your shoes.'

'You going to that food festival thing today?' he wants to know.

'Yes, darling. So I won't see you till tomorrow . . .'

'Oh, cool.' Separation anxiety is a truly terrible thing.

Through our kitchen window I glimpse Will chatting to Tricia over the fence. He breaks away and marches in. 'God, that woman,' he mutters. 'Going on about someone creeping about in our garden the other night. I didn't hear anything, did you?'

I shake my head vehemently. 'No.'

'Some woman screaming and swearing, she said . . .'

'Where?' I feign astonishment.

He shrugs. '*I* don't know. In our borders, she thought. But everything's fine. Nothing's trampled . . .'

I shrug and feign a baffled face, worrying that I'm over-egging it a little, then kiss my family goodbye, grab my overnight bag and virtually pelt for the door.

*

I know it's wrong, and that I should probably have sat down and talked the whole Fraser business over with Rosie and Will. I mean, civilisation wouldn't collapse just because I happened to arrive late at an exhibition centre filled with purveyors of crisps, nuts and other delicacies of the savoury variety. Saul would have called for Ollie as usual and they'd have pottered off to school together. And we'd have decided that Rosie could take the morning off school and discussed it – calmly, levelly, like sensible people. *That's* what we should be doing right now. But I can't face it yet, because I need to figure out how to find the right Fraser Johnson (maybe he *is* the undertaker in St Ives?) and, crucially, how he'll react when I contact him.

To think, that's what Rosie was trying to say while I was prattling on about the world's biggest crisp.

In fact, the crisp *is* pretty impressive, as I discover when I arrive a couple of hours later at the cavernous hangar-style venue in Bournemouth. 'Rupert made it at home,' Dee tells me. 'Baked it in sections and welded it together with some kind of edible glue.' She laughs. 'In fact, I'm not sure it is actually edible.' However, we will be offering plenty of samples: crisp omelettes, dips and even cookies, incorporating crushed crisps, will be concocted in our demonstration kitchen.

'This is looking fantastic,' Rupert enthuses, arriving with Marcelle, his rather terse-looking wife, who's been tasked with transporting a tray of coffees to distribute among us. Meanwhile Rupert hands out brown woollen corsages for us to wear on the bibs of our Archie's aprons (when I say corsages, I actually mean *knitted crisps*, knocked up by Rupert's elderly aunt on the Isle of Skye).

And so the show opens. With so many treats on offer – there are hundreds of stands – the hall is soon bustling with visitors. That's the thing with freebies, I've learned from previous shows: they're grabbed, frenziedly, as if people are scared they're about to run out. The day flashes by in a blur of cooking and chatting and doing my utmost to be a sparkling Archie's ambassador. While Rosie's announcement keeps looming into my mind, luckily I don't have time to dwell upon it.

'You've all been amazing,' Rupert announces as the show draws to a close, presenting each of us with a bottle of champagne.

By the time I leave, I'm feeling rather crisp-like myself (a little fragile, and over-salted, due to copious snacking throughout the day). It feels pleasantly quiet, taking the coast road towards my parents' place; they live in a wind-ravaged cottage a couple of miles out of town. I'm grateful, too, to be staying away overnight. Rosie issue aside, perhaps Will and I just need a little break from each other. Absence, heart fonder, and all that. Well, let's hope so. When my parents suggested I spent the night at their place, I jumped at the chance. Maybe Sabrina will pop round to help Will to polish his cobnuts. She looked so pretty yesterday – all tanned arms and jutty-out collarbones – although, to be fair, Will has given no indication that he fancies her. She's very sweet, and I'm just being paranoid and awful.

I pass the turn-off to the village where Will and I once spent the night in a grand country hotel with stone lions at the gate. It had vast, wooded grounds with a fishing lake, and the most beautiful bedroom I'd ever seen. My parents had treated us, having offered to look after Rosie and Ollie for the night. It was my 30th birthday, and we were refused entry to the hotel restaurant, with Will's Greenspace Heritage T-shirt failing to impress the haughty maître d'. We'd laughed about how country places can be so much stuffier than London restaurants, and decided we could happily live without 'dining' (as it was referred to) in such a formal restaurant. And so we nipped out to the local shop, and assembled a makeshift picnic of bread, cheese, olives and wine, which we consumed, giggling, in our enormous hotel bed, then proceeded to spend all night ravaging each other. We even missed breakfast.

That's what I call being romantic – not spending vast amounts on fancy dinners or enormous bouquets of roses. The memory causes an actual ache, somewhere around the heart region. Would we ever eat messy snacks and drink wine in a hotel bed now, if we got the chance? I doubt it. Will would be concerned about crumbs. Anyway,

I don't really care about that. I just want to feel close to him again.

Of course, there is one, glaringly obvious possibility: that Will's disillusioned with me, with us, with life in general. I've certainly aged significantly since that night in the hotel. There are lines and saggy bits and everything's gone sort of . . . fuzzy. My bottom and boobs are less pert, and I seem to be losing definition on my face, as if someone has altered the focus settings. Boo, the make-up girl, certainly recoiled on seeing me close up: but then, she's used to working with models, not ordinary women with pores and thread veins plainly on display. Surely Will doesn't notice my imperfections – and anyway, I'm *not* hideous. Rupert is always complimenting my appearance. But I'm not especially concerned about how he views me. I mean, I'm not married to my boss.

I'm probably turning into a sex-obsessive. I am greedy for affection and, dammit, the occasional orgasm wouldn't go amiss. It's like the crisp effect. If you're not remotely worried about your weight, then you're probably content with a polite little handful. But as soon as you try to deny yourself, all you can think about is scoffing an entire 'sharing bag', meant for at least two people – which in turn seems so gluttonous that you think, what the hell, and guzzle even more. Liza insists she doesn't care about meeting anyone serious and says she doesn't miss sex, even though she has plenty of admirers as far as I can make out. There's always some yoga buddy of hers asking her for a drink, or to a gig: Liza goes to actual *gigs*, involving acoustic guitars and singer-songwriter types that I've never heard of. However, she reckons it's been so long since she's slept with anyone, the urge has died away.

The opposite seems to be happening with me. Ollie once informed me that sea sponges are asexual – 'It means they can't be bothered to do it, even if they meet a really good-looking sea sponge!' – but I can't imagine reaching that stage, ever. Although, in some ways, it would be a blessed relief.

Anyway, time to banish such tawdry thoughts as I pull up outside my parents' whitewashed house. On spotting my car, Mum rushes out to greet me. I feel my spirits lifting immediately, because here at Withersea Cottage I am neither a wife nor a mum, but just Charlotte which, right now, seems delightfully undemanding.

Mum and I hug tightly, and I tell her she looks fantastic, which is true. She favours a vintage look – casual bits and pieces which could result in a mishmash but work wonderfully with her long, wavy caramel hair and expressive face, bare apart from a dab of sheer lipstick. 'Where's Dad?' I ask as we head into the chalky-white living room. It's dotted with seasidey things: tide-worn pebbles, a wooden dish of shells, and the model boats Dad makes from driftwood.

'He's out sailing with a couple of friends,' Mum replies, 'but he shouldn't be long now. Dinner's almost ready.'

'Oh, heaven,' I enthuse, inhaling the delicious aromas which are wafting through from the kitchen. Mum, like Will, is an excellent cook, although in her case she regards a thick, buttery crust as an essential component to virtually every meal, even at the height of summer. The aroma of melty puff pastry hangs tantalisingly in the air. Then Dad arrives, hair unkempt and face ruddy from the elements, and wraps me in a hug. 'Lovely to see you, Charlotte. How's that gang of yours?'

'Great,' I say, filling them in on our news. 'Rosie's been

taken on by a model agency,' I add, as the three of us sit down to attack Mum's steak and kidney pie.

'Oh, I bet she's so excited,' Mum enthuses.

'Well, Laurie – that's her booker – warned her that they can never guarantee who'll take off, but we'll see what happens when she breaks up for the summer. There's only a few days left of school.'

'You will all come down to see us, won't you?' Mum asks, and I know it's Will she wants to see, as much as me and the kids. She *dotes* on my husband: kind, handsome, infinitely capable Will. Fraser, whom she and Dad regard – understandably – as lower in the food chain than a grub worm, hasn't been mentioned for years.

'Of course we will,' I reply. 'It'll be lovely to all spend some time together.'

'Not booked a holiday this year?' she asks, a trace of sympathy in her eyes.

'Erm, we're a bit tight for cash at the moment,' I admit.

Dad hesitates. 'How's, you know, the job hunting—'

'I'm sure he'll find something soon, Dad.'

'Of course he will,' Mum adds, with absolute confidence. 'He's probably just taking time to be sure he makes the right decision.'

I nod, thinking: hmm, possibly. But who knows? Who knows *anything* anymore? We're clearing up after dinner when my mobile rings. 'Mum, guess what!' It's Rosie. She sounds happy, and my heart soars with relief.

'Hi, sweetheart, everything okay?'

'Yeah. I've got a job!'

I glance at Mum who's regarding me with interest. 'You mean a modelling job?'

'Yes! What else would it be?'

'But I didn't know you'd been on any go-sees . . .'

'I went today, straight after school. Well, I had to come out a bit early and miss last period, history . . . Dad said it was okay . . .'

'Yes, of course it was,' I say quickly, relieved that he appears to have stepped in and made a decision when, usually, every minuscule detail of Rosie and Ollie's lives is left to me to manage. More than anything, though, I'm delighted to hear her cheerful voice again.

'It was great,' she continues breathlessly. 'They took some shots and said I was just right and told me I'd got it, there and then . . .'

'Oh, that's amazing!' I turn to Mum and mouth: *Rosie's got her first modelling job!* Mum grins and clasps her hands together, as excited as a small child.

'So who's it for?' I ask as Dad hands me one of his 'special coffees': a potent Irish kind, swirled with cream and laced with whisky, a mere zillion calories a pop.

'Oh, er . . . some fashion place. Italian. Laurie says they're really high profile and once they like a girl, they use her over and over again. Like, you become *their* girl . . .'

I pause. 'You're sure they're reputable, aren't you?'

'Yeah, 'course they are! Laurie said.'

'But you don't seem sure who it's for—'

'Mum,' she splutters, 'I'm not a child. Can't you just be *happy* for me?'

'I *am* happy,' I say firmly. 'I'm completely overjoyed for you . . .'

'It's on Monday,' she cuts in, 'and I know what you're going to say.'

So I'm that predictable, am I? Although my hackles are rising, I'm trying to retain a sunny demeanour. I don't want to fall out with my daughter on the phone. 'Listen,'

I say, sensing a vein throbbing in my neck, 'it *is* a school day, but as you said, it's almost the end of term . . .'

'Great, so I can do it?'

'Of course you can.' I sip my coffee. Mum is fussing around the living room, straightening things that don't need straightening, while Dad is occupying his favourite armchair and browsing through a sailing magazine.

Tell her well done, he mouths, looking up.

I smile. 'Listen,' I add, 'Grandma and Grandpa are really happy for you and so am I.'

'Thanks, Mum,' she says in a small voice. We finish the call, and Mum perches on the sofa beside me.

'Is everything . . . all right, love?' she asks.

I nod, about to brush off her concern, but the temptation to be honest for once is too great. 'It's just . . . Rosie's at that age, you know.' Mum nods understandingly. 'Or maybe it's me,' I continue, 'or rather, *my* age, that's the problem. Maybe I'm just a bit – you know. Feeling old. Not that there is a *problem* exactly. It's just, we used to be so close, Rosie and me, and now, whatever we're doing or talking about, it always ends up all spiky and bad tempered and sometimes . . .' I shrug, sipping my deliciously boozy coffee, 'I think I'd be better just keeping my mouth shut.'

'No,' Mum says firmly, 'you must always talk to her. It's so important.'

'I know, Mum, and I do try – but it's as if . . .' I pause. 'Maybe teenagers and their parents aren't that compatible, at least for a while. For this bit. What'd be ideal, really, is for us to live on different floors of a huge house and only meet up when they needed us to hand over some cash, or make them something proper to eat . . .'

Dad laughs kindly. 'You've probably got a point there, love.'

'I mean, Ollie's fine,' I add. 'I'm not saying I favour him. Just that we can still talk without him implying that I'm a miserable fun-wrecker.'

'You're not!' Mum exclaims. 'You're a wonderful mum. They're both very lucky, you know.'

I laugh dryly, relieved when she suggests I have a long soak in the bath after being on my feet all day. It's lovely, being pampered a little, as if I am homecoming student. I'm only *slightly* put out that Will didn't come to the phone, just to say hi, as I sink into a cloud of bubbles in my parents' enormous, claw-footed bath. My long, hot soak has a drowsy-making effect, and by eleven I am relieved to head up to bed.

It's not my childhood bedroom. Mum and Dad are prone to wanderlust and have moved several times since I left home. But it's so cosy and comforting that it could be. Huge, puffy duvet, lovely fat pillows and a sharp whiff of the sea: it's perfect and, exhausted from the day's events, I fall asleep instantly in the tiny room.

And at around 2 a.m., I am wide awake.

'Why are you up, Peter? What are you doing?' Mum's voice rings out from their bedroom.

'Just getting a glass of water,' Dad replies. I hear him crossing the landing and making his way downstairs. There's the squeak of an ancient bedroom door, then Mum's soft footsteps padding downstairs, followed by a mumbled exchange in the kitchen.

'Come on, darling, let's just go to bed,' she says. Dad mutters something else, but Mum's voice is firm: 'I just don't see the point in worrying her, Peter.'

'She *should* know. We have to tell her.'

'But why? It'll only upset her . . .'

My heart thuds as I lurch upright. Hearing my parents

making their way back upstairs, I slip out of bed and meet them on the landing. 'Oh, did we wake you?' Mum asks, looking startled.

'No, not really. It doesn't matter. Mum, Dad . . . what's going on?'

'Nothing,' Mum says, smoothing the front of her white lacy nightie. 'Sorry we disturbed you. Just go back to bed, love . . .'

'Dad, what's wrong? You can talk to me, you know. There's nothing you can't tell me.'

He looks down at his feet in their suede moccasin slippers. Oh God, one of them is ill. I've always assumed their lives are pretty perfect, filled with sailing and pastry-making and all the social events they're involved in. 'Dad?' I prompt him.

He looks at Mum, then at me, and says, 'We've had an email, Charlotte.'

An email. My mind whirls with possibilities: They're in terrible debt. They're about to lose their home. One of them has a serious illness . . .

'Well, who from?' I ask impatiently.

Mum purses her lips.

'Could you *please* tell me?'

'I don't think—' she starts.

'Mum, I'm not a child!' Didn't Rosie utter those very few words a few hours ago?

Dad coughs and mumbles, 'It was from that man.'

That man. Well, that hardly narrows it down . . .

'Which man? Is it someone I know?'

'The one who . . .' Mum starts.

'. . . who wouldn't support you when you needed him,' Dad cuts in, as it dawns on me who they're talking about: *he who shall not be named.*

'You mean Fraser?' I exclaim.

Dad nods.

'What did he want? And how on earth did he find you?'

'I don't suppose it was too difficult,' Mum replies, 'with your dad being the sailing club secretary . . .'

'But . . .' I look from Dad to Mum, feeling suddenly, horribly sick. *Has he somehow sensed that Rosie wants to meet him?* 'I guess you've read it,' I murmur.

Mum flushes. 'We did, love, and we probably shouldn't, but we wanted to see—'

'No, it's fine,' I say quickly. 'It doesn't matter. I would have too . . . so can I read it?'

Dad suddenly looks very tired in his rumpled M&S pyjamas. He beckons me into their bedroom where their computer is set up on a rickety table in the corner. My parents have the good grace to switch it on and leave me alone, sitting on a folding chair in the yellowy glow of their ancient desk lamp. They both pad softly downstairs, pretending it's perfectly normal to make a pot of tea at 2.17 a.m.

I peer at his name in their inbox. *Fraser Johnson.* Subject: *For Charlotte.* So he's alive, at least. My heart is hammering away as I click open the mail.

Chapter Eighteen

Dear Charlotte,

Hi, it's me, Fraser. I know it's been an awfully long time. I really don't know how to start so I'll just say what feels right.

I push my bed-hair out of my face. It's a warm, stuffy night, and it feels as if there's not enough air in my parents' bedroom.

I feel terrible barging into your life like this, he goes on, *and hope you don't mind me contacting you via your dad. I remembered you telling me how passionate he was about sailing, so I thought I'd try Googling him. I couldn't believe how easy he was to find. I've looked for you online over the years but assume you're married and have a different surname now. It looked that way in the magazine. I couldn't believe it when I opened it and saw you and your daughter . . .*

My daughter. So he's conveniently airbrushed himself out of the picture. Or perhaps he's genuinely forgotten the two of us, driving down to Brighton as the sun came up, just because it seemed like a good idea. The positive pregnancy test was stashed in my bag, wrapped in tissue, so we could look at it again and again and convince ourselves it was real.

As we sat holding hands on a bench on the seafront, I genuinely believed everything would be okay. So what does he mean, *my* daughter?

. . . *didn't even want the magazine,* he continues, *but the guy at the station was insistent about me taking a copy, and at lunchtime I had a quick look through. And there you were. You look exactly as I remember . . .*

Oh, come on. The combination of Boo's make-up and Parker's lighting probably knocked off a few years, but not seventeen of them.

Of course, there's a tiny chance you're not the Charlotte I knew, in which case I apologise. But I'd bet my life it's you and I'd like to make contact, if that's okay. I know many years have passed. I understand that we both made decisions on the spur of the moment because we were so young and scared. And of course I accept that you might prefer not to be in touch again.

I'd just like you to know that I have never forgotten you.

Love,

Fraser x

I stare at the screen, rage fizzling up in my stomach. I'd gone to bed feeling soothed by Mum's heavenly pie and now I could vomit it right up. My knee-jerk reaction is to reply immediately, asking, What d'you mean, we both made decisions on the spur of the moment? WHAT THE HELL

ARE YOU TALKING ABOUT? Yeah – I'd use shouty capitals, just like that. I hadn't been 'scared', either, as he's so patronisingly put it. Sure, becoming a mother before I'd learnt to drive, or indeed cook anything more taxing than scrambled eggs, hadn't quite been my plan. But it had happened, and I'd loved Fraser, and after he'd been so sweet and reassuring that we could make it work, I wasn't scared at all. He'd even talked about shelving his plans to go into banking and moving down to London, so he could be with me. We'd get a flat, he reckoned, mentioning several areas that might appeal: Notting Hill, Camden, Islington. Money didn't seem to be an issue with him at all.

I exhale loudly, forward his email to my own address, then turn off my parents' computer.

That's better. For once, I haven't leapt in and made an idiot of myself. I have been measured and calm. 'Thanks,' I call downstairs to Mum and Dad. 'I've read it. I'm going back to bed now.'

Mum appears in the hallway, her face ghostly pale as she looks up. 'Are you all right, love?'

'I'm fine, Mum.'

'I . . . I just don't want him upsetting everything all over again.'

'No one's upset,' I say briskly. 'Honestly, it's just a bit of a shock, that's all.' Then, before she has time to come up and be kind and understanding, I scuttle to the little guest room, climb into bed and shut my eyes tightly, as if that will keep Fraser Johnson out of my life.

*

'Hey, how was it?' Will greets me the following lunchtime with a fleeting kiss. The back door is open, sunshine is flooding in, and our kitchen is full of chattering boys all tucking into bowls of strawberry ice cream.

'Great,' I reply. 'Our stand was mobbed all day. Rupert seemed pleased.'

'That's great. Glad to hear it.'

'Will made this,' Saul announces, scraping the dregs from his bowl.

'No, he just got it out of the freezer,' Ollie corrects him.

I chuckle, catching Will's eye. 'Yes, but it's proper stuff with fruit and cream, Ollie. You take it for granted that Dad makes ice cream. You think it's a normal thing everyone has.'

Saul grins. 'It's the best ice cream ever. My dad's too busy to make anything. I wish *he* was unemployed.'

Ouch. Will turns away, busying himself with fixing a punctured bicycle inner tube on the back step. The visiting boys eventually drift off home, and Rosie appears with Nina after an afternoon at the pool. For the rest of the day I'm conscious of going through the motions of catching up with everyone's news, whilst being unable to stop thinking about Fraser's email.

. . . *I have never forgotten you* . . .

Even if it is true, what am I supposed to do with that information? Judging by the tone of his email, it sounds as if he's conveniently forgotten that he chose not to involve himself in the colicky nights and exploding nappies, or the obliteration of verrucas and nits. His sole contributions to Rosie's life can be summed up as provider of sperm, and much enthusiasm (fake, as it turned out) when shown the pregnancy test. Now our child is almost grown up, he's curious, all of a sudden. The bloody nerve of it! And my poor mum and dad, receiving that email out of the blue and wondering what on earth to do for the best.

They'd only met Fraser once: a rather tense occasion, I vividly recall. He was terribly nervous, and although my parents were clearly trying to be welcoming and reasonable, they were obviously thinking: *you swine! Meeting our daughter – our adored only child – on a train and impregnating her about five minutes later!*

At least, that's probably how it seemed to them.

Anyway, the more pressing issue now isn't my parents, but Will, who's crouched on the lawn, and fussing about with bicycle parts. I pull on a sweater – there's a chill in the early evening air – and wander out to join him. 'Hey,' I say, sitting cross-legged beside him on the grass.

He looks round. 'Hi. So, um . . . how were your mum and dad?' I've been back for hours, and he's only just thought to ask.

'Great. It was lovely to see them.' I smile stiffly. 'Isn't it brilliant about Rosie's job on Monday?'

'Yes, I s'pose it is. She's a very happy girl.' At least, I decide, he's *pretending* to be pleased for her. He straightens up and we wander down to the bench together.

'Who's the job for, d'you know?' I ask. 'She was pretty vague on the phone.'

Will shakes his head. 'Some designer, I think. Italian-sounding . . .' We sit together in silence for a few moments. 'So, nothing else going on?' he asks lightly.

Christ, it's as if he *knows*.

'No, why?'

'You just . . . seem a bit . . . edgy.'

I pause, figuring that I could deflect this. I could make up something about being tired from the show yesterday, or not having slept well at Mum and Dad's. 'Um . . . something did happen actually.'

He frowns. 'What?'

I clear my throat. 'Fraser emailed Dad.'

Will's entire body stiffens as he turns to stare at me. 'You *are* kidding.'

'No, Will. I wish I was. He emailed Dad after seeing Rosie and me in that magazine . . .'

'Oh, for fuck's sake!' While I'd hardly expected him to be overjoyed at this news, I hadn't imagined he'd look so . . . *stricken.*

'It's okay,' I say firmly. 'It's not a big deal. I'm just a bit shocked, that's all. I mean, I can't believe he thought he could just drop me a friendly little email after all these years . . .'

I study Will's face. His eyes are guarded, his whole demeanour defensive, as if Fraser Johnson might appear in our garden, pelt into our house and yell, 'Here I am, Rosie! Your real dad! You're going to love me so much more than this shabby imposter with his foraged sorrel which, let's face it, smells weird, doesn't it? Like pee?'

'A friendly little email,' Will repeats.

'I know. It's really weird. Honestly – I never thought I'd hear from him again.'

Will frowns and rubs at his forehead. 'How the hell did he manage to track down your dad?'

'Through the sailing club. Dad's the secretary so I guess he's easy to find . . .'

'So what are you going to do?'

'Nothing,' I say firmly. 'Absolutely nothing at the moment.'

'Does he want to meet Rosie? Is that what he's after?'

'No, that's the oddest thing. It was just, "I saw you

in the magazine, and I wanted to get in touch." There was no mention of meeting her at all. In fact, he referred to her as *my* daughter . . .' I bite my lip as music drifts down from Rosie's room. Ollie's bedroom light is off, but Rosie and Nina, who's staying over, will be up chatting half the night.

'He's fucking unbelievable,' Will mutters.

'Yes, I know. Imagine him seeing her like that, for the first time and almost all grown up . . .'

Will turns to me. 'Shows what kind of person he is. I mean, he could have found us if he'd wanted to. And you know I'd have been fine – well, I'd have accepted it. Him seeing Rosie, I mean, if that's what she wanted.' Will's voice cracks. I go to hug him but he shrugs me away. 'I mean, I wouldn't have been an arsehole about it . . .'

'No, I know, darling,' I say gently. 'We've always been realistic about it, haven't we? That she'll probably want to get to know him at some point . . .'

Will nods. I know that now's the perfect opportunity to add that, in fact, only yesterday morning she said she wanted to meet him. But he looks so crushed, I can't bring myself to spring this on him too. Besides, I need to get things straight in *my* head, before we can start to formulate a proper plan.

He fixes me with a look. His eyes are a startling blue, like sapphires. 'So you're not going to reply, then?'

'What, to his email?' I hesitate. 'I need time to think, Will.'

'What is there to think about?'

'I don't know,' I bluster. 'It's just, if she ever does want to contact him, then I'll have his email address—'

'Great. That'll be handy.' I glance at Will, realising

that it doesn't matter that he's been Rosie's dad for fifteen years, and that he's shown her how to swim, ride her bike and tackle long division. Despite all of that, his Dad-status must still seem as fragile as the finest glass. I don't blame him for feeling that way; Rosie has cooled towards him lately. She's not exactly all over me either. But the difference is, I'll always be her mum, and no one can ever change that.

Will gets up from the bench. 'I'm going to have an early night,' he murmurs. Leaving bike parts scattered all over the lawn, he strolls back into the house.

I could run in after him. I could shout, 'It's okay! I'll delete it! I'll have no contact with him again, ever.' But what about Rosie? He's her father and I can't delete *that*.

In the kitchen, I potter about, attending to jobs we never seem to get around to: shaking crumbs out of the toaster and rounding up various school memos which are scattered about. I refill Guinness's water bottle and replenish his hay. Upstairs, I find Will in our bedroom, pretending to search for a book on the shelf. 'I know this is hard for you,' I say, tentatively.

'It's just a bit of a surprise.' He tugs off his socks and throws them into the laundry basket.

I watch him pulling off his jeans and clambering into bed with his T-shirt and boxers still on. He hasn't even cleaned his teeth, which I suspect is a first: Will is fastidious about such matters. I head for the bathroom and wash and undress, taking a few minutes to compose myself in order to discuss this rationally. Wrapping myself in my dressing gown, I pad through to our room where Will is lying on his back, staring bleakly at the ceiling. 'Are you okay, darling?' I slip in beside him and kiss his cheek.

'I'm fine.'

'Will, the thing is . . .' I start.

'It's all right,' he snaps. 'Reply to him if that's what you want to do.'

'I *don't* want that,' I insist. 'How can you suggest that? That I'm happy about him dropping into our lives again, out of the blue?' My heart is hammering now. Of course he's hurt, I understand that – but it's happened, and we have to deal with it somehow . . .

'I just want the best for Rosie,' Will mutters.

'Of course you do. That's all that matters. But we need to talk—'

He turns away from me. 'I'm just scared, okay? I'm scared of things changing, and what this is going to do to us . . .'

Tears prick my eyes as I find his hand in the dark. 'I'm scared too, Will. I really am.'

His breathing changes. Perhaps he's drifting to sleep, or just pretending – it's impossible to tell. But I hold on tightly to his hand, never wanting to let go.

Chapter Nineteen

All next day, the spectre of Fraser's email hovers in the air between me and Will like a particularly unpleasant smell. We orbit each other politely, to the point at which I'm delighted to escape to work on Monday morning. As it's Rosie's first proper modelling job today, at least she's been reasonably cheerful.

I'm busy at work, thankfully, with lots of upcoming press coverage to finalise. We are supplying crisps to food shoots, setting up interviews with Rupert for business magazines, and launching a major 'design your own flavour' competition. I manage to push the Will/Fraser issue out of my mind, hoping that my husband's mood will have lifted by the time I get home.

As soon as I walk in it's clear that it hasn't. 'Wonder how Rosie's getting on at her shoot?' I ask, pulling off my jacket.

Will shrugs. 'Fine, I expect. You okay with pizza?'

'Sounds great,' I reply, adding, 'look – I've got tons of samples . . .' I start to unload numerous packets of reject crisps from a giant carrier bag. They're not dangerous, or even out of date; just substandard visually, having been bashed around at some point during the bagging process. I mean, they're perfectly *fine*. But as Will eyes the growing pile of packets on the table, I realise it was ridiculously optimistic of me to expect a load of shattered crisps to make things right between us. I suspect that the only thing that'd perk him up would be to call him over so he could watch me deleting Fraser's email, then deleting it from my deleted folder too. But I can't do that. Apart from Rosie wanting to meet him, *I'm* also curious to find out what he's up to these days. And to ask questions too, of course. I am beside myself with curiosity.

'We're getting quite a stockpile,' Will remarks, opening a cupboard to illustrate his point. Sure enough, it's jammed with Archie's premium products. A stranger might surmise that a member of our family was suffering from a hoarding disorder or, quite simply, an obsession with crisps. Trouble is, Will and the kids don't really go for crisps of any kind – sick to the back teeth of them, probably. As a result, we are now 'approaching critical mass', as he puts it.

He picks up a lump of pizza dough from the bowl and drops it on the table with a dull thud. I hate it when he's like this. Maybe it's nothing to do with Fraser's email, or even me, but his age, his hormones – dwindling testosterone levels, perhaps. But of course, a man who's acting all frosty and distant is never hormonal. He's just a bit tired, or *thinking*.

'We should do stuff with the crisps,' I suggest.

'Like what?'

'Well . . . we should be inventive.'

He starts to knead the dough rather aggressively. 'What d'you have in mind?'

'Er . . . I don't know. One of the girls made crisp cookies at the show . . .'

'Crisp cookies,' he repeats, curling his lip as if I'd said *pancakes, with a smearing of dung.*

'It might sound weird,' I continue, 'but the combination of oats and raisins and salty little crispy bits is absolutely delicious . . .'

'Crisp cookies,' Will repeats again, like a malfunctioning robot. '*Crisp cookies?* Are they really a thing?'

'Yes, but it was just an idea,' I mutter, wishing now that I'd left the damn packets at work.

'Hmm,' Will says.

'A crisp pizza could be interesting,' I add lamely. 'Anyway, don't bother cooking for me if you and Ollie have already eaten . . .' That's another thing: I've spotted two dirty plates in the sink. Usually, Will doesn't make dinner until I'm home from work. *Look at me,* his martyred kneading tells me, *making a second meal like a bloody underpaid short-order cook . . .*

'It's fine,' he mutters, fetching his kilner jar of fresh tomato and basil sauce from the fridge. 'Oh, and I meant to say – Tricia's been over, going on about us chipping in to install CCTV out the back . . .'

'CCTV? What would we want that for?'

Will shrugs.

'I mean, we've got nothing to steal,' I point out.

'She was still going on about intruders in our garden . . .'

'Probably just some drunk teenagers,' I remark, pretending to study a packet of Sea Salt and Balsamic as if I've never seen such a thing before.

'Yeah, that's what I said.' He dollops sauce straight from the jar onto the base so it puddles unfetchingly, then mozzarella is ripped up at speed and dropped on. The few remaining leaves of our wilting basil plant are torn off with such force, the whole plant topples out of its little plastic pot. I have witnessed Pizza Express chefs exhibiting more pride in their work.

'We could try crisp omelettes sometime,' I blurt out into the anxious air.

'Uh?'

'Crisp omelettes. They're surprisingly good. Or, d'you remember this from *Blue Peter*, when they covered a loaf with soft cheese and then rolled it in broken crisps, so it looked like a sort of spiky hedgehog?' There's a rap at the door. Grateful to escape Will's withering stare, I rush to answer it.

'Sabrina, hi, come in . . .' As she strides into our kitchen, smiling broadly, I swear Will's stony expression melts: the first glimmer of warmth in forty-eight hours.

'Hope I'm not disturbing you,' she says, looking delightful in a blue patterned wrap dress, hair pulled up with wavy fronds dancing delightfully around her face.

'No, not at all,' I say. 'Come on in. Will's just making pizza . . .'

'Isn't he a *marvel* in the kitchen?' She gazes at my misshapen dinner as he transports it to the oven.

He grins bashfully. 'Would you like one, Sabrina? There's plenty of dough left.'

'Oh . . .' She winces. 'I shouldn't really but Tommy's still away and I was just going to have a sandwich. You know how it is. I hate cooking actually . . .'

'Yes, Charlotte's like that . . .' Hey, what about the thousands of dinners I made when he was gainfully employed at Greenspace Heritage? All the millions of sausages grilled and potatoes mashed? My hair stank of pork, and I nearly gave myself tennis elbow with that darn masher! Granted, they weren't quite the offerings of a kitchen marvel, but no one starved. As Will starts kneading the dough – *caressing* it, actually, with his big, manly hands – I silently forbid myself from opening the fridge, snatching the half-bottle of pinot which I know is nestling there and upending it into my mouth.

'I just wanted to tell you about Zach's next gig,' Sabrina says, perching on the edge of the table. 'They're playing on Thursday night in some divey pub, not too far away from here. Ticket sales are awfully slow, and after all their rehearsing I hate to think of them playing to a couple of bored bar staff plus Tommy and me . . .'

I can tell Will's not fully listening because he's now *fondling* the dough, swooping his hands over its curves while pretending, perhaps, that this isn't the trusty base from our battered old copy of *Jamie's Italian*, but one of Sabrina's pert breasts.

I watch him, agog, and check his face for evidence of arousal. He's flushed, certainly, and his pupils look dilated to me. I lower my gaze to check whether there's any untoward activity in the trouser department. But without going over and peering directly at his crotch, it's impossible to tell.

Sabrina is chattering on about Zach's gig, but I'm finding it hard to focus. Catching me scrutinising him, Will throws me a curious look. Then he rolls out the dough into a perfect circle and gives it a final, unnecessary tweak before lovingly painting on sauce with his pastry brush. Cheese is added, then – the climax of his performance – a liberal dribbling of oil, the posh Tuscan stuff which he's always a bit iffy about me using, and didn't put on *my* pizza. 'There,' he says, sounding exceedingly pleased with himself. I almost expect the pizza to emit a little sigh.

'So, er, Zach's gig,' I prompt Sabrina.

'Oh, yeah. Bit of a disaster-in-waiting, I think. Don't suppose you'd both like to come?' She flashes a hopeful smile. It is, I remind myself, ridiculous to suspect that she fancies Will, or vice versa. She is being friendly and neighbourly and is only inviting us to her son's gig, for goodness' sake.

'Er, yeah,' Will says, sounding less than sure. 'I don't see any reason why not, do you, Charlotte?'

In fact, I can think of one major reason: Zach is a teenager, and I'd imagine his band make teenage music, and we'll feel about a thousand years old. 'Sounds great,' I say firmly.

'What about Rosie?' Sabrina asks. 'She could bring a few friends, boost the numbers—'

'She should be back pretty soon,' Will says. 'I'm sure she'd love to come.'

'It was her first modelling job today,' I explain while Will checks our pizzas in the oven. 'They were shooting at Cambersands. She's being dropped off on the way back.'

'How exciting!' Sabrina says with genuine pleasure. 'Can't wait to hear about it.' Then, right on cue, the door bursts open and in Rosie stomps, muttering a quick hello before clattering up to her room.

I grimace at Will and step out to the hallway. 'Rosie?' I call up. 'How did it go? What were the clothes like?'

'*Nuttin'*,' she barks.

I go back into the kitchen and sigh. 'I know this sounds awful, Sabrina, but sometimes I can't wait until she's about twenty-five and we can talk normally again – you know, communicate, using proper words . . .'

'Tell me about it,' she laughs as Will places our pizzas

on the table. She tears into hers with gusto, making appreciative noises as she munches away.

Will looks at me. 'Sorry yours is a bit burnt.'

'No, it's fine, I like it like this.' I force a smile as I hack through the blackened crust.

'Do you?' Sabrina asks. 'Tommy's like that. Likes everything charred – virtually incinerated. I'm always on at him about it because everyone knows burnt food can cause cancer . . .'

'I'm sure it's fine,' I say, 'and it's not that burnt.' *I mean, it hasn't quite been reduced to ash.*

'Hi.' Rosie has reappeared in the doorway. She is milky-pale and looks utterly worn out.

'So how did it go?' Will asks, handing her a mug of tea. 'Want some pizza? Or something else?'

'We had burgers after the shoot.' Her mouth sets in a grim line.

'So, tell us all about the clothes,' Sabrina chips in. 'What did you wear?'

'Nuttin'.'

I frown at her. 'Nothing? You weren't naked, were you?'

'No,' she splutters, 'I said *knitting*, Mum. We were shooting for a wool company and it was all jumpers and cardis and hats. Can you imagine wearing horrible hairy wool on a day like this?'

'Oh, you poor love,' Sabrina exclaims.

'It was the hottest day of the year,' Rosie bleats. 'I thought I was going to *die*!'

'But I thought it was for some Italian designer?' Will says.

'Yeah, that's what I thought. Laurie said the client was Giordano and I just assumed it was an Italian label, and it turned out it *is* – but for knitting.'

'You mean it's a wool company?' I ask.

'Yeah.' She nods glumly.

'At least it was a job,' Will remarks, 'and you've started earning . . . and it's all experience isn't it?'

Rosie emits a strangled gasp. 'Dad, I'm going to be in a *knitting* magazine! What if people see?' Good lord: one tiddly modelling job and she's already developed a sort of *flounce*.

He shrugs. 'Well, if you're a model, then people are going to see your picture, aren't they? It's an occupational hazard, I'd have thought.'

'Yeah, but wearing a big sweaty jumper with a stupid knitted belt? And *mittens*?'

'Oh, come on,' I say. 'Who's going to see it? Who, out of all of your friends, actually knits?'

She sniffs loudly. 'No one.'

'There you go then,' Will remarks. 'You're perfectly safe. Anyway, like we said from the start, if you feel remotely uncomfortable about it, then just stop. It's totally your call.'

'S'pose so,' Rosie says reluctantly, flopping onto the chair next to Sabrina. '*Look*, though. Look what happened to me.' She pulls up her T-shirt sleeve and shows Sabrina – not me, her own mother, who birthed her – her right armpit.

'Oooh, that's nasty,' Sabrina sympathises.

'A heat rash by the look of it,' I suggest, peering at the mottled skin. 'You need calamine lotion . . .'

'Do we have any?'

'No, but I can get some tomorrow—'

'*We* have,' Sabrina announces, leaping up. 'Had to buy some for Tommy after he lay out in the garden last weekend, burnt himself to a cinder, the silly bugger.' She laughs. 'Too macho for sunscreen. I'll just pop over and get it – oh, and before I forget, Rosie, would you like to come to Zach's gig on Thursday night?'

'Yeah, cool,' she says, rash momentarily forgotten as Ollie wanders in with Saul in his wake, both clutching steaming cartons of chips despite having eaten earlier. Colossal appetites, the pair of them, yet each weighs about the same as a runner bean.

Sabrina darts off, returning with medical supplies and dabbing the lotion onto my daughter's armpit while I watch, pretending to adopt a supervisory role. 'That's much better,' Rosie says gratefully. 'Thanks, Sabrina. It's really cooled it down.'

'Aw, you're welcome,' Sabrina says.

Will chuckles. 'At least someone brings something useful into this house.'

'What d'you mean, Dad?' Rosie asks.

He smirks. 'Mum's brought home a load of reject crisps again, and you'd better watch out—'

'Why?'

'She's planning to turn them into biscuits,' he says, at which everyone hoots with laughter, including me, to show what a jolly good sport I am.

Chapter Twenty

While I might have failed on the calamine lotion front, I have to say I do put on an excellent end-of-term gathering. Something of a tradition – it's always assumed we'll host it, which I love – these events began as jelly-splattered affairs which Tricia and Gerald would observe, fearfully, over the fence (quite possibly giving silent thanks to the fact that they'd settled on raising Nipper rather than producing any human children of their own). These days, Will and I are expected to strew the garden with cushions, pile the table with good things to eat, then quietly melt away into the background, like impeccably-trained staff.

If fact, as I'm a little concerned that Will is beginning to feel like the kitchen serf around here, I've prepared today's food and taken some time off work to give him a break. I'm sure my offspring will be *thrilled* to have me around at the start of the holidays. It's a warm, hazy Wednesday afternoon. Liza has arrived to help out, and Ollie and Rosie's friends have descended – including Zach, who's clearly enjoying being the centre of attention. He is, admittedly, a very good-looking boy, in a rather brooding, malnourished kind of way. He makes the other boys present – perfectly average-sized urban kids – look extremely robust in comparison.

The arrival of a delicate blonde girl causes even more of a stir. 'This is Delph,' Rosie announces. 'We worked together on that shoot . . .'

'That awful shoot!' Delph exclaims, scanning the garden and looking, it has to be said, mightily unimpressed by either the guests or surroundings, it's impossible to tell. She is astonishingly pretty with golden hair which hangs in a silken sheet all the way down to her bum – the world's teeniest bum, I'd wager, clad in denim cut-offs the size of a pencil case.

'What was so bad about it?' Zach asks.

'It was *hell*,' she retorts, at which Ollie – God, I love that boy to pieces – sidles over and says, 'I thought you went to the seaside?'

'Yeah?' Delph rolls her eyes as if to say, *And who are you?*

'We had to wear mittens,' Rosie tells Zach, looking less than comfortable about her new friend making such a fuss.

There's a ripple of laughter. 'So?' Saul says.

'So,' Delph retorts, 'it was hot! Would *you* like to wear mittens on the hottest day of the year?'

'If I was paid, I would,' Ollie replies with a shrug. 'I'd wear a big woolly hat as well. I'd wear *anything* for money—'

'Yeah, well,' Delph retorts, linking Rosie's arm and whisking her away from the riff-raff, 'maybe next time *you* could do it. I'll put a word in for you with my agency. I heard they were looking for annoying brats for Littlewoods' schoolwear adverts . . .'

Blimey, that was unnecessary. I glance at Liza; after

running back and forth with the food, we're taking a breather on a rug at the bottom of the garden. 'Not sure about Rosie's new friend,' I murmur.

'Doesn't seem her usual type,' Liza agrees. We watch as Nina hovers around them, obviously feeling a little pushed aside in favour of the exotic newcomer.

'Liza,' I add, dropping my voice to a whisper, 'something happened when I was at Mum and Dad's . . .'

'What?' She frowns.

'Rosie's dad got in touch. Fraser, I mean . . .'

'No! How?'

'Through Dad. He managed to find his email address. Asked if I want to meet up sometime.'

'You mean, casually? As if you're old school friends or something?'

'Sort of, yes. It was a bit odd actually. He said something about us being young and scared and making mistakes . . .'

She blows out air. 'The mistake he made was fucking off when you needed him.'

I nod. 'Yeah, I know.'

'So what are you going to do?'

'I'm not sure yet. Will didn't take it too well, understandably. But Rosie asked about meeting him recently. It's obviously playing on her mind. I haven't even told Will about that . . .' I cut off abruptly as he approaches with a plate of cookies and three beers.

'Party's a bit different this year,' he observes with a wry smile, handing us a bottle of Corona each and reclining beside us.

I nod. 'Remember when the highlight was the boys building that enormous den? Seems like only last summer . . .'

'We're not completely past it, though,' he adds, offering Liza a cookie. 'We're going to a gig tomorrow night.'

'You're joking,' Liza splutters.

'Unfortunately not,' he says with a grin.

'It's Zach's band,' I explain. 'We've been asked along to boost the numbers.'

Will grimaces. 'Can we possibly get out of it, d'you think?'

'Don't think so,' I say, pleased that he's not exactly overjoyed at the thought of more Sabrina-time. Although I do like her, I was also slightly relieved that she didn't show up today. 'Don't suppose you'd like to come?' I ask Liza.

'Sure, why not?'

'Yeah, you're always out seeing bands,' Will adds. 'You can give us tips on how to behave.'

'Like, do we stage dive?' I ask.

She laughs and bites into a biscuit. 'Just try and look a bit rock 'n' roll, Will.'

'Seriously?' he exclaims with a trace of alarm.

'No, Christ – I'm joking. Just relax and have a good time.' She pauses, munching on her cookie. 'Ooh, these are amazing, Will. Kind of salty-sweet. What's in them?'

'They're all Charlotte's work, actually,' he admits.

'See?' I say, laughing. 'They *are* good. They're crisp cookies. Ready salted with raisins. Will thought I was out of my mind . . .'

I look at him and he smiles back – smiles *properly*, I mean. Fondly, the way he used to. My heart lifts; it's all going to be fine, I tell myself, drinking in the scene in our garden. My culinary experiment worked. As I've never made cookies that people actually wanted to eat before, I take this to be a very good omen indeed. It means Fraser won't contact me again, and Rosie will perform an about-turn and decide she doesn't want to meet him after all.

Most important of all, it means we're okay, me and Will. He is holding my hand now, my gorgeous husband, on this beautiful summer's day.

*

It's been so long since I've been to a gig that I wake up next morning slightly panicked about how it'll be. Not the music, obviously: that'll just *happen*. As long as I face the right direction, and look interested, it doesn't matter whether I enjoy it or not. No, it's the peripheral stuff that's concerning: like, will the venue have a cloakroom or will I have to stand there for hours, clutching my jacket, like when I arrived late at Ollie's school concert and all the seats had been taken? Ugh, the pitying looks I attracted all night, and the comments: 'Are you sure you're okay, Charlotte? Maybe someone could find you a *folding stool*?' All of this hissed in the middle of Sophia Barton's flute solo. I don't want a repeat of that.

Also: clothes. I'd be no problem at all if we were going to see one of those beardy acoustic guys that Liza so enjoys. Hair loose, no make-up, jeans and a top – that's all I'd need to fit in. Actually, maybe not. While a pared-down, folky look is fine if you're willowy of frame, I'm not so sure it works for a rather buxom muncher of crisps.

Hair, I decide. It requires urgent attention. I call Petra, my local hairdresser, and as luck would have it she can fit me in for a cut and colour at four this afternoon. While it is, admittedly, hardly Trevor Sorbie, I always enjoy going to Petra's salon due to the fact that it's comfy and unpretentious and there's plenty of chit-chat: they're the kind of conversations I don't have anywhere else. Beyoncé, online dating, whether juicing is a good thing or just a different way of starving yourself: Petra is a mine of information on such matters and I am always quite happy to sit there, soaking it all in. Less enjoyable is the fact that Petra – who's in her late twenties – always asks, 'So what's happening tonight?' And I always feel obliged to put a spin on such scintillating activities as supervising Ollie's homework or watching a DVD.

At least this time, I am actually doing something notable. 'I'm going to a gig,' I tell her.

And this, it turns out, is my big mistake – because Petra says, 'Oh, right – what sort of music?'

'Kind of indie rock, I think,' I reply, and next thing she's excitedly showing me a shade chart consisting of row upon row of snippets of synthetic hair stuck to a large white card.

'Let's do something different then,' she suggests. 'Something fresher, younger, to lift your look . . .'

'Sure,' I say, swept along by her enthusiasm.

'A rich mahogany with deeper vegetable tones?' I take it she doesn't mean carrot, or any of the less popular, dreary-toned veg: parsnip or celeriac.

'Sounds great,' I say as Petra jabs at one of the hair swatches on the chart. It looks fine, it really does: a rich, glossy brown – what you'd call a proper brunette. As my head wound has finally healed, I can justify today's extravagance as a present to celebrate my recovery. It's only later, when I'm being blow-dried, that I discover what Petra meant by 'vegetable tones': purple. Well, purple-*ish*. Which I don't point out, naturally, because I am the kind of person who never complains when coffee is served lukewarm, or my glass of wine has a lump of cork bobbing about in it. In fact I say, 'Thanks', then proceed to tip generously. The less satisfactory the thing, the more cash I dump on the table, then leave, feeling furious – not with the person responsible but myself, for being such a spineless twerp. How can I possibly encourage Rosie to grow into a strong, confident woman when I can't even say what I think about my own hair?

'Oh, *Mum*.' Rosie is the first to witness my new look when I arrive home.

I blink at her. 'Yes, love, I know.'

She steps towards me. 'You've had it coloured.'

'That's right.'

'Will it wash out?'

My heart drops. 'No, of course it won't. It's a tint.'

'So, um . . . how long will it last?' Her gaze is fixed on the top of my head.

'Until it grows out, I guess, or until I have it coloured again . . .' I shrug. 'Maybe I should go blonde. What colour d'you think it would go, on top of purple? *Mauve*?'

She splutters with laughter. 'It's actually not that bad. It just takes a bit of getting used to.'

'Thanks. Anyway, it'll probably tone down,' I add, feeling more positive now at the thought of us all going for a night out together, in a big gang (apart from Ollie, who's opting instead for a sleepover at Saul's). I'm no sooner ready, dressed in a fitted shirt, black jeans and admittedly very *shiny* purplish hair than Liza's arrived, announcing that my new shade is 'fantastic – no, of course it's not purple, you mad woman. It's gorgeous!' Then Will returns from the shops, still wearing a grubby old gardening T-shirt and scruffy jeans, with a rip at one knee: obviously, he's in no great rush to get ready. 'Oh!' he exclaims, staring at my head. 'Who did that?'

'Um, my hairdresser, obviously. Petra. What d'you think?'

'It's, uhhh . . .' He scratches at an ear. '*Different*.'

'You mean different as in, have I lost my mind?'

'No, of course not.' He glances at Liza and shakes his head. 'God, Charlotte, don't be so paranoid. It's just, um . . . sort of aubergine. Unusual. I kind of like it.' I decide to interpret this as crazed enthusiasm.

'Aubergine,' I tease him. 'So you're saying I look like a *tuber*?'

'The aubergine's not a tuber,' Ollie informs me, marching in from the park. 'It grows from the plant's ovary so technically, it's a fruit. Anyway, I like it, Mum,' he adds, loyally.

'Thanks, darling.'

'And I like *aubergines*,' Will adds, 'and it's very glossy and healthy-looking. If it were a real aubergine it'd win Best in Show.'

'Why, thank you,' I say graciously as he heads upstairs to get ready. Nina arrives, followed by Delph (I can tell by Nina's expression that she'd far prefer Delph *not* to be coming), and now it's just Will we're waiting for, who's been up in the bathroom for ages.

'Is he exfoliating, d'you think?' Liza asks with a smirk.

'What's taking him so long?' Rosie groans.

'No idea.' I give Liza a quick look, wondering if he's had a change of heart about going at all.

Leaving everyone chatting in the kitchen, I head off to investigate and find Will, trotting downstairs. 'Oh!' is all I can say.

Will frowns. 'What is it?'

'Er, nothing. It's just, I've never seen those trousers before . . .'

'They were in a bag of stuff I'd sorted for charity,' he explains. And there, I'm sorry to say, they should have stayed: bound for Oxfam, to be grabbed by a sexy, skinny, twenty-two-year-old bass player . . . not that Will is fat. Or old. It's just . . . he is *not* is your typical leather trouser-wearing man.

We stand and look at each other in the hallway. 'I don't remember you having them,' I remark.

'You keep saying that. You don't know everything I own, do you?'

'No, but—'

'I mean, you haven't done a full inventory of all my possessions?'

I frown, stung by his tetchiness. 'Of course I haven't. They're just . . . a bit startling, that's all.'

'Startling?'

'Yes, like if I came home from work and found you wearing one of those novelty PVC aprons with a picture of a lacy bra and knickers on the front and nothing underneath—' I giggle at the thought.

Will eyes me coldly. 'You're saying leather trousers are in the same ballpark as novelty aprons?'

'No!' I cry, thankful that everyone else is still hanging out in the kitchen. 'I don't mean that at all. Those aprons are awful and your trousers are, er . . .' I tail off, feeling myself starting to sweat. 'They're fine. You look *great* in them.'

'Well, I thought they looked okay,' he mutters.

'They do,' I bluster. 'They do look okay. It's just, I was a bit surprised . . .'

'But it's all right for you to have purple hair?'

'It was supposed to be brown. Mahogany actually. It was a mistake . . .'

'And slather liquid gold all over your face?'

'You know I only said that under pressure!'

Will raises a brow. 'It's okay for you to lie about using something that costs about eight thousand quid for a *tiny* drop, but not for me to wear some old trousers?'

Old, yes. Leather no. Then it hits me: Sabrina was wearing leather trousers the day we first met her. Is he copying her? No, that would be ridiculous. It would mean he's turned into a teenage girl. Maybe being at home for six months, cooking and snipping at things with his secateurs has made him a bit . . . I don't know. Lacking in something? Youth, probably. Excitement. And animal hide. 'Of course it's okay,' I say briskly. 'C'mon, everyone's waiting—'

'Dad, your trousers!' Rosie squeals as we join the others, while Ollie explodes with laughter – my cue to bustle him off, still honking with mirth, to Saul's. Tactfully, Liza merely gives me a quick *what-is-Will-wearing?* look and leaves it at that.

The doorbell goes, and it's Sabrina, wearing a tight, low-cut black dress with a push-up bra, plus a biker jacket (it's beginning to feel like World of Leather around here). 'All set?' she asks brightly. 'Zach's already at the venue and Tommy's headed down there to give them a hand setting up.'

'Yep, we're all ready,' I say, adding, 'great jacket.' It is, actually; she looks more sexy wife of veteran rock star than desperate groupie.

'Thanks. Bought it today. Shouldn't have, but . . .' She shrugs in a *what can you do?* kind of way, and I try not to fixate on her newly ramped-up cleavage.

'What's the venue called?' Liza asks.

'Down Below,' Sabrina replies.

I burst out laughing. 'As in, "I've got an embarrassing problem down below"?'

'Haha, hope not,' she chuckles, adding, 'it's *down below* the Cap and Feather. Bit of a dive but it all adds to the atmosphere, doesn't it?'

''Course it does,' I say blithely, as if Will and I frequent such places all the time.

As it's close enough to walk, we all set off in a straggly group. Predictably, the three girls lag behind so as not to be associated with us, while Sabrina and Will stride ahead. You know you're getting on a bit when you start thinking, Is this age-appropriate? I'm always asking myself those sort of questions: i.e., is this top too low-cut? Do I look ridiculous in a bobble hat? Sabrina clearly doesn't think that way. She wears tiny dresses and has eyelash extensions. She has sex in a garden shed. And she bought that leather jacket today. I can hardly remember going shopping for clothes. The last thing I bought was a set of very plain and functional stainless steel eggcups.

In between the two factions I stroll along with Liza, who's speculating on what the band will be like. 'I saw some stuff of theirs on YouTube,' she says. 'They're pretty good. Think it'll be a great night.' But I'm not fully listening. I can't focus.

All I can think is, maybe it's me. Maybe I just don't get it anymore. Say 'down below' and I think embarrassing gynaecological problems. Ask me to play word association with leather and I think handbag or Chesterfield sofa or, in a trouser context, *possible risk of chafing*. And it strikes me that that's not quite right.

Chapter Twenty-One

In fact, the band *are* pretty good: energetic and supremely confident but so, so young. I feel like their Auntie Mabel, head tipped to one side, thinking, how sweet they are, and how hard they must have practised their songs! Perhaps I could offer to run their fan club, if such things still exist.

'So what d'you think?' A rather sweaty Tommy has appeared at my side, for which I'm grateful as Sabrina and Will have edged their way to the front of the audience, and Liza's at the bar. Obviously, the girls – who've positioned themselves at the other side of the room – don't want me hovering around them either, breathing their air.

'They're great,' I say. 'Zach has a fantastic voice.'

He beams, looking genuinely pleased. 'Yeah. It has that raw quality, you know? And they've put in a lot of hard work.' He sips his beer. 'We're having a bit of a gathering at our place later, if you all fancy coming over? A sort of after-show party . . .'

'Sounds good,' I say.

'Like a drink?'

'I'm okay, thanks,' I say, indicating my almost-full glass.

'What's that – vodka?'

'No, water.' Then, feeling as if I should justify it, I add, 'Been a bit under the weather lately.' Which is easier than explaining, *What with Will's startling trousers, and the slightly disturbing dynamic between my husband and your wife, the temptation to guzzle all the bar's booze would be too much. And the last thing I want is to make a complete arse of myself tonight.*

Tommy wanders off to find his wife who's still at the front, *still* with Will. I get the impression that Tommy doesn't mind a bit; she's just one of those flirty, outgoing types, and I know I'm being completely ridiculous in finding this difficult. I picture Will fondling her pizza and quickly push the image away. Christ, I was never the jealous sort before now. Is it me, who's becoming faintly pathetic? Maybe, if Will was a little less offish with me, I'd be perfectly happy for him to spend all evening yacking happily away to a stunning woman in the kind of teeny black dress I wouldn't even be able to haul over my hips.

I focus hard on the band, letting the music transport me away from my stupid worries. How different Sabrina, Tommy and Zach are from my family. For one thing, Zach is clearly happy for his parents to come along to his gig. Tommy's even involved with the band, and Zach seems content to hang out with his mother too. He's comfortable smoking a joint in front of them, for God's sake. Should Will and I be more like that? I think about how I insisted on accompanying Rosie to the test shoot, and look what happened there: Fraser saw us in that magazine. If I'd let her go on her own, as she'd begged to, then none of that would have happened . . .

And I wouldn't be thinking about him now. Christ, that email. Should I reply, or what? Should I tell him to sod off and stop bothering us, or be reasonable – friendly but distant – seeing as Rosie seems to believe she wants him in her life? I know all of this is painful for Will. I think he'll come round eventually – he has to, really – but we haven't even discussed it again. Anyway, it's not about Will, or even me, really – it's about Rosie. I can't allow her to meet Fraser without checking him out first. I need to know that he's a decent man, who we can accept will be part of her life. If he's fickle, or just idly curious – or clearly deranged – then he can just sling his hook.

I glance over to where Rosie is standing with Nina and Delph. Delph is holding court, and Rosie is laughing raucously. Even across this crowded room I can see that Nina looks like the hanger-on. She's fiercely loyal and fun – a hard-working girl who serves up scamp 'n' king prawn combos at the Harvester, whilst trying to prevent chaos from ensuing at the salad bar. She and Rosie have been firm friends since they were five years old. I catch her deflated expression, and my heart goes out to her.

Delph is of a different breed. I doubt she's ever *seen* a scamp 'n' king prawn combo. She'd probably burst into tears if anyone took her to a Harvester. Modelling has taken her all over the world, and her beauty is otherworldly too: in the unlikely setting of Down Below she looks like a golden fairy. *She* didn't start her career modelling hairy mittens for a knitting brochure; in fact Rosie told me she'd bollocked her agency for even putting her up for that job. 'Delph says I should *never* ever do anything like that again,' Rosie informed me, gravely, as if she was talking about being asked to mop up sick.

Liza reappears at my side and hands me a Coke. 'Pretty good gig,' she remarks, sipping a gin and tonic.

'Yeah,' I say, 'it's kind of . . . *interesting*. I mean, I haven't been to one like this since . . . God, I can't actually remember. Any concerts I've been to with Will, we've had allocated seats and bought programmes.'

She smiles. 'This place is disgusting, though . . .'

'Yeah, it's pretty damp, isn't it? I can actually taste spores.' We laugh and turn to watch as the band launches into another song, more raucous and insistent than the others. It's an excellent song, and I'm having to make a concerted effort not to dance. I feel good, and I haven't even had a proper drink. It doesn't matter that the place is populated almost exclusively by teenage boys, faces untroubled by razors, and skinny girls in even skinnier jeans and little vest tops and copious amounts of black eye liner.

A girl with a silver ring in her nose stands on my foot as she drifts by, and glares at me as if it was my fault for putting it there. 'Sorry!' I say with a grin. Maybe she was just staring because I appear to not have any piercings or tattoos, both of which are in abundance here. In fact, I do have one small tattoo – a tangle of daisies on my right hip, all done and dusted before the effects of the Amsterdam space cake had worn off. Fraser had egged me on to get it. He'd had a small devil inked onto his shoulder – he'd shown it to me before we'd even reached Paris. Not that I regret getting mine. I regret *nothing,* I think defiantly. *Je ne regrette rien!* And I'm not even drunk! I can come to a gig and my husband can zoom off and spend the whole evening glued to

Sabrina's side and I can stand here sipping Coke and it's *fine*.

'This is good, isn't it?' Sabrina's beside me now, tailed by Will. It's the band's final song, and then something happens which kills the atmosphere stone dead. The lights go on before they've even finished playing. In the dark, the cellar at least had a sleazy sort of atmosphere, which could almost be described as exotic. Now it's cruelly illuminated by fluorescent strips. I look around. Many eyes are upon us: this clump of middle-aged people who've blundered into a gig. Actually, Sabrina and Liza sort of fit in – as does Tommy. He's clutching a bunch of cables, so he belongs here. He has a job to do.

I glance at Will. We look like the parents who've returned a day early from holiday and walked in to find their home full of unfamiliar teenagers guzzling all the drink and stubbing out fags in the pot pourri. *We only came to swell the numbers!* I want to explain to a gawping boy with a fuzzy, gingery chin. I glimpse my pallid expression with my ridiculous hair in a cracked mirrored pillar. So that's what I'd look like embalmed, I muse, hoping it's just the terribly unkind lighting that's making me look that way. I seem to be blaming a lot of things on 'the light' these days.

'Just going to the loo,' I tell Liza. In fact, I don't really need it. What I do need are a few moments to rev myself up for the party at Sabrina and Tommy's, as Will seems keen to go back to their place. His trousers seem to be impregnating him with an unusual eagerness to party.

As I stride into the ladies', the floor of which is entirely covered with sodden loo roll, a boy and a girl emerge, dishevelled, from one of the cubicles. Surely they haven't just done it, in a stinky basement loo? It seems terribly insalubrious but then, what do I know? And only a few days ago I was seriously considering persuading Will to do it with me in our shed.

Disconcertingly, as if I'm not here, the couple start snogging hungrily against the chipped basins. I make for a cubicle, inadvertently setting off the roaring hand dryer as I brush past. 'Oh my God!' the girl screams, as if she's been shot. I bolt the wobbly door and plonk myself down on the clammy plastic toilet lid, wondering if it would be so terrible to make my excuses and not to go to the party after all.

I can't, of course. My family is going (well, apart from Ollie, who I'd give anything to swap places with right now. Saul still nurtures a slightly furtive love of Lego. I'd rather be building an elaborate space station from coloured bricks than be parked on this rather manky-looking loo). Anyway, it would look pathetic to just limp off home.

I get up from the loo and stride out, feigning confidence. Things are looking brighter already, I tell myself: the snogging couple have disappeared, and when I find everyone, they're ready to leave. We all make our way up the spiral metal staircase to street level, where the night air feels fresher than I can ever remember. After the fungal atmosphere of Down Below, it could be the Cotswolds. 'What a talented son you have,' I tell Sabrina, meaning it, as we make our way home.

She smiles proudly. 'Thanks. They were great, weren't they?'

'They really were,' Liza says, and Will murmurs in agreement. Maybe it'll be fun, I decide, back at Sabrina and Tommy's: a big group of us, all ages, having fun together instead of Will and I reading our books or watching a box set. In fact, by the time we reach their place I am quite in the mood for a party. Even Will's trousers seem less startling now. Perhaps they just took a bit of getting used to.

'Sorry about the mess,' Sabrina trills as she lets us in, although this time there are no overflowing packing cases, or bottles strewn all over the dining table: just a gold vase filled with enormous white lilies emitting a pungent perfume.

'Wow,' I say. Although they're not quite my thing – I prefer a jumble of flowers cut from the garden – I can't deny that it's an impressive display.

'From Tommy,' Sabrina announces with a grin. 'It's my birthday.'

'Oh, why didn't you say?' Will exclaims, turning to me and whispering, 'We should have got her something.'

'I know,' I mouth back, remembering him suggesting that we celebrated my 38th birthday by having the cracks filled in our house. *Stop this,* I tell myself sternly. *You're a grown woman, not a teenager.*

'I wish we'd known,' Will witters on as Sabrina wanders off to fetch drinks.

'About what?'

'Her birthday!'

Oh, for Christ's sake. I'm sure she won't mind getting the Tiffany necklace a couple of days late. 'It doesn't matter, Will,' I mutter. 'She wouldn't have expected anything from us . . .'

'I just think it would've been nice—'

'Can we leave it please?' I hiss, at which he mutters something unintelligible. Oh, I know I'm being ridiculous. It's probably due to the fact that, now I've had time to mull things over, I realise I am not completely appalled by the fact that Fraser emailed me. Curiosity, that's all it is: he meant the world to me once. And, because I know I shouldn't even be *entertaining* such thoughts, I'm trying to convince myself that Will – loyal Will, who makes his own strawberry ice cream – is behaving in a similarly devious manner.

He turns away and falls into conversation with one of the men I vaguely remember from the barbecue. I join Liza and Sabrina, and soon the music's cranked up; Tommy has appointed himself as DJ for the night, much to the amusement of Zach's mates. It soon turns into quite a party, yet I can't quite throw myself into it. Looks like Nina can't either. I catch her, dolefully checking her phone, while Rosie and Delph are locked in intense conversation.

It's nearly midnight when my mobile rings. My stomach does a little lurch when I see that it's Maria, Saul's mum. 'Hi, Maria. Everything okay?'

'Yes, don't worry, it's nothing really. I know you're out tonight. It's just, Ollie's not very well. I'm sorry . . .'

'Oh, I'll come and get him right away . . .' Will gives me a quizzical look as I start to pull on my jacket.

'I'm happy for him to stay,' Maria says quickly, 'and he keeps saying he wants to, but he feels terribly hot—'

'No problem,' I say. 'I'll be ten minutes at the most.'

'What's wrong?' Will asks, frowning as I finish the call.

'Ollie's not well. Sounds like he's running a temperature . . .'

'I'll go and get him,' Will says.

I shake my head. 'It's fine. I'd rather go, honestly. You stay here and have fun.' I feel bad now, as I kiss his cheek, for my iffy reaction to his trousers and the surges of jealousy I keep experiencing over him just being friendly to Sabrina, when I virtually hauled him over the street to meet her in the first place.

I *really* must grow up.

'I'm going to pick up Ollie,' I tell Rosie. 'Are you girls ready to come back to ours now?'

She looks as appalled as if I'd suggested cutting up her food. 'We can come home on our own, Mum, when we're ready.'

'Okay, fine. Don't stay too late, though.' I hesitate, realising how silly I'm being. Will's here, and Liza too. Nothing untoward is going to happen. So I say my goodbyes and stride down the street towards Saul's place, where I find my boy perched on the sofa, jacket on already, looking slightly shrunken. 'Hi, Mum,' he grunts.

'Hi, darling. Oh, you poor love. C'mon, let's get you home . . .'

'I'll drive you,' says Maria, a generous woman who's managed to bring up no less than four children, seemingly without ever raising her voice.

I smile, grateful for her kindness. 'Don't worry. We'll be home in two minutes and a breath of fresh air will do him good.' I hug her goodbye.

'Such a shame to spoil your night.'

'It hasn't,' I say truthfully. 'Honestly, I'd had enough.'

Back home, it's clear that Ollie still feels ropey as he lets me fuss around him – tucking him into bed and dabbing at his clammy forehead with a flannel. I miss being able to pamper my kids. I don't mean the everyday stuff like washing their clothes or making them fried egg on toast. I mean being . . . *motherly.* Nursey, almost. I fetch Calpol and perch on the edge of his bed until he starts to doze, then I head downstairs and wonder what to do next.

Twenty minutes later, Rosie and Delph tumble in in an explosion of giggles. 'Hi girls,' I say, wondering if they've been drinking, and deciding not to interrogate them – they're fine, actually. Just high spirited. 'Where's Nina?' I ask.

'Gone home,' Rosie says airily.

'Really? But I thought she was coming back to ours—'

'Her *dad* picked her up,' Delph adds with a smirk, as if this were the most humiliating thing ever.

I frown at Rosie. 'You did invite her to stay, didn't you? I mean, I hope she didn't feel left out . . .'

'Mum, she's *sixteen*,' Rosie scoffs, rolling her eyes in Delph's direction. 'Of course she didn't feel left out. She was just being a bit . . . I dunno . . .' She shrugs and turns to Delph. 'C'mon, let's go up to my room.'

'Can I get you anything?' I call after them. 'D'you want me to bring you up some water?'

'Nah, 's all right,' Rosie mutters.

Then, on the landing – and clearly not caring that I'm within earshot – Delph says, 'So what d'you think of Sabrina?'

'She's really nice,' Rosie replies.

'Isn't she *orange*, though? Like, she's just had a cheap spray tan?'

'Er, I guess so,' Rosie says, sounding unconvinced.

'She's tangerine,' Delph adds, giggling, 'or satsuma. Or *mandarin*. What's the difference anyway? I never understand the difference between all the little orange fruits . . .' There's much laughter as they clatter into Rosie's room, banging the door behind them.

As I shower off the mouldy whiff from Down Below – the *venue*, that is, which I've now decided ranks as the worst name ever for a venue – I mull over what's just happened. Rosie might be tricky, but she rarely has a bad word to say about anyone; it's one of her loveliest qualities. I can't believe she's being so dismissive about Nina either. And Delph should ask Ollie about tangerines, I think huffily. *He* knows about fruit.

Back downstairs, I rummage around in the kitchen for something to eat. I don't fancy crisps. I *especially* don't fancy Lobster Bisque flavour. Something warm and soothing is needed . . . I spot a jar of Ovaltine, untouched for years, and make myself a steaming mugful. Carrying it through to the living room, I perch on the window ledge in the dark, enjoying the malty sweetness of my drink.

From here I can see straight into Tommy and Sabrina's living room. Like ours, their place has a big bay window facing the street. Looks like more people have arrived for the party, as the room is pretty crowded now. Although it looks fun, I'd actually rather be sitting here, enjoying the stillness before going to bed. I sip my drink, thinking, well, tonight wasn't so bad. They're fun, generous people and I really need to get a grip on myself.

Their front door opens and Liza emerges, turning to wave at someone in the hallway, then strides off, slender and leggy with her long, light brown hair wafting behind her. I wonder how long Will's planning to stay. A few people are dancing in the living room now: middle-aged dancing, otherwise known as 'throwing shapes'. Just as well the girls aren't witnessing this. Rosie can't tolerate adults dancing – even me singing along to the radio seems to cause her actual physical pain these days – and, fortunately, Will rarely succumbs.

He is now, though. Blimey, some fancy shapes are

being thrown. Hexagons, maybe. Or – Ollie's favourite – dodecahedrons, multi-faceted with stabbing motions of the arms, as if he's trying to swat away moths. Highly unusual behaviour, but it's definitely Will, gyrating his leather-clad hips and waving his arms in a curious melding of eras and styles.

It'll do him good, I tell myself. It'll get those endorphins flying through his system and hopefully put a smile back on his face. He needs to let off steam – to cast off the shackles of domesticity and pizza-kneading and all that. Christ, I'd be drunk too if I'd spent the best part of six months lashed to the cooker and tugging up dandelions. I'd be going berserk, actually. I might even be giving that recruitment advert for traffic wardens some serious thought. I'd encounter hostility every single day, but would it really be any different from living with a teenager?

That's it, I decide: Rosie regards me with at best suspicion, and at worst, outright hostility, as if I am about to fine her – when in fact I am a pretty easy-going mother just going about my daily business. Anyway, Will and I must sit down and have a proper chat about what's happening with his job applications, and whether he should widen the net a little – be open to possibilities . . . Maybe he could be a landscape gardener? Or a pizza chef?

In Tommy and Sabrina's living room other guests briefly appear, then dip out of sight. The room seems to empty completely, then Will strides back in, not all by himself but clutching a woman tightly to his chest. Her long, tousled hair is mussed all over her face; I have no idea who she is. Bile rises in my throat as he twirls her round in a passionate embrace.

I don't mean a tango or any other kind of sexy Latin thing, which would be okay – sort of. I mean, of course he can dance with other women if he wants to. It's just, he never dances with *anyone* – not even me – unless he can possibly avoid it. He'll go round gathering up glasses, or even start washing up; anything rather than be bullied into throwing himself around to some 70s disco tune with a load of pissed adults in someone's living room. It's just not his thing. At least, I thought it wasn't, just as I'd never imagined him breaking into Chrissie Hynde's wardrobe from 1979 and stealing her trousers . . .

Anyway, if we're going to be technical about it, this isn't really dancing at all. It's actually foreplay: i.e., a lot of steamy clutching and – ugh – burying his head between her breasts which jut out from her torso, like weapons. Who *is* this woman? Sabrina, or one of her friends? Is it that Abs woman? All I can make out is a slender body with pneumatic tits and a big tussle of hair being tossed about the place.

A cluster of people have appeared in the room and seem to be laughing or applauding. Maybe this is the kind of party game Sabrina and Tommy are into? Perhaps shed sex is just the tip of the iceberg and they're planning some kind of orgy scenario? The Ovaltine tastes sickly at the back of my throat.

I should get dressed and go over and usher him home, before he makes a complete tit of himself. But I can't face marching in, as if I'm his irate mother. Anyway, I told him to stay and enjoy himself. What I *should* do is stop torturing myself, and staring at this ridiculous spectacle, idiot wife that I am with my stupid aubergine hair. I don't even like aubergines. What's the point of a vegetable – sorry, *fruit* – that you have to sprinkle with salt so as to draw the bitterness out? I *am* bitter, though. I'm as bitter as the bitterest aubergine, I decide, as tears fuzz my eyes.

I get up and stride away from the window, then carry my mug upstairs, hoping my husband is at least horribly sweaty and chafey in those leather trousers. I hope he wakes up tomorrow with a terrible crotch rash and has to slosh the rest of that calamine lotion (*Sabrina's* calamine lotion) all over his dick. I am already planning my strategy: to be calm and aloof while he lies in bed, horribly hung over and clawing at his angry toilet parts. He has *never* danced with me that way. Not that I'd want him to – but still. I sip the dregs of my tepid Ovaltine. A bit of milky skin sticks to my lip.

In our bedroom now, I undress and pull my dressing gown tightly around me, then fetch my laptop and climb into bed with it. Sitting up, cross-legged, I click it on and skim through my inbox. There it is: the message from Fraser.

I know many years have passed. I understand that we both made decisions on the spur of the moment because we were so young and scared . . .

Tears are spilling onto my cheeks now. I rub them away with the back of my hand. All I can see is Will, pressing his face between that woman's pointy tits, like a dog trying to snaffle a biscuit that's slipped between the sofa cushions. What was he thinking? How drunk *is* he? I've been sloshed, yes. Very recently in fact. But I only paddled about in creosote and scared our neighbours.

I fully understand if you'd rather not be in touch again. I'd just like you to know that I have never forgotten you . . .

*

Before I can even consider what I'm doing, as if I have no control over my fingers at all, I type,

Hello Fraser,

Dad passed on your email. Yes, it's me – I'm Charlotte Bristow now. Quite a surprise to put it mildly but good to hear from you all the same. Anyway, here I am.

Charlotte

Chapter Twenty-Two

Will is home. The dancing bear has returned from the woods, having caroused with She-Bear – she's probably *blown on his porridge* – and is now making his way unsteadily to the kitchen. At least, I think he is. I am lying, ears pricked, in bed. It's 2.07 a.m. and I haven't slept at all. So what to do next?

Obvious options appear to be: 1. continue to lie here, pretending to be asleep and thus avoiding confrontation, possibly forever. Or, 2. storm downstairs and tell him precisely what I saw. No – can't do that. I will *not* admit that, while he attempted to devour some woman's cleavage, I was staring out through the window, sipping Ovaltine.

No, I shall just pretend I didn't see a thing. I'll carry on with my life, taking care of the kids and going to work; I shall be a model of dignity. On a positive note, at least none of the kids have woken up, despite him clattering about downstairs. It would be bad enough, Rosie and Ollie finding out – but we have a visitor here, who barely knows us. I could do without Delph finding out about Will's erotic display and spreading it around the modelling world about what an embarrassment Rosie's dad is. Things are tense enough around here as it is.

'Uhhh . . .' There's a groan from the stairs. Another sound comes: whimpering, like a small injured dog. I slip out of bed and creep towards the landing.

Will is lying in a heap on the stairs. His hair is askew, plastered to his forehead with sweat, and there's a drink spillage on the front of his T-shirt. I observe the scene, wondering why I feel so different about my husband, who clearly needs urgent assistance, from when one of the children has hurt themselves or been upset for some reason. It *is* different, though. Kids need you. They might be unfeeling and selfish and make you crave strong drink, in huge quantities, but they don't do it on purpose. Once, when I had to fill in a form at the doctors' reception, I pulled out a tampon instead of a pen from my bag and tried to write with it. 'That's not a pen,' Ollie yelled. 'That's one of them things ladies stick up their bums!' Mortifying, yes, but he was only trying to *help*.

Will flinches and moans again. God, I'm going to have to deal with this. 'Will,' I whisper, crouching beside him, 'are you okay?'

'Urrrr,' he mumbles.

'You need to get up. You can't sleep here. One of the kids'll see . . .'

He hugs at the stair. ''S'all right. Did you email him then?'

'What?'

'Him. Fraser. Did you say he can see her?' He fixes me with a glazed stare.

'I did reply,' I murmur, 'but let's not talk about that now—'

'Why not? We need to, it's important!'

'*Shhhh*,' I hiss at him, terrified that Rosie will overhear. 'I know it is, but we're not discussing it now, on the stairs, when you're off your face. You must be kidding. Come to bed, Will. I'll get you some water—'

'I did something bad,' he cuts in.

'Yes, I know, I saw—'

'No, you didn't, you don't know . . .' What *is* he on about now? Maybe him smooching with that woman was just the warm-up, and he went off and did it with her in the downstairs loo or out in the garden or something. Or even in the shed! Which would be horrific, obviously . . . but right now, all I care about is shovelling him off to bed.

'Come on, Will. We'll talk about it tomorrow.' He remains inert. 'You're going to wake everyone up,' I hiss.

'I'm sorry,' he warbles. 'I'm so, so sorry, Charlotte . . .' Slowly, I manage to coax my now trembling husband up into a sitting position.

'Don't worry, I've got you,' I whisper. 'Now try to stand up . . .'

Obediently, he stands. His eyes look strange – unfocused and not quite there – and he's sweating profusely. There's been another spillage, I realise now, down the left leg of his trousers. It all adds up to a highly attractive package. Trying to contain my annoyance, I manage to guide him through to our bedroom and onto the edge of our bed, where he sits, head bowed, looking down at his shoes. 'Will,' I murmur, 'how much did you drink?'

'Not much. Just a bit.'

'But you look completely out of it.'

He grimaces and flops back onto the bed. 'I'm having a really bad time.'

'What d'you mean? What have you *done*?' I peer at his face, wondering if it will ever regain its normal, healthy hue.

'Tommy said it'd be fine, he still does it on special occasions—'

'What,' I snap, 'shag strange women in downstairs bathrooms?'

He gawps at me, uncomprehending. 'I didn't . . .'

'What did you do, then?'

'I took an E.'

It takes a moment for this to sink in. 'You took an *E*? For God's sake, Will! What is this, 1988?'

'No, but Tommy said—'

'You're a bit too old to succumb to peer pressure,' I exclaim. 'Do they do this regularly then, with Zach and his friends in the house?'

'No, they'd all gone off to some other party—' He stops abruptly and lurches off the bed, clattering to the bathroom where he retches loudly into the loo.

I scurry after him – he's left the door wide open – and find him propped unsteadily against the washbasin. 'Dad?' Rosie is standing in the doorway now, her face stricken. 'What's happening? What's wrong with him, Mum?'

Delph appears beside her in a tiny vest and pair of pink knickers. 'Ew, God, has your dad just puked?'

'It's nothing,' I say quickly. 'He's fine, girls. Just go back to bed . . .'

Ollie's door opens and he pads towards us, rubbing at an eye with his fist. 'Is Dad sick? Has he caught what I've got?'

'Go back to your rooms,' I say firmly. 'Come on, there's nothing to see—'

'Has he got a fever?' Ollie wants to know. 'Maybe you should take his temperature . . .'

Hmm, where could I possibly stick the thermometer . . .

'Sorry,' Will mutters. 'Sorry, everyone. I'm fine. I'm just a bit, uh, tired . . .' He glowers at me, as if *I'm* the one who's guzzled class As and vomited, then he totters out of the bathroom and stumbles downstairs, mumbling, 'Just leave me alone.'

With a shrug, Ollie shuffles off to bed. I look at Delph, then at Rosie, who are making no move to go anywhere. '*Mum?*' Rosie mouths at me. 'What the hell's wrong with Dad?'

'Is he pissed?' Delph asks with a smirk.

'No, he's not pissed,' I reply.

'What is it then?' Rosie demands.

I rearrange my face in the hope of conveying an expression of extreme calm. 'I'm not sure, darling, but it's nothing to worry about. It's probably just something he ate.'

*

We are driving. Or, rather, I am; Will is huddled in the passenger seat, his face a strange colour that I don't know the name of. It's a sort of peaky, greenish-grey, like something from a Farrow and Ball colour chart. Bone or Elephant's Breath. I think Tricia might have chosen it for their back door. And it's *fine*, for woodwork, but not so great for a face.

I don't know where we're going but we had to do *something*. We couldn't stay in the house, with the kids gawping and firing questions and refusing to go back to bed – and on no account do I want Rosie and Ollie finding out that their father has been merrily chomping down ecstasy. The fuss they made, about me nibbling one measly little herbal bun . . . what would they make of this? All I could think of was to throw on some jeans, plus a sweater over my pyjama top, and explain that I was taking Dad out for 'some air'. I bundled my dazed, frightened husband into the car and drove him away, as if he were a fretful baby who was refusing to go to sleep.

'Where are we going?' Will mutters.

'I don't know.' I glance out to my right. An elderly man is leaning against a wheelie bin, smoking, and a young couple are wandering along arm in arm.

'Are you taking me to hospital?' he asks in a small voice.

'No. Unless you think I need to? Are you saying you need your stomach pumped? Because I'm sure that could be arranged, Will—'

'No thank you,' he snaps. We slump into silence as he lowers the passenger window. Looks like he's perking up a little. It was only an E, after all, which I presume to mean singular, so maybe it's wearing off already. Let's hope it doesn't have any worrying side effects. While I don't profess to be up-to-date on such matters – witness my 'pot' faux pas – I assume it was manufactured in someone's kitchen in Britain rather than smuggled into the country stuffed up someone's arse. But what if it was? What if it's travelled through an entire digestive system? I stop at red lights and study Will's face. He looks, whilst not the epitome of rude health, not quite on the brink of death either. 'Maybe we should go home,' he suggests flatly.

'In a bit,' I reply. 'Let's . . . oh, I don't know. I don't know what I'm doing, Will. Look – that café's open . . .'

'Looks horrible.'

'Yes, well, I'm not feeling too fussy right now. I'm not exactly insisting on a Michelin star. Let's just go and have a cup of tea.' Perhaps, I reflect as I park in front of the café, I'm just a tedious, Ovaltine-sipping middle-aged woman who needs to take a look at herself. He thinks: party time! Gimme drugs. I think: what I'd really love now is a nice hot beverage.

The all-night café has yellowing polystyrene ceiling tiles and smeary red Formica tables. At 3.17 a.m. it is devoid of any other customers. We are served by a man with a mop of black, oil-slicked hair and a strong whiff of cigarettes on his breath. 'What d'you want?' he asks.

A cup of tea and a divorce. 'A pot of tea please.'

'Right. And you?' He darts a look at Will.

'Just-a-glass-of-tap-water-thank-you.'

The man frowns. 'That's all?'

'Yes thank you,' Will says wearily.

'It's just, you can't sit here for hours drinking tap water . . .'

I lean towards Will. 'Maybe have something to eat. Something plain. It might settle your stomach . . .' I grab the sticky laminated menu and quickly scan it: virtually everything is fried. What does Rupert say the word 'fry' conjures up? 'Greasy, artery-clogging and frankly pretty horrid.'

'How about tomatoes on toast?' I suggest, as if Will is incapable of deciding for himself.

'What kind of tomatoes are they?' Will asks the man.

He peers at Will. 'They're *tomatoes.*'

'Yes, but—'

'They're tomatoes,' the man mutters, 'out of a tin.'

‘Oh,’ Will says bleakly.

‘Sounds *great*,’ I say over-enthusiastically, feeling more and more like Will’s carer by the second, and turning back to him the instant the man has gone. ‘What kind did you think they’d be?’

Will shrugs and fiddles with the greasy pepper pot.

‘It was hardly likely to be some rare breed pedigree thing garnished with fresh basil.’

He blinks at me. ‘You don’t get breeds of tomatoes. They’re not cattle, Charlotte. You get *varieties*.’

‘Sorry,’ I say hotly. ‘Anyway . . .’ I clear my throat, grateful that café man has disappeared into the kitchen, ‘you said earlier that you did something bad . . .’

‘Uh?’

‘At Sabrina and Tommy’s. You said you did a bad thing and I assume it wasn’t drawing on the walls or pulling someone’s hair or—’

‘I told you,’ he hisses, leaning towards me, ‘I took that . . . *stuff*.’

‘Yes, and apart from that, I happened to look out and see you dancing.’ I am aware of blinking rapidly.

‘What?’

‘I mean, when I say dancing, you were actually clamped together with some woman, virtually having sex.’

Will looks aghast. ‘What are you on about?’

I inhale deeply as our drinks, and Will’s tomatoes on toast, are plonked down in front of us. There are splatters of pinkish juice all over the plate, suggesting that the tomatoes were thrown at the toast from a great height. ‘I *saw* you, Will,’ I add as the man marches off. ‘I know it sounds pathetic but I happened to glance out and there you were, doing this hot, sexy dance with a woman . . .’

'I don't do hot sexy dancing,' he barks, causing the man to snigger from behind the counter.

'No, I didn't think so either but I saw it with my own eyes. It was hot, Will. *Steaming*. It's a wonder you didn't melt your trousers . . .'

He is staring at me. I know I should stop, and that the café man is standing there, smirking openly at us. But I can't.

'Leather doesn't melt,' Will mutters.

'Was it Sabrina? Is that who you were dancing with?'

He shakes his head vehemently, like one of those velvety toy dogs you see in the backs of cars. 'You think I fancy *Sabrina*?'

'I have no idea, Will. Maybe you do!'

'You've gone bloody insane,' he declares.

I sip my weak tea. 'She is very attractive. And it's fine, if you *are* attracted to her. I mean, at least I'd know . . .' I tail off.

'I definitely wasn't dancing with Sabrina.' He lifts his glass of water with a quivering hand. 'At least, I don't think I was.'

'Well, I saw you with *someone* . . .'

'Yes, you've said that. I think we've established that fact.'

'So who was it?'

Will sighs. 'Look, it's all a bit hazy, okay? Can we stop discussing this now, please? I'm not feeling too good.'

I glare down at his untouched snack. There are two plastic bottles on our table: a red one for ketchup and a yellow one, on which someone has written in fat black felt tip SALAD CREAM. Will is studying it as if it were a fascinating artefact in a museum. A Roman condiment, perhaps. His face softens, and there's a flicker of something in his eyes – regret, perhaps, as if he might be on the verge of saying sorry, and let's forget it and just go home . . . And maybe, I think, I've misread the whole situation, and all he was doing was messing about. So what if he took a stupid drug and danced like a lunatic? We all do mad things sometimes. What about me, getting myself covered in creosote?

'Will?' I say tentatively.

He wrenches his gaze away from the table. 'Can you believe it?' he says.

'Believe what?'

'That.' He jabs a shaky finger towards the yellow bottle.

'What about it?'

'They actually have salad cream here.'

I gawp at him. Thankfully, the man has disappeared again. He doesn't strike me as someone who'd take kindly to having his sauces mocked. 'So?' I ask.

'Who has salad cream in this day and age?'

For some reason, this throwaway comment enrages me far more than it should. 'It's just a dressing, Will. Some people like it, you know. I mean, it's not an illegal substance.' *Unlike some other things I could name.*

He shrugs. 'It's disgusting.'

'No it's not. My parents always had salad cream. Still do, probably, and it's perfectly okay for them. In fact, if I had a bit of lettuce in front of me right now I'd *drown* it in salad cream, and bloody delicious it'd be too!'

He reels back in his chair. 'Jesus, I only—'

'It says a lot!' I exclaim. 'It really does, Will. You have no idea what it says about you . . .'

'What the hell—'

'Your attitude towards salad cream,' I rant on, 'gives

away more about you as a person than you realise, and it's *not* very flattering—'

'My attitude to salad cream?' He is staring at me now, clearly having recovered from his chemically-enhanced adventure. In fact, he's actually *smirking* at me, after nuzzling some woman's sticky-out tits and throwing up in our washbasin in front of our kids, *and* a visitor, who's a personal friend of Marc Jacobs by all accounts. Without stopping to think what I'm doing, I've grabbed the salad cream bottle, pointed it at Will like a weapon and given it an almighty squeeze.

'What the fuck, Charlotte!' He leaps up and stares, dismayed, at his T-shirt. It's splattered with yellow goo. The retro creamy condiment is dripping slowly downwards, and there's a little daub of it on the front of his trousers, as if a bird has plopped there. Grabbing my bag, I pull out my purse, slam a tenner on the table and march out of the café, with my husband in pursuit.

'You are fucking crazy,' he snarls as we climb into the car.

'Probably, yes.'

'You're a bloody child. You've never grown up, that's your problem—'

'And you've behaved perfectly maturely tonight,' I snap back.

'What about you? I seem to remember you getting pissed in the garden with Liza and Sabrina and bashing your head on the door. When did you last see me so drunk I fell over and hurt myself?' I cannot respond to that. I just drive on, my knuckles shining white as I grip the steering wheel. My mouth tastes foul; I think the milk in my tea was off.

'At least I'm not injured,' he adds piously. *No, but you may be, before the night's out.*

I am so furious now, I can hardly breathe, let alone utter actual words. How could I have imagined myself with him in a saucy shed situation, cushioned only by a sack of chicken manure fertiliser? I actually thought it might be sexy, doing it with him in a small, enclosed space filled with spiders. Christ, I wouldn't get naked with him now if we were offered an entire floor of the Savoy. Anyway, he's probably getting his excitement elsewhere. I bet dancing wasn't all he did tonight. What does he enjoy? Foraging. Maybe that's what he was doing. Foraging about in that woman's pants . . .

The flat London sky is beginning to lighten. 'So,' he blurts out, 'did you email him back?' My stomach lurches.

'Email who back?' I ask, knowing precisely who he means.

'Your ex.'

I nod. 'Yes, I did.'

'Is Rosie going to meet him, then?'

'I suppose so,' I say quietly. 'In fact, she's said she wants to . . .'

Even without looking I can sense his expression changing. 'What – recently?'

'Yes, just before I set off for Bournemouth . . .'

'Why didn't you tell me?' he exclaims.

'Because . . . I knew you'd be upset.'

'For Christ's sake, Charlotte – this is *massive.* It'll change our whole lives. Didn't you think I should know?'

I inhale deeply, catching a vinegary whiff from the salad cream. 'Yes, of course I did. And I know I should've told you straight away. But at the moment – well, for a while actually, but especially since you left work, I've found it really hard to talk to you . . .'

'So it's my fault then,' he snaps.

'It's no one's fault,' I reply, trying to keep my voice steady. 'It's not about blaming anyone. It's just happened, like we always knew it would. And she's asked about Fraser before, you know that—'

'Yeah, just innocent, childish questions—'

'But she's not a child anymore,' I cut in, my eyes filling with tears. 'She wants to meet Fraser, to find out what he's like . . .' I pause. 'It's only natural, Will. I mean, we've talked about this, and we said we'd help her to find him and deal with it together . . .'

'That was different,' he says flatly, and I realise now that of course, he's right: he was fine about Rosie meeting Fraser *in theory*. But it's not in theory anymore; it's real. We fall into silence as I turn into our road and park in front of our house. It occurs to me, as we stomp indoors, that this probably wasn't what Sabrina had in mind when she said we needed a date night.

Chapter Twenty-Three

Dear Charlotte,
Lovely to hear from you. And quite a surprise, to be honest. I wasn't sure whether you'd want to contact me or if your dad would even pass it on. So, where to start? I know it's been a hell of a long time but I've wanted to get in touch so many times over the years. I've just never quite known how to go about it, or how you'd react if I did. The truth is, I never stopped thinking about you . . .

I've wondered about him over the years too – or, more accurately, why he asked Mummy to write me that letter. And the possibilities I've come up with are:

1. She was horrified at the thought of him becoming a young dad when he had 'a promising future ahead of him' (obviously, as far as she was concerned, I didn't have any future at all) and forbade him to see me. And although he was nineteen, and perfectly

capable of travelling all over Europe by himself, he was a good boy and did as she asked.

2. He asked her to write it because he was too embarrassed to admit that he'd found himself another girlfriend called Perdita with a swishy mane of golden hair and a cabinet full of gymkhana trophies.

As my husband sleeps off his chemically-induced hangover, I am feeling unusually measured and calm. The kids are having a lie-in too, and there's an aura of stillness as I stretch out on the sofa with my laptop and read on.

So how are things are in your life? I assume you're married and fantastically successful. You were always so smart – far smarter than me when it came to travelling around and finding somewhere to stay and getting us sorted. Remember that room I found us in Pigalle and it turned out to be a brothel, with a peephole in the wall and all those frantic noises in the night? And the time I left my passport in that bar? Anyway, you know how to contact me now. I'd love to see you for a coffee, just to catch up. But of course I understand completely if you'd rather not—

At the sound of someone coming downstairs, I quickly shut my laptop. 'Hi, Mum. Is Dad all right?' Ollie wanders in and flops down beside me.

'Yes, he's fine, love. At least, he will be. He just needs to sleep it off.'

He nods. 'It's good that he was sick, if he's got food poisoning.'

'Yes.'

'Being sick's how the body gets rid of bacteria before it can be absorbed in the bloodstream. It's what we're designed to do. The diaphragm goes up and down and the abdomen contracts and food shoots out, it's called projectile vomiting—'

'Yes, Ollie, I know.' I muster a smile and test his forehead with the flat of my hand. 'So how are you feeling? You were awfully hot last night.'

'I'm fine now.'

'That's good, darling.' I put my arm around him as he rests his head on my shoulder. It's a breezy, sunny morning, and I'm seized by an urge to get out of the house, away from Will for a few hours. 'D'you want to do something today?' I ask.

'Yeah, like what?'

'I don't know. You're on holiday, we've got the whole day ahead of us.' I shrug. 'We can do anything really.'

Ollie sits up. Such a handsome boy with his clear, grey-blue eyes, a scattering of freckles and a big, wide smile. 'All right. Shall we go swimming? To that big new place with the flumes?'

'Um . . . are you sure that's what you want to do, after having a temperature last night?'

'Yeah, I'm fine! Can Saul come?'

'Yes, of course he can. I'll call Maria now . . .'

'Um, Mum?' he says as I place my laptop on the table. 'You're not going to, er . . . swim *with* us, are you?'

I laugh. 'No, don't worry. I'm not planning to put you to shame with my record-beating front crawl.'

He laughs. 'I mean, you don't even have to come. We'd be fine going on our own.'

'Listen,' I say, scrolling for Maria's number on my phone, 'I'll take you but I won't put so much as a toe in the water, okay? I'll see if Liza wants to come too and we can have a coffee in the café.' After dispatching a glass of water and toast to the sick bay – which Will accepts with rather sheepish thanks – we set off, collecting Saul and Liza on the way.

Compared to last night's greasy spoon, the swimming pool's café is an oasis of loveliness. Slightly over-heated, perhaps, but at least it's making me sweat out my ill feelings towards Will. 'You're kidding,' Liza exclaims. 'Will took ecstasy? *Your* Will? Are you sure?'

'Yeah, I know. It's completely bizarre.'

'But people don't start taking drugs at forty-one years old. They kind of . . . build up to it. In fact, no – they might have a go at it when they're young, then they get to a point when they start tapering off because they can't handle it anymore and they're scared of looking stupid.'

'Well,' I retort, 'there's been no building up or tapering off with him. He's just dived in and done it. Voluntarily, too. I mean, I'm assuming Tommy didn't sit on him and force it into his mouth . . . God, I wonder what his mother would say?'

Liza splutters. 'I still can't believe it. He seemed fine when I was there. A bit pissed, sure, but okay. Why did he do it, d'you think?'

I shrug. 'No idea. In fact, I don't really care. I'm more concerned about the fact that I don't seem to know him at all. Don't you think that's a bit . . . *worrying*?'

'Oh, come on.' She touches my arm. 'It was just one mad night . . .'

'I saw him dancing with someone too,' I add, going on to describe his erotic display, and our jolly jaunt to the all-night café where I squirted him with salad cream.

She convulses with horrified laughter. 'He must've

been off his head. If he took ecstasy on top of all the beers he'd had at the venue . . . It doesn't *mean* anything.'

I shrug and cup my coffee. 'That's what they all say.'

'It's true, though. God, Charlotte, you know he'd never do anything to jeopardise the two of you. He might not always show it, but you know he's devoted to you. And he was only *dancing* . . .'

'Yes, but the dance involved him squashing his head in her cleavage.'

'Oh.' We both glance down at the pool where Ollie and Saul are lying on floats, drifting languidly like a couple of middle-aged friends on sun loungers. 'Maybe it was the leather trousers that sent him a bit mad,' Liza adds.

'Yeah, possibly,' I say, managing a smile. 'Um . . . there's something else. I've heard from Fraser again . . .'

She frowns, studying me. 'You want to see him, don't you?'

'Sort of. Yes, I suppose I do . . .'

'Because Will was off his face?'

'Of course not! That's nothing to do with it at all.'

'Because . . .' Liza adds, obviously choosing her words carefully, 'you wouldn't make such a monumental decision on the basis of him acting like an idiot just for one night . . . would you?'

'No,' I declare, a shade too loudly. A little boy in a buggy slides a choc ice out of his mouth and stares at us.

'So you wouldn't do it for . . . *revenge* or anything?'

'Of course not,' I insist. 'I'd see him because he's Rosie's dad. You know she wants to make contact with him . . .'

Liza nods.

'Well, if I meet him first, I'll be able to suss out if he's a decent man and if it's okay for Rosie to get to know him.'

'Well, that makes sense,' she says cautiously.

I turn to watch a woman dive, in a perfect arc, into the deep end. I'm feeling better already, about Will's indiscretion; it no longer feels like an earth-shattering event. Liza has the knack of helping me to put things in some kind of perspective. Plus, I'm no longer racked with guilt over my email exchange with Fraser. If I do meet him, it'll only be to check out whether he'll be a positive presence in Rosie's life. I'd be conducting an assessment – *interviewing* him, if you like. It all feels quite sensible and grown up.

Out of the corner of my eye, I spot Ollie hauling himself out of the pool. He sees me and Liza and waves. 'How lovely that he still acknowledges you in public,' she says with a smile.

'Yes, I know. He's a great boy.'

She turns to me with a look that tells me a difficult question is coming. 'So, if you do arrange to meet Fraser, will you tell Will?'

I hesitate. 'Yes, but *after* I've met him, I think. There's no point in a big drama now – and anyway, we're hardly on the best of terms . . .'

'Well, if you're sure you feel okay about that.'

I drain my cup, watching an exhausted-looking woman chasing two excitable young children who make straight for the vending machine. They proceed to shake it, as if that'll make all the Galaxy bars tumble out. 'I'm not sure about anything, Liza,' I say. 'It just feels like something I have to do.'

*

Will appears to be on best behaviour when I arrive home with the boys. 'Sorry about last night,' he says as we start to prepare dinner together. I notice that he has left a small pause, into which I am perhaps supposed to insert, *And I'm sorry too, for being so immature as to squirt you with 70s condiment. It was wrong and I am thoroughly ashamed of myself.* But I don't. Anyway, a call from Rosie's agency quickly dispels any lingering hint of tension.

'I've got a casting on Monday,' she announces. 'It's a massive job. I can't believe it!'

'That's fantastic,' I say, hugging her. 'What's it for?'

'Billboards. An ad campaign for that new mall they're building, the one that's going to be bigger than Bluewater . . .' I beam at her, delighted to see my daughter looking so radiant and happy.

'Well done, darling,' Will says, clearly not grasping its significance.

'I probably won't get it,' she adds, trying to rein in her excitement, 'but Laurie said they're really keen to see me. Oh, and those knitting people wanted me again, for another pattern book or something, but I said I'm not doing that.'

I frown at her. 'You turned down a job? Are you sure that was okay?'

'Yeah. Delph said it wouldn't do my profile any good . . .' How bizarre, to hear my daughter talking of having a *profile.* She brightens again. 'Anyway, I really want this other one. The billboard thing, I mean. Laurie thinks I'm their kind of girl . . .' Her face bursts into a huge smile.

'Well, that's that, then,' I exclaim. 'Sounds like you'll get the job!' We dissolve into whoops of excitement, Will's saucy dancing and Fraser's emails disappearing from my mind, at least for now.

Chapter Twenty-Four

The house is all quiet early on Saturday morning as I curl up on the sofa and compose an email.

Hi Fraser,

Thanks for your email. Yes, I think meeting for coffee would be a good idea as, obviously, we have things to discuss. Are you still in Manchester? I'm in East London. Are you down here often? Let me know what works for you.

Charlotte

Hi Charlotte, comes the speedy reply.

Lovely to hear from you again. I'm so glad you want to meet. As I've mentioned before, I have wanted to get in touch with you for years now, and seeing the magazine was the trigger I needed.

I divide my time between Cheshire and London these days. I've been working in the City the past few years and I have a flat in Battersea. Anyway, I'd love to know more about your life now, and your family and what you're doing . . . but I guess you'll tell me if and when you feel ready.

Also, I want you to know I don't blame you one bit.

Yours,

Fraser x

I frown at his last sentence. Blame me for what? For getting pregnant after we'd only known each other for a few short months? This implies I *stole* his sperm and impregnated myself, and that the poor mite had nothing to do with it. Or does he mean me scoffing that space cake? I *love* cake, always have, and didn't imagine anything involving eggs, flour and butter – innocently baked – would result in me sliding off a chair in a café and lying on the floor laughing. Has he decided to forgive me for that?

Another email pings in: *I know this is a long shot but I have some time off next week . . . is there any chance we could meet up then? Or would that be completely out of the question?*

It's wrong, I know it is. But I need to see him.

Okay, I type, *how about Caffe Nero in Long Acre on Monday, 2 p.m.?*

Good choice, I decide. Huge, busy and impersonal.

Perfect, he replies, see you then. Fx

Business concluded, I have a rather stilted breakfast with Will – the kids have yet to emerge from their rooms – then head out to the local shops. I can't be around Will right now. I know it's terrible, arranging to meet Fraser in secret when I took time off to hang out with my family and be useful at home. I wouldn't feel quite as guilt-ridden if I didn't experience a whoosh of excitement whenever an email from Fraser pops in. Although he irritates me slightly – what with 'dividing his time' between two homes, the posh knob – my heart still leaps every time he gets in touch. I wish I could treat his emails in the same way as the relentless INCREASE GIRTH AND LENGTH NOW!! spam which floods my inbox daily. But I can't.

I *have* to see Fraser. I need to know why he cut off contact so abruptly, and why he just stopped wanting me. And I'm kidding myself by pretending it's all for Rosie. Perhaps – despite insisting that I don't care, that I *despise* him, actually – the truth is that I've never truly got over the miserable, spineless rat-bag deserter after all.

I stroll past our local, rather uninspired shops, and walk for another twenty minutes or so to the villagey area with its fancy boutiques and artisan bakers. There's a homewares shop which seems to sell little more than antique cut-glass perfume bottles and brocade cushions. There are galleries, shockingly pricey boutiques and fancy delicatessens. I buy a sourdough loaf with the density of sandstone, and an apple tart in a flat white box from a new French patisserie.

Greengrocer's next. Here, I carefully avoid choosing anything which Will is capable of growing at home: lettuce, for instance. That's the effect my correspondence with Fraser is having on me. It's making me paranoid about the tiniest things. For instance, if I bought, say, some rocket, would Will glower at it and remark, 'But we have plenty in our garden . . . or aren't my leaves good enough for you?'

God, it's exhausting. Who'd have thought salad could be controversial? If I could only rattle off a quick email to Fraser saying BUGGER OFF OUT OF MY LIFE, then at least I wouldn't feel so bad, even though I haven't really done anything – *yet.* Whereas my husband, as I keep reminding myself, gobbled mind-altering chemicals and made a complete spectacle of himself with a mystery female in full view of our street.

I glance down at a wicker basket laden with mangoes. At least I'm on safe ground with fruit, because Will doesn't grow any yet, apart from plums, which are yet to appear. In fact, being in close proximity to so much over-priced produce is making me feel a little more wholesome. It occurs to me, as I fondle various prime specimens, that that's precisely what I am actually doing here: i.e., not buying mangoes because anyone particularly likes them (disappointing flesh-to-stone ratio) but because it's the kind of thing good mothers/wives do. They take their mangoes home and cut them up and everyone sits around slurping them in the garden. That would impress Tricia – to see all of us enjoying the sunshine, whilst snacking on exotic fruit.

Yep, that's what we'll do. Mangoes are far more pleasing than reject crisps. Starting to make my way home, I decide to try to make amends with Will as soon as I get back. As he's kindly pointed out, I am perfectly capable of making an arse of myself too; witness my drunken head gash. Feeling more positive now, I stop off to buy a bottle of Chablis for us to enjoy in the garden later. I shall present these fine offerings to him as peacemaking gifts. Maybe a relaxed evening together will help to thaw things between us. Yet, as I stride along with my expensive provisions, I still feel like a very bad person indeed.

I have asked Fraser to meet me for coffee behind Will's back. Glancing down into my bag, I'm wondering now if Will even likes sourdough. Didn't he comment once that it was 'heavy'? Then I see it, parked on the gravelled forecourt outside the church: a white van, with *Donate Blood Here* on its side. *That's* what I could do. That would cancel out the guilt, more effectively than any amount of produce from Roots 'n' Fruits.

I stop and watch people drifting in and out of the church. It might be my imagination, but they look like good people. They save human lives, after all. As I make my way towards the entrance, it occurs to me that, if they drain off some of my bad blood – the guilt-tinged blood that's currently bubbling through my veins – then my body will replace it with nice clean fresh stuff. And perhaps, miraculously, the new blood my body produces will stop me wanting to see Fraser quite so much.

There's a small queue at the booking-in desk. 'Have you donated blood before?' the woman asks.

'Yes,' I reply, 'but a long time ago.' I give her my details and she checks the screen and finds me. I'm given a form, and perch on a plastic chair at the end of the row while I fill it in. A young woman with a swingy blonde bob takes me into a little booth where she pricks my thumb with a hand-held machine. She studies the digital display. 'Ah, sorry,' she says, 'your haemoglobin's too low.' She smiles reassuringly. 'Your iron level – it's nothing to worry about, but I'm afraid you can't donate blood today.'

For some reason, even though I know I'm being silly – it could probably be rectified by scoffing a pile of spinach which, as luck would have it, Will grows in abundance – I am hugely disappointed by this news. Everywhere I look, posters are pinned up saying DONATE

BLOOD TODAY AND SAVE A LIFE. I want to donate mine, but no one wants it. And it's not really about iron. I know this. It's because I am a terrible person who's planning to sneak off and meet her ex.

I glance around the hall where row upon row of people are lying on beds, having their lovely iron-rich blood drained out of them. At one end of the room a cluster of people are sipping tea, tucking into chocolate biscuits and having a jolly chat. There are bursts of laughter. It looks an outing in itself.

'Charlotte! Whoo-hoo!'

I scan the hall. 'Over here!' I arrange my face into a smile as Sabrina strides towards me, chomping away on a Wagon Wheel.

'Hi, Sabrina. I was just leaving actually—'

'Oh, we can walk home together if you're heading back. God, don't you *love* Wagon Wheels? I'd forgotten how good they are!'

'Actually,' I tell her, 'I haven't been able to give blood. There wasn't enough iron in it, apparently.'

'Aw, aren't they fussy these days?' she asks as we step outside.

'Seems like it,' I say, wondering if Sabrina took ecstasy the other night too. If so, it seems a little unfair that a whole armful of blood has been drained out of her when mine hasn't had a sniff of an illegal drug since that measly little muffin in 1996.

'So how come you're not at work?' she asks as we make our way home.

'I've taken some time off, seeing as it's the start of the holidays.'

She smiles. 'Quite right too. Bet Will's pleased . . .'

'Yes, he seems to be. Um . . . Sabrina? Can I ask you

something about the other night? After Zach's gig, I mean?'

She nods. 'Sure.'

I'm not about to lower myself to admitting that I stood there, sipping my malted drink while my husband flailed about with another woman. Maybe it *was* Sabrina. I no longer care. Bet they were all off their faces and hardly remember anything anyway. Liza was right – even if it was her, it didn't mean anything. But I do need to know how Will came to mistake a Thursday night in an ordinary East London terraced house for a rave in a field – *twenty-five years ago*. I hadn't even realised people still took ecstasy. According to Rosie, these days it's all about smoking 'cheese'.

I glance at Sabrina who seems perfectly bright and perky, even with depleted blood. 'It's just, Will was pretty out of it when he came home that night,' I venture.

She glances at me. 'Oh, God. Sorry about that. I wasn't sure he'd be able to handle it. But he seemed like he needed to let his hair down, you know?'

Yep, what he *really* needed was a pill that would make him cuddle the stairs and cry like a little baby.

'A mate of Tommy's brought them,' she adds. 'We don't indulge. Well, not often. You can't at our age, can you?'

'Er, no,' I say, as if Will and I are faced with a similar dilemma on a regular basis.

'Anyway,' she adds breezily, 'as long as he was okay . . .'

'Well, no, he was sick actually.'

'God, really? Poor Will!'

'He's recovered now,' I add quickly.

She smiles. 'Well, at least he had fun. I wish you'd been able to stay. We saw quite a different side to him, y'know. He's a scream.' He is indeed. 'Fancy a coffee?' she adds as we reach our street.

'Sure,' I say, deciding the wine can wait. Maybe Sabrina will shed some more light on what was going on with Will the other night.

'I think Rosie's at our place, hanging out with Zach . . .'

'Oh, that's nice.' *What are they doing?* I want to ask. Will, I notice, seems to have relinquished his role as Highly Protective Dad. This shift in attitude appears to have coincided with his new-found love of leather trousers and dirty dancing. Not to worry, though, because it's all cheery smiles as Sabrina lets us in, and we find Rosie and Zach in the kitchen, drinking tea and munching toast. The scene could not appear more innocent if a game of Ludo were set out on the table. 'Hey, Mum,' Rosie says with a big smile.

'Hi, darling. I just ran into Sabrina at the blood bank.'

'Mum's got this *thing* about giving blood,' Zach remarks with a smirk.

'No, I haven't,' she retorts. 'I just needed to get out. Been working on sketches for the new collection since six this morning . . .' She grins at me. 'Want to come up and see?'

'I'd love to,' I say. 'C'mon, Rosie, let's have a look.' We all head up to the loft conversion, which is more grotto than studio – a magpie's nest lined with snowy feathers and glittery beads. Light floods in through a large Velux window. Wedding dress sketches are pinned on the walls, and lengths of velvet ribbon and lace hang from row upon row of brass hooks. 'What a beautiful room,' I exclaim.

'It's amazing,' Rosie agrees, touching scraps of marabou feather strewn over a full-length mirror with an ornate gilt frame. Then she flits back downstairs – clearly, Zach is more enticing than drawings of dresses – leaving Sabrina and I alone.

'So what d'you think?' She shows me her latest sketches on her drawing board. They are lavish creations, frothy with feathers and tulle and intricately embellished. While they're not quite my taste, for a woman who wanted a fantasy dress – the frock of fairytales – they would be perfect.

'I think they're gorgeous,' I say truthfully.

'Well, I hope so. This is the kind of thing we do best – the full-on, traditional bride, really.' She pauses. 'Look, Charlotte, I didn't mean to be flippant about Will being sick the other night. I'm sorry, we shouldn't have encouraged him.'

I shrug. 'He's a grown man, Sabrina. It was no one else's fault.'

'Well, he was quite keen, you know, to try one . . .'

'Idiot,' I say with a grin.

'They're all the same, darling.' She hugs me, and I decide right then that Sabrina wasn't Will's saucy dance partner. She just couldn't be. She's too open and damn well *nice* to have virtually copulated with him and then be super-friendly to my face. And if he has a bit of a thing for her, and wants to impress her – hence the leather trouser aberration? Well, we're all allowed to have crushes. They make us feel young and alive. Which makes me feel *slightly* better about meeting up with the first man I ever loved.

*

I find Will in the garden. His arm, warm and lightly tanned, brushes against mine as we sit side by side on the bench. He looks especially handsome today, his white T-shirt showing off his honeyed skin to best effect.

'Rosie and Zach seem pretty close,' I muse.

Will nods. 'He seems like a decent boy. D'you think they're going out or just hanging out together?'

'God knows. She won't give anything away.' I watch a bee crawl into a mottled pink foxglove. 'She's probably snogged him,' I add.

'What? I'll bloody kill him . . .' Will breaks into a laugh.

Christ, I thought he was serious for a second.

'I'll *maim* that boy if he's kissed our girl,' he adds. *Our girl.* It warms my heart, the way he says it. There's still time to email Fraser and say I've changed my mind about that coffee.

'D'you think you can still get those iron chastity belts?' I ask with a smile.

'Not sure,' Will says. 'I could have a go at making one . . .'

'It was a hell of a lot easier when all she wanted to do was play Boggle,' I add.

'Yeah. Is she still over at his place?'

I nod. 'He's probably just showing her his collection of definitive stamps.'

'That's what I was thinking. Or hoping, at least.' We dream up more things they're doing – playing dominoes or Kerplunk – then Rosie texts to say she'll have dinner at Zach's, and Ollie heads off for a horror film marathon at Saul's. So this balmy Saturday evening is all about us, just like those long-ago evenings when we had no one to please but ourselves. Instead of cooking we just eat the sourdough with cheese, followed by mangoes and wine, sitting on the back step in the evening sun.

Later, we bring out a rug and lie on the lawn, aware of Gerald humming to himself as he scrubs out their bird bath. We fall into a dozy, companionable silence on this beautiful evening. I no longer care about the saucy dance or the drugs; maybe Will wanted to try ecstasy just the once, because it sounded interesting and fun – like the time I had a fish pedicure. God, it was disgusting, those nibbly, slithery things shoaling around my feet. I couldn't wait to get out.

Anyway, none of that matters now. I rest my head on Will's chest, deciding to tell him about Fraser as soon as I get back from Caffè Nero on Monday. There shouldn't be secrets. I *must* be nicer to him; I still wince at the thought of that salad cream. In fact, if we could enjoy evenings like this more often, I don't think I'd ever fret about the state of our marriage. Kids, a home to run, Will being out of work . . . is it any wonder we've fallen into a rut? These days, it's virtually impossible to have a conversation in private.

Later still, when the kids are home and asleep, I snuggle up to Will in bed. Maybe, I think, he might be feeling more, um, *relaxed* after our lovely evening together. So I make a move, and for a moment I think, this is good, he hasn't done that toasting-fork-flinching thing – then he looks at me and says, 'Still feeling a bit worn out from the other night actually.'

It would seem that my husband's hangovers now last *two* days.

Chapter Twenty-Five

Monday morning, and there's been a major volcanic eruption in London E11. 'Look at it, Mum!' Rosie wails, prodding at her chin. 'I *can't* go out like this . . .' She assesses the true horror of the situation in the reflective surface of our stainless steel kettle.

'It's just a blemish, love,' I remark. 'A tiny pimple. You can hardly see it with the naked eye.' In fact, it's more medium than tiny, as blemishes go. But still, hardly a national crisis.

She flumps down onto a kitchen chair. 'Don't patronise me, Mum. I can see what it is. It's not even a flat one. It sticks right up. Why did this have to happen today?'

'I'm not patronising you,' I retort. 'It *is* a pimple, Rosie. What else d'you want me to call it?'

'How about Roger?' Will says, smirking as he ambles into the kitchen. 'Or Barry? Or Dave?'

Rosie scowls and touches it gingerly. It's her casting today, for the shopping mall, no less. Her face could be on billboards all over London. 'Very funny, Dad,' she mutters.

'C'mon,' he offers, patting her hunched shoulder, 'it's really not that big.'

'Look, I know it's massive, okay? So let's just leave it at that.'

Will shrugs and rolls his eyes at me.

'Yeah,' Ollie says, breezing into the kitchen in his pyjamas, '*my* eyes are naked, and I can see it.'

'Thanks a lot,' Rosie snaps.

He snatches a piece of toast from the plate on the table and rips a bite out of it. 'You could probably see it from outer space,' he adds helpfully.

Rosie splutters. 'Can you make him go away, Mum? *Please?*'

I look at her. 'He does live here, love. Where d'you expect him to go?'

She groans loudly. 'Well, I'm not going to the casting today.'

'But you were so excited—'

'The thing is, Ro,' Ollie cuts in, munching away, 'you should be pleased about that spot.'

She glares at him.

'Spots are good,' he goes on, ''cause there's this stuff called sebum – oil, basically – and it blocks the pore and gets infected with bacteria. D'you know why it's swelled up with that little yellow bit on top?'

'What yellow bit?' Rosie glares at him as if he has slithered out from under the fridge.

'It's 'cause the white cells know there's bad stuff happening. They're all gathering together, like an army, and they're gonna fight it . . .'

Rosie closes her eyes, as if in prayer.

'. . . and that yellow bit's keeping it all inside and protected, like a lid.'

'I don't care what my cells are doing,' she snaps, 'and I don't want a fucking *lid* . . .'

'Rosie!' Will snaps. 'That's completely unnecessary.'

'Stop making such a huge drama out of it,' I add. 'You want to be a model and put yourself up for big jobs like this?'

'Yeah, 'course I do—'

'Well,' I charge on, 'that means being a bit more grown up and not over-reacting to every little thing—'

'Like seeds,' Ollie chuckles, jabbing at the jam jar on the table. 'We have to have this horrible jelly-type jam 'cause Rosie hates seeds . . .'

'Never mind seeds, Ollie.' I turn back to my daughter. 'It's not a big deal. A little dab of concealer and you'll be fine.'

'You're not meant to wear make-up on castings,' she retorts. 'Remember what happened at the agency when they made me scrub my face?'

'Yes, because that was *loads* of make-up and we're just talking about the teeniest dab of cover-up.'

'Anyway,' Will adds, 'surely they're used to seeing teenage girls?'

'Yuh?' she says with a shrug.

'Well,' he goes on, 'they'll be well aware that spots are just part of life . . .'

'And if you get the job and you've still got the spot,' Ollie adds, 'like, if it's the sort that lasts ages and ages, basically *scarring* the skin, then they can just Photoshop it out.'

'Oh, right,' she rounds on him, 'so you're the expert now?'

He nods. 'I know about Photoshop, yeah. We did that photography project and Mr Bailey got it on his computer and showed us—'

'And skin?' she snaps. 'So you're a dermatologist too?'

Ollie's face clouds. 'No, we just did the structure of skin at school, the dermis, the epidermis . . .'

'*Fascinating*.' With that, she flounces out of the kitchen, banging the door behind her.

'Christ,' Will mutters.

'I don't know what's going on with her,' I murmur, pouring a coffee.

Ollie shrugs. 'This toast's a bit bendy, Mum.'

'Yes, that's because it was made about an hour ago.' I sigh loudly and drop fresh slices into the toaster. 'I'm going up to see her. She needs to calm down. If she doesn't go to this casting she'll be really upset . . .'

'But that won't be *our* fault,' Ollie calls after me.

I find her hunched on her bed, picking at her nails, having freed her hair from its scrunchie so it falls all around her face, like a demented curtain. Perching beside her, I gently push a swathe of it out of her eyes. 'Hon, it *will* cover up. Come on, let me help you.'

She peers at me, bleary eyed. 'What d'you know about spots? You never get any.'

'That's because I'm thirty-eight, and I'm getting lines and wrinkles instead. Crevices, basically. Remember that geography trip you went on to Yorkshire last year? To Malham Cove?'

She nods.

'What was that thing there again? You did a study on it, drew all those cross-sectional diagrams—'

She smiles, despite herself. 'A geographic fissure.'

'Yes, well, that's what I'm looking at these days: *geographic fissures*, running from my nose to my mouth and right across my forehead, like furrows in a field.' I squeeze her hand. 'I'd be delighted to just have the odd spot to deal with, to be honest.'

Her smile lifts a little more. 'You don't have fissures, Mum. You've got lovely skin.'

'Well, it's not as fresh as it once was, but that's okay. I'm not obsessed with looking younger. I mean, it's not as if I'd *dream* of spending hundreds of quid on some stupid gold particle serum . . .'

She emits an actual laugh.

'So, come on – get your make-up bag and let's have a look . . .'

Reluctantly, she uncurls herself from her bed and fetches a red polka-dot purse from a drawer, from which she extracts a cheap concealer. It's a worrying shade of pink, like Windolene. 'D'you have some foundation as well? We might need to blend something to get the right shade.' She rummages through a box of bottles and tubs, finally pulling out a tube. I blend two products together on the back of my hand, then, using a small brush, dab a little onto the offending blemish. It's still there – just. But much reduced.

'That *is* better,' she says, almost begrudgingly, inspecting her face in her dressing table mirror. 'You can hardly see it unless you peer really close.'

'And no one's going to do that,' I reassure her, 'so you can get ready and go to your casting now.'

She turns and smiles and, in a gesture that almost causes my heart to burst, flings her arms around me. 'Thanks so much, Mum. I love you.'

'I love you too, darling.' And she's off, amidst good lucks from Will and me, and Ollie yelling after her, helpfully, 'I hope it *erupts* when you're at the casting and lava bursts out.'

Our house seems to empty very quickly after she's gone. Will is summonsed by his mother to clean her patio, which is apparently marred by a small patch of moss (sounds like a crisis on a par with Rosie's blemish). Then Maria and Saul arrive to whisk the boys off to a climbing wall in Victoria Park. Good, dutiful Will, assisting his mother, and good mum Maria, offering the boys a day of fun: so many kind, helpful people, which makes me feel even more despicable, sneaking off to meet Fraser. But it's only *coffee*, right? Nothing can happen in Caffè Nero with tons of people about on a rather grey Monday afternoon. I'll just be curt and polite and find out whether he might be prepared to meet Rosie at some point. Then straight home.

I'll be back before Will's even finished tackling that moss.

*

I set off in jeans, a plain pale grey T-shirt and not a scrap of make-up: i.e., nothing that might convey that I am excited about seeing Fraser and want him to find me attractive. In fact, I hope to give the opposite impression: that I'm a busy woman with a happy and fulfilled life and *no time for mascara*, thank you very much. This man certainly does not deserve lipstick.

It's only on the Tube that I start to fear that I may not be able to pull this off. I'm nervous – *hand-shakingly* nervous, in fact, as if I'm on my way to a job interview which, if I don't get it, will result in our home being repossessed and us having to give away Guinness because we can't even afford his dry food.

Seven years ago, I drove out to Essex to be interviewed for the position of Marketing Director of Crisps. *No need to be scared,* I told myself, having bought crippling black patent shoes and a rather uninspiring navy blue suit from Wallis for the occasion. *It doesn't matter if you get this job or not. There are plenty of others. Even if they offer it to you, you might not want it.*

I'd been a bag of nerves when I set off. My hands had been so sweaty I'd had to wipe them on the bit of old shirt I used to clean my windscreen. Miraculously, though, by the time I pulled into the car park at Archie's, I'd started to feel a whole lot better. I'd managed to shrink the interview right down in my mind until it had become a tiny, insignificant thing. Somehow, I'd wrung all the scariness out of it.

That's what I'm trying to do right now. I am attempting to shrink meeting Fraser down to a tiny chore which must be attended to, and will be forgotten as soon as it's done. No reason to feel edgy, I remind myself. As the train rattles along I try to picture a bloated Fraser, covered in warts with wiry hairs bushing out of his nostrils. Those posh teeth, I decide, will look weirdly fake against his battered old face, which has been worn to wrinkly folds from numerous exotic holidays.

When I knew him he dressed like a student in knackered old Levi's or baggy khaki shorts, and faded T-shirts proclaiming his love for Bowie, The Velvet Underground and Iggy Pop. These have now, I decide rather gleefully, been replaced by stiff striped shirts and chinos, classic posh boy attire. He's a Thomas Pink man, I reckon. As for shoes, I'm seeing moccasin-type things in quease-making mustard leather. *Fraser is a jerk,* I repeat in my head. *Fraser is a deserting bastardy arsehole.* I'll tell Will all about him as soon as he's back from Gloria's. Yes, he'll be annoyed, but I'll explain that it was something I had to do, and we'll delight in slagging him off together and discussing how hateful he is. It might even make us feel closer, united in our disdain of the dumper-of-pregnant-girls.

Anyway, it's only coffee, I remind myself as I get off the train.

It's drizzling when I step out of the station, and I can sense my hair frizzing instantly. Purple frizz, like a thistle. Attractive. No brush in my bag either (although what do I care about my hair being a mess?) and, for some reason, I didn't think to bring a jacket or even a cardi, probably because my mind was on other things. Like being a sneak and a liar and deceiving my husband, *and* Rosie, and – oh, God . . .

Now I actually feel quite sick. Vomiting in Long Acre is not an ideal option (too close to Face Models, for one thing: that would be lovely, splattering out my breakfast on the pavement just as a supermodel – or, worse still, Laurie – swished by). Instead, I take several deep breaths to steady my nerves as I step into Caffè Nero.

I give the place a quick scan and order a flat white and an almond croissant which I know I'll be unable to eat. As if I'll be tucking into baked goods when encountering the man who fathered my daughter then proceeded to smash my heart to pieces. Finding a small vacant table right at the back, I mop up spilt coffee from my saucer with a paper napkin.

Thus settled, with a clear view of the door, I arrange myself to look as nonchalant as possible. My aim is to appear as if I am just having a brief pit stop in between shopping in Gap and braving Marks and Spencer's food hall. The only signs that I might be slightly on edge are the fact that I keep glancing at the door, as if expecting the police to burst in and arrest me. Plus, I'm picking away at the pinprick on my thumb where they tested my substandard blood.

Don't be nervous, I tell myself. *He ruined your life,*

remember? At least, until you got over the cowardly dick-head mummy's boy – which didn't take long.

It doesn't work. No shrinking is happening at all.

Maybe I won't even recognise him? He might have lost all his hair, or grown a colossal beard; men change more than women as they grow older, don't they? I remember my own frizzy hair and try to pat it down. And that's when I see him, when I'm mid-pat, as if testing a cake for done-ness.

Fraser Johnson has walked in. He stops and glances around the café. Although it pains me to admit it, he's not bloated or hideously disfigured in any way. There are no warts – at least, none are obviously visible – or nasal sproutings. He is just Fraser, looking anxious and a little older, but still the boy I loved madly. And it feels as if there's a bird – something small and pecky, like a chaffinch – repeatedly hitting against my ribcage. *Be angry*, I tell myself. *Remember how deeply you hate this man.*

My cheeks are sizzling hot, no doubt tomato-hued and clashing nicely with my aubergine hair. *Startling colour combo!* as Tricia might say. And now he's seen me and his face bursts into a smile. It's a genuine smile with no tinge of guilt that I can detect. He certainly doesn't look mortified, or even sheepish. He wends his way between tables towards me. I try to fix on a *you-bastard-deserter* expression but I can't. My mouth won't do what I want it to do. And although I'm doing my best to beam disdain – hatred, even – that's not happening either. I, too, am smiling. I can't control my own face.

He walks towards me, all long, gangly legs and blue, blue eyes. The Japanese girl at the next table glances up at him in appreciation but he doesn't appear to notice. He looks down at me and says, 'God, Charlotte, it's been so long.'

Chapter Twenty-Six

'Yes, it has, hasn't it?' is all I can think of to say.

He glances at my half-empty cup and untouched croissant. 'Er, can I get you anything? Another coffee?'

'No, I'm fine, thanks.' Fine, apart from the fact that I shouldn't be here at all. Imagine, thinking I could make everything all right by stopping off to give blood and buying mangoes. What am I doing here, while my husband is on his hands and knees, scraping away at Gloria's patio with a trowel?

'Won't be a sec,' Fraser says, heading for the counter. *Please be longer than that,* I urge him, *because I need time to compose myself, to calm this chaffinch in my chest and remember how to breathe.* I twiddle with a hangnail, now picturing Ollie and Saul scaling the climbing wall in Victoria Park, urging each other to go higher and higher while Maria watches anxiously from a discreet distance. I push the image away but it's replaced by Rosie, walking nervously into the casting and hoping to God her concealer hasn't worn off.

Christ, what kind of mother am I?

Fraser returns with a black coffee. He takes the seat opposite and rakes a hand through neatly-cut blond hair. 'I don't know where to start really,' he says with an awkward laugh.

'Neither do I.' There's a pause, and it feels as if the whole of this huge, busy café has gone silent.

'I hope you didn't mind me emailing,' he adds.

'It was a surprise,' I say quickly, 'but if I'd minded I wouldn't have replied.'

'Yeah, I guess.' Fraser glances down and fiddles with his cup. He looks younger than his years; I know he's thirty-six, two years younger than me. But his face is unlined and his hair is showing no sign of retreating. He has the slim, rangy body of a younger man, and is wearing a smart red-and-blue checked shirt and dark jeans. I have already confirmed that his shoes are perfectly ordinary – shiny and black – and not some kind of mustard fiascos.

Fraser clears his throat. 'So, er . . . your dad's still into sailing?'

How odd that he remembers. But then, we'd filled each other in on every minute detail about our lives, during those long train journeys through Europe. 'Yes, he is,' I reply. 'Can't imagine him ever giving that up . . .'

'That's good.' He inspects his hands. 'And . . . Rosie's a model.'

I nod.

'Amazing.'

'Uh-huh,' I reply, wondering when we might stop speaking in small, simple sentences. We sound like a Ladybird book.

Tension flickers in Fraser's eyes. This isn't easy for him either, I realise. Well, nor should it be. *He* wasn't palmed off with a cheque and a packet of bird seed. We fall silent and I catch the Japanese girl at the next table giving us a quick look. *Uh-oh,* she's thinking, *date's not going well.* Fraser sips his coffee, making a little slurpy noise because it's too hot. He's probably scalded his lip.

And then he says it. He fixes me with a direct stare as if seeing me properly for the first time since he walked in and says, 'Look, I'm sorry about the way things turned out . . .'

I cough involuntarily. 'Well, yes, I suppose you are. But it's a bit late really. I mean, seventeen years too late. Which is quite a long time, don't you think?'

The girl keeps swivelling her head around in our direction. 'What d'you mean?' Fraser asks, frowning.

I stare at him for a moment. 'How can you say that as if you don't know?'

'But . . .' He tails off. 'From what I heard . . . well, I just thought . . .'

'What did you think?' I ask sharply.

'You . . . you'd decided to go through with it,' he goes on, 'and seemed like you had everything sorted . . .'

'So you just stepped away,' I cut in, '*conveniently*.' Fraser exhales and looks around the café. God, I could slap him now. I had it all sorted, did I? He makes it sound like buying a new kettle. He has no idea what it was like pacing around a tiny flat at 2 a.m. with a wailing baby and no one to turn to. None of my friends had children. I sensed that they were bewildered by the whole baby business, and who could blame them? One time, on a rare night out, I had a couple of wines and found myself raving about this amazing machine Mum and Dad had bought me, which gobbled up stinky nappies and turned them into odourless bricks. 'Genius!'

I babbled, then caught Rachel and Gabby glancing at each other in a 'What the hell's happened to Charlotte?' kind of way. Later, as I stood at the bar, I heard Gabby chuckling, 'I hope to God she stops going on about those shitty bricks!' And the two of them dissolved into laughter. None of this happened to Fraser. I pick up my croissant and take the tiniest bite.

'I thought it was what you wanted,' Fraser murmurs.

'You thought I wanted to be abandoned like that? When I was *pregnant*?' I must have blasted that out because I catch the girl at the next table staring openly. She quickly looks away.

'Well, it's what you said,' Fraser replies, clearly trying to remain calm, 'that time you phoned and spoke to Mum. You made that pretty clear. I mean, it's not what *I* wanted but—'

'What d'you mean, when I phoned?' I cut in. 'You changed your number, remember? Or at least, I assume you did because I couldn't get through. Anyway, I got your mum's letter and that spelled everything out for me and . . .' I shrug. To my horror, my eyes are brimming with tears.

Fraser has turned pale. 'What letter?'

'You know, the one your mum sent – with the bird seed. Don't pretend you don't know . . .'

'I really don't. I have no idea what you're talking about, Charlotte. What d'you mean, bird seed?'

'You know – the stuff you buy to put in those little holders so the birds can—'

'Yes, I know what bird seed is,' he says quickly. 'I just don't understand what it has to do with anything.'

I am sitting very still, aware of all the chatter around us and hoping that the rather stuffy atmosphere in this café will help to evaporate the liquid now wobbling dangerously in my eyes. Why am *I* upset, when he's the one who ran away? I don't care about him. I have Will, and we have gorgeous children and live in a lovely home with wonky walls and a beautiful garden. I need nothing from this man.

'Fraser,' I say, adopting an oddly patient voice, 'your mum wrote to me and said that in no circumstances should I try to contact you again. She said you had great prospects, and I suppose what she meant was that sticking with me, and becoming a dad – a real dad, I mean, who was there and involved and actually *cared* – would ruin your life . . .'

He stares at me. 'I . . . I had no idea.'

'And she sent me the bird seed as an incredibly witty little joke,' I go on, bitterness creeping into my voice now, 'along with a cheque for ten thousand quid, which was very kind of her.'

Fraser leans towards me. 'She sent you *money*?'

I nod. Miraculously, my eyes have dried up and I feel strong, perhaps fortified by that tiny nibble of croissant. In fact, I am completely fine. I pick it up and take an enormous bite just to show him how fucking fine I am.

'What for?' Fraser asks.

'Well, for the baby, I suppose.'

'For . . . the baby?' he repeats.

'Yes, to help us. But I didn't want her money so I tore it up and sent it back.' I use a finger to sweep up the crumbs on my plate into a neat little pile.

'Charlotte . . .' Fraser starts. Now, startlingly, *his* eyes are wet. Moisture is trapped in his lower lashes, like dew on grass.

'Anyway, it's been fine,' I continue briskly. 'My parents helped loads when she was little, and then I met Will and we had another child—'

'*Another* child,' he repeats, fixing his gaze on mine. 'Honestly, I didn't know.'

I frown at him. The Japanese girl has left, and her table has been taken by an exhausted-looking middle-aged couple whose copious carrier bags clutter the space around them. 'What didn't you know?' I ask.

'That you . . . *had* the baby.' He half speaks, half whispers it.

And that's when it starts to wobble: the towering stack of Jenga bricks I've held in my mind for all these years – his change of heart or sudden panic attack or whatever it was, and him asking his mother to write to me and then – the worst part – never once caring enough to get in touch just to ask, 'So, how was the birth?' Or, later, 'How's my child doing? Is she talking yet? What are her favourite things to do?'

At this moment, with the couple at the next table complaining that Hamley's isn't as good as it used to be, a tiny doubt starts to flicker in my mind. For the first time, I wonder if perhaps that's not quite how it happened. I look at Fraser as he rubs at his eyes.

'You mean,' I say hesitantly, 'you thought I didn't go through with it?'

He nods. His lips are pressed together. It's as if he doesn't trust himself to speak.

'You thought I had an abortion?'

'Yes.' His voice is soft, gravelly. He picks up a sugar cube and grinds its rough surface with a thumbnail. 'That's what Mum said – that you'd phoned and told her and said you never wanted to see me again.'

I feel as if I have been kicked, very sharply, in the stomach. 'Jesus.'

'I know. I don't know what to say.' He looks utterly distraught.

'Well,' I say, my voice wavering, 'that didn't happen. I had Rosie and she's sixteen now . . .'

His Adam's apple bobs as he swallows. 'But it said in the magazine that she was fifteen—'

'Yes, they got that wrong. The journalist was a bit slapdash.'

'God, Charlotte. When I saw the two of you I just assumed you must have met someone else and got pregnant pretty quickly . . .'

I shake my head. 'Rosie's yours, Fraser. I mean . . .' I shrug. 'In the biological sense.'

'I really don't know what to say . . .'

'. . . And I never phoned your mum. I've never spoken to her in my life. Didn't you think it was odd when your phone number changed?'

'Christ, I don't know – she did that a couple of times. Said we'd been getting nuisance calls . . . what was that about bird seed again?'

I roll a piece of croissant between my fingers. 'Um . . . I wrote to you saying something about wanting to be a pigeon so I could crap on your head.'

'Oh,' he says hollowly, dropping the sugar cube into his coffee. 'D'you feel like that now?'

'What, that I want to be a pigeon?'

'I mean angry. Let down. I don't know . . .' I look at him, this handsome man who looks barely a day older than the last time I saw him, when I'd hugged him goodbye at Euston station. *It'll be okay*, he'd said, kissing me. *We'll be together and make it work. I love you.*

All these years, I've held a version of events in my head. And that's not what happened at all. How might things have turned out if his mother had never interfered? No, I *can't* think that way. I must go home, right now, and be a good mother and wife. I scramble up from my seat and throw my bag over my shoulder.

'What are you doing?' Fraser asks, alarmed.

'I need to go home. I shouldn't be here with you . . .'

'Charlotte, please.' He jumps up and grasps at my arm. 'Please don't go. Look, I don't really see Mum anymore. Haven't spoken to her properly for years. She and Dad have separated—'

'Well,' I blurt out, 'if you do speak to her you can tell that, when Rosie was a toddler, one of our favourite things was to feed the birds in the park. You wouldn't believe how tame they were. We used to always take bread but then I found the packet of seeds in a drawer so we took that. So her present came in useful after all . . .' I turn away, horrified that everything's gone blurry – the staff behind the counter, the shuffling queue and the rows of muffins in their paper cases.

'Charlotte, wait!' Fraser says, hurrying after me towards the door. 'Don't rush off like this . . .' And now my tears are spilling over. I charge out of Caffè Nero with Fraser in pursuit, remembering when Ollie put the plug in the washbasin and left the taps running to prove that our overflow system worked effectively. Only now there's no overflow. Just my face, which is completely wet as I spin back towards Fraser and say, 'I'm sorry, but I can't talk about this anymore.'

Chapter Twenty-Seven

'Turned out it wasn't just the patio,' Will announces on his return home, 'but a bird table as well. Trust my bloody sister. She'd ordered Mum this ridiculous table with platforms at different levels, and a little house on top – a sort of Swiss chalet – but of course it was flatpack and she needed me to build the damn thing.'

I force out a laugh. Although he's in unusually good humour – perhaps it's perked him up, feeling needed and useful – I'm finding it hard to focus on multi-tiered bird tables and how his mum made him deep-clean her patio with some awful environment-ruining stinky stuff after he'd scraped off the moss.

All I can think is: *Fraser didn't know he had a child. He never deserted us after all. How would things be today if we'd made it work and brought up our baby together?* I keep replaying that morning, when we'd watched the sky lighten from Brighton seafront, and peered at the positive pregnancy test over and over, hardly able to believe it bore a thin blue line. We'd made a baby! The hormones in my pee that I'd peed onto this little stick told us so! And I think about all the times Fraser said he loved me. Maybe it wasn't all lies.

I feel chilled to my bones, even though the afternoon has turned oppressively muggy. Pottering around the kitchen, I try to find something useful to do.

'I mean,' Will goes on, 'do birds actually care what their table looks like?'

'No, I guess not . . .'

'. . . As long as there's bird seed on it?'

Agh no. Do not talk about bird seed. 'Well, it sounds quite impressive,' I say. 'I might have to go round for a look.'

Will chuckles as I start to set the table for dinner. 'If I'd known you'd be that interested, I'd have taken a picture on my phone.'

'I would have liked that,' I say, with a small laugh.

'Charlotte?'

I fix on a bright smile. 'Yes?'

'Are you . . . *okay*?'

'Yes, I'm fine! Why d'you ask?'

He peers at my face. I can feel the deceit radiating out of my every pore. I'm trying to be normal, fetching chilli sauce and orange juice from the fridge, while still reeling in shock over what I learned today; that Fraser didn't bother to find out when the baby was born because he didn't know she *was* born. I'd be no more shocked to have discovered that Dad wasn't really my dad, and that my actual father was one of those obscure members of the Luxembourg royal family that you see in *Hello!* magazine.

'You just seem a bit weird,' Will remarks.

I glide across the kitchen to fetch glasses. 'In what way?'

'Um . . . you're talking strangely, as if English wasn't your first language and you're trying to get to grips with the tenses.'

'I don't know what you mean,' I bluster.

He throws me another quizzical look. 'Actually, you sound like a prim telephone operator from the 1950s . . .'

'Stop analysing me,' I say hotly as the front door opens. Rosie bursts in, all smiles and flushed cheeks. I have never been so delighted to see her.

'Guess what!' she announces. 'They want me for the billboard campaign. Can you believe it?'

'That's fantastic,' I exclaim, hugging her. 'I didn't think you'd hear so soon.'

'Neither did I,' she says, snatching an apple from the bowl and crunching into it, 'but they called Laurie as soon as they'd seen me and it's happening! I'm going to be on billboards all over the South East!' She throws her arms around Will, then me – again – and even Ollie as he bowls in, tired and sunny-faced after his day out. Rosie hasn't mentioned meeting Fraser again, since our heated exchange after Zach's gig. Maybe this big ad campaign will take her mind off things, until I decide what the heck to do now.

'Have fun at the climbing wall, Ollie?' Will asks.

'Yeah, it was great,' our son enthuses. As we tuck into Will's delicious Thai stir fry, I try to convince myself that my own 'day out' wasn't a big deal really. We didn't even make plans to meet again.

So why haven't I told Will? We don't keep secrets from each other generally. At least, I don't – not to sound like some paragon of virtue, but because I genuinely haven't got up to anything even remotely devious in all the years we've been together. And . . . well, now I have. And I haven't the faintest idea of what to do next. One thing I *do* know, though, is that I'm definitely not allowed to be angry about leather trouser night anymore.

*

I meet Liza next morning to tell her how Arlene Johnson effectively erased Rosie and me from her son's life. 'I can't believe she did that,' she exclaims, clutching her glass of green juice.

'Neither can I,' I say. 'It's inhuman, really. That was his child! And her *grandchild*. What's she's basically done is denied Rosie any sort of relationship with Fraser—'

'I'd want to get on a train right now and confront her . . . where does she live again?'

'Not sure. They used to be just outside Manchester, but Fraser said he's not really in touch with her anymore.'

Liza exhales loudly. She's teaching classes today but I've managed to grab her for a quick chat in the yoga studio café. We are surrounded by beautiful, slender beings who appear to be so utterly at peace with themselves, I can't imagine any of them has ever done anything at all deceptive. 'Well,' Liza adds, 'I'd want to point out that she completely altered the course of your life, *and* denied her own son the chance of being a dad—' She stops short. 'I don't mean, you know, that Will hasn't been a *brilliant* father . . .'

I nod.

'And maybe,' she goes on, 'this is how things were meant to happen. I mean, if she hadn't interfered . . .'

'*Everything* would have been different.' I, too, have

ordered a juice, only mine isn't green, but a violent purplish colour to match my hair.

Liza looks at me. 'You don't regret the way things have turned out, do you?'

'Of course not,' I say, with more certainty than I feel.

'Does Fraser have any other children?'

'No idea. I don't know anything about him apart from the fact that he works in London – something financial – and has a place in Cheshire too. We didn't talk about anything other than the Rosie situation . . .' I take another sip of my juice. It involves beetroot and tastes rather soily; I'd hoped it might help to purify my thoughts but it seems to be failing on that count.

'So what are you going to do?' Liza asks.

'I'll tell Will, but I need to pick my moment. You know how he is these days.'

She nods. 'Did you ever find out what went on at Sabrina's that night? After I'd left, I mean?'

'No.' I drop my voice to a murmur. 'He's adamant that nothing was going on with any woman, and I must've imagined it all, hallucinated maybe . . .' I pause.

'What's going on with him, d'you think?'

I shrug. 'A mid-life thing, maybe? I've no idea. I mean, *ecstasy,* Liza. Will's never even smoked a ciggie, let alone a joint. That's one of the things I loved about him, when we met – that he seemed like such a proper, sorted grown-up who enjoyed a few beers or glasses of wine but could handle *life*, you know?'

She nods. 'Unlike Fraser.'

'Well, yes, I mean, I thought he'd just run away.'

'He still did really,' she points out. 'He just accepted his mum's version of events and never called you to see if you were okay, or to try and help in any way. He just slunk away, like his mum wanted him to.'

'You're right.' I check my watch. 'God, sorry, I've taken up all your break—'

She pulls a regretful face. 'It's fine, but I'd better go . . .' I leave her to take her next class.

'The thing to remember,' I hear another instructor saying as I pass one of the studios, 'is that it's all about the breath. Calm, steady breathing. In . . . and out. In . . . and out . . .' If only it were that simple.

*

When I arrive home, Will is huddled over his laptop at the kitchen table. 'Any luck?' I say, without thinking.

'What with?' Will's gaze remains fixed on the screen. Looks like some environmental thing. Aware that it's highly annoying to peer over someone's shoulder, I move away.

'Oh, I don't know. Just . . . stuff.'

'No,' he says wearily, 'I *don't* have any news about jobs yet.' He picks up his laptop and disappears to the garden with it. Well, fine.

I hang out with Ollie – Rosie is out on another casting – and we find ourselves making cookies together, which I'd have assumed he'd grown out of long ago. Pleasingly, though, he seems to enjoy messing about in the kitchen with me, and insists that we make a batch of crisp cookies – 'like you did for the party' – as well as his previously favoured chocolate chip variety. Then Saul shows up, and the two of them rush off to the park, with handfuls of still-warm cookies.

Alone now, I head upstairs and click on my own laptop

in our bedroom. Satisfied that all is quiet in the house, I check my emails.

All junk, apart from one from Fraser.

Can't stop thinking about what we talked about yesterday. Need to see you again. Would that be okay? Can I call you?

F x

How can I say no, after what he told me? *Yes,* I reply, *we definitely need to talk. Here's my number . . .*

It takes me three attempts to type it correctly. I press send, my heart hammering like a caffeinated thing, knowing that no amount of yoga-type breathing could calm me now.

Chapter Twenty-Eight

I'd felt bad about not booking more time off work to coincide with the summer holidays. However, now I'm on my way to the office, on a breezy Wednesday morning, it's something of a relief. It's excruciating being around Will, trying to figure out the best way to tell him about my meeting with Fraser.

I know I'm being cowardly, and that I should have told him everything as soon as Fraser and I arranged to have coffee. Maybe I would have, if this had happened long ago, when I felt close to Will and we kept each other abreast of the minutiae of each other's lives. But we don't anymore. It's the eggshell thing: never knowing quite how he'll react. Not that I'm making excuses. This is no longer just about Rosie, I've realised, remembering how my heart started thumping alarmingly when Fraser walked into Caffè Nero: strikingly handsome in a blond, blue-eyed way, a little hesitant, and just as I'd remembered him. Even now, my stomach does a little spin at the thought. I take a moment to sit in my car in Archie's car park, before forcing myself to banish all Fraser-related thoughts and head in to work, where I shall try to behave like a normal person.

However, it appears all's not well at Archie Towers either. Dee seems distracted as she runs through everything that's happened during my time off. 'Rupert's been weird,' she says, tension flickering in her eyes.

'In what way?'

'Kind of distracted and grumpy. Maybe he was missing you.' She emits a small, mirthless snigger.

'Doubt it,' I say, pouring our coffees, and startled by her gloomy expression when I place hers on her desk. 'Has it been that bad?' I ask. 'Has he had a go at you?'

'No, no, it's not that. In fact, um . . . can I tell you something? It's actually nothing to do with Rupert at all . . .'

'What is it, then? Are you okay?' I pull up a chair beside her. 'Dee?' I prompt her.

She exhales. '*Please* don't say anything. Oh God, Charlotte, I have to tell someone . . .'

'You can tell me,' I say gently, adding, to lighten the mood, 'Don't say you've been going around saying fry instead of cook.'

Dee musters a small smile. 'I wish it *was* that. It's . . . here, let me show you.' She opens her desk drawer and extracts an envelope which has already been ripped open. She pulls out a postcard and hands it to me.

It depicts two teddy bears in wellies, kissing. The curly writing above the picture reads *I love you beary, beary much*. 'That's, er, sweet,' I say. 'Is it from Mike?'

Dee shakes her ahead. 'No, it was on my desk this morning when I came in.'

'Who put it there? D'you have any idea?'

She flushes cherry-pink and nods. 'Not Rupert?' I gasp.

'God, no! Read the other side . . .'

I flip the card over and read, in rather jittery biro writing: *You are so lovely, Dee. Frank xxx*

'Frank? You mean *fryer* Frank?'

'Yeah,' she mutters.

'He snuck up here and put this on your desk?'

She nods.

'*Frank* put it there?' I almost laugh as I picture the big, handsome Spanish man, all dark eyes and five o'clock shadow in his fat-splattered Archie's apron, Silk Cut dangling from his mouth. I'd never have had him down for a teddy bear card sort of man. Not a *beary-beary-much* type at all.

'Yep,' Dee says grimly.

I look at her. 'So . . . does he have a thing about you or something? What is this – a sort of non-Valentine's day Valentine?'

Dee turns even redder. I've noticed this about blondes: when they blush, there's no hiding it. 'Sort of,' she replies as it begins to make sense: her uncomfortable squirming when I was setting up my picnic scene, and how tricky it was to choose pictures in which she didn't look completely mortified.

'Are you having a . . . a *thing* with Frank?' I gasp.

She bites her lip. 'No, no, not at all . . .'

'Are you sure? Because the card seems so—'

'It's nothing,' she cuts in, 'well, nothing much. God, I don't know. We get along, he's lovely, we're friends . . .'

'Yes, I know you are,' I say.

'. . . And there was this thing, last week, when you were off . . .'

'What kind of thing?'

'Well, er . . . we had a bit of a sort of, um . . . kiss

sort-of-thing.' I am amazed by this. Dee, who always seems so thrilled to be making a home with Mike.

'Where did you kiss?' I whisper, aware of Jen chatting to someone in the shop downstairs. Sounds like we actually have customers.

'On the mouth,' she whispers back.

'No, I meant where, um, *geographically—*'

'Oh! In the spud store.'

'The spud store?' I splutter involuntarily. 'But it's so . . . dark in there. And it smells kind of earthy . . .' Actually, maybe it has that sort of shed-like appeal . . .

'I know,' she says sheepishly, fiddling with her hair.

'What are you going to do?' I ask, desperate to know more: Rosie was right when she said I take an unnatural interest in other people's lives.

'Oh God, I don't know. He's gorgeous. Very sexy. I never planned it, you know. We were just having a smoke and then we found ourselves in there . . .' Like the way I *found myself* replying to Fraser and then arranging to meet, and keeping the whole thing secret . . . how horribly easy it is to tumble into doing all kinds of illicit stuff, without actually intending to. 'You think I'm awful,' she bleats.

'No, of course I don't.'

'But it's so deceitful! I live with Mike, and I love him, and we're *really* happy . . .'

'Dee,' I say, hearing Rupert arriving downstairs, 'don't beat yourself up about it. It was only a kiss.'

'You don't think it counts? As cheating, I mean?'

'No, it absolutely doesn't.' As if I have the faintest idea about anything.

'What would *you* do, if you'd done something – I don't know, kissed someone, or had a fling . . . would you tell Will?'

Making my way to my own desk, I try to formulate a sensible reply. 'I haven't a clue. I guess it'd depend on the situation . . .'

'The difference is,' she declares, 'you'd never do anything so stupid. I feel like such an idiot, Charlotte. I mean, what was I *thinking*?'

I muster what I hope is a big, reassuring smile. 'It was only a kiss, Dee,' I repeat, deciding that now's not the time to tell her the spud store has CCTV.

*

How amazing, I reflect on the drive home, that she thinks I've got it all sorted. I suppose, to Dee, I must give the impression of being a proper grown-up. When you look at the facts, I guess I am; married with two children, one of whom has already earned an eye-popping day rate for looking pretty – albeit in scratchy mittens – but everyone has to start somewhere. When I was Dee's age I'd have assumed a thirty-eight-year-old woman would have life pretty sussed. I used to think that, by that stage, I'd have a fantastic relationship with a lovely, intelligent, funny and sexy man (that didn't seem like too much to ask).

Will is all of those things. Okay, the sense of humour has waned a little, but anyone's would, if everyone kept asking about the job situation, and whether they'd 'heard anything yet'.

My mobile rings. Expecting it to be Will, asking me to pick up something from Tesco Metro, I pull over onto the forecourt of a shabby carpet warehouse. It's stopped ringing by the time I've parked, and it's not Will. I call the number.

'Charlotte?' the man says, and of course it's him. My heart starts pounding. I wish it wouldn't do that. I should be able to control my own internal organs.

'Hello, Fraser,' I croak.

'I, er . . . I hope it's not a bad time . . .'

I fix my gaze on the rows of rolled-up carpets piled up haphazardly in the window of the store. 'No, it's okay.'

He clears his throat. 'I had to call you. I can't stop thinking about everything . . .'

Neither can I, I think, although right now all I want is to go home and pour myself a big glass of wine and sit chatting with Will in the evening sun, like we did over our sourdough and mango picnic. I want to do normal, regular things, like Tricia and Gerald next door. Well, maybe not quite like them. But *our* sort of normal: that's what I need in my life right now.

'Me too,' I tell Fraser. 'It's on my mind the whole time.'

'It's like . . . everything's changed,' he adds.

'Yes, I know.'

'I can't believe she did that. My mum, I mean—'

'Fraser,' I cut in, 'did you ever receive any letters from me? After your mum said I'd made that call?'

'Er . . . no?' He phrases it as a question. 'Did you write?'

Of course I did, idiot. That's what people did in those days. We wrote crazy letters on Basildon Bond notepaper – outpourings of love, then anger, and sometimes we even cried on the letters, thinking, good, I've made it all wet! That'll make the paper all wrinkly and he'll realise how devastated I am! THAT'LL SHOW HIM.

'A few times, yes,' I reply in an airy tone.

A small pause. 'Mum must've got to your letters first.'

I inhale deeply and start the engine. 'I need to go, Fraser. I don't want to discuss this on the phone.'

'Please, can't we talk? When can I see you again?'

'I don't know—'

'I *need* to talk to you, Charlotte. Does Rosie know anything about me?'

'Yes, of course she does. Well, a bit. She doesn't know anything about your life, and neither do I—'

'But I want you to,' he cuts in. 'I feel terrible, you know. I haven't been able to sleep since I saw you. I've taken time off work. God knows what Rosie thinks of me . . .'

I cringe every time he mentions her name. *He's* not her dad. Will is. Fraser Johnson has never dabbed Savlon onto a bleeding knee or cheered her up with a packet of neon-bright Haribos after a jab at the doctor's. He never had to acquaint himself with the machine that turned stinky nappies into bricks – which were never, as promised, 'odourless' – or stripped a child's bed at 4.30 a.m. after she'd puked all over the sheets. At least, I don't imagine he has. As he's never mentioned kids, I assume he doesn't have any. He's breezed through life, 'dividing his time' between London and Cheshire, while I divided my time between the swings in the park and my cluttered kitchen.

'Can I see Rosie?' he asks.

No, no, no. This isn't the way we'd planned it. We were going to handle this calmly, Will and I, and talk it over when the time was right. 'Maybe,' I say warily. 'I'll have to discuss it with her.'

'When?'

'When we're ready, Fraser,' I say, abruptly finishing the call and pulling off the forecourt – without looking properly, and causing a driver of a gleaming red Porsche to toot irritably. *It's okay,* I tell myself, trying to steady my breathing as I drive home. I'll tell Will straight away – or at least, as soon as we can talk in private. That's the thing with teens. It's not the sex thing that's tricky, as Sabrina believes. It's having a private adult conversation, without Ollie or Rosie barging in and demanding to know what we're talking about. As if we're that fascinating! I mean, often it's just Will musing over whether he needs a haircut, or me reminding him to buy a present for Gloria's birthday.

By the time I pull up in our street, I have it all planned out: what I'll say, and where I'll say it. We'll sit in the garden. It's a warm, muggy evening; the air feels heavy and damp. We'll need wine to refresh us.

I step into the house and find Will in the kitchen. 'Hi,' I say, kissing his cheek, which he merely allows as if I am a distant cousin.

'Everything okay?' I ask brightly.

'Yeah.' Dinner smells delicious; after all this time, I am still always hugely impressed when he manages to do something terribly clever with marinades. Any fancy flavourings I add to food seem to evaporate in the oven. I have the incredible knack of turning the most thrilling-sounding Jamie Oliver dish into a joyless school dinner.

Something catches my eye as Will checks the oven. Curiously, my stained canvas shoes are sitting neatly paired up on the table, as if on display. Beside them rests Ollie's shiny silver torch, now pieced back together, as good as new. 'Oh,' I say. 'You found my shoes.' I smile, trying to convey how pleased I am to be reunited with my Converse rip-offs (Primark, £6.99).

'Yes, they were in the shed.' Will gives me a significant look.

'And Ollie's torch! He'll be so pleased.'

'That was in the shed too. Your shoes were sitting on the workbench and the torch was broken on the floor. I fixed it, though—'

'That's good,' I say, my heart rattling alarmingly.

'Charlotte . . . what were you doing in there? These shoes are covered in creosote and someone had tried, very badly, to mop it all up. I nearly fell over the empty tin. What was going on?'

'Nothing,' I say quickly. Will throws me a quizzical look. 'Well, um,' I add, feeling my cheeks blazing, 'this is a bit embarrassing. Remember that night, when I had drinks with Liza and Sabrina and I told you I'd bashed my head against the door?'

He nods, frowning. This is all wrong. He doesn't look like the man I was planning to have a lovely evening with, sipping chilled white wine in the garden, while I told him about Fraser – which, of course, he'd be hugely understanding about. He looks like a teacher who's pretty annoyed because someone hid a slice of salami inside a history textbook.

'Er, that's not *quite* what happened,' I mutter.

'What are you talking about?' Rosie and Ollie are both playing music in their rooms. Two different tracks mingle confusingly, which would annoy me normally, but now I'm relieved they're otherwise engaged.

'I was sort of . . . exploring it,' I explain.

'Exploring it? What is there to explore? There's hardly anything in it. What were you *doing* in there?'

'Oh, there are loads of things,' I rattle on. 'I was amazed at how much stuff you'd managed to pack into it. All those tins and tubs . . . blood and bone fertiliser! And hormone rooting powder! It all sounds a bit . . .

lewd, doesn't it?' I laugh awkwardly, aware that, once upon a time, I'd have told him immediately what I'd been up to. While he might have teased me for being a raving lunatic, we'd have sniggered about it and possibly even done it in there, in a 'why the hell not?' sort of way. We did that kind of thing, back in the stone age.

Will is studying me as if he's not quite sure who I am. 'But you *never* go in the shed.'

'That's because it's your domain, darling,' I say, touching his arm. He flinches as if I'd poked him with a fish.

He shakes his head. 'I just don't get it. The shoes, the torch, the creosote . . .'

'Well, er,' I start, sensing my cheeks sizzling even hotter, 'I was kind of thinking, maybe it might be nice to, er, try something a bit different. And I thought . . . you know. It might be quite fun.'

A wasp drifts in through the open window. He bats it away. 'What d'you mean, different?'

'You know. Just . . . *different*.'

He still looks confused. What does he *think* I'm talking about? Switching our online shop from Tesco to Asda? Or trying the Berries & Cherries Dorset Cereal instead of the nutty kind we usually have? This is ridiculous. Why can't I just spit it out? Will has seen me naked millions of times, in all kinds of ungainly positions. He's watched me push a baby out of my vagina, for goodness' sake.

'I mean for a sort of sex thing,' I murmur, my cheeks radiating a fierce heat.

His brows shoot up. 'A sex thing? What, in the shed?'

'Yes, I thought it might be fun.' I laugh self-deprecatingly. He continues to study me with an icy glare.

'You mean . . . you think our sex life's boring?'

'No! Of course I don't. It's lovely. It's just that . . . you know.' Will blinks at me. This is *excruciating*. 'We don't do it very often these days,' I say, all in a rush, 'and I was starting to worry and I thought—'

Will frowns. 'It hasn't been *that* long.'

'It has, Will. I mean, the last time was Mother's Day . . .'

'D'you make a note of this kind of thing? D'you keep a log?'

'No,' I protest, 'of course not—' I take his hand but he pulls it away.

'D'you have a *file* on this?'

'Don't be silly. It's just, these things tend to lodge in my head. You know – special occasion sex. And I'm not blaming you—'

'Well, thanks!' he blusters.

'. . . I'm saying it's not your fault at all. It's not anyone's fault. It's just us, the way things are. And I'd started to think, maybe we could . . . *vary* things, so I was investigating the shed as a possible location . . .' My top lip is sprouting sweat, I can feel it glistening there.

'You want to do it in our shed,' he says, holding my gaze.

'Well, no actually,' I say, lapsing into a jokey tone, 'that's what's funny because I had to conclude, after my *extensive* research, that its potential as a potentially erotic location is limited.' I laugh, loudly and alone.

'You must think I'm an idiot,' Will says.

'No, of course I don't—'

'You've been in there, and you knocked the creosote over—'

'Well deduced!' I say with a ridiculous grin. 'That's exactly what happened . . .'

'—Because,' he hisses, flinging the back door open and stomping out to the garden, 'you were messing about in there with *another man*.'

Chapter Twenty-Nine

For a moment, I just stand there. He can't think that. He can't really believe it. He has too much time to think and brood, that's all, being stuck at home for so long. I find him sitting on the bench, glaring at our shed, as if my imaginary lover might still be cowering in there, terrified to come out. 'Will,' I say tentatively, perching beside him, 'you don't really believe that, do you?' He shrinks away, as if I reek of something unpleasant.

'What else am I supposed to think?'

'I told you! I know it sounds mad, but I was only prowling about to assess it, to see if—'

'You're obviously lying,' he interrupts. 'You're bright red, and it's all so convoluted—'

'Yes,' I cut in, 'because I know how stupid it sounds and what a bloody ridiculous thing it was to do.' I stare down at the ground. Here we are, in our beautiful garden as planned, although the glasses of chilled white wine are absent. As is any mention of Fraser, obviously. It's not the right time. When will it *ever* be the right time?

'It was a bit,' Will mutters.

'Okay, but it's a bit of a jump to assume I'm having a fling, isn't it? D'you honestly think I'd do that?' I picture myself, just an hour ago, talking to Fraser in the Carpet Land car park. 'I know it sounds mad,' I add, 'but, honestly, Will – I've told you what I was doing. That's *exactly* what happened—'

'Oh, right, when you banged your head against the door . . .'

'Actually, the creosote can fell on my head.'

He slides his gaze towards me. 'Really?'

'Yes,' I mutter. 'It has a really sharp edge. It could have been a lot worse . . .'

He observes me, failing to show any sympathy. 'So you lied about that, then.'

'Yes. I'm sorry.' We fall into silence.

'You've been weird lately,' he ventures finally.

I nod. 'I know. It's just, something's—' I break off as Gerald strides out into his garden.

'Lovely evening,' he says brightly.

Will nods. 'Yes it is,' I reply. I watch as our neighbour bobs down, then reappears clutching a green plastic sieve. He gives it a little shake.

'Only way to get the stones out,' he says with a grin.

I'm aware that weeding should be done – and mowing, obviously – but sieving the soil? Is this a thing? 'You're very dedicated, Gerald,' I remark.

'Yes, well, I do what I can. Any luck with jobs yet, Will? Anything in the offing?'

I glance at Will. 'Erm, I'm looking into a few things,' he replies.

Gerald nods, wiping a lick of sweat from his brow with a gloved hand. 'Very competitive these days and of course, you're not getting any younger . . .'

'Yes, that's right.' Will smiles tightly.

'. . . I mean, if there are two candidates, one in their forties and one of twenty-eight, no prizes for guessing who they'll go for . . .'

'Yep, I'm aware of that,' Will cuts in. I glance at him. A vein seems to be throbbing in his neck.

Gerald jiggles his sieve. 'It's unfair, of course. Discriminatory really. I mean, look at you, Will, with decades of life experience and, er—' He tails off, as if unable to think of any more admirable qualities my husband might possess. 'Glad I'm not in your shoes,' he adds. 'I don't envy you one bit. Tricia and I are lucky in that our jobs are secure and the mortgage is paid off . . .'

'You are lucky,' Will agrees. *Smug fucker,* I sense him adding silently.

Gerald picks a bit of gravel out of the sieve and examines it before tossing it aside. 'Had any more intruders in your garden? We've been worried, since we heard all that screaming—'

'No, nothing,' I say quickly, jumping up and scuttling towards the house, as if I might have suddenly remembered a pan of milk simmering on the hob.

Will follows, and there's a distinct air of grumpiness as we prepare dinner together. Although he is virtually silent as we eat, Ollie's chattiness masks any awkwardness. 'When are you gonna get more modelling jobs, Rosie?' he enquires.

'Dunno,' she replies.

'Are you working for those mitten people again?'

'No, I'm not.' She rolls her eyes and adds, turning to me, 'Another wool company want to see me, Mum. Laurie says I should go. She reckons I'm great for the knitting market. What does that even *mean*?'

'I've no idea,' I say. 'But it's all work, isn't it? And experience?'

She drops her knife onto her plate. 'What d'you think, Dad?'

Will frowns. 'Does it really matter whether you're working for a fashion magazine or a knitting company? I'd have thought it was all pretty similar—'

'Of course it's not similar!' she cries shrilly. 'Delph says you have to be really careful when you start out, or you'll be branded as one of those naff girls, a catalogue girl—'

Bloody Delph . . .

'But *she* modelled mittens,' Ollie reminds her.

'Yeah, by mistake, idiot . . .'

I look at my daughter, wishing now that I'd whisked her out of Forever 21 before Laurie could press that card into my hand. We should have listened to Gloria's warnings about the foil dress poking and never let her do it. She seems so defensive these days, and unusually intolerant of her little brother. I'd never have imagined that mittens could be viewed as so controversial. Christ, it seems like only last week that she owned a pair: Fairisle pattern, lovingly knitted by my mum. Rosie had cried, I recall, when she'd left one on the bus.

'I'd rather have gloves,' Ollie muses. 'I mean, why would anyone choose to wear something that stops them using each finger individually?'

'Can we stop discussing mittens?' she barks. They batter back and forth, sniping and snapping until Ollie stomps off to his room, and Rosie heads out to meet Zach to go to the movies again. This time, we let her go with no prior quizzing. If she's old enough for the knitting market, then she is perfectly capable of trotting off to the cinema with a boy.

I watch Will as he carefully waters his tomato plants on the kitchen shelf. Does he really think I'd sneak into our shed with another man? The very idea is so ludicrous I can't even bring myself to be angry with him. I start to sort laundry, replaying Dee's confession today: *snogging in the spud store*. Not very Archie Towers-type behaviour, admittedly – but still, it was just a blip. On the other hand, my meet-up and phone conversation with Fraser are starting to seem like a huge deal. It no longer feels like 'only coffee'. There's no *only* about it. What the hell am I playing at?

Will is in the utility room now, gathering tools to fix a bit of loose fence that Tricia has been grumbling about. The toy garage pops into my mind, with its working lift. Rosie had always preferred her collection of vehicles to the curly-haired doll Grandma Gloria had given her, and was delighted when Will had presented it to her. 'Thank you, Daddy!' she cried, throwing her arms around him. He had always been Daddy, right from the start. Although – naturally – I'd introduced him as Will, she never seemed to consider the possibility of calling him by name.

A lump forms in my throat as he emerges clutching a hammer and a box of nails. 'What?' he says simply, studying my face.

'Will,' I start, 'there's something I have to tell you.'

'I *knew* there was. What is it?'

'It's not what you think,' I murmur. 'It's . . . it's Fraser.'

His face darkens. 'Has he contacted you again?'

I nod. 'Yes, he has. We've, um, emailed a few times . . .'

'That's who you were with in the shed!'

I stare at Will. His eyes are narrowed, his cheeks flushed. So that's what he thinks – that I invited my ex round for a quickie in the shed, knocking down a can of creosote in our excitement . . . for God's sake. I can't tell him about the coffee in Caffè Nero – not now, when he's being so irrational.

'Of course I wasn't,' I say firmly. 'That's just ridiculous. God, Will, how did it get like this between us?'

'Like what?' he counters.

'Like . . . *you* know. This. I really don't want to list all the incidents which illustrate how we haven't been getting along . . .'

'No,' he says firmly, 'do tell me. Tell me everything you're unhappy about.'

I swallow hard. 'Okay – the night you gobbled a load of drugs . . .'

'Oh, yeah, you were charming that night, weren't you? Reading the riot act in that café—'

'I've *never* read you the riot act,' I exclaim. 'I was pissed off, yes, when I saw you dancing with that woman at Sabrina's—'

'And then you squirted me with salad cream. That was mature! How d'you think that made me feel?'

'I don't know how you feel about *anything*,' I shoot back, 'because you never tell me.'

Tears fuzz my vision as I turn away. Sodding salad cream. Will he still be bringing that up when we're in our eighties? No, because he'll have left me by then and I'll be a batty old woman, unable to forgive myself for wrecking my marriage over a secret coffee with my ex.

Will dumps the hammer and nails on the kitchen table and clicks on his laptop. Maybe he's about to Google 'quickie divorce'. I try to gauge his expression as his laptop rouses itself, creakily; it's a rickety old machine, 'steam-powered', he reckons. In fact, he merely opens his Facebook page. Considering the terse exchange we've just had, this is rather insulting. But then, who am I to judge? Of course he's hurt and upset, and I can't imagine how he'd feel if he knew how my heart leaps every time I glimpse Fraser's name in my inbox.

Assuming our conversation is over, I busy myself by pairing up Rosie's socks. Not my favourite job usually, but the repetitive task is at least helping to bring down my heart rate to a normal-ish level. I dart a quick look at the laptop again. Still Facebook. Not Will's page, I realise now, but Sabrina's: so they're Facebook friends. That's fine – of course it is. And I'd be friends with her too, if I was on it. Will is scrolling down her timeline. I glance casually over his shoulder, in a way that I hope seems companionable, rather than prying. There are pictures of Zach and his band, plus various pierced and pallid members of the audience at Down Below. I turn away and sort Will and Ollie's pants into two tidy piles.

When I glance back, there's a gallery of wedding dresses on the screen, modelled by one of the younger women – blonde and bronzed, with prominent collarbones – from Sabrina and Tommy's housewarming party. In another shot, Tommy is blowing a kiss at the camera and waving a bottle of beer. There's a moody close-up of Zach, strumming a guitar, looking every inch the indie boy pin-up.

Then more of the gig we went to. I know it's that night because Sabrina is wearing her plunging black dress and leather jacket. I spot Liza in a couple of shots; they must have been taken back at Sabrina and Tommy's place, after I'd gone to collect Ollie.

There's one of Will, looking a bit pissed but happy, wearing a squiffy grin. Enjoying himself, obviously, while I was sipping my Ovaltine and having poisonous thoughts. And there's one of him and a woman in a fierce embrace.

My heart seems to stop. 'Sabrina's just put these up,' Will says flatly.

'Oh, um . . . right! They look really fun.'

He glances at me, then indicates the screen. 'Is that the person you were talking about when you mentioned hot, steamy dancing?'

I study the picture he's pointing at. It's not a real woman – I can see that now. The camera flash has bounced off her pink, shiny face and her little red mouth is an 'o' of surprise. 'Er . . . yes, I think it is.'

It's Chloe, Tommy's pretend girlfriend. I squirted salad cream at my husband for dancing with a blow-up doll.

Chapter Thirty

Thursday morning, and I'm still in the dog house. At least, I assume I am. My plan was to get up super-early and make Will a lavish cooked breakfast – full English with black pudding, his favourite – but he was off on his bike before I'd even got the frying pan out.

I can't get over the fact that I ranted at him for smooching with what was effectively a lilo, with tits and a face. Although I've apologised a thousand times, he's obviously still miffed about it. Still, today isn't all bad. It's Rosie's big shoot, for the billboards for the new shopping mall. I hope Will comes back in time to wish her luck. Maybe then, when she's set off, we can talk things over in a calm, rational way. Although he hasn't mentioned Fraser again, I'm aware that we urgently need to clear the air.

Ollie appears, still in PJs, and starts plundering the kitchen for cereal, groaning when he opens the crisp cupboard and a packet tumbles out. Some are probably out of date by now. 'Nothing worse than a stale crisp,' Rupert announced during a meeting, to which I wanted to reply, 'Actually lots of things are worse: war, or losing all your loved ones in a house fire.' But I just agreed that an ageing crisp is a truly terrible thing.

Ollie sighs loudly. 'Where's Dad?'

'He's gone out on his bike, love.'

'This early? Why?'

'No idea,' I say, dropping two slices of bread into the toaster and adding, 'I hope he's back soon, though. It's Rosie's big shoot today and I need to leave for work.'

'I'm fine here by myself,' he says airily.

'I know you are, Ollie, for a little while. But not all day.' Hmm. Could Will be planning to stay out for hours, just to make things difficult?

'Mum!' Rosie strides into the kitchen, still in her dressing gown with her hair unwashed and roughly pulled back into a wonky ponytail. 'I can't find Guinness. Have you seen him?'

'He'll be in there, love,' I say, indicating the utility room.

'He's not. I've already checked. The door was left open last night—'

'Not the back door?' I exclaim.

'No, the utility room. Didn't you make sure it was shut before you went to bed?'

I start scanning the kitchen, checking under the cooker and fridge. 'I'm not sure,' I reply. 'I can't remember—'

'Why not?' she cries. *Because my marriage was falling apart, that's why. Because I was so humiliated over that stupid blow-up doll that I omitted to perform my nightly duties of turning off a billion lights and securing Guinness in the utility room for the night.*

'I'm not the only person who's capable of shutting a door around here,' I mutter, continuing to hunt for our pet. 'There are four of us and everyone's able-bodied. In fact, I've been meaning to say, how about involving yourselves in poo-collecting duties once in a while?' Rosie and Ollie give me blank looks. 'I mean,' I rant on, unable to stop myself, 'I accepted it when you were little – that you couldn't be expected to scoop out poo from his hutch, and that was fine. But you're not little now, and he's pretty much moved in with us, and if you're going to let him hop all over the house, dropping his, er . . . *droppings* everywhere, you're going to have to—'

'We could make him a nappy,' Ollie interrupts with a smirk. 'A sort of mini bunny Pamper.'

'I'm serious,' I say, trying to calm my voice. 'I mean, I've dealt with every single pellet that's dropped out of his bum for nearly ten years now. How long do rabbits live?'

'You want him to *die*?' Rosie gasps.

'No, of course not!'

Ollie sighs loudly. 'He might be dead already if someone left the front door open. He could've been run over, or maybe a cat's got him—'

'Oh God,' Rosie shrieks. While she and Ollie check the bedrooms, I search behind sofas and bookshelves and a great pile of muddy trainers by the back door. What makes us think that pet ownership is beneficial to children? Oh, they'll learn to care about something other than themselves, we reason. They'll develop empathy and practical skills. They'll have someone to talk to and confide in when they start to view us – their doting, ever-obliging parents – as hideous wreckers of fun. We never consider that, when things go wrong, it's completely traumatic for everyone.

Ollie's voice drifts down from the landing. 'Maybe he's escaped to the wilds?'

'What d'you mean, the wilds?' Rosie retorts. 'This is London. There *aren't* any wilds.'

'Yes, there are,' he argues. 'What about where Dad found those puffballs? Where was that again?'

'What's that got to do with anything?' Rosie stomps downstairs with Ollie in pursuit.

I study her anguished face. 'He'll turn up,' I try to reassure her. 'He's probably squished himself into some tiny space and he'll come out when he's hungry.'

'Well, I'm not going anywhere until he's found.'

'But what about your shoot?'

She shakes her head firmly. 'I'm not doing it. I'm not going. How could I possibly concentrate on modelling clothes with Guinness missing?'

'But you're booked, Rosie!' I exclaim. 'You can't just not go—'

'It's probably best that you don't,' Ollie observes, ''cause your face is all blotchy and red . . . imagine *that* blown up twenty feet high.'

'Shut up,' she roars.

'No one would shop there,' he adds sagely. 'So, as an advertising campaign, it would fail.'

The front door opens and Will wheels in his bike. 'Everything okay?' he asks vaguely.

'No,' I mutter. 'Guinness is missing. I – well, *someone* – must have left the utility door open last night. He could be anywhere in the house. Sorry, Will, but I really need to go. I'm running late as it is . . .'

'Oh, Christ,' he says.

'And Rosie's saying she won't do this job today until he's found . . .' I glance at her. This is so unlike Rosie. She used to feel bad about being late for a birthday, and now she's planning to let everyone down: the photographer, the client and God knows who else will be waiting for her, at colossal expense. Still, it's her call. 'This'll look really bad for you,' I add, snatching my bag from a chair. 'I know you're upset, but they *chose* you, Rosie. You're the girl they want. What'll they do when you just don't show?'

She shrugs. 'Get someone else, I guess.'

'At such short notice?'

'Mum, I'm *not* going—'

'Okay,' Will snaps. 'Deal with it then, Ro. Call Laurie and explain why.'

'I can't do that! I'm useless at lying. She'll know right away . . .' She turns to me. 'Mum, will *you* phone? Say I'm ill?'

'Oh, so I'm really good at lying, am I?' I sense my cheeks flaring pink. 'No, that's not fair. If you're not going to show up, you'll have to take responsibility for it yourself.'

'Please, Mum! *Please*. I'll never ask for anything ever again . . .'

I look at her – her bottom lip is trembling, like a little child's – and sense Will assessing the scene. He's waiting, observing, to see if I'll crumble. I feel like a teacher delivering a lesson under the steady gaze of an Ofsted inspector.

'All right,' I say with a sigh. 'Never mind about me needing to get to work. I'll call her. What d'you want me to say?'

'I don't know. Anything!'

Incredibly helpful. Perhaps to lessen my humiliation, Will at least strides out of the kitchen. I grab my phone and call Laurie's mobile. It's only modelling, I tell myself as I wait for her to pick up. Only a girl having her photo taken for a massive poster campaign, to advertise a sparkling new mall that's cost billions of pounds. But hey, in the grand scheme of things, it doesn't matter. Nobody's died – well, a small furred mammal might have, or been savaged by that snappy little purse with teeth next door, but let's not even *think* about that . . .

'This can't be happening,' Lauren barks when I explain the situation. 'Does she realise how important this is? How crucial to her career? It'll propel her onto a whole new level—'

'I realise that,' I cut in, glaring at Rosie, who's picking little pieces from the soft interior of a home-baked loaf on the worktop, and morosely posting them into her mouth. 'But she really isn't well enough. I'm so sorry.'

'Is it a stomach thing? Because if it is, I'm sure it'll settle if she has a glass of water and something to eat, something plain, a bit of toast . . .'

'No, it's not a stomach thing.'

'What is it then? Tell me I'm not hearing this—'

'It's a sort of . . . all-over thing.'

Laurie groans. 'If she has a fever, as long as she *looks* okay, then just tell her to pull herself together—'

Oh, how very caring! *We nurture our girls*, Laurie said, the day we first met her, when what she actually meant was, *As long as they're capable of standing up and moving their faces a bit, we don't give a shit if they're running a temperature of 102 degrees* . . . Of course, Rosie is in fact in fine physical health. She has now successfully hollowed out an entire cob loaf.

'She can't get out of bed,' I tell Laurie. 'I'm sorry but there's no way she can work today.'

'Look, if it's boyfriend trouble—'

'It's *not* boyfriend trouble.'

'Period pain? They drive me mad, these girls, at the mercy of their menstrual cycles. I keep telling them, "Darlings, pop an ibuprofen and get on with it . . ."'

'It's not period pain either. Ibuprofen won't do any good at all.'

Laurie tuts. 'Well, as her agent I'm saying she *must* work today . . .'

'And as her mum,' I cut in, startled at how determined I sound, 'I'm saying she can't. Look, I know this is terribly inconvenient—'

'Inconvenient? Understatement of the year!' With that, the call ends. I glare at Rosie who has now resumed checking the kitchen again for her elusive pet.

'Well, that was horrible,' I announce.

She grimaces. 'What d'you think'll happen?'

I shrug. 'I've no idea, but she didn't sound impressed. I'm not sure she believed me, actually. Maybe she thinks you've just had an attack of nerves . . .'

'No,' she insists as Will reappears, 'you were great. Totally convincing.' She turns to him. 'Mum's a *brilliant* liar!'

'Oh.' He throws me a blank look. 'Well, that's great. Really glad to hear it.'

'It's good to know I'm useful for something,' I witter, feeling actually sick, 'but I really have to go to work now . . .' I kiss Will on the cheek, then turn to kiss Rosie.

'You really *are* the best mum in the world,' she says, throwing her arms around me and burying her hot, sticky face in my hair.

Chapter Thirty-One

Rupert is still not his usual buoyant self. There's been no missive this week, no perky email peppered with exclamation marks and jolly emoticons. Any conversations we've had have been snatched and, when I try to update him on upcoming press coverage – with Archie's products featuring in several highly-prized food magazines – he appears to be barely listening. 'Everything okay, Rupert?' I ask as he dithers around, picking up the small framed picture of Rosie and Ollie from my desk and squinting at it, as if he's not entirely sure what it is, before setting it back in its place.

'Er, just quite a bit on at the moment,' he replies.

'Anything Dee and I can help with?' I catch her eye across our office. Although I'm still feeling pretty rattled about covering for Rosie this morning, I'm trying to maintain a calm and professional air.

'No,' he says, 'everything's fine . . . sort of.' He musters a stoical smile. 'Well, better get on.' Dee and I look at each other as he lollops away, aware that our amiable boss is actually not fine at all.

'Weird,' she says.

'Something's going on,' I remark, simultaneously texting Will: *Any bunny sighting?*

Nope, pings back his reply.

'So how are . . . things anyway?' I ask Dee. 'At home, I mean . . .'

She pushes back her fair hair and traps it into a ponytail with her hand. 'God, I don't know, Charlotte. I don't know what to do. I'm avoiding Frank at the moment . . . and I think Mike knows something's wrong,' she adds.

'You mean, he knows about Frank?'

'No – I mean there's nothing *to* know, not really. But he's aware that things are different . . .' She tails off, then adds, 'I feel so bad – not because of Frank, not really, but seeing Mike trying so hard, suggesting things I might like, that we could do together . . .'

'Like what?' I ask.

'Well, we always have a KFC on a Friday night, it's a thing we do – the Bargain Bucket. It's his favourite. And the other night, I must've seemed preoccupied because he kept saying, "Dee, are you okay? Are you fed up? D'you want to do something different this weekend?" And I said, "Yeah," thinking, let's *do* something, that'll help – and you know what he suggested?'

I shake my head. Her eyes are shining with sadness or frustration, I'm not sure which. 'He said, "Let's not have the Bargain Bucket this week, let's have something else – we'll have the Ultimate Dips Box instead."' She laughs mirthlessly. I am momentarily lost for words. Will would rather saw off his own foot than have a KFC.

'It's just his way of showing he cares,' I suggest.

Dee nods. 'You're right, and you know, I do love him,

but I've stopped thinking of him in a . . . you know. *That* way.' She lets her hair drop.

'You mean, you feel like flatmates?' I venture.

'Yes, exactly. He's like my best friend who I happen to live with, and have a laugh with, and get all cosy with on a Friday night, which is lovely, you know – I mean, that's what *you* do, isn't it? You and Will. You're great together – rock-solid, even after all these years. You're happy to stay in and just be together . . .'

I'm aware of a twisting sensation in my stomach. 'Erm, yes, mostly . . .'

'So why can't I be content with what I have? I mean, it's what I thought I wanted – the nice sofa and cushions and box sets and takeaway and all that.' She studies my face. 'You have all that and you're happy.'

'Yes,' I say, prickling with unease, 'but we're way older than you, and we have a family, so of course we're not out partying all the time.' An image of Will, weeping on the stairs after chomping those pills, flickers into my mind. 'Maybe it's all happened too quickly,' I add. 'I mean, moving in with Mike, the whole domestic thing . . .'

'You were only twenty-two when you had Rosie,' she reminds me, as if I represent the blueprint of how things should be.

'Yes, but that wasn't planned, remember? There's no way I'd have thought, right, never mind that I've nearly finished my course, and have a job offer already, working in the publicity department at the British Museum – because I'm going to be a mum. And, because I can't imagine how I could afford full-time childcare, I'm going to turn down that job and sit at home in a tiny flat with a baby instead.' I catch myself. 'I don't mean that I've ever regretted having Rosie.'

'I know you haven't,' Dee says. I watch as she gets up from her desk to make coffee, ignoring a call on her mobile. What a remarkable front she puts on, pretending to love planning meals for Mike, and poring over cake tins and rose-patterned tablecloths. I know we're all supposed to find solace in cooking and baking these days, but – crisp cookie triumph aside – I don't seem to be able to train myself to enjoy such pursuits. As previously noted, my cooking is the type offered in school canteens and at the lower end of the scale of old people's homes. Will roasts a chicken and it's a thing of wonder: succulent, with irresistible golden, crispy skin. Mine is a perfectly serviceable, plain old bird, eaten but unremarked upon. And what has Will done, I muse, as Dee starts tapping at her keyboard, since he's been out of work? He's tried to raise our standards on the domestic front – not just to make himself feel useful, but because he knows it's not an area I'm particularly fond of. He is simply doing his best.

I turn to my own screen but can't focus on the press release I need to send out today. Poor Will, I reflect, doing all that stuff, unappreciated. I glance over at Dee who's peering at her own screen, making a clicking noise with her tongue. Mike thinks he's doing the right thing, trying to treat her, and show her how loved she is; his willingness to upgrade to the Ultimate Dips Box is, in some ways, like Will and his home-baked cob loaves and perfect Jamie Oliver thin-crust pizzas (well, *Sabrina's* perfect thin-crust pizza). He does all of this because he cares and loves us, and he absolutely doesn't deserve a wife who sneaks off to meet her ex (only coffee!) behind his back and squirts salad cream on his favourite T-shirt.

My body prickles with shame at how humiliated he

looked when I raised the subject of our barely existent sex life. Maybe that's just what happens, when you've been together as long as we have: that side of life wilts, like the sprigs of mint Will picked from the garden, stuck in a glass on the worktop and forgot to use. Sabrina reckons she and Tommy are at it constantly like nubile little bunnies ('You know what men are like. Insatiable!') but maybe she's exaggerating? Anyway, everyone assumes the grass is always greener when, in fact, it rarely is. And Sabrina and Tommy are so different to Will and me, it's crazy to compare us.

Hell, talking of bunnies, where *is* Guinness? I call Will at lunchtime, relieved when he answers, despite there still being no sign of our absent pet. 'How's Rosie?' I ask.

'She seems okay.'

'She's not worried about not turning up for that job?'

'No idea,' Will says. 'She hasn't mentioned it again.'

'Hmmm. She's obviously really concerned then.'

'Yeah.' He laughs dryly, and I'm overcome by an urge to hug him and say, *please* can we try to work things out? Can we start being kind to each other again?

I arrive home to find Ollie, Saul and a cluster of their friends all lolling in the garden, sipping lemonade, having formed a search party for Guinness. 'No luck, Mum,' Ollie reports with a shrug. I thank the boys for trying anyway, and head indoors to greet Will with a kiss.

'Still nothing,' he says. 'I'm afraid it's not looking good. I think he must've got out of the house somehow.'

I glance out of the kitchen window. 'Ollie seems to be quite stoical about it.'

'Yeah.' Will smiles. 'I think he quite likes the idea of Guinness breaking out into the wild, going feral . . .'

'And what about Rosie?'

'She decided to cheer herself up with a bit of retail therapy. She and Zach have gone to the West End . . .' He hesitates, as if about to add something else.

'Everything else okay?' I ask.

'Um, yeah. It's just . . .' He glances out to the garden, then back at me. 'I've, er . . . got a bit of news.'

I study his face. 'You mean good news?'

He flushes. 'Sort of. I'm going for an interview next week.'

Without thinking, I throw my arms around him. 'Really? That's brilliant, Will! Where is it?' I peel myself off him and stand back.

'Er . . . it's quite a long way away, actually.'

'Well, that's okay, isn't it? I mean, it was quite a trek, wasn't it, working in Hammersmith—'

'It's not Hammersmith, Charlotte.' As he falls silent, something stirs inside me: a smidgeon of doubt that perhaps this isn't the joyous occasion I'd imagined it would be.

'Well, where is it? And what's the job?'

'It's um . . . a directorship.'

'Wow, that's fantastic! Finally, someone's realised how much you have to offer—'

'I've had lots actually,' he interrupts. I stare at him, uncomprehending.

'You mean *interviews*?'

'Yeah.'

'But you never said . . .'

'You never asked,' he says flatly.

I study my husband, wondering how we've managed to end up so chilly and distant with each other. He couldn't even find it in himself to tell me when he'd had interviews. And to think: I've assumed he was spending all his time here at home, or out on his bike, or pottering about locally. Rowdy laughter drifts in through the window, then Ollie bursts in, smelling of grass and sunshine and announcing that they're all off to the park.

'I didn't want to seem like I was nagging,' I tell Will as soon as they've all clattered out. 'I thought you had enough of that from your mum.'

'Well, anyway,' he says matter-of-factly, 'this is a second interview.'

'Great! Wow. So they're really keen, then.' I try to seem pleased, and not show how hurtful this information is to me.

'Hard to tell really,' he says, 'but it'll be good to meet them face to face. The first interview was on Skype . . .'

So Will sat in this very house, being interviewed, and didn't feel like mentioning it to me when I came home from work. I wonder if that was the day I arrived home laden with reject crisps, or came in babbling on about Rupert's golden retriever, who's becoming more and more flatulent by the day, or some other scintillating gossip from the world of salty snacks. 'So what's the job?' I ask, keeping my tone light. 'Is it with a charity?'

Will nods. 'It's called the Seal Protection Trust. Conservation and protection are a big part of it, but they're putting more resources into education, working with schools and running regular boat trips, even sea life safaris—'

'Seals? But there aren't any seals in London, are there?' I laugh, feeling suddenly foolish, blurting out a question that a five-year-old might ask. 'Apart from at the zoo,' I add. 'The job's not with the zoo, is it?'

'No, Charlotte. It's, um . . . in Scotland. The job's based up on the east coast, north of Inverness.'

I stare at him, wondering how he could have kept

this from me. Something catches my eye in the garden; just a crow, eyeing me defiantly from the fence. 'But what about school?' I ask. 'D'you think it'd be okay to uproot them now? I mean, it might be all right for Ollie, but this is such a crucial time for Rosie, with needing the results for a veterinary course . . .' Will starts to speak, but I interrupt: 'And what about their friends and Rosie's modelling? I know that shouldn't be the deciding factor, but can you imagine how she'll react if we tell her, "Actually sweetheart, we're leaving London and moving hundreds of miles north to the middle of nowhere where you won't know a soul . . ."' I tail off and blink at Will.

'The thing is, Charlotte—'

'And what about this house?' I blurt out. 'Would we sell it, d'you think, or let it out?'

'Listen, the house isn't—'

'And your mum? D'you think she'd move to Scotland too? I mean, I know she's fine at the moment, but she does rely on you for all those little jobs, and I can't imagine your sister stepping in, can you?'

Will opens his mouth and closes it again, like a fish.

'What about *my* job? I know it's only crisps, Will, but it's all I have at the moment . . .'

'Charlotte,' he cuts in, more firmly this time, '*if* I get it, and nothing's certain yet—'

'So . . . when are you going?'

'First thing Monday,' he replies. 'The interview's after lunch, but they want me to spend a few days getting to know the staff and the area, going out with field workers to get a real sense of what they do. So I'll be gone for a few days . . .'

'How long exactly?'

'Well, um, a week,' he replies.

Just like that, with no discussion. Of course, I didn't discuss my secret little meeting in Caffè Nero either. I snuck off while Will was dutifully cleansing Gloria's patio of its pesky moss. 'So where are you staying?' I ask bleakly.

'They're putting me up in a B&B in some tiny place near the headquarters. It's the only one in the village, I think . . .'

'Will,' I say, 'it sounds like they absolutely want you for this job. Surely no one gets a week's accommodation and travel unless . . . I take it they're paying for your flight?'

'Uh-huh.' It's his sheepish expression – which says, I actually want this job very much – that gives him away. With a wave of dread, I also realise what this means for us. 'Charlotte,' Will starts, 'if I get it, I'm not planning for us all to move north.'

My heart feels as if it is being crushed like a tin can. 'Oh,' I say faintly.

'I mean . . . I think it'd be best for you and the kids to stay here.' He pushes back his hair, avoiding my gaze.

'You mean, *you'd* move? Just you, by yourself?'

Will nods. 'That's what I'm thinking.'

'You mean . . . without *us*?' I'm trying to be strong, and behave like women do in romcoms when they're being left. Terse conversation over, they stride off in their clicky heels and do something drastic – something that makes a bold statement – like having their waist-length hair cut off and emerging from the salon with a chic, impish crop. I don't feel like that sort of woman. I have purplish shoulder-length hair and would worry that, if I were to chop it all off, I wouldn't even look like an aubergine anymore. I'd be a potato. One of those prized Maris Pipers from Mickey's farm.

'I didn't plan this, you know,' Will says simply.

'But you did!' I protest. 'Of course you did. You applied for a job hundreds of miles away, knowing what it'd mean for us. Why did you even do that?' My voice cracks, and I will myself not to cry. *I will not be a blubbery cry baby. I will be strong! Let him go wherever he wants to. We'll cope. We'll even look after the garden. I'll finally get to grips with our temperamental lawnmower and throw hormone rooting powder on anything that looks like a proper plant. There is nothing we need Will to do for us!*

'Look,' he says gently, 'I know this sounds stupid, but I can't tell you how crap it's been, applying for all these posts and getting nowhere, or getting *nearly* somewhere, then being told, "Oh, sorry, you didn't have quite the skill set we were looking for." Then I'd snoop about online and find that the person they'd taken on was virtually half my age . . .'

'Come on, Will, you're only forty-one. It's hardly geriatric!'

'Well, it is when you're job-hunting,' he insists. 'I hate to say it, but Gerald was right. I'd started to think I was on the bloody scrapheap, Charlotte. So, when I saw this directorship post I just thought, sod it, why not apply and see what happens, never expecting to even get an interview. It was a mad, impulsive thing to do. I didn't even think they'd call . . .'

'And then they did,' I bleat.

'Yeah. I was amazed. And I started to think, maybe I have a chance here and, if I do get it . . .' He breaks off the shrugs. 'Well, maybe it'd be good for us too.'

'*How* is it good for us?' I exclaim. 'You'd be in Scotland and we'd be down here. How can that possibly be a good thing?'

'I mean, to have a bit of space from each other,' Will says, still unable to look at me properly.

'You think we need space?'

'Yeah, I think maybe we do.'

'It's not *that* bad!' I cry, trying to keep the tears in by sheer willpower alone, and realising that maybe he's right: is that really the best I can come up with? That our marriage isn't 'that bad'?

'I think we've both let things drift,' he says gently.

'You're right. We have.' Tears are dripping down my cheeks as I think about our VAT return sex life, and how he flinches if I try to touch him. I've assumed it's just a result of us growing older, and being together for fifteen years – but maybe it's not. Maybe it's more serious than that, and I haven't had the courage to admit it.

'So,' Will says, 'what d'you think?'

What do I *think*? As if we're talking about whether we eat too much butter and should switch to Flora instead? I look at him, knowing I'm as much to blame as Will is for this state of affairs. What right do I have to be outraged by his secret interview, with all the sneaking around I've done lately? Will should know about my coffee with Fraser, and that pretty soon, I think Rosie should meet him too. We need to be open and honest like proper grown-ups and stop tip-toeing around each other. I'm about to blurt all this out, and to say that we all love him and need him here, and how can Rosie possibly cope with the Fraser situation without him? But the front door opens, and Rosie and Zach stride in, arms draped around each other, closely followed by Ollie and his gang from the park.

I greet everyone, then delve into a kitchen drawer, fling

takeaway menus on the table and hand Rosie all the money I have in my purse. 'Order anything you like,' I say quickly.

I turn to Will and grab his hand. 'Can we go out?' I murmur. 'Can we go somewhere so it's just us?'

Chapter Thirty-Two

We haven't been to Parliament Hill for years, not since we bought Rosie a box kite and Will showed her how to fly it. Having never managed to manoeuvre any kind of kite successfully, I was blown away by how Will made it look so easy. Even Ollie crying when he wasn't allowed to control it all by himself didn't spoil the day.

This evening is a little different. We didn't discuss where we might go 'to talk'. We just climbed into the car and set off, and here's where we ended up. Although the evening has turned cooler, there are plenty of families out walking, and small children chasing each other, squealing with delight; it's a scene plucked straight from Archie's website. The only thing that's not quite right is the couple – Will and me – who are walking a little apart. Let's just say we are not emitting the jolliness which Rupert describes as 'the real essence of what we're all about'.

'Will,' I say carefully, as we march up the hill, 'is this anything to do with the shed?'

He gives me a bewildered look.

'Finding my shoes in there,' I explain, 'and assuming I was having a fling or something . . .'

He groans. 'God, no. I applied way before that. Look, I'm sorry about that. I don't know what I was thinking, accusing you . . .' He stuffs his hands into his jeans pockets.

'You asked if I'd been in there with Fraser,' I add, giving him a quick look.

'Yeah, I know. I'm sorry, it was a mad thing to say. I think I just had a bit of . . . I don't know . . . cabin fever.'

Hence applying for a job far, far away – to break out of that little cabin of ours. It still seems rather extreme. Most people, when they experience that hemmed-in feeling, go out and get drunk, or book a holiday or, in Sabrina's case, donate blood. 'So you don't think I really did that.'

'No! Christ, of course not.'

We walk in silence for a few moments. 'Actually, Will . . . I *have* met Fraser.'

He stops and stares at me. 'You met him? Where?'

'In Caffè Nero in Covent Garden . . .'

'And you didn't tell me?'

'No, and I'm sorry. I know I should have, but I didn't. It's just, you seemed so upset, the first time he emailed me . . .'

'So it was *my* fault, was it?'

I go to touch his arm but he shrinks away. 'I'm not saying that. It's not anyone's fault. It was a spur-of-the-moment thing—'

'So when did you meet him?' Will snaps.

'On Monday, when you were at your mum's getting the moss off her patio.'

He actually gasps at this. 'Great! Just as well she had me building that bloody bird table as well, huh? To give you plenty of time?'

'It wasn't like that,' I protest. 'It was just something I felt I had to do.' My cheeks are blazing, and a young mum and her little boy, with a purple kite tucked under his arm, give me a curious look as we march past.

'Why's that lady cross?' the child pipes up.

'Shush, darling. It's none of our business . . .'

'Why's that man shouting about a bird table?'

I glance back. She is tugging him along by a hand. 'Never mind, Lucas. Come on, if we don't hurry up we'll never get to fly this kite . . .'

'Why not?'

'Because the wind'll all be gone, that's why . . .' Their voices fade.

'It's the deceit,' Will mutters. 'The fact that you snuck off and met him and didn't say anything, before you went, or even afterwards . . .'

'I know, and I'm sorry. I feel really crap about it, Will.'

'I suppose this shows I'm doing the right thing, then,' he growls.

'What, by leaving? Is *that* what you're doing? I still don't understand. Is it really about the job, or something else? Would you be leaving anyway?'

'I don't *know* what I'm doing,' he rages. 'Look, why didn't you just tell me before you went?'

Because I was scared, is the truth. Because of the eggshell thing, feeling as if I spend my entire life stepping carefully around you, as if the ground beneath my feet is incredibly fragile and pale, speckled blue . . .

'I knew you'd be upset,' I murmur. 'It was really quick,

and a bit awkward, to be honest—' I break off as he turns away from me suddenly. 'Where are you going?'

'Back to the car.' We stomp down the hill in silence. This is it, I decide: I've lost him. He'll be offered this job, and meet a bevvy of beautiful girls, all dedicating themselves to the welfare of the creatures of the sea. They'll have creamy, Celtic skin and in-depth knowledge of the behaviour of puffins. He'll meet an elfin girl with one of those alluring Gaelic names, like Mhairi or Eilidh – the ones with h's in confusing places which I'm never sure how to pronounce.

I climb into the driver's seat and put the key in the ignition. A tiny leaf is clinging to the top of Will's head. Normally I'd pick it off, but he's emitting powerful *don't-touch-me* vibes.

'The thing is, Will,' I start, trying to order my thoughts, 'it didn't quite happen the way I thought it did. With Rosie, I mean. And Fraser.'

'What d'you mean?' he asks gruffly.

'I mean, he didn't just leave us. Well, he did, but not the way I thought he did.' I clear my throat. 'His mum told him I'd phoned to say I hadn't gone through with the pregnancy, that I'd had an abortion—'

In an instant, his expression changes and the anger fades. His eyes focus on mine. 'Christ, Charlotte.'

'Yes, I know.'

He pauses, and for a moment, I think he's going to reach for my hand, but instead, he rubs his eyes and sighs loudly. 'So he never knew he had a child?'

I shake my head. 'Even when he saw us in that magazine, he didn't realise she was his.'

Will frowns. 'Isn't he very good at maths then? Or doesn't he know how long the human gestation period is?'

I throw him a sharp look. 'They got her age wrong in the interview, remember? They said she was fifteen so he assumed I'd got pregnant by someone else . . .'

'Charming. So what now? I s'pose he's going to be part of our family, is he?'

'Will, *please.* We've always known she'd want to meet him at some point . . .'

'Yeah, when *we* felt it was right. I always imagined we'd be in control of the situation, you know? So we could talk to her first, and decide if it was the right thing to try and track him down . . .'

'It's just the way it's happened,' I insist. 'I know it's not perfect, but then, nothing is.'

'No, it certainly isn't.' He turns away, staring pointedly out of the side window, as I switch on the ignition and pull out.

As we drive home in silence I try to adjust to the possibility of my husband leaving me. To think, I've felt mildly rejected when he's edged over to the far side of the bed. And now he wants to relocate as far away as humanly possible from me, whilst clinging on to the very northernmost tip of mainland Britain. Hell, why not go the whole hog and move to the Shetland Isles, or Iceland, or the North Pole? Sure, it'd be chilly, but with his two identical cashmere sweaters – presented by his mother and me on his birthday – and worn on top of each other, I'm sure he'd be perfectly cosy.

'What shall we tell the kids?' I ask finally, as we near our own street.

'I think we should just be completely honest.' *Unlike you,* he adds silently.

'Fine, but how d'you think they'll react?'

'I think they'll be okay,' he says, blithely, as if we are about to break the news that we are choosing a new colour for our front door.

Zach and Ollie's friends have gone, and we are greeted by evidence of extreme over-ordering from our local Indian. 'Want some, Mum?' Ollie asks, indicating the cartons of cold curry strewn over the coffee table in the living room. 'There's tons left. Look – we got Peshwari naan just for you . . .'

'Thanks,' I murmur, trying to look pleased.

'Where did you go anyway?' Rosie wants to know.

'Uh, just out for a drive,' Will says.

'A drive,' Ollie sniggers. 'That's such an old peopley thing to do. I mean, what's the point?'

'It's enjoyable,' I fib, because he's right: there was no point at all. Will's mind is made up and, even if he doesn't get this job, he's obviously decided to cast the net far and wide in his search for employment. Well, fine. To show Will how completely *fine* I am, I grab the untouched naan and rip off a huge piece.

'Don't understand why you like Peshwari,' Ollie scoffs. 'It's sweet and almondy. It's all wrong in a bread-type scenario.'

'It's delicious,' I retort, although right now, with Will revving himself up to tell the kids about his plans, I don't remotely feel like eating. My teeth sink into the spongy bread. Although I'm sure it *is* delicious, and that the Bombay Star hasn't altered its recipe, right now it seems to have the taste and texture of an insole.

'Want some more?' Ollie asks, waggling the oily dough in my face.

'No, hon, I've had enough.' I glance at Will, who is

finishing what's left of the chicken korma (*he's* not having any trouble eating, I note).

He clears his throat. 'Erm, I've got a bit of news,' he says, proceeding to tell them about zipping off to Inverness on Monday. Straight away, I realise that my anticipated awful, tearful scene isn't going to happen because, rather cleverly, Will is presenting the possibility of this new job – 'and it's not definite, not at all,' he keeps stressing, although of course it's virtually in the bag – as a fantastic opportunity for boundless family fun.

'Sounds great,' Rosie marvels. 'God, Dad – a director! That's some promotion . . .'

'I'd love to go there,' Ollie adds.

'Well, you can,' Will enthuses, crunching a poppadom, 'if I get the job . . .' He is on the verge of leaving us. How can he keep on stuffing his face, forking great chunks of chicken into his gob like he hasn't eaten for weeks? 'It's so wild and beautiful up there,' he adds, biting into the last onion bhaji.

'How d'you know?' Ollie asks. 'You said the first interview was on Skype.'

'Yes,' Will says, 'but we had lots of holidays up there when I was a kid. I had an aunt up there, remember? Grandma Gloria's sister who lived in Dornoch.' Ah yes, I remember him describing Aunt Helen: tough, robust, her hair pulled back into a no-nonsense bun, in stark contrast to Gloria's beauty contest glamour. Then he's off again: enthusing over white sand beaches and turreted castles peeping out from dense pine forests, while I try to pick a bit of naan out of my right molar.

Maybe it *is* for the best, I decide. What kind of marriage is this, if all this planning has been going on and he hasn't thought to involve me in any of it? I try to catch his eye as he talks. It's as if I am not even in the room.

'But if you get it,' Rosie says, frowning, 'when would we actually see you?'

'I'd be home some weekends,' Will says, still avoiding looking at me at all, 'and you could come up, of course. It's only a ninety-minute flight. You'll be there before you've even finished your tub of Pringles . . .'

'Are Pringles free on planes?' asks Ollie, who can barely remember flying anywhere.

'Er, I think so,' Will replies. 'Probably. Honestly, you'll love it. It's not just seals up there, you know. There are dolphins, porpoises, minke whales . . . even ospreys. D'you know what they're like, Ollie?'

'Yeah, they're massive birds of prey.'

'. . . with nests the size of rafts,' Will surges on, 'big enough for a grown man to float in . . .'

'Cool!' Ollie exclaims.

'Could we fly on our own, Dad?' Rosie asks. 'Without Mum, I mean? I'm old enough . . .' It feels as if that wretched piece of naan has lodged itself in my throat.

'Sure,' Will says. I get up from the sofa, stride through to the kitchen and open the fridge. Although I take out a bottle of fizzy water, wine is what I want. Wine, of any kind at all – at this point I'm not fussy – tipped hastily down my throat. Tragically, there doesn't seem to be any. Why is this so? We always have a bottle or two hanging about. We should have another stash, hidden away: *emergency wine.*

By the time I rejoin my family, they are busily planning many jaunts. These appear to involve independent travel and boat trips while, presumably, I am left at home to trundle back and forth to a crisp factory in

Essex and conduct an endless, fruitless search for our lost rabbit. They don't realise – and nor would I want them to – that Will's thrilling adventure is actually his way of leaving me.

Unable to join in with the jolly conversation, I wander off to re-check Guinness's sleeping quarters, then slope back into the kitchen, feeling all at sea here, in my own house: redundant, really.

'*Can* we go, Dad?' Ollie's voice rings through the house. 'Can I bring Saul as well?'

'I don't see why not,' Will replies.

I sit alone at the kitchen table, sipping my glass of water. In fact, I'd rather be here than squashed on the sofa with Will and the kids. I can't bear to watch him being cheery, poppadom-crunching Dad when he's on the brink of ending our marriage. I can hear it all, despite being in a different room – do they *always* talk so loudly? Will is on about basking sharks now; gentle creatures who glide through the sea, mouths wide open to allow billions of plankton to float in. It's like a nature documentary without pictures.

A sea sponge, *that's* the kind of sea creature I'll be. What little factlet did Ollie tell me about them again? That they can't be bothered to do it, even if they meet a really good-looking sea sponge, haha! Well, I reflect, glimpsing Tricia through our kitchen window, pegging out Gerald's enormous Madras-checked underpants, maybe that wouldn't be so bad. I'd just bob about, bothering no one. I wouldn't even think about sex or love or being fancied; I'd just be *there*.

Yep, that's what I'll be, I decide, grabbing my bag and slipping out quietly to the off-licence for wine.

They're still chattering away in the living room when

I come back. I don't think anyone's even noticed that I've been out. So I pour a big glass and take it upstairs, where I sprawl on our bed with my laptop and Google 'distance London Inverness'.

559 miles, it says, which suggests that Will craves more than 'a bit of space'.

Chapter Thirty-Three

I'm not sure how Will and I get through the period leading up to him stepping onto that plane, where the living is easy and the Pringles are free. Actually they're not; they are £1.80, sour cream or paprika – not a Lobster Bisque to be had – from what EasyJet grandly term their in-flight 'bistro'. I know this because I've checked.

This is the kind of person I have become: an obsessive checker of details, in between glaring at Will's best suit which hangs, interview-ready and sheathed in clear plastic, on our wardrobe door. It's very smart: charcoal, with a fine, paler stripe. I've rarely seen him wearing a suit at all, and am almost tempted to ask him to model it for me, just so I can hold in my head an image of a different Will – assured, professional, Director Will – in case I never get a chance to see him that way. But I suspect he'd think I was taking the piss, and I'm at pains to avoid any more bickering before he leaves.

In fact, it feels as if our life is being carefully stage-managed to minimise any difficult moments. Will is being extremely polite and rather sweet to me, as if I have just returned from a lengthy stay in hospital. I almost expect him to bring me grapes, or a copy of *Woman's Weekly*. And when I spot him peering at grey seals on his laptop, he quickly shuts down the page as if it's porn.

On Friday morning – a work day, when I'd usually snatch a piece of toast – I am presented with perfectly soft and melty scrambled eggs, accessorised with snipped chives. I look at the chives, wishing I could interpret them as evidence that Will loves me madly and that I'm forgiven for meeting Fraser and being such a thundering disappointment of late. But I can't. Whichever way I look at them, they are just flecks of oniony herb.

Anyway, I have no appetite whatsoever, so the eggs remain barely touched. Perhaps this is one advantage of Will and I having 'space'. My favourite work skirt now sits at hip level, rather than digging into my waist; even my matronly sausage-boob seems to have deflated. My face looks a little slimmer than how it appeared in *Front* magazine, even without Boo's endeavours with all that blusher and shader. I wouldn't say it's an improvement, though. I look tense and faintly unwell, and definitely lacking in cheek glow and eye sparkle. One small consolation is the fact that Sabrina, Tommy and Zach have gone away to visit Tommy's mother. I seem to run into Sabrina constantly these days, and she's the type to home in on a change in appearance. Although I do enjoy her company, I'd rather not have to explain what's going on. Now yet, anyway. I do, however, manage a snatched phone conversation with Liza when I arrive at work.

'I know it's not great,' she says, 'but if he does get the job, he can still come home at weekends, can't he?'

'That seems to be what he's planning,' I admit.

'It might even be good for you,' she suggests. Hmm.

Absence makes the heart grow fonder and all that. 'It's doable, isn't it?' she adds.

'I suppose so,' I say reluctantly, thinking it *would* be okay, if Will was desperately upset at the prospect of being parted from me. But he's not; in fact he seems positively buoyant. Weirdly, it's almost like having my old Will back, when he was happy, beavering away at Greenspace Heritage, and never did that nostril-flaring thing at me.

In the office now, I barely look up from my screen, apart from to briefly speculate with Dee as to why Rupert is so antsy, and joke whether he's gone off us, his 'favourite girls', because he's barely stopped to say hello. We don't mention Frank, or the *beary-beary-much* card. I wonder if it's still in Dee's drawer. For days now she's said nothing about soft furnishings, or the shortlist of tile colours she and Mike have arrived at for their bathroom. We don't speak of any of that. We just clatter away on our computers and make many calls. Rupert fails to put in an appearance all day; I leave a message with Rhona, his secretary, explaining that I'll have to take some time off next week, with Will not being around. I also leave a message on Rupert's mobile, reiterating that things are tricky at home, which he fails to respond to.

Back at home, it's sort of similar, in that Will and I don't discuss anything serious either. Not Fraser, not Scotland, not the plight of the bottlenose dolphin. At the weekend, we have some 'family outings', as Rosie disparagingly calls them – although she seems to enjoy our trip to a pop art exhibition, and a meander around Portobello Road, which we haven't done together for years.

We are a family, I remind myself, as we sit in the

sunshine clutching cartons of falafel. And we'll still be a family when Will is in Scotland. Plenty of dads do that – work away from their partner and kids. We are strong enough to cope. Trouble is, I have a horrible feeling that Will is viewing this not as something to 'deal with', but as an escape.

Rosie and Ollie barely stir in their beds on Monday morning as I tell them I'm taking their dad to Gatwick. Hardly surprising: it's 6 a.m. Although Will had planned to take a cab, I have insisted on driving him. From Inverness airport he'll pick up a hire car and drive north, along the beautiful coastline he spent many hours showing the kids; ribbons of white sand, and all that wildlife.

I have adopted a matter-of-fact demeanour, although the effort of maintaining it is causing my left eye to reverberate disconcertingly. My stomach is churning, and it's all I can do to focus on the road ahead. We don't talk a great deal on the journey, and when we do it's about the traffic (not too heavy) and the weather (breezy, pleasantly fresh). Will is obviously trying to rein in his excitement.

Well, sod it all, I decide, after a brief, slightly awkward goodbye at the departure gate. I hope he gets the job. He *needs* it; he's wilting away, fiddling about with his lettuces and herbs. While I know he'll make sure he still sees the kids ('You'll be there before you've even finished your tub of Pringles!'), I know what'll happen with us. Never mind our friend minke whale, with her alluring curves and elegant fins. He's bound to impress the local *human* lovelies too, 'hot dad' that he is.

In the airport car park, I'm just about to climb into my car when my mobile rings. 'Charlotte?' Rupert says. 'Can you talk right now?'

'Yes,' I reply, 'and I'm glad you called. Look, Rupert, I'm sorry about this—'

'What about?'

'About asking for more time off without warning. You see, Will's had to go away and I can't expect Rosie to look after Ollie all week—'

'Just take time off,' he cuts in. 'It's fine, no problem. The thing is . . .'

'Will's applying for a job in Scotland,' I blurt out, because I feel as if I can.

'God, is he? Is that, um . . . a good thing?'

'I don't know,' I admit, climbing into my car, relieved that I work for a cuddly operation like Archie's, not a vast, faceless company where holidays must be requested months in advance. 'Well, not really,' I add. 'I mean, if he gets it, he's planning to move north and the kids and I will stay in London. So, anyway,' I babble on, trying to sound jovial and light, 'you won't be getting rid of me that easily.'

I focus on a battered old buff-coloured Morris Minor which is trundling slowly around the car park. Rupert, I realise, has gone quiet. 'Sorry to babble on,' I say. 'You wanted to talk to me . . .'

'Yeah. The, er . . . the thing is, Charlotte, there's something I have to tell you. I'm having this meeting—'

'Not a gathering?' I chip in, inanely.

'Um, well, whatever it is, I'm getting all the staff' – so we're staff now, not teamsters – 'to explain what's happening at Archie's.' A small pause. The faint whiff of apple is still detectable in my car, even though I've tried to de-fruit it numerous times.

'So what's happening?' I ask faintly.

Rupert coughs. 'We're being taken over, Charlotte. I'm so sorry. I wish I was telling you this in person . . .'

'You mean you're selling the company?'

'Yes, to Fielding Foods—' Oh, my God. Fielding foods are huge: they make *everything*. Well, nearly everything: biscuits, breakfast cereals, nasty pasta sauces which seem to bear no relation to actual real, fresh tomatoes apart from being red – Will would rather eat plain, bald pasta rather than slathering it in that filthy stuff . . . my mind grinds to a halt. They also make crisps, of course: the cheap, everyday kind (ready salted, salt & vin, etc) sold singly in newsagents and in multipacks in every supermarket in the land. '. . . Been on the cards for some time now,' Rupert goes on, 'but, you know, confidentiality and all that . . .'

I watch as the Morris Minor parks up and a family tumbles out, baggage-less and seeming excited, as they all stride towards the terminal; must be meeting someone from a flight. How much more joyous the arrivals area is to the goodbye zone. '. . . We'll be part of one of the biggest food manufacturers in Britain,' Rupert adds, his voice straining with the effort of making this sound like a great thing.

'So what does this mean?' I ask, as fine rain starts to spit at my windscreen. 'For the staff, I mean? The, er, teamsters?'

'Well, they're keeping the Archie's brand of course, which is fantastic. But . . .' – and here it comes – 'operations are being centralised so production is being relocated to their main plant in the East Midlands.' All these un-Archie's words: *operations, production, plant* . . . '. . . And I hate to tell you,' Rupert adds, 'but PR and marketing are all going to be centralised too . . .'

I listen to my boss's bumbling apologies and he goes on to stress how *valued* I am, and how he'll ensure that

I'm handsomely rewarded with a generous redundancy package, plus glowing references of course, that goes without saying . . . and all I can think is: *Fielding Foods*. They are as far from cuddly knitted crisp corsages as it's possible to be. But it's okay, I tell Rupert, it's okay, really. I know these things happen. I do understand.

'I'm so glad you're seeing it this way,' he says, sounding genuinely distressed.

Well, what else am I supposed to do? In a few short hours my husband will be arriving at his B&B in that quaint little postcard village, and changing into his suit (secretly, I have always found him ultra-fanciable in a suit). And soon after that, he'll be told he is now officially Director of Seals.

While I am officially redundant.

These things happen, I repeat silently in my head, on the drizzly journey home.

Chapter Thirty-Four

In fact, I do have a job: Director-in-chief of Bunny Hunt. As the kids profess to have 'run out of ideas' of where Guinness might be, I re-check every hidey-hole I can think of. It's keeping me busy, at least. But, as it involves rummaging about in the more unsavoury crannies of our house, it's pretty thankless, grubby work. Lonely, too. Ollie seems to have given up the hunt, and Rosie is spending pretty much all of her time in her room, muttering to God knows who on her phone. Delph or Zach, probably, although I'd like to think it might be Nina. I know Rosie's upset – about Guinness, certainly, who's been missing for five days now, and possibly Will, despite her cheeriness when he broke the news – and I wish I could do something to lift her spirits. Aren't parents supposed to be able to make everything better? My suggestion that she might like to ask Nina round, so they could hang out together, was met with a blank look. 'I'm *fine*, Mum,' she said, unconvincingly.

Feeling cabin-feverish, I break off and change into my sole tracksuit and trainers for a speed-walk around the park. Decreased appetite, and now exercise – I'll soon be fitting into what the fashion industry terms 'sample sizes' (see, I'm learning fast). Anyway, I reflect, as someone in the distance waves to attract my attention, that's one upside of the Fielding Foods takeover. I will no longer have the perpetual temptation of premium crisps sitting under my nose. Rupert has called again to explain that I won't be expected to go back in to work. I should just pop in in a few days' time, 'when the dust has settled', to 'go over my "package"' with him. We even laughed at that.

As the waving person approaches I realise it's Helen, Nina's mum, who's all smiles. 'Haven't seen you for ages,' she says. 'How's things?'

Fine, is what I should say. 'I've just been made redundant,' I blurt out, which causes Helen, who has a proper job – she's a social worker, it's a job that *matters* – to put a hand on my arm and say, 'Oh, God, how awful. Shall we grab a coffee? D'you have time?' All the time in the world, as it happens. So we head to the café in the park, which always smells of bacon, even when there's no indication of bacon being cooked.

I fill her in on the swallowing up of cuddly Archie's by an enormous conglomerate in the East Midlands. 'What'll you do?' she says, all wide, sympathetic eyes.

'I have no idea. Haven't even had time to think. Anyway, I'm not holding you up, am I?'

'No, no, I've got the week off. Thought I should spend a bit of time with Nina. She's um . . .' Helen's cheeks flush beneath her mass of nut-brown curls.

'Is she okay?' I ask, frowning.

'Um . . . she's a bit down, actually, but I don't want to load this on you, not when you've had that awful news . . .' My heart seems to slip a bit lower than where it should be.

'Any reason?' I know, before she even replies, what it is.

Helen takes a sip from her mug. 'Look, I know how it is, Charlotte. The age the girls are – they grow apart, they're all so fickle at this stage. I hear Rosie has a boyfriend now, and she's modelling. That's fantastic.'

I muster a smile, almost wishing she wasn't being so understanding. I mean, the girls have been best friends since they were five years old. What if Delph drops Rosie, and Zach loses interest and moves on elsewhere? 'I'm sorry she's not seeing much of Nina,' I venture. 'I've tried to encourage her. It's just so hard to get through to her at the moment . . .'

She smiles. 'Oh, I know what it's like. To be honest, I don't think it's really Rosie's fault. It's that Delph girl—'

Oh, hell. 'Has something happened?'

'Well, er . . .' Helen stirs her coffee unnecessarily. 'She wasn't very nice to Nina, actually.'

'When was this?'

'The night you all went to that gig. It was just a few snidey comments, about her weight, mostly—'

'Her weight?' I gasp. 'What on earth did she say?'

Helen shrugs. 'Just that, you know . . . she'd look better if she lost a bit . . .'

'Oh, my God.' I am horrified. Nina is lovely; a perfectly proportioned teenage girl.

'Delph said she had fat arms,' Helen adds. 'She's worn long sleeves ever since—'

'That's awful,' I exclaim. 'I'm mortified, Helen. I don't know what to say. Rosie seems entranced by Delph. I wish she wasn't, but that's how it is at the moment . . .'

'It's okay,' Helen says quickly. 'I didn't know whether

to say anything and, anyway, it's really not your fault, or Rosie's—'

I look at her, picturing our daughters together at age eight, when Will and I took them to Lego Land; and at eleven, when they set off for their first day at secondary school . . . weirdly, although I didn't cry at the departure gate this morning – or even when Rupert told me I'd lost my job – I could cry now. 'I feel terrible,' I add.

Helen slips her bag onto her shoulder. 'Don't, honestly.' I drain my cup and, as we part company outside the café, I tell myself that it's okay, *these things happen.* 'Nina's making some new friends at the Harvester,' Helen adds, giving me a fleeting hug before striding away.

*

I arrive home to find Rosie messily gathering snacks together in the kitchen: biscuits, toast and jam, even bowls of crisps, which she wouldn't entertain normally. Perhaps she senses that our supply of freebies will soon run dry . . .

'Hungry?' I ask lightly.

'Yeah, starving. Delph's upstairs. I'll just take this lot up.' Ah, the weight-assessor. The body confidence guru for teenage girls. Rosie piles everything – plus two glasses of chocolate milk – on a tray and carries it out of the kitchen. I purse my lips and hope I won't be put in a position of having to feign friendliness with our guest. 'Oh, Mum,' Rosie calls back, 'Dad called.'

I charge through to the hallway and look up. 'What did he say?'

She is halfway up the stairs, balancing the tray precariously. 'He said he's fine.'

'Oh. Great. Er, are you sure you can manage that tray?'

'Yeah, 's'fine.'

I blink at her. 'Did he say how the interview went?'

'Yeah, really well, I think,' she says casually, as if it's of no real consequence.

'I saw Nina's mum in the park,' I add as she starts to make her way up to the landing. 'She said Nina's feeling a bit down at the moment, maybe you should give her a call—'

'Mum,' Rosie says firmly, without turning around, 'I don't really want to get into all that right now, okay?' She disappears to her room.

I sit on the stairs, wondering what I'm supposed to do now. I mean, I can't dissuade her from seeing Delph. One even faintly negative comment from me would cause her to adore the girl even more. A burst of raucous laughter comes from Rosie's room. It's *cruel* laughter I hear – the kind a poor, bewildered lady in the park might be subjected to, if her skirt was tucked into her big knickers. I try to beam up stern vibes to alert Rosie as to how disappointed I am, that she's dropped loyal Nina for a vacuous girl who's criticised her best friend – her *real* best friend I mean – when Delph herself is definitely verging on malnourished, in my opinion. Maybe Rosie's concerned about her – hence all the biscuits and crisps and chocolate milk?

With a sigh, I pull out my phone from my jeans pocket and call Will. His calm, mellow voice explains that I may leave a message. *No thanks*, I think bitterly.

'D'you think I look, like, *old* or something?' Rosie's voice rings out from her room.

''Course not,' Delph retorts. 'You're insane. How can you even think that?'

'Well, the mitten shoot, and them telling Laurie I'm perfect for the knitting market . . .'

'Don't take any notice of that,' Delph replies. 'You look sixteen, seventeen or eighteen, tops. That's just bread-and-butter work, my agent calls it. No one sees it and no one cares. It's just money, Ro. God, you sound like my mum. She's always going, "Do I look ancient to you? Am I too old for a bikini? Or a denim jacket?" Drives me mad!' They both hoot with shrill laughter.

'How old's your mum?' Rosie enquires.

'Dunno. About forty-five, I think – goes on about the menopause anyway. I think it's happening. She's been dead moody. Crying over nothing and moaning that her hair's drying out . . .'

'Does that happen?' Rosie asks, sounding alarmed.

'God, yeah. And not just that. Your skin withers and you shrivel up down there . . .'

'No!'

'Yeah. Sex gets, like, *really* painful . . .'

'That's disgusting,' Rosie says. Christ, aren't they aware of how loudly they talk?

'Well, it's true,' Delph declares. 'Mum told me. We have a really honest relationship. We're more like sisters really . . . are you like that with your mum?'

'Not really,' Rosie replies, at which my heart sinks.

'D'you think she's having her menopause yet?'

'Dunno. Probably.' Bloody hell, I am only thirty-eight. I am in my *prime*! I could produce a couple more babies if I got a move on, although in view of my situation right now, this is highly unlikely. 'So what else happens?' Rosie asks as I gather myself up and creep back downstairs.

'Oh, all kinds of shit. Your face gets hairy 'cause your

oestrogen's running out. Basically, you become more like a man.'

In the kitchen now, with the door firmly shut, I peer at my reflection in our kettle. Can't see any hairs sticking out of my chin, but then it is a bit smeary so I grab an Archie's tea towel and give it a wipe, then lean in for a closer look. Now I see it: a lone hair jutting out, just below the left corner of my mouth. An actual menopause symptom. An *old lady sprouting*. Why hasn't Will told me? He probably hasn't noticed. I doubt he'd detect anything untoward if the lower half of my face was entirely smothered by matted fur. I pull at the hair ineffectually, which makes my eyes sting, then rummage in the drawer for scissors and snip it off.

The girls are heading downstairs now, giggling away as if they don't have a care in the world – which is, of course, how it should be. They are young. They are gorgeous. They have thirty-odd years before anything remotely menopausal starts happening to them. I have lost my job, just as my husband is planning to leave me and become a Director and, to top it all, I am growing a beard. When should I tell them about my redundancy, I wonder? Not now. Ollie is at Saul's, and Rosie is too busy discussing my imminent shrivelling to be concerned with the trivial matter of us being able to pay the mortgage and, you know, *live*.

The kitchen door flies open. 'We're going out for a coffee,' Rosie announces.

Coffee, which she has always dismissed as bitter and disgusting . . . 'Okay,' I say. 'Take your phone, would you?'

'Sure,' she says pleasantly, perhaps pitying me for my withering insides.

Delph waggles her fingers at me by way of saying goodbye. 'Don't worry,' she tells Rosie as they leave. 'By the time it starts happening to us, they'll have invented a cure for all that stuff.'

Chapter Thirty-Five

'It'll be *fine*,' Sabrina assures me later, as we're installed on my sofa, tucking into the wine she's brought. 'Tommy was away loads when Zach was little, and to be honest, sometimes it was easier not to have him around. Life was simpler. You know how men just clutter up the place?'

'S'pose so,' I say with a smile, grateful now that she's come round. Why can't I breeze through life, seemingly unrattled by anything, the way Sabrina does?

'Me and Zach would have picky little dinners,' she goes on. 'Just bits and bobs thrown on a plate. It was brilliant. I mean, Tommy's great, but he's hard work, you know? Loud. Messy. Like a big, boisterous adolescent . . .'

I top up her glass. 'And how was it when he came back?'

'Great,' she enthuses, her fine gold bracelets jangling, ''cause we'd had some space.' Ah, the space issue again. 'It'd, y'know, *reignite* things,' she adds with a grin. 'That might happen with you and Will. But you know what the best thing was?'

'No, what?'

'He always brought presents.' Her eyes sparkle. 'Bet Will comes back laden with stuff.'

'I don't really want presents,' I say firmly. 'This place is crammed with stuff, Sabrina . . .'

'But you must want *something*. Everyone loves a treat. Come on, what would yours be?'

I shrug. 'Oh, nothing much. Just the ability to rewind our lives to where we were before Will lost his job. He loved Greenspace, you know. He was a different man then. I'd go back to the time before this Scotland job, before seals and porpoises . . .'

In fact, I decide, I'd magically transport us even further back than that – to when Ollie was a baby, and Rosie was six, and we were all crammed into our two-bedroomed flat in Hackney. There was no garden or shed – no mysterious hormone powder then – just a tiny balcony with a wobbly clothes horse parked on it, draped with babygrows and sleepsuits with poppers up the front, and the only tool set we owned came out of a Christmas cracker. I don't tell Sabrina that part, though, just as I haven't mentioned my meet-up with Fraser: I can't risk her telling Zach, and Rosie hearing about it that way.

In fact, it's not quite true that there's nothing I want. A call, a text – that would do: just a sweet message from Will. In fact, what I'd really love is something to arrive through the old-fashioned post – like a card with two cuddling teddies on the front, and 'I love you beary, beary much' in swirly silver type beneath them. Of course, that's not Will's style at all, nor mine. What is *happening* to me?

'So how d'you think things are going with Zach and Rosie?' I ask, to change the subject.

'Oh, she's an adorable girl,' Sabrina enthuses. 'He really

likes her, you know, but then . . .' She pauses. 'They're young and he has a lot of friends . . .'

Please let's not have a heartbroken girl on top of all of this. 'Rosie's never had a proper boyfriend before,' I remark.

Sabrina nods. 'Well, I think it's just casual between them.'

'That's probably for the best.' I top up our glasses, adding, 'You know, I can remember exactly how I was – at Rosie's age, I mean.'

'Oh, me too.'

'They think we're ancient, though, don't they? And that we have no idea what their lives are like?'

She nods vehemently.

'I heard Rosie and Delph discussing the menopause today,' I add, 'about everything withering up: hair, internal organs, vagina . . .'

'Christ no,' she shrieks, dissolving into laughter.

'Rosie reckons I'm menopausal.' I smirk and sip my wine.

'God,' Sabrina exclaims, 'you'd pass for thirty. Seriously. You're so lucky, you know. You don't need make-up, fake tan, all that.' She glances down at her own bronzed limbs.

'It would probably help,' I say with a shrug. 'I just never seem to get around to stuff like that.'

'That's the thing, though. Bet you're one of those women who looks great even when they've just got out of bed . . .' I protest that I don't, that I'm quite the horror really, but she charges on: 'It takes me an hour every morning to look like this, you know. That's probably why it was always a relief when Tommy was away, 'cause I didn't have to go through the rigmarole of getting up before him, to put my face on . . .'

I stare at her. 'You mean, you put on your make-up before Tommy wakes up?'

'Yeah,' she sniggers. 'Just a bit, you know: brows, lashes, touch of tinted moisturiser. He's never actually seen me without it. He probably wouldn't recognise me with a bare face.' We laugh, and drink more wine, and out of the blue, she throws her arms around me, a little squiffily. 'Better get back,' she says finally, at around ten-thirty. 'Got to sort through some orders for tomorrow . . . but listen, you and Will – this Scotland job could be the best thing that's ever happened to you.'

Maybe she's right, I reflect, heading up to bed. Somehow, though, I can't imagine things 'reigniting' if Will gets the job and only comes home for the odd weekend. Would we sleep in the same bed? I'd imagine we would – there's nowhere else and, after all, we haven't officially split up. We would just be 'having a bit of space'. Maybe he's planning to divide our bed in two with an electrified fence? In fact, it seems more likely that Rosie and Ollie will be flying up to see him in Scotland instead. What will I do during those empty weekends? Start yoga again? Or dig out our old board games and play Cluedo by myself, or Buckaroo?

Rosie's light is on; rather than disturbing her I just call out goodnight through the door.

'Night, Mum,' she says sleepily.

I peer into Ollie's room, where he is curled up fast asleep on his bed, fully dressed, his cheeks flushed from being outdoors all day. No point in waking him and telling him to put on PJs. No harm in sleeping in a T-shirt and shorts.

Maybe, I think, padding quietly to my bedroom, this is what Sabrina meant about life being simpler when your husband's away. We, too, had a perfectly acceptable picky dinner – cold chicken and couscous discovered in the fridge. I found some only slightly wrinkly cooking apples in the veg rack and made a crumble. A small thing, which Will would do without thinking, but pleasant too. I enjoyed making it. I'd suggest that that makes me a proper grown-up, but I have no idea what that means anymore. Is it Dee, at twenty-four, pretending to love shopping for cushions and scented oil burners? Or Sabrina, who's well into her forties, yet can't bring herself to let her own husband see her bare-faced? Then there's Rosie who, at sixteen years old, is right for the *knitting market*. It's hugely confusing.

My mobile trills, and my heart leaps when I see Will's number displayed. 'Hi, how are you?' It comes out more eagerly than I'd intended.

'Good. Fine.'

'How was the interview?' I ask.

'Um, yeah, I think it went pretty well . . .'

'Any news yet?' Christ, I sound like his mother.

'No, not yet.' Awkward pause.

'I've been calling you,' I add.

'Yeah, I know. Sorry. It's been a bit, uh, hectic . . .'

I lie back on our bed and stretch out, taking up all the space. To my right, on the floor, is a heap of Will's old clothes, ready to be taken to charity. There are bobbly old sweaters, faded T-shirts and several pairs of jeans worn out from Will spending so much time on his knees in the garden, planting, weeding, thinning out.

'Will,' I say, 'I've been made redundant. Rupert's sold Archie's. The company's moving up to the Midlands and even if I wanted to go – which I don't – there won't be a marketing department anymore . . .'

'Oh, God,' he exclaims. 'That's awful. Surely he can't just do that, with no warning—'

'He can,' I cut in, 'and he has. And it's okay. Well, it's not great, of course, but I'll manage. Maybe it was time to move on anyway. And at least I won't be bringing home any more reject crisps . . .'

He laughs softly. 'I'm really sorry, Charlotte. That's a total fucker, it really is . . . what d'you think you'll do?'

'I have no idea,' I reply. About anything, in fact, I want to add. My mind is an utter void.

'Are you sure you're okay?' he asks.

'Yes, I s'pose so.' Silence hangs in the air between us. Perhaps the absence/fonder thing doesn't apply to Will. 'D'you want to speak to the kids?' I ask.

'Er, sure, if it's not too late?'

'I think I just heard Rosie. Hang on a sec.' I get up and find her emerging from the bathroom. 'Is it Dad?' she asks, clearly delighted as I hand her the phone.

'Yep.' She takes it to her room and shuts the door. So that's that, then: the end of my conversation with Will. Not that we had much to say to each other anyway. Rather than going to bed and listening to her chattering away, I perch on a chair at the small desk in the corner of our room – next to Will's still untouched birthday turntable and speakers – and click on my laptop. As usual, my emails are all junk – except one.

Dear Charlotte,

Hi, me again. Can we spend some proper time together? I can't stop thinking about everything we discussed. Would you spend a day with me? Or is that too much to ask?

Please get in touch.

Love,

Fraser x

A whole day? It would be tricky to arrange, and sneaking around isn't my usual style: look where 'only coffee' got me. But then, Will isn't here. He is over 500 miles away, and all he'd tell me about his interview is that it went 'pretty well'. What the hell does that mean?

Hello, Fraser, I start to type. Then I stop. My heart, too, seems to have juddered to a halt. Rosie is standing behind me. I didn't even hear her come into my room. 'Hi, love,' I croak, swivelling to face her.

Her face is unreadable as she holds out my phone. 'Here you go.'

'That was pretty quick.' I smile and take it from her.

'Yeah, Dad's a bit tired.' She is making no move to go back to her room.

Her eyes flick to my screen. I look at her as she scans the lines. 'Fraser?' she says faintly. 'Mum . . . are you emailing my real dad?'

Chapter Thirty-Six

'He's been in touch,' I murmur. 'He emailed Grandpa after seeing us in that magazine together.'

'Oh my God, Mum!' she gasps. 'Why didn't you say?'

'Because . . .' I sense my face glowing hot. 'I wanted to talk it over with Dad first, so we could decide what to do.'

She drops heavily onto the edge of my bed, wide-eyed, cheeks flushed. I am poised for an outburst: *You should have told me straight away! Why d'you treat me like a child?* But it doesn't come. She pushes a strand of hair out of her face and asks, in a quiet voice, 'So what does Dad think?'

My cheeks burn. 'Well, um . . . he's not exactly delighted, love. You have to understand how weird this is for him.'

She nods. 'Yeah, I can imagine. Poor Dad.'

I sit beside her and squeeze her hand. 'But don't worry. I'm sure everything'll work out.' A white lie – so tiny it doesn't count.

Rosie springs up again. 'Mum, I can't believe this! I'm going to meet Fraser! I am, aren't I?'

'Erm, well . . . yes.' Of course she is. There's no way around it now.

'When?' she demands, eyes shining. At this moment, I am so glad Will is up north with his minke whales.

I get up and hug her, then pull back and study her face. 'Look, Rosie – I've already met him. We had coffee last week . . .'

'Did you? Why didn't you tell me?'

'Well, erm . . . it felt important to see him, to check him out, before you met up with him. D'you understand that?'

She grimaces. 'What, in case he was an axe-wielding maniac?'

I raise a small smile. 'I suppose so. It *had* been a long time, you know . . .'

'Did you talk about me?'

'Yes, of course we did . . .'

'Oh, Mum, I'm so excited!'

'And I want to meet him again,' I go on, trying to sound as if I know what I'm doing, and that I have everything under control, 'because we still have stuff to talk about. And after that I think, yes, it'll be fine for you to meet up . . .'

Of course it is. It's also terrifying, but right now I'm relieved that she's too full of excitement to even think about being angry at me for keeping all of this from her.

'What was he like?' she wants to know.

I pause. 'Just the same, I guess. The same as I remembered. Older, obviously . . .'

'Does he have any more kids? Do I have any half-brothers and sisters?'

'I don't know, sweetheart.'

She stares at me. 'You didn't even ask? What did you talk about, then?'

'Quite a lot, actually . . .'

Her expression changes, and all the joy drains out of her face. 'Does he want to see me though? I mean, he's never tried to. Why would he want to get to know me now?'

I swallow hard, wondering how to explain the most important part. 'The thing is, darling, he didn't know he had a daughter.'

'What? What d'you mean?'

'I mean, he knew I was pregnant, and it seemed like he wanted to make it work – he was delighted, you know, about the pregnancy, about you . . .'

She frowns. 'So what happened?'

'Well, um . . . his mum wasn't happy. She told him I'd called, and that I hadn't gone through with the pregnancy and never wanted to see him again—'

'So she lied?' Rosie gasps.

'Yes.'

'She said you'd had an abortion? What a cow! Why did she do that?'

'Because . . .' I break off. 'I don't know. But he was young – only three years older than you are now . . .'

'So what? What difference does that make?'

'I guess she was being protective.'

'Yeah, there's being protective,' she snaps, 'like you and Dad insisting on coming to the agency with me, and interrogating me and Zach when we were only going to the cinema and—'

'Listen,' I cut in, 'I never met her, so I have no idea what was going on in her head. But the fact is, he accepted what she said, and he didn't try to see me after that. So maybe he *wasn't* ready. And we were fine, me and you – we got on with our lives and then I met Dad . . .'

Her eyes fill with tears. 'I miss Dad.'

'So do I, sweetheart,' I say, taking her hand again.

We sit back down in silence, side by side on the edge of my bed, then she kisses my cheek and says, 'I'm going to bed, Mum.'

I look at her. 'Are you okay?'

'Yeah, I am.' She musters a smile, then makes her way to the door. 'Will you tell Fraser,' she adds, 'that I'd like to meet him?'

'Of course I will,' I say.

Hearing her bedroom door close, I return to the email and type quickly:

Yes, I think we should spend some time together as we have a lot to discuss. When is good for you? Also, I've told Rosie I've seen you and she is keen to meet you at some point – would you be okay with that? But I think just you and I should talk first. I might be able to ask Rosie to look after her brother for the day. Where were you thinking of meeting?

Charlotte

He replies within seconds.

Hi Charlotte,

I'm not going to work this week. I can't until I've seen you. Can I meet you tomorrow, or is that too short notice? I don't want to pressurise you. Just say what you'd like to do – anything is fine with me. I did have an idea, though – would you like to have a day in Brighton with me? Or would that be too weird? I could pick you up somewhere that's convenient . . .

A sudden movement makes me flinch away from the screen. At first I think I imagined it; but no – something definitely moved. There it goes again. The pile of charity shop clothes twitched. Mice, is my first thought. If this is what happens when Will goes up north for a week, what'll we have on our hands if he's based up there permanently? Rodent infestations. And while Gloria wouldn't say it out loud, I know exactly what she'd be thinking: *Standards haven't half slipped since Will left . . .*

I step gingerly towards the heap of old T-shirts and sweaters. It's not that I'm afraid of mice – at least, not the domesticated type, like Saul has, which seem to spend most of their time scuttling in and out of a toilet roll tube. Admittedly, I'm not crazy about the kind that sneak into houses and shoot out without warning, having gnawed through an electrical cable.

I edge closer, glimpsing Will's black leather trousers, bundled up between some ratty old jeans. So he's getting rid of them. In fact, they're not *that* bad. Will was clearly as unsure as I was about going to Zach's gig; while I was having my hair tinted aubergine, hoping it'd make me 'blend in' with young people, he was probably raking through his old clothes for something suitably youth-making.

I leap back as the clothes move again. What if it's not mice, but rats? I can picture Tricia and Gerald's appalled expressions as a van pulls up outside our house with VERMIN EXTERMINATION in huge letters on its side. Heart galloping now, I glance around the room for something to poke the pile with. I have to get the thing out, or *things*: maybe they've been breeding in there. All that sex going on – wild rompings, all night long, mere feet away from where I sleep.

I creep down to the kitchen, grab our floor brush and hurry back upstairs with it. Using the non-bristle end, I give the pile a sharp jab. 'Come out!' I address the pile in a wavery voice. Nothing. 'Get *out*!' I command, more firmly now, determined to show that I'm not a pathetic woman who falls to bits when her husband deserts her. The pile shudders again. Christ, it's *alive*—

'What is it?' Ollie cries from the doorway. 'What are you doing, Mum?'

'Nothing, Ollie, just go back to bed—'

There's a thudding of feet as Rosie hurries towards us. 'Mum, what's going on?'

'Mum's hitting the clothes with the brush!' Ollie announces.

'Why? What's happening?' She clasps a hand to her mouth.

'I don't know,' I mutter. 'Something moved . . .' Casting the brush aside, I stride towards the pile, determined to show my children that their mother is made of stern stuff. I pull clothes off the pile – the old, worn-out sweaters and T-shirts and leather trousers – until they're flung all over the floor, as if there's been some frantic, *What on earth shall I wear?* crisis going on, until all that's left where the charity pile was is a large, rather startled rabbit, eyeing us with surprise.

'Guinness!' Rosie yells. 'He's here!' She scoops him up and cradles him in her arms.

'He must be starving, Mum,' Ollie says reproachfully. 'What's he been eating all this time?'

Gathering up Will's clothes, I pause to inspect the leather trousers. They were in mint condition when he wore them. Now they're punctured by small raggedy holes; evidence of Guinness's feasting. I hold them up. 'Look at this. He's bitten right through the crotch.'

'That's disgusting!' Rosie howls. 'My God, Mum . . .' She dissolves into laughter.

'At least Dad can't ever wear them again,' Ollie splutters, when he's finally capable of speech.

Chapter Thirty-Seven

Fraser drives a gleaming black BMW that smells as if it rolled off the production line about an hour ago. There's no fermenting fruit whiff, no crushed Ribena cartons scattered about my feet, no chewing gum wrappers or crisp packets stuffed into the 'bin' (i.e. door compartment). I glance at Fraser, who is driving with the smooth composure of someone who'd passed his test first time, and was bought a brand new car by his parents for his eighteenth birthday. As we leave the suburban sprawl behind us, it occurs to me that I still know virtually nothing about him as an adult man.

'So it was no problem coming out today?' he asks.

'No – Rosie's keeping an eye on Ollie.'

'That was good of her. Is she generally pretty helpful, then?'

She's his daughter, whom he's never met, and he wants to know if she's helpful? Don't ask me that. Ask me if she's smart or clever or funny or kind. Ask me what she's *like*. He's nervous, I think, and immaculately dressed: black jeans, plus a pale blue shirt that's so perfectly pressed, I wonder if he has an ironing lady. 'She can be, when she wants to be,' I start, 'but you know what teenagers are like . . .'

Does he, though? Probably not. Maybe he finds them annoying with their fondness for hanging about, music hissing tinnily from their headphones. 'Depends what it is,' I babble on. 'She does help, if I ask – you know, about seventeen times. But we have a rabbit and the deal was, she'd look after him – I mean, not all by herself, she was only six when we got him – but now she's more than capable of shovelling up a few pellets. I mean, they're fine, they don't even smell really . . .'

God, make me stop. It's the first proper day I've spent with Fraser since 1996 and I'm describing Guinness's poos.

'I can imagine that's irritating,' Fraser offers, 'but I have no experience of that kind of thing. I don't have kids.' He quickly corrects himself. 'Any *other* kids, I mean . . .'

'Are you married?' I ask, giving him a quick look. He is actually incredibly youthful looking, I decide. I think he's had a haircut since that coffee in Covent Garden. It looks expensive, even though it's just a short, regular cut.

'Was,' he says. 'Well, still am technically. We're separated.'

I nod and gaze out of the window, wondering what Will would think if he could see me now, heading for Brighton in what he'd probably describe as a 'wanker's car'. Ours have always been old and temperamental, with piles of detritus stashed in the boot. Anyway, as Will has failed to reply to the message I left first thing this morning – 'Just to see if there's any news!' I chirped, like a fond aunt – I haven't felt obliged to update him on this latest development.

The sky is pale blue, streaked by thin white clouds that look as if they've been sprayed with an aerosol. Since we set off, conversation hasn't exactly flowed easily. As arranged, Fraser picked me up around the corner from my house, at the entrance to the park. Although Rosie and Ollie know what I'm doing today, I wanted to avoid a terrible awkward first meeting on our doorstep.

'So what's Rosie's little brother like?' Fraser asks.

'Ollie?' I say, as if I am a supply teacher who's been asked about a pupil I'm barely acquainted with. 'He's, um . . . pretty smart. Into science and stuff, biology, experiments . . . he's desperate for a proper professional microscope.'

Fraser chuckles, perhaps formulating his next question. I feel as if I am being interviewed, and the next one will be, 'So, Charlotte, what would you say are your main strengths and weaknesses?'

Strengths: Scrabble. Eating. Enthusing about crisps to journalists. Being 'a good sort', as Rupert puts it.

Weaknesses: Chronic ditheriness. Worrying over insignificant things. Tendency to obsess over when this man beside me might next get in touch, despite being married and old enough to know better.

Fraser and I seem to have run out of things to say. How on earth are we going to fill a whole day? I envisage an awkward stroll along the beach, and lunch, and making some kind of 'plan' regarding Rosie, before he drops me back home.

Right now, I wish I *was* at home. Perhaps he feels the same. He clears his throat and gives me an anxious look. 'This is the weirdest thing that's ever happened to me,' he murmurs.

To *him*? What about Rosie? Then, as if reading my

thoughts he adds, 'I don't mean that in a *poor me* sort of way. I don't mean that at all. I'm sorry, Charlotte – I'm just trying to explain why this feels so awkward, and why I'm being so crap, really—'

'No you're not,' I say quickly.

'I am. I'm being completely useless, inadequate . . . all I could think was, we need time together. We can't sort all this out over a coffee in a busy café in about twenty minutes. It's fucking serious, Charlotte. I want to get it right, I don't want to screw up again—' His voice wavers as he focuses determinedly ahead.

'Fraser,' I say hesitantly, 'why didn't you ever try to contact me? After your mum told you I'd phoned, I mean . . .'

He takes a moment to consider this. 'I know it sounds ridiculous now, but I just believed what she said. My mother, I mean. It was a complete shock. I was devastated, you know. But then I thought, well, you must've had a change of heart, and panicked and thought it'd mess up your life – that *I'd* mess it up. I thought maybe your parents had stepped in, and persuaded you that you didn't have to go ahead . . .'

I picture Mum, pacing around in my flat with my baby propped over her shoulder, winding her, and a spurt of curdled white stuff shooting out of Rosie's little pink mouth and landing on Mum's emerald green linen dress. I'd apologised madly and tried to dab it off with a wet cloth. 'It's only from Oxfam,' she'd said, forgetting she'd told me what a find she considered it: vintage Jaeger.

'No, they didn't do that,' I say. 'They were brilliant, though. They came up to London as often as they could, and forced me to go out and meet friends, virtually manhandling me out of the door . . .'

I realise with a start that Fraser's eyes are moist. 'Well, I got that wrong, then. Honestly, I just thought maybe I'd make things worse by trying to stay in touch, when it sounded as if you just wanted me out of your life.'

I nod, wondering how things would have turned out if he'd tried just once, and made a single call.

'I was an idiot,' he mutters.

'No, you weren't. You were nineteen years old and had no reason to think your mum was lying.'

He nods. 'So when did you meet Will?'

'When Rosie was eighteen months old. Mum and Dad were babysitting and I'd gone to a comedy club with some friends. In fact, I hadn't wanted to go at all, thought I'd have nothing to talk about apart from baby stuff . . .' I laugh. 'Which was true, actually.' I glance at him. 'So, did you never want children?' It feels intrusive – maybe he and his wife couldn't have kids – but it feels important to know.

'I did,' he says firmly. 'I always wanted them, but Elise always said it wasn't the right time, career-wise – she had a great PA job and was hoping to move up into office management. And then' – he's smiling now – 'she started to show Chihuahuas . . .'

'Chihuahuas?' I repeat.

He chuckles. 'Yeah. And that started to take up all her free time – the training, the grooming, the endless fucking blow drying and nail clipping and traipsing from show to show . . .' He breaks off. 'Anyway, you were saying how you met Will—'

'Yes, at the comedy club. His friends had been heckling – not Will, he's not the type – and he'd wandered off to get a drink and we started chatting . . .' I sense a twinge of unease and quickly push it aside. Where is he now?

Over 500 miles away, impressing the pants off the charity people. 'He's been a brilliant dad,' I add firmly.

'I'm sure he has. Rosie seems like a lovely girl.'

I want to point out that he doesn't know that; all he knows is what he read in *Front* magazine. 'She is,' I say. 'She's a *brilliant* girl.' I glance at him. 'What did you think when you saw our picture?'

'Oh, God, you both looked beautiful . . .'

'Well, Rosie did.'

'You too,' he insists. 'You were just as I remembered – apart from the hair of course, that was—'

I laugh. 'I think the hairdresser on the shoot was going for some Brian May out of Queen look.'

He flashes me a big, fond smile. 'Honestly, that's not what I thought . . .'

'Remember we both hated Queen?' I prompt him.

'God, yeah! That's how we started talking' As we both chuckle at the memory, it feels as if something clever happens with the air conditioning in this new-smelling car, as any remaining tension fades instantly. 'Those Liverpudlian guys,' he adds, 'murdering "Bohemian Rhapsody" . . .'

'You said if they carried on to the Beelzebub bit you might actually throw up . . .'

We are both laughing as we pick over details we'd forgotten until now: the woman we met, a stoical solo traveller who'd been all over the world yet still referred to a couchette as a 'courgette'; our final night together in Paris when funds had run low – I was virtually broke by then, and Fraser's bank card wouldn't work – and all we'd had to eat was a couple of pickled eggs from a jar on the shelf behind the bar.

By the time we reach the outskirts of Brighton, I've

almost forgotten that today is all about Rosie and Fraser, and what we need to do for the best. Right now, with the bright sky above us, I feel as if I've been snatched from my life as a grown-up woman, a hutch-cleaning serf and a marketeer of crisps, and dropped somewhere else entirely.

The beach is milling with children running in and out of the waves. Although we're already two weeks into the school holidays, it still feels as if everyone is delighted to be let out, freed from lunchbox-packing routines. In our family-friendly corner of East London, the local mums tend to muddle through, having hordes of kids over for the day when other parents are working. 'Gosh, I hope this isn't going to be a regular thing,' Tricia remarked once, as Rosie and Ollie and a huge bunch of friends tore around our dishevelled garden, screaming and throwing water balloons at each other. 'For your sake, I mean,' she added quickly. 'You must be exhausted!' In fact, I loved those full-on, mass-catering days when the sun blazed down and everyone was filthy and soaked to the skin. I was less keen when Rosie and her friends took to hibernating in her room on glorious sunny afternoons, shouting, 'Just leave it outside my door, Mum!' when I announced that pizza was ready, as if I were a Domino's delivery girl.

We find a spot on the beach and kick off our shoes, close to a family who are setting out a picnic. I look at Fraser, remembering the only other time we were here together: the morning after pregnancy test day. How excited we were. How giddy and thrilled because, naturally, we hadn't the faintest idea of what lay ahead. 'Remember that picnic we had in Paris,' Fraser muses, 'in the Jardin des Tuileries? The cake picnic?'

'Yes, because neither of us much liked the savoury part of picnics so we thought we wouldn't bother with that bit.'

Fraser laughs. 'How mature.'

'Raspberry tarts,' I remind him, 'and those layered things with the flaky pastry and squidgy cream stuff inside.'

'Millefeuilles,' he says, accent perfect. 'It means a hundred leaves.'

'Your French was good. Mine was atrocious . . .'

He looks at me, as if about to say, *No, you amazed me with your linguistic skills*, then laughs. 'Well, that street seller did look horrified when you said, "Une piece de pasteque, s'il vous plait . . ."'

'I know!' I exclaim. 'As if I'd said something disgusting or suggested we did something incredibly *dirty* with his watermelon . . .'

Fraser snorts with laughter. 'Like what?'

I shrug. 'I don't know. Inserted it somewhere?'

We are creasing up with laughter now. 'My God,' Fraser says, 'you haven't changed a bit.'

'Neither have you,' I say, and it's true: the finely honed cheekbones and elegant, curvaceous mouth bring to mind one of those ancient statues you see in a museum – all curly haired and pouty, the kind you look at and think, God, those Renaissance types were all right. What did Laurie say again on scouting day? *You have amazing bone structure, Rosie*. Well, it's no surprise. Although we've often been told she's so like Will, there's no mistaking who her real father is.

Fraser fetches ice creams which melt so quickly I spend the next few minutes catching vanilla drips with my tongue. We lapse into comfortable silence, and when

I turn to glance at him, he is looking directly at me, as if amazed to find me here. 'Remember the last time we were here?' he asks softly.

'Yes, of course I do.'

He inhales deeply. 'I . . . I want to make things right between us, Charlotte.'

I nod, understanding. It's not just about him and Rosie, but us too. 'So do I,' I murmur.

'D'you think we can?'

'I don't know.' Then I add, 'Maybe, yes.'

A couple of little boys run to the sea, squealing and giggling, pursued by a girl who doesn't look more than twenty: their nanny, perhaps. A relaxed-looking older woman on a blanket waves at them. 'Come in, Mummy!' one of the boys shouts.

'Maybe later,' she calls back. It always amazes me when nanny does all the charging about while Mum sits there, smiling vaguely before turning back to her paperback.

'I feel bad, Fraser,' I say, 'about being here with you.'

'Do you? I wish you didn't . . .' My heart jumps as he gives my hand a reassuring squeeze. It's okay – it's *daytime*. On a score of badness it's about twenty points lower than snogging a colleague in the spud store. I think about the last time I tried to touch Will, and he flinched away, as if I'd poked him with a stick with a bit of poo on the end.

'It's just, I didn't tell Will about seeing you today,' I add. My hand is sticky, I think, from the ice cream, and my heart is rattling away as if I've just guzzled a can of Red Bull.

'I don't want to cause problems between you,' Fraser says.

'You're not. It's not about you, not really. Will and I have a few, um, issues going on at the moment . . .'

'Oh, I'm sorry.' A teenage couple has arrived now, and proceed to splash each other in the sea and shriek with laughter. They could be us, Fraser and me – two young people, not even fully grown up, before lawnmowers and mortgages and angry husbands running away to Scotland. I'm no longer middle-aged Charlotte, thinking, *Is this it? Is this as good as it gets?*

Fraser is still holding my hand. I no longer feel bad; my heart is soaring, like the seagulls above. Right now, on this glorious August day, I'm the girl I was back in '96, with no mortgage or shed or wonky pelvic floor, when it felt as if anything was possible.

Chapter Thirty-Eight

I had a flatmate – a roommate, in fact – at the time when I met Fraser. Beverley Savage was a no-nonsense girl with wiry red hair who'd recently dumped her boyfriend for being 'too deep', and 'always reading'. Although she could have afforded it, she hadn't wanted to go Inter-railing with me. 'It's crap, Europe,' she'd declared, even though the furthest she'd been from mainland Britain was the Isle of Man.

'Remember that time Bev was banging on the bathroom door?' Fraser asks, lapsing into an exaggerated Yorkshire accent: '"Lemme in! Am *bustin'* for a wee . . ."' We convulse with laughter as we head back towards town in search of something to eat. This is better. We're being silly. My heart rate seems to have returned to its normal speed.

'"Warra ya doin' in there?"' I bark back, in Bev Savage's voice. '"Yer better not be at it. That's disgustin'. If you don't 'urry up am gonna wee in the sink . . ."'

In fact, we hadn't been 'at it', at least, not at that precise moment. We'd been messing about – partially undressed, admittedly – in the bedroom Bev and I shared, until we'd heard that terrible sound: her key in the front door lock. 'She's back,' I'd shrieked, and we'd charged into the mouldering bathroom with its salmon-coloured tiles and actual fungi sprouting through the carpet.

Still laughing at the memory, we buy a picnicky lunch from a posh deli and sit on a bench on the seafront. Everything we've bought is in little pots, and I'm trying not to daub myself while ferrying small bits of stuffed pepper to my mouth with a wooden fork. 'Tell me about Will,' Fraser says. A piece of oily pepper pings off my fork and lands on my top, another non-special one – navy blue, with a small daisy pattern – chosen to show that I wasn't excited about our day together at all. 'Maybe I shouldn't ask,' he adds, 'but—'

'It's okay. You can ask whatever you want. He's actually away for a job interview at the moment. It's in Scotland . . .'

'Really?'

I nod. 'It was a bit of a shock, to be honest. I didn't even know he'd applied for it.'

'Wow . . . so, um . . . will you all move north?'

'No, no, that's not the plan,' I say firmly. 'We'd stay in London – me and the kids, I mean . . .'

'Oh, I'm so glad. Sorry. God, that sounds awful. It's just . . .' He pauses. 'It feels like I've only just found you again.' His words knock the breath out of me. Found *me*? Isn't this supposed to be all about Rosie?

'It's sort of complicated,' I mutter.

'But . . . he wants to move away from you, and the kids?'

I'm primed to spout the line we'll tell his mother and sister – and anyone else we don't feel able to be honest with – if he gets the job: *He's only accepting it because he hasn't been able to find anything closer to home. It's a great position, after all, and he'll visit* . . . But Fraser isn't Gloria, or my sister-in law. 'He . . . he says we need a break, actually,' I add, unable to stop myself.

'You're splitting up?'

'Well, not officially . . .' Fraser listens without interrupting as I explain how things have been lately: the angry-mowing and pill-gobbling and weeping on the stair carpet. He remains silent, sitting so close on this sun-faded bench that I can sense the warmth from him. I tell him about assaulting my husband with squirty salad cream, and how I mistook a blow-up doll for a real woman; I tell him everything, because it feels as if I can. Even though all of this makes me sound quite ridiculous, I can't stop.

And then I do, abruptly. I study his face to figure out if he's appalled, or thinking, *Shit, Charlotte's completely deranged. Better make an excuse and get her back to London, pronto* . . . 'God, Charlotte,' is all he says.

'I know. It's all been a bit . . . eventful.'

'Yeah. Sounds like it. I thought things were pretty crazy with me and Elise and the Chihuahuas.'

A smile tweaks my lips. I think about telling him about Guinness, gnawing through the crotch of Will's leather trousers, but then he might think, Jesus, she married a leather trouser man, and I don't want Will to seem tragically middle-aged, the kind who wears his hair long to compensate for it thinning on top, because he's not like that at all.

'So,' I say, turning to Fraser, 'what about you and Rosie?'

'Well, I'd love to see her of course. But I don't want this whole thing to freak her out.'

'It won't,' I say firmly, 'and it's not a thing – I mean, *you're* not a thing. You're her dad.'

He nods, as if momentarily overwhelmed by the fact. 'So . . . what d'you think's best?'

I consider this as we watch a runner powering effortlessly along the promenade, a black and white collie dog scampering beside him on its lead. They are keeping pace perfectly, both focused ahead as if they exercise together every day. What will Rosie make of Fraser? Will they connect in any way? Awful therapy-type speak, I know, but I'm not sure how else to put it. 'Bond' feels too strong, something built up over years of playing and drawing and building Lego together.

'We should arrange for you to meet,' I say.

'Just the two of us? Or d'you think you should be there too?'

I picture Will and I shuffling into Face Models with Rosie. *Quite the family outing!* Laurie quipped.

'No, I think it'd be better for her to see you by herself. I'll come into town and meet up with her afterwards.'

Fraser smiles warmly. 'You've really thought this through, haven't you?'

Of course I have, I'm her mum. Although all I say is, 'Yes.'

*

We are driving home to London in the grown-up car. I don't want to go back. I want to carry on talking, as we have been the whole journey. I want Fraser to get a picture of what Rosie is like. It feels strange, condensing her sixteen years into random anecdotes and descriptions, but I'm doing my best. I break off and text her. *All okay at home?*

Yeah, she replies, *Ollie being annoying but OK. How's it going?*

Good, I text back, *will tell all,* knowing that that's not entirely true. Of course I won't tell her how wonderful it is just to be myself, without that treading-on-eggshells feeling, and how ridiculously happy I feel today: no longer middle-aged, Ovaltine-sipping Charlotte, heading for old-lady facial sproutings, but young and ridiculously free.

'We're pretty near my place,' he adds as the traffic slows to a crawl. 'We could stop off, get a takeaway. How does that sound?'

It sounds like heaven. And it's something I *definitely* shouldn't do. 'I'm not sure,' I murmur.

'There's a fantastic Indian at the end of my road,' he adds. 'Best in South London, apparently. I'll drive you home straight afterwards . . .'

A quick curry together: what harm can it do? 'Okay,' I say, 'but I'd better not be too long. I don't want to get back late.'

He smiles. 'Great. I've really loved today, you know.'

'Me too,' I say truthfully, wondering how Will would react he if he could see me now, in this 'wanker's car', and quickly banishing the thought.

Fraser's place is one of those huge ground-floor flats I glance into sometimes and think, *Where's all the clutter?* It's calm and airy, with tall Victorian sash windows and a sense that everything has been carefully chosen, rather than grabbed in IKEA in a tearing hurry.

'I'll show you the garden,' he says, letting us out through the back door, then disappearing back inside for a bottle of Chablis and another of sparkling water. Wine for me, water for him. He sets them down on a small wrought iron table. 'Thanks,' I say gratefully, fishing out my phone as it bleeps.

'Rosie again,' I tell Fraser. 'It's not like her to be so communicative.'

Ollie's gone to Saul's, it reads. *They're having big family barbecue. Can he stay the night? I said it was OK. I'm on my way to Delph's. She says I can stay over. That OK?*

I glance at Fraser, then back at my phone. *All fine,* I reply.

'Everything all right?' Fraser asks.

'Yes, seems like they've got their social lives sorted for tonight. They're both staying over with friends.' He looks at me. Although I've only had a few sips of wine, I feel dizzy and light. Maybe it's not the wine at all.

'Charlotte . . .' he starts hesitantly, 'I . . . I don't know how to be a dad.'

'It doesn't matter.'

'Yes it does. What if she's angry? How much does she know?'

I sip my wine. 'I told her you didn't know anything about her, that you didn't even know I'd had the baby. And anyway, no one knows how to be a parent. I didn't. Still don't, really. There's no rule book, unfortunately. I wish there was. I wish there was a whole booklet thing printed in seventeen languages like you get with a new camera . . .' I pause. Actually, I don't, because I have never read a single instruction manual in my entire life. 'I get things wrong all the time,' I add. 'I annoy her, I get in her way, I badger her for information . . .'

'Well,' he says, 'I think you're amazing.'

I laugh awkwardly. 'I'm not, I'm—'

'Yes, you are. You're beautiful and clever and funny and—'

Then he stops, and his lips are on mine, and it's the loveliest kiss I can remember. It feels as if the world has stopped.

We pull away, as if shocked by what we've just done. 'God, Charlotte,' he murmurs. 'I hope that didn't seem—'

'No, it was . . . lovely,' I say, my head swimming.

'But you're married. I know you're having problems right now, but still . . .' He breaks off and kisses me again, very gently. I pull away.

You're right, I'm married, are the words that should be falling out of my mouth. *Will might be exploring those white sand beaches right now, but he is still my husband, so I absolutely shouldn't be doing this* . . . I focus on the rectangular lawn and neat borders filled with small, well-behaved shrubs. While not quite as precision-planted as Tricia and Gerald's garden, it still looks exceptionally well-tended. Maybe Fraser has a gardener as well as an ironing lady.

'It's okay,' I say quietly. 'I wanted to come here. I wasn't ready to go home yet.'

Fraser takes my hand in his. 'I loved you, you know. I couldn't believe it when Mum said you'd called. It destroyed me, actually. Remember I was all set to go into banking? Well, I pissed around instead, working in a video store and doing odd jobs here and there for a couple of years, until my parents forced me to get my act together . . .'

I start to reply that I was pretty devastated too, when my phone pings again. It's another text from Rosie: *OMG you should see Delph's house it has a POOL!!!*

I slip my phone back in my pocket.

‘Everything okay?’ Fraser asks.

‘Rosie’s new model friend has a pool,’ I explain. ‘Who on earth has a pool in London—’ I stop abruptly. My heart soars as the first man I ever loved kisses me again.

Chapter Thirty-Nine

We haven't had time to get a takeaway. The Indian at the end of Fraser's road might be the best in South London but we haven't been there, or even phoned for a delivery because we've been kissing fervently, like teenagers who think they've just invented this incredibly thrilling act. In between the kissing there's been a bit of talking and drinking of wine. At least, *I've* had two large glasses. Fraser hasn't because the plan is still that he'll drive me home tonight.

Both of us know that this won't happen.

It's not just coffee, there's no 'just' about it. Everything I do here seems to be a massive deal. I go to the bathroom and think, *I am peeing in Fraser's loo.* I wash my hands at his washbasin using his posh Molton Brown liquid soap. Back home, our bar soap in the bathroom somehow manages to be slimy on one side and all cracked and dried out on the other: 'Our science experiment,' as Ollie calls it.

There's a wall cabinet with a mirrored door. I peer at my reflection; I should look terrible, awash with stress and remorse but I just look happy. There are no fresh facial sproutings, I am delighted to note. Even my geographical fissures seem to have melted away.

I could stay here tonight. I could do this. The kids are out for the night and Will is in Scotland, with whales.

I open the cabinet and peer inside. There are Neal's Yard toiletries in their distinctive dark blue bottles, and some kind of shaving preparation in a circular wooden tub, like a mini Camembert.

And a packet of condoms. Condoms, in a little gold packet, like a fortune cookie! I haven't encountered one since prehistoric times. It was probably made from animal hide, rhinoceros skin or something. I've had a coil, simple and functional like a very ordinary, old-fashioned kettle. When I first got it, Will joked that if I faced the right way it could probably pick up Radio Moscow.

No, no, no, I must *not* think of Will. Or, if I do, it must only be in negative terms, like him flinching at my touch, and sneering at salad cream. I close the cabinet door, and when I rejoin Fraser in the living room he has topped up my wine, and poured an enormous glass for himself, which means he's not planning to drive me home after all.

His sofa is a huge expanse of pale grey, unsullied by spillages and scuff marks. While I'd never actually do this, I know for certain that if I lifted the seat cushions there'd be no broken Bic biros or crisp crumbs lurking underneath. 'Come here,' Fraser says softly, taking me in his arms and kissing me. I think of the condoms in the bathroom. My whole body swills with nerves and desire.

He breaks away. 'Let's go to bed,' he says.

I look at him. Christ, *bed* – involving nudity and sex. Which bra do I have on again? The reasonably pretty black one, or the tragic off-white thing that was never the same after I washed it with my jeans? My phone buzzes in my bag, and I leap away to retrieve it, panicking as I always do when I'm away from the kids that something terrible has happened, even though it never has, and they're not babies anymore.

It's a text from Will. I feel sick, as if he can see me through my phone with my just-snogged face. There's no written message, just a picture, which I click open, not realising at first that Fraser is peering over my shoulder, gaze fixed on the screen. 'Sorry,' he says, jolting back. 'I just thought maybe something was wrong.'

I turn to him, frowning. 'What, with the kids?'

'Yeah.' This is extremely confusing. Being Rosie's biological father doesn't mean it's his place to worry about her, or Ollie for that matter. I focus on the picture on my phone.

'What is it?' Fraser asks.

'It's . . . a mushroom.'

He guffaws. 'Oh, is *that* what it is? For a moment I thought it was a penis . . .'

I feel as if I can't quite move my body properly, as if every movement is slow and awkward and must be carefully thought about. I sit there, looking at the screen. Will, *my* Will, is thinking about me. He has sent me a photo of a mushroom.

'It's a shaggy inkcap,' I say quietly.

Fraser laughs again. 'How d'you know? You're full of surprises, Charlotte, but I'd never have thought of you as a mushroom collector. I mean I knew you *cultivated* them, you and Bev in that horrible flat, on the damp bathroom carpet . . .'

Very slowly, I place my phone on the low blonde wood coffee table in front of us. Did he get the condoms in for us, I wonder? How could he possibly have known I'd come back here?

'I know its name,' I say, 'because they're pretty rare and he'll have been excited to find it.'

'Who? Your son?'

He can't even remember his name. 'No, Will, my husband.'

Fraser smirks. 'You're married to a mushroom collector.'

It's as if a switch has been flicked, and instead of feeling deliciously wanton I now feel very strongly that I don't want to be here, and that I need to be back at home. I edge away from him on the sofa.

'Honestly,' he adds, grinning, 'I was worried for a moment. I thought some pervert had sent you a picture of his dick.'

I breathe in and out, slowly and deeply like yoga types do. 'Yes, I s'pose they are a bit phallic. But I'd be worried if I ever encountered one looking like that. I mean, I'd probably suggest an urgent trip to the clinic . . .'

'Yeah,' he sniggers, edging towards me and wrapping an arm around my shoulders.

I look down at the pale grey fluffy rug. I am no longer picturing myself throwing off my clothes and landing in a passionate tumble on Fraser's bed. I am imagining Will roaming about in the Scottish countryside and spotting that mushroom, and carefully picking it. He was excited about his find and wanted to share it with me.

This means he no longer thinks of me as a condiment-squirting maniac. It also means I *have* to see him. I stand up, pushing back my dishevelled hair. 'Fraser,' I say, meeting his quizzical gaze, 'would you mind calling me a cab?'

Chapter Forty

I am woken by rain battering at my bedroom window. As Rosie has yet to return from Delph's, I haven't been able to fill her in on my day out with Fraser. Not that I plan to tell her everything. Just that he's a decent man, who cares about her very much, and that we both agree that it would be good for them to get to know each other. We were both a bit sheepish and embarrassed as I left last night, apologising unnecessarily and parting with a slightly awkward hug. 'We just got a bit carried away,' Fraser said with a rueful smile, and I decided then that I *do* like him, and that I'm happy for Rosie to have him in her life. However, I'm not wildly impressed that he can't tell the difference between a shaggy inkcap and a human penis.

A couple of hours later she appears with Delph in tow, both of them giggling and muttering unintelligibly, as if communicating in some mysterious language spoken only by young, beautiful people with modelling contracts. They fail to acknowledge Ollie as he strides in, full of all the great things that have been happening at Saul's house – 'He's got his own TV now! Everyone has. Can I have one?'

'We can maybe think about it for Christmas,' I say vaguely, but Ollie isn't listening. He is watching the girls as they slather thick slices of bread with jam.

'We normally have home-made bread,' he announces, 'but Dad's away and Mum can't make it so we've just got the normal stuff . . .'

'I don't think Delph needs to know that, Ollie,' Rosie retorts, breaking off to take a call on her mobile. She frowns and mutters before tossing her phone onto the table. 'That was Laurie,' she adds.

'Oh, d'you have a casting?' I ask. 'Or a job?'

She shrugs. 'Dunno. She just said could I pop into the agency.'

'Well,' I say, 'I suppose next time you're in town . . .'

'She said today,' Rosie adds, 'if it's convenient.'

'You need a better agency,' Delph declares. 'They're not pushing you enough, Ro. I'm booked all next week. I'm off to Tuscany with *Vogue* . . .'

Rosie musters a bright smile. 'Yeah, well, maybe she wants to talk about the direction she wants me to go in or something.' Actually, I think, the direction I'd suggest is the one you seemed to be following before modelling, before Delph, when you read a book now and again instead of flicking listlessly through fashion magazines, and deigned to have the occasional pleasant conversation with me.

'I'm sure it'll be fine,' I say ineffectually.

'Yeah, well, I might as well go now.'

'I'll come into town with you,' Delph announces. 'I'm getting a rose-petal facial at two o'clock. Have you ever had one?'

'Er, no,' Rosie says, as if she's considered it but hasn't got around to it yet.

'Oh, you should!' Delph asserts. 'They lay these pink petals all over your face and the goodness – y'know, the *essence* of flowers – seeps into your skin and then they exfoliate it all off.'

'Skin does that naturally anyway,' Ollie retorts. 'It falls off all the time. There are flakes of it all over this house.'

Delph winces. 'Well, that's charming.' With that, the girls gather themselves together and swish off in a cloud of heady perfume. Perfectly timed, I must say, for the first step of my plan.

*

'Right,' I tell Ollie, 'we're going on a trip.'

'What kind of trip?' he asks, all excited.

'We're going camping.'

'Great!' Thankfully, Ollie still regards sleeping in our leaky old tent as a fantastic treat. 'Where are we going?' he wants to know.

'Well, the plan is, the first night we'll stay in Northumberland, that's in the north-east of—'

'I know where Northumberland is,' he retorts.

'And then,' I continue, 'we'll carry on up to Scotland—'

'To see Dad?'

'Yes.'

'Cool, what did he say? Is he looking forward to seeing us?'

I hesitate, wondering how to put this. 'He doesn't know, sweetheart. I want it to be a surprise . . .'

'He's been gone for three days now. He hasn't phoned

for ages! We haven't even told him about finding Guinness.'

'I know, darling,' I say briskly, 'but his mind'll be full of this job and he's probably getting to know the area . . .'

'If he's that busy,' Ollie says, looking wary now, 'd'you think he'll want us just turning up?'

I smile at my boy, who's turning browner by the day. 'Of course he will,' I say firmly, hoping to God that I'm right. 'So, can you get some clothes together? Enough for three or four days?'

'Yeah,' he says, scampering off. I have yet to tell Ollie and Rosie about being made redundant from Archie's; I don't want to spring it upon them yet, until we know what's happening with Will's job. However, this is why we are driving and camping, rather than flying and staying in a hotel. It's a budget trip, which I'm hoping they will view as an adventure.

I call Gloria to ask if she'll look after Guinness. 'I'll bring him over,' I explain. 'You won't need to do anything apart from feed him . . .'

'I *suppose* that's okay,' she replies warily, as if our small furred mammal is prone to launching vicious attacks.

The presence of a giant, navy blue people carrier outside Gloria's pebble-dashed home signals the presence of Sally, Will's younger sister. Despite living in the Cotswolds – a mere couple of hours away – she and her family deign to visit Gloria around three times a year.

'You're looking so well,' Sally exclaims, attempting to hug me while I grip Guinness's open-topped box. 'Oh, isn't he cute? I do admire you, Charlotte, letting the kids have pets. I won't allow it. The smell! Ew!' She wrinkles her nose, then quickly corrects herself, as if remembering that she owns several ponies. 'Not that this little chap smells *at all.*' She sniffs the air above him. 'Mm, all I can smell is hay, actually. Lovely and sweet and countryish.' Gloria emerges from the kitchen and quickly peers into Guinness's box, then teeters back as if he were an unexploded bomb. I leave our pet in the porch as we all head into the chintzy living room.

'You're growing into such a handsome man,' Sally gushes, giving Ollie's hair an enthusiastic ruffle. 'And where's Rosie today? And my dashing big brother?'

'Will's away for an interview,' I start, deciding not to go into the whole story.

'An interview?' Gloria repeats. 'Thank heavens for that!' She turns to her daughter. 'I've told you, Sally, how worried I've been about Will, stuck at home, tied to the kitchen . . .'

'. . . And Rosie's gone into town,' I cut in. 'Her model agency have asked to see her.'

'Oh yes, Mum's filled us in on all of that,' Sally remarks as Ollie and I say our hellos to Marty, Sally's husband who, in his brown cardigan and slacks, almost merges with Gloria's chocolate velour sofa. Also present is Bruno, their scowling seven-year-old son, who is, according to Sally's previous reports, in the top one percentile of something or other, although I'm not quite sure what that means.

'Hi Bruno, how's things?' I look down at the small, chubby-cheeked boy who is sprawled belly-down on his grandma's cream rug, prodding at his iPad.

'All right,' he replies dully, picking at his ear and failing to shift his gaze from the screen.

'What's that you're playing, Bruno?' Ollie asks gamely, for which I could hug him.

'Just a thing,' he replies.

'Oh,' Ollie says with a smirk. 'It looks good.'

'It's only for one player,' Bruno snaps, gathering himself up from the floor and relocating to a shadowy corner behind the sofa.

Sally beams in an *isn't he adorable?* sort of way. 'So, about Rosie modelling,' she says, motioning for us to sit with Marty on the sofa. 'D'you feel okay about it? I mean, thrusting her into the public eye with the dangers of horrible predatory photographers and all that?' Although she's still smiling, rather manically, a little furrow has appeared between her meticulously pencilled brows. I'm itching to remind Sally that her own mother paraded about in nothing more than heels, a sash and swimsuit at beauty contests, but Gloria's hovering about, and I don't want to bring up that thing about the poky-fingered *Sorrington Bugle* man.

'We thought about it carefully,' I say firmly, wondering how soon we can get the hell out of here without appearing rude. 'But, you know, her exams had finished and we thought, if she's going to give it a try, then the summer break's probably the best time.'

Sally gives me a pained look. 'It just seems a bit . . . shallow, I suppose. I mean there's more to Rosie than that. She's *quite* bright, isn't she?' *Although not on a par with the genius currently mouth-breathing loudly behind the sofa . . .*

'Yes, but it's just a sideline, like a summer job. She wants to be a vet . . .'

'A summer job where you're not allowed to eat!' Sally chuckles, shaking her head in wonderment.

'Well, it was a family decision. Anyway, we really should get back. Lots of packing to do . . . um, Gloria, I've left Guinness in his box in the porch, but I thought maybe I could put him in your shed? Would that be okay? I've brought his dry food and his water bottle so he'll be fine—'

'And his run,' Ollie adds.

Gloria frowns. 'His *run*?'

'The big wire mesh thing Dad made,' Ollie explains. 'I'll drag it out onto your lawn. As long as it's not raining, Guinness likes to spend most of his day in it.'

Gloria looks nonplussed. 'His run will be *on* my lawn? Will the grass be harmed?'

'Not at all,' I say firmly.

'Well, he'll poo, obviously,' Ollie says cheerfully, 'but it's like fertiliser, it's *good* for grass, it puts nutrients in and nitrates and stuff, and he'll keep it nice and short . . .'

Gloria frowns. 'So where are you going on holiday?' Sally asks, tailing us to the back garden as we sort out Guinness's temporary accommodation.

'Just camping,' I reply.

'Oh, aren't you brave! You are a one, Charlotte. I couldn't spend one night in a tent. We're going to Florida again. But camping sounds so much more, er, *earthy.* I take my hat off to you.'

Ollie keeps quoting Sally the whole drive home. 'You are a one, Charlotte!' he pipes up, making me crease up with laughter every time.

We arrive home to find Rosie slumped on the sofa, flipping channels between something about crop circles – 'an area of high incidences of paranormal activity,' the narrator says gravely – and a low-budget cookery show on which several people are cooing over a plate bearing a very plain-looking slab of cod. 'Didn't expect you back so soon,' I say, kissing the top of her head.

'It was a quick meeting,' she mutters, settling now on a show about the perils of online relationships.

'This programme's so stupid,' Ollie announces. 'They meet people online who look like models or dancers or whatever, and surprise surprise, the person can never manage to meet up face to face . . . like, wouldn't you be suspicious?'

Rosie throws him an icy look.

'And then,' Ollie continues, 'they *do* meet, 'cause the presenters arrange it, and the guy she thought was a male model turns out to be really old – like, *forty-two* or something, with a massive beer gut and some kind of horrible skin disease—'

With a groan, Rosie turns off the TV. 'Are you okay?' I ask.

She shrugs and picks at a fingernail.

'Did Laurie suggest how you might get more jobs?'

'No she didn't, okay?' I step back, startled, as Rosie leaps up from the sofa. 'She didn't suggest anything, Mum. Well she did, but it wasn't *that* . . .' With a strangled sob, she runs out of the room and thunders upstairs, slamming her bedroom door behind her.

Ollie and I stare at each other. 'Wait down here,' I murmur.

I find her hunched on her bed, tapping away at her phone and refusing to look up at me. 'Sweetheart,' I say, perching beside her, 'what happened today?'

'Nothing,' she mumbles, face half-covered by hair.

I look at her, wondering how to coax her to tell me what happened without making things worse. It never used to be like this. Rosie would tell me everything. 'Did you have a nice time at Nina's?' I'd ask, and she'd reply, 'Yeah, we made a sponge cake and then we had an idea to make it look like a bed with an icing duvet, so we did that, and guess what! Nina's got a trampoline . . .'

And now? She's a closed book. I lick my dry lips and glance around her room. There's a clutter of scented candles and bottles of perfume and books and pens on her dressing table. A white ceramic hand, its elongated fingers draped with jewellery, is perched on a small plate bearing a half-eaten Maryland cookie.

'They dropped me,' she announces suddenly.

'You mean the agency?'

'Yup.'

'Really? Why?'

She shrugs, casting her phone aside on the rumpled duvet.

'Was it because you didn't turn up for that job?'

'No, of course not,' she exclaims. 'It's just, she – Laurie, I mean – started going on about my homely face. That's what she said, Mum – that I'm homely! What does that even mean?'

I look at my lovely daughter whose eyes are brimming with tears. 'Oh, darling, I have no idea . . .'

'Well,' she charges on, 'that's why the mitten people liked me, she said, and she thinks I'm not really right for fashion – that I'd be better modelling for home catalogues, like standing in kitchens and conservatories and all that, being the teenage daughter perched at the breakfast bar, she said, that's how *homely* I am—'

'That's nonsense,' I retort, glancing round for evidence of how wrong Laurie is. I point at our decommissioned cat-shaped biscuit barrel which Rosie stores her hair accessories in. 'That's homely. *I'm* homely, probably. Grandma Maggie and Grandpa Peter, they're homely. Grandma Gloria . . . well, maybe not so much. But you're only sixteen, Rosie. How can she possibly say—'

'Anyway,' she interrupts, 'Laurie reckons I'd be better with another agency, one that specialise in those sort of girls – the homely kind. She's got a friend who runs that kind of agency. "Her girls are always working!" she said . . .'

'Maybe that's not such a bad thing,' I suggest, putting an arm around her narrow shoulders.

'You think I want to be in sofa adverts?'

I don't answer that. Nina would be delighted to, I reflect, instead of doing all those extra shifts at the Harvester. We lapse into silence. Ollie has put the TV back on downstairs – it's blaring at what Rosie calls 'old people's volume' – and it sounds as if Gerald is giving his lawn one of its thrice-weekly mowings. Nipper, who takes issue with the mower, is yapping insistently.

'It's not what I thought, Mum,' Rosie mumbles.

'You mean modelling?'

She nods. 'I thought I'd get to travel and stuff. Meet people, wear lovely clothes, be in magazines . . .'

'You have been in one,' I remind her.

'Yeah, with you.' She raises the tiniest smile.

'Hmm. Sorry about that. I couldn't stop myself, you know, *muscling in* . . .'

She lets out a small, hollow laugh. 'That was the best part actually, that first shoot. Well, compared to standing there sweating like mad on a beach and getting a rash from the wool. I thought it'd be a bit more . . .'

'Glamorous?'

'Yeah.' She shrugs again, as if shaking off the day's disappointment. 'Anyway,' she adds, 'what happened with Fraser?'

Odd that she's only just asking now. Perhaps the

burning desire to meet him has cooled a little. Or maybe being described as 'homely' is of more immediate concern.

'It was fine,' I say, sensing my cheeks flush. 'We got on well, and he wants to meet you, if you still do—'

'Yeah, 'course I do! When?'

'Soon. We'll sort something out, okay? We'll talk it over with Dad . . .'

'But Dad's in Scotland.'

I pause, wondering how she'll react to my plan. 'Yes, and we're going up to see him – you, me and Ollie. That's where we were when you came home. We'd been to Grandma Gloria's to drop off Guinness . . .'

'Are we going to fly?' she asks, still thrilled by the possibility.

I shake my head. 'We'll have to drive, I'm afraid.'

'So Dad gets to fly and we have to go in your smelly old car?'

'Well, yes – it's the only one I have at the moment.'

She nods, looking a little shamefaced. 'All right.'

'And we're going to camp,' I add.

'Camp?' she exclaims. 'Oh, Mum, do I *have* to come?'

'Yes, you do. You can bring a friend if you like. The tent's huge, remember . . .'

'You're really selling it to me, Mum,' she groans.

'What about Nina? D'you think she'd like to come?'

Her face clouds. 'Um, things are a bit weird at the moment . . .'

'Delph then?'

'You think Delph'd want to sleep in a stinky old tent?'

I sigh and get up from her bed, deciding not to get drawn into this. In my own bedroom I pluck Will's leather trousers from the charity pile and take them through to show Rosie. 'I thought we could take these with us to Scotland,' I add.

'Oh my God, Mum,' she says, giggling. 'Does he know what happened? Was he upset?'

'No, he doesn't know. I, er, haven't had a chance to tell him.' I pause, wondering *why* he hasn't been in contact: I'd have appreciated a call, seeing as I've just lost my job, and it's so unlike him not to keep in touch with the kids. No response to my text, either, when I joked about being impressed by the size of his inkcap. Am I doing the right thing by dragging Rosie and Ollie all the way to Scotland with a leaky old tent? Christ, I hope this won't blow up in my face.

'Can't we stay in hotels?' Rosie asks hopefully.

I shake my head. 'Sorry, no. Look, love, things are tricky at the moment. I've been made redundant from Archie's.'

'No!' she gasps. 'God, Mum. What are you going to do?'

I muster a big smile. 'I'll find something else, don't worry. But in the meantime, we'll have to be pretty careful. Anyway, camping's fun . . .'

'Sure it is,' she says with a wry smile.

'And we're leaving early tomorrow,' I add, 'so could you pack a bag tonight?'

*

It's midnight by the time I've gathered my own clothes together, and unearthed our camping stove, sleeping bags and roll-out mats from the cupboard under the stairs. The tent isn't there, though. Must be in the attic, requiring me to lug the ladder upstairs and clamber in through the hatch on the landing, whilst trying not to disturb the kids.

I click on the light, scanning the travel cots and car seats and Ollie's old activity arch with all the Winnie the Pooh characters dangling off it, thickly furred with dust. There are boxes of books, a long-deceased Amstrad computer and our fake Christmas tree, used only once since Gloria remarked, 'Pity you didn't get a real one!' and which was regarded as substandard by the children ever since. That was the Christmas when she also announced that it was a shame we hadn't had the children christened. 'Does that mean I don't have a name?' bleated Ollie, who was only four at the time.

I prowl around in the gloom of the single bare bulb, picking up long-forgotten books – I have no idea why we've kept them all – and a clear plastic sack of fairy story cassettes which both Rosie and Ollie insisted on listening to over and over in bed every night.

Dust catches in my throat as I spot a shiny silver biscuit tin sitting beside our tent. It's full of photos from a pre-digital age that seem to mainly depict our early family holidays. I crouch down, flipping through them, realising how much younger Will and I looked then. In one photo – I'm not sure where it was taken – the four of us are on a beach. I'm wearing a bikini and Will's in trunks. This was before the kids started making vomiting noises on glimpsing us in our swimwear. We looked pretty good, I think. Will is deeply tanned and looks as if he's casually flopped an arm around my shoulders. We must have asked a stranger to take it. In another, obviously taken on the same day, we are all smiley and happy with our arms wrapped around each other in the dunes. Tears prick my eyes.

I flick through more photos, stopping when I find the only one I kept of Fraser and me; I lied when I told Rosie I didn't have any. I was scared of upsetting Will by showing it to her, and I suppose I've pretended it sort of melted away in the attic. My hair is very long, with what looks like a self-cut fringe, and he looks extremely handsome with his messy fair hair and bright, white smile. We are standing on a footbridge spanning a canal in Amsterdam – another picture taken by an obliging passerby.

I place the rest of the photos back in the tin, except this one. Then, being as quiet as I can, I carry it – plus our enormous, unwieldy tent in its nylon sack – down the ladder and deposit it on the landing. I climb back up to replace the hatch, then prop the ladder against the landing wall and go down to the kitchen.

There, I take out our kitchen scissors and cut up the photo of the young, smiley couple in love. I don't need it anymore. Rosie doesn't need to see it either because soon, she will meet him for real.

Chapter Forty-One

We set off just before 6 a.m. and arrive at our campsite, tucked behind a dramatic sweep of Northumberland coast, just after lunch. Cranky from being confined in the car for so long, Rosie and Ollie grudgingly help to pitch our tent; in fact, it's Ollie who barks instructions, while I wrestle with poles and acres of rustling nylon. 'Delph's going to Italy on Monday,' Rosie reminds me. She has assumed a flat expression as if I have dragged her to a B&Q car park.

Thankfully, though, the grey sky clears, the sun peeps out, and to my surprise, Rosie pulls off her sandals and heads for the sea to paddle. She's soon joined by Ollie. I watch from the dunes with my bare toes tucked in the soft, warm sand as they mess about in the shallows, the way they used to. It's already starting to feel like a family holiday. The only difference is, Will isn't here.

After drying off, we head into the village in search of fish and chips. There's a pretty Norman church, an old-fashioned sweet shop and a proper butchers, manned by a jovial-looking chap in a navy and white striped apron.

It's all very pleasing – *homely*, in fact. A cluster of elderly ladies are chatting outside a bakery. I have yet to spot anyone under the age of fifty here. The place has a sleepy, amiable air, plucked straight from a children's storybook; several passersby have already said hello, and commented on the beautiful afternoon.

We buy fish and chips to eat back at the campsite. 'I was thinking, Mum,' Rosie says, crunching batter, 'I need a job. A proper one, I mean – not going to castings and having someone pretending to look at your book and flipping through it in about two seconds . . .'

'You're going to look for a summer job, then?'

'Yeah. As soon as we get back.'

'Maybe Nina could put in a word for you?' I suggest.

I expect her to scoff at my crappy idea. 'Yeah. I feel kind of bad, actually. I haven't seen much of her lately—'

'If you get a job at the Harvester,' Ollie interrupts, 'does that mean we'd all get a discount at the salad cart?'

'You always say cart,' Rosie sniggers. 'It's salad *bar*.'

'Salad cart makes it sound like it's for hooved beasts,' I remark, which makes the two of them giggle.

This is all right, I decide. It's not Florida; in fact I'm not sure Sally would even class it as a proper holiday. I just hope Will doesn't mind us descending on him tomorrow. Since the mushroom picture there's been no communication from him. I'd thought the shaggy inkcap was a sort of peace offering, but it looks like I read too much into it. This would suggest that he really does want a clean break, i.e., possibly one that goes on and on forever and is actually more commonly known as *divorce*.

Bloody hell. I can't even bear to think about that. But right now, although I'm pretty sure he'll be delighted to see the kids, I'm not at all certain he'll feel quite the same way about me.

*

As a trio, we are more effective at disassembling a tent than erecting one, and after a pretty restless night we are on our way to Scotland before any other campers have emerged from their tents. The atmosphere as we drive north is cheerful and jokey, especially after a stop-off for breakfast. They can't wait to see their dad, I realise, with a sharp pang. They've missed him, perhaps more than they've even realised.

The second campsite I've booked is more of a wild and windy affair, without a shop or any facilities, apart from a bleak-looking shower block, a mile or so from the charity's headquarters. Once our tent has been pitched, we go for a walk along the rugged coastline. I try Will's mobile as the kids dawdle behind, but it goes to voicemail. 'Hi, Will,' I start, 'it's me. Just wondered how things are going . . .' Friendly auntie again. 'I, er . . . well, I have a bit of a surprise,' I add, 'so could you call me please?' Then I ring off.

'Mum, look!' Ollie yells. 'Look over there. Seals!'

I turn and stare. 'Wow,' I exclaim, amazed at how inert they seem, flumped on the mottled rocks. Slowly, one of them rouses itself and flops into the sea.

'They're, like, so lazy,' he chuckles.

'They're amazing,' Rosie marvels, taking pictures with her phone.

We stand and watch them for ages. I can see why Will was lured up here, but the thought of him settling here, without us, makes me feel as if my heart could burst.

'I'm starving, Mum,' Ollie announces as we head back to camp.

'There's a shop in the village,' I tell him. 'Let's go and fetch supplies.'

'I'll stay here,' Rosie says, ducking into the tent. 'I'm *exhausted* after that walk.'

'She's so feeble,' Ollie sniggers as we set off to buy rolls, sausages and a newspaper from the village store. In a sleepy café, I buy takeaway hot chocolates for the kids and a large, strong coffee for me. 'When are we gonna see Dad?' Ollie wants to know as we step back outside.

'Soon. Today, I hope.'

'Does he know we're here yet?'

'Er, no. I haven't been able to get hold of him, love.'

'Where's he staying?' Ollie wants to know.

'At a B&B,' I reply, 'somewhere in the village. It's called Glen something. Glenholm, I think . . .'

'Let's find it!' he says gleefully.

I frown. 'I'd rather speak to him first, rather than just turning up—'

'C'mon, Mum,' he argues. 'He'll be dead pleased.' I look at my son, who's clearly desperate to see his dad. And of course, we should try to track him down: why are we here, if not to see him? We peer at every house all the way back, and finally we spot Glenholm guest house: an immaculate pebble-dashed modern bungalow, with an enormous lilac bush in the front garden.

My stomach clenches. Maybe we shouldn't have come after all. I could have taken the kids camping to France instead. After all, there's no hurry to get back to London, now I no longer have a job to go to. I sip my coffee, burning my lip.

'*Mum*,' Ollie's voice cuts through my thoughts. 'Why aren't you listening? I said, I've got an idea. Instead of knocking, let's go back to the campsite and fetch his leather trousers and leave them here on the doorstep as a joke.'

'That would just be weird,' I chuckle. 'That'd freak him out. He'd think he had some creepy, crotch-eating stalker . . .'

'Go on, let's do it! It'd be so funny. Let's get them . . .' I love him for this, his boyish enthusiasm, but I'm still not sure it's the smartest idea.

However, back at the campsite Rosie agrees that it's an excellent plan and, after we've cooked a late lunch on our camping stove, she proceeds to wrap the trousers in the newspaper I haven't even read yet. 'This is mad,' Rosie giggles. 'He's gonna totally freak out.'

'Wish we could see his face,' Ollie chortles, 'when he finds it.' He rips off the blank side of the map from our Northumberland campsite and writes: FOR WILL BRISTOW.

'I'll take it,' I say.

'Can I have a cake from the café in the village?' Ollie asks. 'I'm still hungry.'

'You're a pig, Ollie,' Rosie retorts. 'How can anyone eat so much?' I leave them bickering – albeit fairly good-naturedly – as I head back to the village with our eccentric parcel tucked under my arm, and its label in my jeans pocket.

There's no one around the B&B as I place it on the doorstep. I stride away, trying to affect a casual air, as if I am merely exploring the village. The café is much busier now, milling with robust outdoorsy types with rucksacks and enormous walking boots. I go in and wait in a queue at the counter. Then, as I glance around, someone catches my eye, who isn't quite so outdoorsy. At least, unlike the serious walkers, he doesn't look as if he eats lumps of granite for lunch.

It's Will, sitting at a small table across from an extremely attractive young woman. She has one of those fresh, almost luminous faces which simply doesn't need make-up, and her long auburn hair is secured in a neat plait which snakes down her back. She is breathtakingly lovely, and it's definitely a *real* woman this time – not a blow-up doll. She and Will are so wrapped up in chatting over their coffee that they don't notice me asking for a slice of chocolate cake. I pay quickly, dropping my change, which clatters onto the counter. I gather it up, stuff it into my pocket and zoom for the door with my head down, almost dropping my paper bag of cake as I hurtle outside.

So he's made a new friend. Maybe it is 'only coffee'. Or perhaps he's shown her his shaggy inkcap too. It hasn't taken long, I decide bleakly as I stride back to the campsite, for Will to make himself thoroughly at home.

Chapter Forty-Two

To stop myself from obsessing about Will and the auburn beauty, I suggest a dip in the sea. While Ollie is keen, Rosie reckons it'll be freezing and is appalled that I brought her swimsuit without telling her. 'I'm capable of doing my own packing, Mum,' she grumbles, before sloping off to get changed in the shower block.

She's right; the sea is shockingly cold. We scream as the waves crash over us, but soon it's wonderfully exhilarating, swimming in the clear, cool water with the bright sun above. The kids don't even seem too appalled by the sight of me in my swimsuit. I don't think I have ever felt so alive. Or freezing, actually, when we finally emerge from the sea; we are shivering so much, the only thing for it is to light a fire, which thrills Ollie. Thank God one of my children still delights in making things burn.

Having dried off and dressed, we meander along the beach, with the big bag of sausages, rolls and ketchup we bought at the local sells-anything shop. While Ollie excels at finding driftwood, it's Rosie who manages to get the blaze going: 'We learnt this in Scouts,' she announces as we all huddle around it.

It's Rosie, too, who spots him, making his way down to what is now 'our' cove. 'Look,' she yells, squinting into the distance, 'it's Dad!'

I swing round to see Will sauntering towards us, an unreadable expression on his face. Then he breaks into a smile.

'We've missed you, Dad,' Ollie says, running towards him.

Will hugs him tightly. 'I've missed you too. And you, Rosie. I had no idea you were planning to come—' He breaks off and wraps his arm around the two of them, then turns to me.

'Hi,' he says, kissing my cheek. 'This is quite a surprise . . .'

'A good one, I hope,' I say feebly as smoke gusts in my face.

'Um . . . yes, of course it is.'

'Did you find your present?' Ollie wants to know.

Will pulls a confused face. 'Er . . . yeah. I was a bit taken aback, to be honest . . .'

'It was Mum's idea,' Ollie fibs, laughing. 'She made us do it.'

'Sure I did,' I say, sensing my cheeks glowing, not from the heat of the fire – which is dying down quickly – but because I feel so . . . *ridiculous*.

'How about you two get some more driftwood?' Will suggests, for which I am grateful. They hurry away obediently. He has always had that knack with the kids: to get them beavering away, involved in a project.

'It's like those field trips you used to take them on,' I

remark, watching them scouring the upper reaches of the cove.

Will nods. 'That's what I was thinking.'

I look at him, hardly daring to ask. 'So . . . I assume they've offered you the job?'

Will nods. 'Yep, they have. They did straight away, actually.'

Then why the heck didn't you let me know? 'I'm really pleased for you,' I say briskly. 'I just thought, you know, it'd be nice for the kids to have a break, with us not going away this summer. So we decided to come up and see you. I hope that's okay, and that we're not getting in the way—'

'Of course you're not,' he cuts in. 'It's just . . . I don't really know what to make of things, Charlotte.'

I run my hands through the tiny, ground-up shells. 'What things?'

Will sighs loudly. 'Those trousers. The way you packaged them up and left them on the doorstep like that, with the note on, held down by a stone. That's fucking *weird* behaviour.'

'It was Ollie's idea actually,' I say quickly. 'Honestly, he just thought it'd be funny—'

'It's pretty bizarre,' Will says tersely. 'I mean, I'd worked out this plan, and I thought you and me . . .' He tails off. 'Then I opened the package.'

I stare at him, uncomprehending.

'. . . I mean,' he goes on, 'I thought we could figure this out, but now you've made your point . . .' He frowns. 'I know you don't like those trousers but you didn't have to take the kitchen scissors to them—'

'I didn't!' I protest.

'Hacking out the crotch,' he exclaims, picking up a

stone and tossing it across the beach. 'It's a pretty violent gesture. In fact it's kind of bunny-boiling behaviour. It wouldn't take a psychologist to figure out what you were trying to say . . .'

I look at him, aghast. He thinks I'm a crotch-hacker? 'Will,' I start, 'I didn't mean—'

'Obviously, you did, and I get the message, okay?'

'Could you listen to me?' I snap. 'I *didn't* cut up your trousers. What kind of person d'you think I am?'

He shakes his head sadly. 'I'm getting the message that—'

'There's no *message*, because I didn't do it. It wasn't me, all right? Guinness did it. That's where he'd been hiding – behind that pile of clothes you'd put out ready for charity. He'd gnawed away at the leather. We thought it was funny. I actually thought you might too.' *Sorry,* I fume silently, *for a moment there I must've confused the old Will, who possessed a fine sense of humour, with the one who is sitting all stony-faced at my side. The one who has cosy coffees with other women . . .*

Will is looking at me curiously, as if I might be making this up. 'Guinness,' he says slowly, 'ate my trousers?'

I nod glumly. 'Well, he just had a bit of a nibble really. You know how he likes to gnaw at things. I doubt if he actually ingested it.' Now he'll start on about how I should have kept our rabbit secure because, after all, I am in charge of pooping matters and pretty much everything else concerning our pet.

'For fuck's sake.' He says this so quietly, I'm not sure if I heard him correctly.

'If you're upset,' I mutter, 'they can probably be mended. We could find another pair in a charity shop and cut out a piece and—' I break off, realising that Will is staring at me, and that his mouth is starting to quiver, as if he's having to summon every ounce of willpower not to laugh.

'You think that'd be a good look, do you? To have a big patch sewn on, where the crotch was?'

I clear my throat. 'Well, if it was done very neatly . . .'

Will splutters. 'Maybe the patch could be a different colour, like yellow or pink. You know – to add interest, as they say in fashion circles . . .'

'Maybe,' I say.

He starts to laugh. 'I don't *want* to mend them, Charlotte. Christ, d'you think I was planning to wear those things again?'

'Well, you wore them to Zach's gig—'

'Yeah.' He pushes back his dark hair. 'What the hell was I thinking?'

I shrug. 'You actually looked pretty, er . . . I mean, you *can* carry them off, sort of, in certain types of situation—'

'They were bloody ridiculous,' he retorts. 'You know why I dug them out? After meeting Tommy and his mates . . . I mean, I *like* them, they're a laugh, but—'

'What does this have to do with Tommy?'

'You know. The tight jeans, the band T-shirts and studded belts . . .'

'You were trying to fit in with them?' I ask incredulously.

Will smiles. 'Not exactly. I mean, as an older man—'

'You're talking as if you're about seventy,' I chuckle.

He shrugs. 'Yeah. Well, that's what I was thinking – that maybe I'd got a bit staid. You know, a bit dad-jeans, sad old fucker kind of thing. Then I found those trousers and I thought – hang on, if they still fit . . .'

'Which they did,' I remark with a smile.

Will laughs self-consciously. 'I think I just had a moment of madness actually. Rosie did say I know sod all about fashion.'

'It's all very confusing,' I murmur. 'The age thing, I mean. God knows how we're supposed to be. Like our car, remember? The first one we chose together?'

'God, yeah . . .' He looks dreamy for a moment.

'The vintage Saab, burnt orange with the leather seats . . .'

'And we decided to swap it for something more grown-up and family-friendly,' he adds.

'And ugly, frankly,' I say with a hollow laugh. 'It was the sensible thing to do, but wasn't it sad when that nice couple in the fifties outfits came round and drove away in it?'

Will pokes a smooth, weathered stick into the sand. 'Kind of.'

'Didn't you feel like they were driving off with your youth?'

'Not really,' he says, 'because being with you, and our family, was more important than any car.'

A lump forms in my throat. I watch the kids, chatting away at the water's edge. It's lovely to see. But being here still feels like the end of something.

'But what about the job?' I prompt Will. 'You said you've accepted it?'

'Yes, I have.'

'I thought you would,' I say, keeping my voice steady. 'But I have to tell you, this has been so hurtful, Will. All this silence, not knowing what was going on . . . why didn't you call?'

He pauses before answering. 'Yeah. I'm sorry. It's

just . . . I did need some space, not from you, or at least not *just* from you – I mean, from everything. From life back at home . . .'

'Why?'

We sit in silence for what feels like a very long time. 'You've said things haven't been right with us, and it's true – they haven't. I just needed to figure out why it's been like this, and what was actually going on.' I picture myself kissing Fraser in that bland, beige living room. My stomach twists with shame. '. . . At least I thought I did,' Will continues. 'But as the days went on, all I could think about really was . . .' He turns to look at me. '*You.* I missed you. I missed the kids too, obviously – but it was you I kept thinking about, especially at night.' He laughs softly. 'It is beautiful up here. But I've been bloody lonely.'

I want to reach out and touch him, but can still sense an invisible barrier between us, which would give me an arm-jolting shock if I tried to pass my hand through it. 'What about the job, though?' I ask. 'I mean, a directorship,' I add, trying to sound pleased. 'That's fantastic, Will.'

Will nods. So, despite professing to miss me madly, he still doesn't want me. He hasn't wanted me for months, and I will never again be a sexual being. I'm a withering, middle-aged woman with my ancient coil lying there like a shipwreck, covered in barnacles and the occasional shoal of small, bottom-feeding fish drifting through.

'I do want it,' he adds, taking my hand now, 'but I can't be away from you.'

I look at him. How handsome he looks, rather more windblown than his usual London self. It suits him. He looks at home here amongst the wild coastline and rapidly changing skies.

'What d'you mean?' I ask. 'I mean, how could that possibly work, when the charity's up here?'

'I am going to join them,' he replies, 'but I'm going to be based in London. I'll have to come up one week a month . . .'

'You mean,' I say incredulously, 'you'll work from home the rest of the time?'

'A bit, but you know – I've been at home a lot these past few months . . .' He smiles awkwardly.

'It hasn't been easy,' I suggest.

'Not really. Well, maybe I could have handled it better. I know I've been bloody hard to live with.'

I bite my lip, not knowing what to say. 'Anyway,' he adds, 'they're expanding into Devon, Cornwall and the Norfolk coast, so there'd be a lot of travel. I was hoping you could come on some of the trips – the kids too, while they still want to be with us . . .' He pauses.

I pick up a stick and poke at the remains of our fire. 'Will,' I start, 'I saw you having coffee with someone today. In that café in the village. The one all the walkers go to—'

'Well, it is the only one,' he says. 'That was Joanna, from the charity. We were discussing the final details, before I headed back down south . . .'

On a Saturday, though? They were talking shop on a *Saturday*?

'They're a dedicated lot,' he adds, as if reading my thoughts. 'It's not exactly nine-to-five.'

'No, of course not.'

His face softens as he squeezes my hand.

'We did go for lunch a couple of days ago,' he adds, as every cell in my body seems to shrivel, just as Delph said it would – although I bet even she didn't imagine it'd happen so suddenly. 'To talk about work,' he adds firmly. 'Honestly, that's all it was . . .'

'She's very beautiful,' I remark, feeling ridiculous.

'Is she?' He feigns amazement.

I laugh. 'Oh, come on, Will . . .'

'Seriously,' he says, 'there's been a lot to talk about, with me being mainly based down south.' The rush of the sea fills my ears.

'*Can* it work?' I ask, my voice cracking. 'With us, I mean?'

His arm curls around me. 'Of course it can,' he says.

Chapter Forty-Three

'Don't worry,' Will says as we stroll aimlessly around Soho on a muggy Saturday afternoon. 'She's old enough to make decisions and we had to let this happen. All that really matters is that she feels okay.'

'Yes, I know.' We have been back from Scotland for two weeks now. This is the first time Fraser has had a 'window' in which to meet his daughter. 'Crazy at work,' he said in his last email, thankfully omitting to mention what happened between us at his flat. I haven't told Will that Fraser and I kissed, although he does know about our day together in Brighton. There's no need, I've decided, not when it didn't mean a thing.

Will, Ollie and I parted company with Rosie over an hour ago. Unable to settle to anything, we buy takeaway noodles to eat on a bench in Soho Square.

The park is filled with family groups, tourists prodding at their phones, and a large, excitable French school party who have descended with their packed lunches. I look at Will and Ollie, who have fallen into a discussion about microscopes. I am hugely impressed by Will's ability to give his full attention to our son's forthcoming present, even though Ollie's birthday isn't until December. No one but me would detect the hint of anxiety in his blue eyes, or notice the way he keeps glancing around the park to see if Rosie's coming. I've texted her to let her know where we are, and to ask her to meet us here, half-hoping she'd hint how things were going when she texted back. *Great,* was all she said.

'Sure you still want one?' Will is saying. 'It's a serious piece of kit, you know. D'you think you'll actually use it?'

'Yeah,' Ollie replies, although there's a trace of something in his voice – a slight waning of the enthusiasm he'd displayed a few weeks ago. 'Or,' he adds, 'maybe I could have an iPod instead.' Catching the look of disappointment on his dad's face, he grins and says, 'Or both! That'd be great . . .'

'Still four months to your birthday,' Will says quickly, catching my eye. 'Plenty of time to decide . . . look, there's Rosie!' He gets up and waves, and she hurries towards us.

'Hi,' she says with a smile.

'How did it go?' I ask in an overly casual way, as if she's just met a friend from school.

'Okay,' she says briskly. I glance at Will as we leave the square, still in awe of how he is managing to hold it together today.

'We were talking about what Ollie wants for his birthday,' he says in an overly jovial manner, falling into step beside her.

'But it's not for ages,' she remarks.

'No,' he says, 'but we were just, you know . . . *thinking* . . .'

'Anyway,' I add, 'yours is only two weeks away and you haven't said what you'd like to do.' *What did you think of him?* I want to ask her, so desperately it's making my heart race. *Were you disappointed? Was it an anti-climax? Or were you so bowled over by him you'll become super-close and won't have time for Will, who's your real dad, let's never forget that . . .*

I can almost *see* the tension radiating from Will. 'There's that new Japanese place, Rosie,' he says lightly. 'Maybe we could have a quick look today, see if you fancy it?' I sense him catching himself as we make our way along Old Compton Street. 'I mean, that's if you want to go out with us for your birthday. Maybe you'd rather just do something with your friends? That's okay. I mean, I'm not *assuming* . . .'

'It's fine, Dad,' she says.

He glances at me as we walk, then turns back to Rosie. 'I don't want to force a family outing on you . . .'

She laughs. 'It's *fine*. Really. Stop going on.' We check out the restaurant. With its deep red walls and black lacquered tables, it meets with Rosie's approval.

'Is it all raw fish?' Ollie asks glumly, staring in.

'No, of course not,' she retorts. 'Who says you're coming anyway?'

They start to bicker, and I catch Ollie muttering, 'Did you like him then? Or was he weird? Why haven't you said anything about him?'

'Just leave it,' she snaps.

I reach for Will's hand. 'Listen, you two,' he says, a trace of tension in his voice, 'I'd planned a treat for this afternoon but if this is the mood, perhaps we won't bother . . .'

'What is it?' Ollie asks.

'Never mind,' Will says. 'Anyway, let me know how many are coming, Rosie. You can bring some friends, maybe Nina or Zach or . . .' He tails off. Either he can't remember Delph's name, or is hoping Rosie won't notice the admission. 'Bring anyone you like,' he adds, coming to a stop outside a smart boutique hotel in Dean Street. 'We don't need to come at all . . .'

'Dad,' she says, frowning now, 'I'd love us to go out as a family for my birthday like we always do. But yeah, it'd be nice to ask Nina too. I feel bad, y'know, after that night at Zach's gig. We haven't spoken since then. I've tried to call but, I don't know, her phone's always been out of charge or something . . .'

'Maybe you should go round to see her,' I suggest. Rosie nods.

'See if she wants to come, then I can book it,' Will adds, clearly as desperate as I am to know about her meeting with Fraser. Why can't she just *tell* us?

'Er, why are we all standing here?' Ollie asks, stuffing his hands into his pockets.

Will nods towards the hotel's elegant facade. 'I, um, booked a table for us in here. I heard they do a lovely afternoon tea.'

'Really, Dad?' Rosie asks, clearly delighted as we all file in.

We have tea and tiny cucumber sandwiches and miniature scones and cakes, all presented on multi-tiered stands. 'Oh my God,' Rosie exclaims as tiny French pastries arrive, 'this is heaven, Dad. What made you think of it?'

'I just thought we all deserved a treat today,' he says simply, and I realise now why he planned this: to make today, meeting-Fraser day, seem like a special thing, something to celebrate. He's done it to show that he's fine about everything, and that he's not going to sulk or make things difficult. I reach for his hand and hold it tightly.

'So, um, how are things going with Zach?' I ask, to fill a lull in conversation. She has still told us precisely nothing about her meeting with Fraser. I sip my tea and try to look relaxed, as if today is nothing out of the ordinary at all.

Rosie sighs, biting into a tiny chocolate éclair. 'He's all right. We're just friends, though . . .'

'I thought you seemed keen?' Will says, then corrects himself. 'But of course it's none of our business—'

'Dad, are you all right?' she asks, frowning.

He gives her a bewildered look. 'Yes, of course, I'm fine.'

'You seem a bit nervy, that's all . . .' Hmm, and why might that be? Doesn't she *realise*?

She grins at me. 'Zach's sweet and everything, but he's a bit of a stoner, Mum.'

'Yes, I know he likes his pot,' I say to amuse her.

'You mean his cheese, Mum,' Ollie sniggers. 'His *assassin of youth*.'

Rosie looks thoughtful. 'But it's not just that. He's . . .' She tails off. 'He's a bit, well . . .' My mind races. Pushy, persistent? I glance at Will, imagining him mentally preparing his 200-page prospective-boyfriend-of-darling-Rosie questionnaire.

'A bit what?' I prompt her.

She exhales loudly. 'A bit thick, to be honest. We were round there, and Sabrina and her friend Abs were watching a DVD. Me and Zach stood there watching it for a minute and he said, "What's this?" And his mum said, "*Titanic*." You know the film one with Leonardo diCaprio?'

I smile. 'Yes, of course I do.'

'Well,' she adds, laughing now, 'he said, "Oh, one of them stupid romcoms, they're so predictable – everyone knows they're gonna survive."'

I blink at her. 'You mean he didn't know it actually happened?'

'No! That's the thing, Mum. He'd never heard of it. Well, he had, but he thought it was just a made-up story about Leonardo diCaprio and Kate Winslet kissing on a ship . . .'

'My God,' Ollie scoffs, 'I've known about the *Titanic* since I was, like, five years old!'

'Yeah,' she sniggers, 'you know everything, genius boy . . .'

'Who *doesn't* know that?' he retorts. I glance at Rosie as they fall into teasing each other, wondering when she'll divulge at least *something* about meeting Fraser today. I can't understand it at all. We polish off every morsel from the stand – at least, Rosie and Ollie do; Will and I barely eat a thing – and by the time we leave, Fraser's name still hasn't come up.

'So, how did it go today?' It's Will who asks her as we step out into Dean Street.

She gives him a bemused look. 'What, with Fraser?' His name hangs like a smell above us.

'Yeah,' he says casually.

She bunches her hands into the pockets of her skinny black jeans. 'He was all right. He was nice. We chatted a bit, you know?'

I glance at her, trying to detect any hint of upset, or a sense that it was too overwhelming and that she needs time to think, to process it all . . . but there's nothing. She links an arm through Will's as we head for the Tube. 'He's a nice guy,' she says lightly, 'but he's not you, is he? I mean, I'll never know him like I know you. You'll always be my Dad.'

I get a sense then that I should hang back, and give them a few moments together without me chipping in, wanting to know every detail. As Ollie and I fall a little way behind, I see Will kiss the top of Rosie's head. They are chatting as they walk, all awkwardness gone. I wish I could see his face. But this is their moment, and I slow my pace even further to give them the chance to talk.

Realising Ollie is no longer ambling along beside me, I glance round to see that he's hanging back too, as if to disassociate himself from us, his mortifying family.

'Come *on*, Ollie,' I call back.

He looks away, his flat expression telling me, *I don't need to walk with you, Mum. I'm not going to get lost, you know. I'm not going to run into traffic.* So I'm alone now, although not in a bad way. My family are here; it's just that everyone needs their little bit of space.

Up ahead, a slender, olive-skinned woman with swathes of dark glossy hair is hurrying towards Rosie and Will. She calls out and waves to attract their attention. Ever the nosy mother – I know, I can't help myself – I quicken my pace to catch up. Will and Rosie have stopped chatting and are looking expectantly at her.

'Excuse me,' the woman says, catching her breath as she turns to Rosie. 'I hope you don't mind me stopping you, but I work for a model agency called Carol Mortimer Management. Have you ever thought of being a model? I think you'd be perfect for a fashion agency like ours.'

Rosie hesitates, then a big, bright smile lights up her face. Sometimes, her loveliness knocks the breath out of me. Will takes my hand and threads his fingers through mine.

Rosie glances at me, then back at the stranger. 'Thanks,' she says, 'that's a really nice thing to say. But I really don't think—'

'Oh, please consider it,' the woman says, already pulling out a card from her bag. 'You have the face, the height, and your eyes are amazing—'

'No, really, it's not for me,' Rosie says, leaving her looking a little crestfallen as the four of us stroll away, all together now, on this beautiful summer's afternoon.

Chapter Forty-Four

I set off for my interview, not in a gloomy grey suit this time but a smart red shift dress from Hobbs, low, elegant black heels (lent by Sabrina) and a smart black jacket I found lurking in my wardrobe. My hair has been coloured to great effect by Rosie, banishing the last traces of aubergine. So it's been a sort of team effort. I'm a little jittery on the way into town, but it's okay. There are no sweaty hands this time, and I'm not having to pretend that I don't care about this job.

I do, very much. And I'm fine with the size of it. It's huge, actually; a high-profile launch of a digital magazine, and they need a Marketing Director. I've been putting in a few hours a week helping Sabrina to publicise Crystal Brides. But while I'm happy to help her out, I'm looking to get stuck into something new and exciting that'll really push me.

'About time you got yourself a proper job,' Rosie teased this morning. I could have leapt on the defensive, and reminded her that my *un-proper* job has funded everything from school trips to every stitch of clothing she wears, not forgetting the tiny things like hair clips and deodorant and scented candles. But I didn't. I just laughed and kissed her and set off.

I arrive at the offices just off Bond Street. It's a huge, golden sandstone building, and extremely well-groomed men and women are striding in and out. They look confident and purposeful. It's a fresh, breezy morning, and the sun is beating down from a clear blue sky. Taking a deep breath, I hold my head high and walk in.

The interview is long and intense and, when I finally come out, I am dizzy from talking about myself, and running late. In fact, when the interview was arranged, I'd been tempted to say the date wasn't suitable, as it was my daughter's birthday – but of course the woman from Deacon Publishing didn't need to know that. So I'd said it was fine, and now I'm running through Soho, all in a sweat.

By the time I reach the restaurant for lunch, everyone is already there: Will, Rosie, Ollie and Nina. We have invited Gloria too, but she is running even later than me. 'Mum's held up at the hairdressers,' Will says with a grin, getting up and kissing me. 'So, how did it go?'

I exhale loudly. 'God, I don't know. It's so hard to tell. But I think it went well . . .' I turn and hug Rosie. 'Happy birthday, sweetheart. Sorry I had to rush off this morning.'

'That's okay. You look great, Mum. Bet you've got the job . . .'

'Well, let's hope so,' I say, as the waiter comes over to talk us through the incredibly complicated menu: none of us has the faintest idea what anything is. But it's all beautiful – so pretty to look at that we all hesitate before piling in (except Ollie, who dives in as if he hasn't been fed for weeks). We are just finishing off when my mobile rings.

'Sorry,' I say, 'I'd better take this . . .' I march to the

door and step outside. It's Kate, the woman who interviewed me.

'Hi, Charlotte, are you okay to talk just now?'

'Yes, I'm fine,' I say, glancing in through the restaurant window where Will is up on his feet now, getting Nina and Rosie to sit closer, arms around each other, for a photo.

'We'd like to offer you the position of Marketing Director,' she says.

'Oh! I didn't think I'd hear so quickly—'

'It was an easy decision to make,' Kate adds, proceeding to talk about my start date, and that she'd like me to pop in and go through my contract, and all that stuff – stuff which I'm extremely happy about, of course, but can barely process right now.

I take a moment to breathe when we've finished the call. When I step back inside the restaurant, all eyes are on a huge white cake, ablaze with candles and decorated with icing roses, which is being carried to our table.

'Oh, Mum!' Rosie cries, feigning mortification but clearly thrilled, 'did you have to?'

'Yeah,' Will says, getting up and hugging me, 'did you have to ask them to do a cake? It's so embarrassing!'

I laugh, realising that of course he arranged it. 'I got it,' I whisper into his ear. 'I got the job, Will.'

'That's fantastic,' he says, hugging me. 'You're brilliant, you know that? You're so clever and smart and of *course* they want you. I knew all along . . .' Then he kisses me again, in front of everyone in this busy restaurant.

For once, the kids don't look appalled. In fact they haven't even noticed our outrageous display of affection. Nina and Ollie are singing happy birthday, and strangers are glancing around and joining in as our daughter blows out seventeen candles on this, the loveliest of days.